A FEAST OF YOU

A Feast of You

Sorcha Grace

Praise for A TASTE OF YOU

"With a deliciously sexy hero, a heroine with unforgettable spice, and mouthwatering sensuality, Sorcha Grace's *A Taste of You* will have you begging for seconds. Absolutely delectable."

—J. Kenner, *New York Times* bestselling author of RELEASE ME, CLAIM ME, and COMPLETE ME

"More than just a taste of sexy here. Scorching hot flames have burned up dinner! Witty and fun, *A Taste of You* by Sorcha Grace is a satisfying, sensual read not to be missed."

—Raine Miller, *New York Times* Bestselling Author

"Fans of Sylvia Day and E.L. James will find a lot to like about the mysterious William Lambourne and will root for a heroine who deserves a second chance at love. An intriguing start to a saucy new trilogy."

—Roni Loren, National bestselling author of FALL INTO YOU

"Yummy! Imagine Christian Grey with warm chocolate and you have William Lambourne. Add a complex heroine who gives love another try and you have *A Taste of You*. This steamy romance will take you through twists and turns and have you cheering for love to prevail. I can't wait to read what's next for William and Catherine!"

—Aleatha Romig, Author of the bestselling CONSEQUENCES series

A FEAST OF YOU

To M, S, and D. Thanks for the inspiration.

ONE

Chicago looked like it had snowed pink and red. I'd never liked Valentine's Day—men wearing silly red socks with hearts on them, the cheap drugstore candy, the ridiculous cards—but I had to admit, this year I didn't mind it so much. Sure, all the hearts and cupids and over-the-top, once-a-year expressions of love were still kind of lame, but I was looking forward to celebrating in a few hours with William.

Maybe that's why it seemed so fitting that I was on my way to Willowgrass. Chicago's hottest new restaurant was where it had all began for William and me. Just five or so weeks ago—*had it really only been that long?*—I'd tripped outside the restaurant as I'd left a meeting. Who would have thought my clumsiness would set just about everything in my life on a totally new course? I couldn't have predicted, much less imagined, where I'd be today. Or who I'd be with.

Stormy Eyes.

I remembered looking up at him as I'd scrambled to pick up the contents of my bag that had spilled all over the uneven patch of sidewalk when I tripped. Taking in his thick, wavy bedroom hair; his chiseled features; his eyes that seemed to change from smoky grey to vivid blue. He was the most beautiful man I've ever seen, and the entire package had just about rendered me speechless that first night. And now Stormy Eyes—William Maddox Lambourne—was all mine. I couldn't help but smile at that thought.

Mine.

The setting sun glinted off the windows of Willowgrass as the car came to a halt in front of the restaurant, and I allowed my gaze to drift up to the burnished W on the sign. It looked the same as the first time I saw it, even though so many things in my life were different now. Take, for example, my ride. The first time I'd arrived in a cab with Beckett. This time, I was sitting in the backseat of a very large, chauffeured, black Mercedes sedan. I wasn't accompanied by my best friend, but by a private security officer who was my constant shadow.

Asa Singer was a member of William's security team, and like the others William employed, Asa was a cross between commando and linebacker. I could see Asa's reflection in the restaurant's windows as we got out of the car. He was about six foot five, olive-skinned, and handsome. He was also built like a Mac truck and incredibly imposing in his *Men in Black* suit, which strained across his chest and huge shoulders. The guy looked lethal, which was exactly what William had been going for when he'd assigned Asa to me, I was sure.

Asa was friendlier than some of the other guys on the security team, which was to say he actually answered my questions instead of sitting in stoic silence when we were together. He'd told me he'd served in the Israeli Special Forces before turning to private security work. I knew he carried a weapon, but looking at him now, I wondered where he kept it holstered. Hopefully I'd never have to find out.

I'd definitely been on my guard since the break-in at my condo last week. I was lucky—nothing had been stolen—but a violation of privacy like that does things to a girl. Plus, there was the creep factor of receiving a mysterious envelope filled with surveillance photos of me. Just thinking about it made the little hairs on the back of my neck stand up.

William had seen the envelope of clandestine pictures of me going about my daily routine just hours after he and I had exchanged our first 'I love yous.' When he'd revealed that he'd received similar photos, that had been bad enough. I'd wondered what the fuck was going on. But once we got the call that my condo had been broken into, that had been it. William had insisted that I not only stay at his penthouse, but be guarded at all times until this whole scary mess could be sorted out.

I'd protested. I mean, I had my own place that I loved, but I'd known I didn't stand a chance against William once his mind was made up. Truthfully, I was pretty freaked out, too, so I hadn't argued with him all that hard. It was weird to know a stranger had been secretly watching me and following me, capturing my every move in digital.

William had said he'd do whatever it took to keep me safe and this past week, I'd tried to remember that his intentions were good, even when his controlling tendencies started to drive me a bit nuts. It was William's way of showing me he loved me, that I was precious to him, and I loved him back for that. But his idea of safety wasn't always practical. Right now it meant my Volvo was parked in his building's garage and off limits, so Asa or another member of William's team drove me around. I didn't mind the chauffeur or the bodyguard most of the time, but I was starting to miss my freedom. Sometimes it seemed like I couldn't even go to the bathroom without asking for permission.

There were perks, however, like William and I playing house in his luxurious 56th-floor penthouse. It was only temporary, but waking up next to William—or under him—every morning was the kind of feast for my erotic senses that I could happily indulge in indefinitely. I was loving all the little domestic things I hadn't experienced for years, like taking showers together or watching William get dressed in the morning. Most of all, I loved waiting for William to come home every night. He never seemed too tired after work and he found plenty of time to exhaust himself in bed with me until we fell asleep.

Of course, I missed my condo, my runs along the lakefront, and walking through Lincoln Park. But I felt safe and protected at the penthouse and a little bit like a princess. William had given me complete freedom in his home and even set up a workspace for me in his study. His cook did all the shopping and cooking, unless William decided to whip up one of his own delicious concoctions. The housekeeper made certain the entire place was meticulously clean and as neat and tidy as a five-star hotel. If I wanted a run, I headed downstairs to the building's top-of-the-line gym. If I needed something, Rajesh, the building concierge, was happy to make sure I got it. He called me Miss Catherine and behaved as though I'd been living there all my life.

After our disastrous trip a few weeks ago to William's estate in Napa Valley, I'd expected to chafe a bit under this house arrest. At Casa di Rosabela, I'd beat my wings like a bird in a gilded cage, confused and abandoned. If I was being honest, I'd admit that I had freaked out and overreacted, riding on an emotional rollercoaster completely of my own making. But it was totally different this time—*I* was different—and so far, lockdown at the penthouse had been pretty awesome. It helped that I was sharing my cell with the man I loved. And all the incredible sex helped me forget why all the security was necessary in the first place.

Asa cleared his throat, and I realized I was still staring at the Willowgrass sign. Caught daydreaming about William, *again*, I gave Asa a sheepish smile and stepped into the warmth of the restaurant. It looked the same, but it had taken on an aura of success. As a photographer, I was an expert observer and I'd sensed Willowgrass was destined for greatness the first time I walked in back in January. And I hadn't been wrong. Ben Lee's restaurant was a huge hit now and the house was packed, lines out the door, night after night.

"Catherine!"

I smiled as Ben's sister, Amanda, came forward to greet me. She looked as lovely as ever in a short red dress and towering black platform heels. As petite as she was, I was more than a head taller, and when we hugged I told her I loved her dress.

"You're the one who looks fabulous," she said with a genuine smile. In confusion, I glanced down. Nothing on me was red or screamed Valentine's Day. I wore black skinny jeans and ankle boots and had on a long black sweater under my wool coat, but Amanda couldn't have seen it. As usual, my brown hair was pulled back in a ponytail.

"Not your clothes," Amanda said and laughed. "*You.* You look so happy."

I *was* happy, though it was almost embarrassing that it was so obvious. "How could I not be happy?" I asked, unable to hold back my smile. "This place smells amazing. Ben's cooking up something incredible, I bet."

Amanda's gaze flicked to Asa, and I turned to him. "This is Asa Singer. He's keeping me company today." I'd started explaining the security personnel that way because it invited fewer questions and seemed to put everyone at ease.

"Welcome!" Amanda said. Asa just nodded, his eyes scanning the restaurant as though an attacker might jump out at any moment.

"So where is he?" I asked Amanda.

She rolled her eyes. "Where do you think? The kitchen, of course. You know the way."

I headed back toward the kitchen, pausing at the bar and gesturing to a stool. "I'll just be a minute, Asa. Wait for me here?"

He frowned. I knew he didn't like letting me out of his sight, but there was a fine line between protecting and smothering. Asa sat stiffly at the bar. Pulling off my gloves and stuffing them into the pockets of my coat, I continued into the kitchen, walking into the now-familiar space. This was the first place William and I had kissed, and I couldn't stop my gaze from sliding to the walk-in freezer where we'd shared that hot embrace.

The kitchen was a hive of activity and line cooks bustled around doing prep work for the dinner service, which would begin soon. Valentine's Day was one of the busiest nights of the year for most restaurants and no one seemed to give me a second glance amidst the purposeful chaos.

"Cat!"

I turned at the familiar voice. It wasn't Ben but my best friend Beckett, exactly who I was looking for. "Are you still here?" I asked mockingly, giving him a hug and a kiss on the cheek.

"Of course I am. I'm always here lately," he joked, holding my shoulders and smiling down at me. "This is my home away from home."

"I thought my place was your home away from home," I said with a smile. Beckett loved using the AGA in my kitchen to test out new recipes.

He shrugged. "It gets lonely now that you're not there. When are you going to have me over to that castle you're living in?"

"How about this weekend?" I said. "I'll give you the grand tour. Are you usually free for dinner?"

He nodded. "I'm here at dark o'clock and home by four or so."

"Ah, baker's hours, Ben is lucky to have you, even for a few weeks."

Beckett had recently landed the job of his dreams as head pastry chef at Patisserie LeClerc, a Parisian-style bakery conceived by Emil LeClerc, a very famous French chef and restaurateur. Bistro LeClerc, the chef's signature Chicago restaurant, and its sister *patisserie*, were currently under construction in Lincoln Park. Until the opening, Beckett was using Willowgrass as his test kitchen to master Chef LeClerc's recipes, and the lucky patrons of Willowgrass got to enjoy his efforts.

"It's after five now," I said with a glance at the black and silver Patek Philippe watch that William had given me. "I didn't think you'd still be here."

"I've been helping Ben's pastry chef. There's a fixed menu, but both dinner services are sold out and that's a lot of desserts. Plus, I wasn't going to miss the chance to see my favorite girl's face when I reveal *the pie*." He put his hands up as though the words were emblazoned on bright lights along Broadway. They probably should have been. Beckett made the best key lime pie I'd ever tasted, and I'd asked him to make one as my Valentine's Day gift to William.

For the past week I'd been agonizing over the age-old question of what to get the man who had everything, because, in this case, billionaire William really *did* have everything. The light bulb had gone off when, in passing, William had let it slip that key lime pie was his favorite dessert. If he liked key lime pie, he was going to go orgasmic when he tasted *Beckett's* key lime pie.

"Ready?" Beckett took my hand and led me to a stainless steel table a bit away from the hustle of the line cooks. Clearly Beckett had deliberately set the scene. Lights shone down on the single pie in the center of the table. I must have sighed appreciatively because Beckett grinned and said, "I know."

It was seriously the most beautiful pie I'd ever seen. The meringue was artfully sculpted into an array of tiny peaks and valleys, with the tips of the little points lightly toasted to perfection. A meticulous graham cracker crust peeked out from the top edge of the pie pan, and in the center, a few delicate slices of candied lime sparkled and crowned the creation. It looked incredible and almost too good to eat. "I'm drooling, Beckett. You've outdone yourself."

"My produce guy really came through with the key limes. Leave it to you to ask for fresh key limes in February, but with what you're paying, I could afford to have them flown in from Florida this morning. Now I need your assurance that you'll pay for my hand surgery. I think I got carpal tunnel from squeezing all those tiny little limes. And it's my right hand. You know what that means."

I rolled my eyes. Beckett was still Beckett. He glanced out the now-open double doors into the main dining room, then back at me.

"Who's the muscle at the bar, Cat? He's pretty hot. Maybe you should introduce us."

I glanced at Asa, who was still looking out of place at the bar, and then back at the lovely pie. "That's Asa Singer. He's my driver and protector today."

"So romantic. Just like Whitney Houston and Kevin Costner in *The Bodyguard*."

"Yeah. Without the singing or the romance, though."

Beckett leaned on the table and sighed. "I'm glad William is taking your protection so seriously. You were practically hysterical when you called me about what went down at your condo last week. Scared the shit out of me. You apparently scared the shit out of your boyfriend, too, which is a good thing given his response."

I didn't want to talk about the break-in or about William's security measures, so I switched subjects. "What do you and Alec have planned for tonight? Don't you need to get home and get ready?"

Beckett blushed, and my mouth dropped in shock. Beckett never blushed.

"Alec has a surprise for me."

"A surprise? How romantic!"

Beckett straightened and then leaned back on the table again. "I'm supposed to show up at his place at eight. He said I won't be cooking."

"Intriguing."

Beckett fidgeted with the table's corner and...blushed. Again! Beckett had confessed he might be in love with Alec. From all I'd seen, Alec really cared for him too. I was happy to see Beckett happy and finally falling for someone.

The two of us had spent many Valentine's Days bemoaning our single status. While I'd always kind of gagged at the Hallmark holiday, Beckett really went in for the hearts and flowers and romance of the day. He went for that in real life too.

I gave his arm a squeeze. "Enjoy tonight, love. You deserve it. You deserve to be wined and dined and treated like a king."

"Or queen." Beckett cackled, and I laughed. "What's on your Valentine's Day agenda?" he asked, then held up a hand. "If it involves the kitchen floor, don't tell me. I haven't been barefoot in your kitchen since your *pain au chocolat* reveal." He gave me a wicked smirk, which I countered with a playful smack.

"No kitchen floors. We're having a quiet night in…with pie." I gestured to the decadent culinary masterpiece before me.

"Ha! You two sex maniacs don't know how to do 'quiet.'" He leaned close, speaking in a whisper. "Just so you know, that graham cracker crust doesn't belong in certain places. Hint, hint."

Now I could feel my cheeks heat. "Obviously I tell you way too much about my sex life."

"And you'd better not stop! Any idea what William's getting you? More diamonds? Your own plane? Maybe an island?"

"Oh, yeah, right."

"Seriously, if he gives you an island, can we go this weekend? I'm so over the snow and the cold. I could totally use some beach time."

"He's not getting me an island, Beckett. Actually, we decided no gifts."

Beckett staggered back in mock horror. "Are you fucking kidding me, Cat? What's wrong with you? Your boyfriend is one of the richest men in the country, and he's head over heels in love with you. Of course he's going to get you a fabulously expensive present. Let him spoil you because he can. Stop fighting it."

I hadn't thought of it that way. I just hadn't been able to think of anything to get William, until the pie, so I'd suggested we not do a gift exchange. William had seemed to agree. I blushed again, remembering how William had then changed the topic with several lingering kisses that turned into a lot more. I cleared my throat. "Well, I'm not expecting anything other than a nice night at home with my boyfriend."

"Don't forget the pie!"

"Right. Of course. A quiet night and delicious pie."

Beckett waggled his eyebrows. I'd never seen anyone, outside of a cartoon, waggle their eyebrows like Beckett.

"Pie we're going to eat off of plates, with forks, like civilized people."

"Keep telling yourself that, Cat. And call me tomorrow with all the messy details."

"Hey, you'd better have details too," I said while he produced a white cardboard cake box and carefully slid the pie into it.

We kissed goodbye, and I headed back into the restaurant, carrying my cake box tied with a shiny red satin ribbon. Asa stood and trailed right behind me, doing his best guard dog imitation.

TWO

Thanks to Asa's cutthroat driving, we arrived at William's penthouse just a short time later. Asa rode up in the elevator with me, and when the door slid open, revealing William's expansive foyer, he motioned for me to stand back while he secured the perimeter—or whatever it was those special ops guys did. As I waited, Laird bounded forward, barking excitedly. He was my real guard dog, and I still felt a wave of relief every time I saw him.

I really thought I'd lost Laird. When Minerva had called about the break-in my condo and told me that Laird was missing, my heart had stopped. Laird had been Jace's dog, then our dog, and then one of the few things connected to Jace that I'd brought to Chicago when I moved from Santa Cruz almost a year ago. So much of my life in Santa Cruz was fading into hazy memory, but Laird was a living, breathing, barking reminder that it had all been real and that it had mattered. I'd been so relieved when a DePaul student had called and said Laird had followed her home from the library. She'd been up late studying, so she'd let him sleep at her place and then called first thing the next morning. I hadn't cared about anything else in my condo. I could have replaced everything but Laird.

Laird had easily adjusted to life in the penthouse and his new "family." Asa motioned for me to exit the elevator, and Laird's nails clicked on the marble floor as he followed Asa and begged for attention. I set the cake box on a side table and grabbed Laird's collar. "Settle down, boy."

Asa gave me an appreciative look and said, "I'll take Laird for a walk."

When Laird heard *walk*, he barked again, the sound echoing through the cavernous space. "Thanks," I said, scratching Laird behind the ears. The irony that William's high-paid security experts had also proved to be expert dog walkers wasn't lost on me. I didn't mind walking Laird, but William had argued that he didn't want me strolling around the Gold Coast alone. Rather than take a security member with me, it was easier just to let Asa—or George or Anthony—do the dog walking. And since in Laird's estimation, nothing save table scraps beat a walk, my dog had a whole slew of new best friends.

After Asa pronounced the penthouse safe and left with Laird, I moved the pie to the kitchen, then headed to the master suite. I planned to take a long soak in a scented bubble bath before getting ready. Though we were planning a quiet night, that didn't mean there couldn't be a little excitement. Lingerie and Valentine's Day went together like chocolate and more chocolate, and I had a sexy red ensemble to slip into. William was going to love it.

*****

William arrived home just after seven o'clock. With his tie loosened and his hair adorably tousled, I felt the familiar urge to run my fingers through his thick, dark curls. Even after a full day of mastering the universe, his charcoal suit looked impeccable, as did the man wearing it.

I'd slipped into my racy new lingerie and pulled on a pair of distressed boyfriend jeans and a cute black sequined top I'd bought at Zara a few years ago. Strappy black stilettos would have looked great, but we were staying in, so my feet were bare, showing off my newly pedicured red toenails.

We met in the living room and I went easily into his arms. I was greeted with, "There's my beautiful girl," as he pulled me tighter against him and slanted his mouth over mine.

He would have given me a quick kiss, but I didn't pull away, allowing my lips to linger and my tongue to gently entwine with his as a promise of what was to come. My hands slid over his muscled chest and down his rock-hard biceps. He smelled delicious, as always, and looked like he'd come from a photo shoot for *GQ*. "You look good enough to eat," I purred.

"You look pretty great yourself." He gave my ass a quick pat and moved away. I waited for a *Happy Valentine's Day*, but he was already leafing through his mail.

"What would you like to do for dinner?" I asked, trying to sound casual.

William shuffled an envelope to the back of the stack. "I already grabbed something," he said. "I had a meeting and had to skip lunch."

Okay. We'd agreed on a quiet night, but I thought we'd at least have dinner together. Maybe I'd misunderstood. I wasn't going to make a big deal out of it, and I said, "Great. Well, I have dessert then."

"That's nice." He was still looking at the damn mail.

"I thought so."

Something in my tone finally made him look up, and he frowned. "Dessert? On a Wednesday night? That's a little odd. What's going on?"

I blinked at him. Had he seriously forgotten what day it was? Here I was with pie and sexy lingerie, ready to celebrate our first Valentine's Day together, and he thought it was just any other Wednesday. I put my hands on my hips. "It's not *just* Wednesday," I said icily. "It's Valentine's Day, remember?"

"Valentine's Day? Are you sure?" But he couldn't stop himself from smiling.

He was totally messing with me. "William!"

He started laughing. "Of course I remember. Practically every woman in the building had flowers delivered. And I ran into more than a few guys who were freaking out about what to buy their wives or girlfriends." He pulled me into his arms again, sliding his hands over my hips. "Even if I'd wanted to forget—which I didn't— I would have been reminded."

"Lucky for you we said no gifts."

"Yes, lucky me."

I grinned at him. "Though I might have a little something for you," I teased. "Guess."

"Oh, really?" His fingers made small circles on my hips, dipping lower to caress my ass. "A heart filled with chocolates?"

"No, but it is red." I lifted a hand to my shirt and slowly undid a button to reveal a red bra strap. William's eyes, now a smoky grey, followed the movement.

"My favorite color. A tie?"

I undid another button, revealing the lace. "No…"

His hands cupped my bottom, pulling me against him. "Silk boxers?"

"You're getting closer."

"And you're taking way too long with those buttons." He gripped the fabric in his hands and yanked it open. Buttons and a few sequins went flying, and I gasped with surprise and also a little bit of pleasure.

"That was silk."

"I'll buy you another," he said as he buried his lips against my neck, trailing a line of kisses down to the V between my breasts. "Where did you get this?" He moved back to take me in with his hot gaze. My nipples hardened, and I knew he could see the effect he was having on me since the lace was sheer.

"Oh, just something I had in the back of my closet." The truth was it had taken three separate shopping trips to find the perfect ensemble. The La Perla bra was made of delicate scarlet botanical lace. It was beautiful and more than a little risqué and it cupped my breasts to perfection.

"Like hell." He flicked the buttons of my jeans open and slid them over my hips, then groaned. "Crotchless?"

The matching thong was as indecent as a $90 tiny piece of handmade, red, Italian lace meant to conceal nothing could be. The set was simply scorching and when I'd seen it and imagined William's reaction to it, I'd had to have it. "You like?" I purred.

William's hungry eyes traveled up and down the length of me. "Oh, I like. Very much," he growled.

I kicked my jeans off, returned to his embrace and pressed against him. Our mouths met in a hot tangle of lips and tongues while his hands slid down my ass and then between my legs to cup my bare sex. His pelvis rocked into me, pressing the length of his now very hard cock against my exposed flesh. I moaned as he covered my aching nipples with his hot mouth. He swirled the taut points under the lace with his tongue until I was panting. Only then did he give me what I wanted, sucking a nipple into his mouth so that an electric current of pleasure rocked through me.

"Harder," I cried, but he always knew what I wanted, and he pulled away, teasing my hard point and working it with his tongue. I was wet now, the dampness making my thighs sleek, and when he sucked my nipple into his mouth again, I almost lost it right then and there.

"Don't you dare," he commanded, and I whimpered.

I wanted to demand that he fuck me, but no one demanded anything of William. He'd only draw out the torture if I got too bossy, so I focused on holding back my orgasm and letting it build.

"Good girl," he said, his mouth still on my breast, one hand on my butt and one wrapped around my back. "Your tits look amazing in this, but I'm tempted to…" He trailed off then bared his tooth. Taking the delicate lace in his mouth he ripped it and exposed my nipple to the air. He licked it then blew, and I shivered.

"You realize this lingerie was very expensive," I said as he ripped the lace above my other nipple.

"I'm improving it." He kissed me again, his tongue sliding between my lips as his fingers fondled me. The heat building between my legs made me rock harder against him. Mercifully, his hand slipped down, and I felt his warm fingers slide between my bare folds. "You're so wet, Catherine," he murmured against my mouth. "So sleek and wet." One finger slid slowly into me, and my walls clenched around him.

"Oh please," I murmured breathlessly. If anyone had asked me if I was the sort to beg, I would have said never in a million years. But William made me beg, and he made me like it.

"Not yet, beautiful girl, I want to taste you."

The next thing I knew I was off my feet and being carried across the room. He settled me on the edge of the couch, pushing my legs open and kneeling between them. He bent and I braced for the feel of his mouth. When it didn't come, I looked down at him. He was watching me, a mischievous look in his eyes. "William," I said, my tone pleading.

"Your hands, Catherine."

I realized I had my hard nipples between my fingers, stimulating them while I waited for him to give me release.

"Put them down." His eyes still sparkled as he spoke softly and directly in that dark, uncompromising voice that made me shiver from head to toe. "If you move them, I'll have to do something about it. Keep them at your side."

I lowered my hands and gripped the suede material of the couch on either side of me. Obedience was worth everything it cost me because of the dark pleasure it always brought. I craved that kind of pleasure more and more now.

His mouth descended on me, his tongue scraping over my sensitive bead. I bucked, arching my hips to give him better access. His tongue dipped inside me and the heat was heavenly. God, I loved this.

"You are my favorite delicacy," William whispered, pressing his cheek to my inner thigh. His lips were glistening with my moisture and I wanted to reach down and run my fingers through his thick, dark curls, but I kept my hands where he'd ordered them to stay. "I'll never get enough of you," he muttered, then his tongue was inside me again, sliding out to stroke my swollen clit and then back in. My hips moved with William's rhythm as his eager tongue licked me, bringing me closer and closer to the edge. But I wouldn't come. Not until he permitted it. My legs were shaking, and I was making small whimpering sounds. Finally, his tongue probed deep and, with his teeth scraping lightly against me, he said, "Come."

I jerked and let go, feeling the waves of pleasure crash over me. At some point I was aware that William had moved away. I looked up, noting he was still fully dressed. He opened his expensive trousers and pulled out his hard cock. It was beautiful. Long and thick, it jutted out magnificently. A pearl of semen already crowned the tip, and my hips arched toward him in welcome.

He entered me hard and fast, and on the heels of my first orgasm, I felt myself building toward another, even more powerful. He rocked into me again and I put arms around his neck. He growled, "Naughty girl." He captured my hands and, clasping my wrists, he raised them over my head, pinning me to the couch as he fucked me and I deliciously surrendered.

He thrust savagely at first, but then he slowed, his eyes on mine as he moved slowly and deliberately. His hips rolled, pressing and stroking those places deep inside that made my toes curl. I mewled like a kitten as his cock swelled. He was close, but he didn't speed up and he didn't lose eye contact. His eyes were so impossibly dark as they searched mine. I saw love there and tenderness and need. I hoped I reflected it back.

"Now," he murmured, kissing me gently. "Come with me."

He thrust again, and I came apart.

*****

I wore William's shirt and he wore nothing but his trousers while we ate key lime pie. "This is the best gift I've ever received," he said, forking up another mouthful of Beckett's sweet creation. I had to admit, Beckett had outdone himself. William had lied about already eating. He'd had a four-course dinner delivered from one of his favorite French restaurants and had paired it with a bottle of delicious *pouilly-fuisse*, which was crisp and refreshing.

William had gone on about the wine, of course. I'd loved watching his eyes light up as he spoke passionately about Chardonnay grapes and wanting to try producing a similar kind of white at WML Vineyards and aging it in real oak casks, which I learned was unusual these days. I'd had one slice of Beckett's decadent pie and couldn't eat another bite. William, on the other hand, was on his second piece of pie. He licked a bit of meringue off his lips, and I started thinking about how that cream would taste on his cock.

"Before your thoughts turn in that, much appreciated, direction," he said, reading me perfectly, as always, "I have a present for you."

"You already gave me your gift. Dinner was delicious. And before dinner, well, that was..." my voice dropped off as I coyly looked up at him through my lashes.

He chuckled. "Another gift then." He reached for his coat and pulled a business envelope from the inside pocket.

"William! We said no gifts."

He handed me the envelope. "*You* said no gifts. And need I remind you, you didn't even adhere to your own stipulation." He gestured to the half-eaten pie. "Not that I mind." He nodded to the envelope. "Open it."

With a little frisson of excitement, I tore the envelope open and unfolded the paper. The first thing I saw was an aerial shot of a tropical island. I looked at William, then back at the photo. It couldn't be. "Have you been talking to Beckett?" I asked.

"No. Why?"

I leafed through the pages, which described the private Caribbean island and all of its amenities. "Oh my God. You really did get me an island."

"I thought you'd be more surprised."

I shook my head. "I'm in shock. An island, William?"

"Only through the weekend," he clarified, as if that made it a lesser gift. "We can leave whenever we want—tonight, tomorrow morning."

"To our own island?"

He nodded. "Just you and me. Thousands of miles away from here, where it's warm and sunny. The whole weekend all to ourselves, days and days where I can keep you chained to my bed and have my wicked way with you."

I laughed. "That sounds delicious."

He raised his brows. "It will be. But let's bring the pie just in case."

God, I loved this man.

How could I not?

THREE

"I don't think Laird even missed me," I said after giving my dog another hug. Laird barely noticed. He was too busy playing with his favorite Kong toy. William closed the door to his massive closet and glanced over.

"George said Asa and Anthony took turns taking him on walks and hanging with him. He wasn't lonely."

"I'm glad." I gave Laird a last pat, which he ignored, and then I all but melted when William put his hands on my shoulders and massaged. I sighed. "I can't possibly have any tension left in my muscles. Not after four days on Tropos."

"Good," William said, kissing my neck. Delicious shivers ran through me as his stubble scraped lightly against my tender skin. He moved away and carried his toiletry bag to the bathroom. I watched his easy, familiar walk and appreciated how his faded jeans rested so dangerously low on his hips. He was effortlessly sexy and I never tired of watching him. I'd gotten used to him strutting around naked on the island, and now I missed seeing his defined, sinewy muscles flex under his gorgeously tanned skin.

We'd had the entire island to ourselves, and our getaway had been the perfect Valentine's Day present. Like William, I'd spent pretty much the entire vacation naked. We'd flown to a British

Virgin island on one of William's private jets, then we were helicoptered to nearby Tropos. The tiny island was owned by some titled English business tycoon and it was incredibly luxurious—and incredibly private. It could accommodate up to thirty guests, but it had been just me and William—and the very discrete staff—on the island during our stay. We hadn't had to worry about anyone seeing us sunbathing in the nude or making out in the warm Caribbean waters.

Had anyone been watching us, they would have gotten an eyeful, as we'd done a lot more than just make out. I'd always known William had a voracious sexual appetite, but I hadn't realized exactly just how voracious. I'd lost count of the number of times we'd had sex, and I don't think there was a place on the island or in the opulent Balinese-style house we hadn't made use of—the beach, the pool, the Jacuzzi, a chaise, the shower, a hammock, the garden, the kitchen. It had been decadent and glorious. We'd spent long afternoons out of the heat of the day in a huge, teak, four-poster bed draped with a gauzy white canopy and curtains. The house had open galleries on every side so the tropical breeze and gentle lapping of the surf had provided the soundtrack, and a dazzling white beach and the cerulean blue ocean were literally just steps away. I'd seen a lot of beaches in my life, but nothing as beautiful as that.

Except maybe William.

He'd been so relaxed and open on Tropos. It wasn't just the sex. That would never be a problem between us. It was the hours we'd spent talking and laughing together that had felt so right. We'd both forgotten all of our problems back in Chicago and we'd connected in a way we hadn't before.

I hadn't had any of the doubts I'd had on our Napa trip and I'd tried hard not to overthink things and to just feel. And what I'd felt was love. I'd *felt* loved by William, cherished and adored even. And I loved William just as deeply as I'd loved Jace, maybe even more so. Admitting that didn't feel like any kind of betrayal now. Jace was dead and I deserved to find happiness again. And I was really lucky because I had.

I stood and pulled my hair out of its ponytail then fished around in my suitcases for something warm to wear to bed. Even with the heated floors, the master suite seemed cold after four days in the Caribbean. I could hear William in the bathroom, putting his things away, turning on the water to brush his teeth, and it all sounded so familiar. I remembered getting ready for bed like this with Jace and that same feeling of comfortable companionship came over me. But my relationship with William was very different from my marriage. It was more mature, more grounded. I'd been just out of college when Jace and I had married, but I'd grown up a lot since he'd died and I wanted different things now.

As if he'd heard me thinking about him, I glanced up and found William leaning on the bathroom's doorframe, watching me. "It's been hard for you," he said.

"What do you mean?" Nothing had been difficult on Tropos. Just the opposite, in fact.

He moved into the room. "The break-in at your condo, living here, having a bodyguard follow you everywhere you go."

"Oh, that." It had been nice to forget all of that for a few days, and it would be nice to forget it permanently. Now that we were back in Chicago, it struck me again how quickly my life had changed since William and I met. Most of those changes had been good, but not all.

He gestured toward my two suitcases, which I'd propped open at the foot of the bed. "You haven't even really unpacked. I cleared space in the closet for you, but you aren't using it."

"I haven't had time."

William raised a brow. Yeah. We both knew that wasn't true. I sighed. "I don't know. It feels strange, I guess. That's your closet."

"Catherine—"

I held up a hand. "I know what you're going to say. I should treat this like my home. I'm welcome here. All that."

"If you know it, why don't you do it?"

I shrugged. "Because this isn't my place. It's yours, and I guess I like the reminder that I'll be going back to my own condo soon." Before he could interrupt or argue, I hurried to finish. "Everything has happened so fast. And I was only here for a week after the break-in and then we went to Tropos. I thought everything would be cleared up in a few days, and I'd be back home by now."

William crossed to me and took me in his arms. It always felt like coming home when he held me, which was probably one of the reasons I tended to forget how weird it was that we were living together already.

"Like I said, I know it's been hard for you." His deep voice vibrated through me since he was holding me close against his sculpted chest. "I spoke with the police before we left for the Caribbean and they were still investigating the incident at your condo. George is putting everything he has into finding who sent those pictures. I'll get another update first thing in the morning."

I smiled up at him. "Thanks. Do you think my description of the guy I saw in my building helped at all?" The morning of the break-in, I'd let in a repairman who said he was there to fix a leaky pipe. But it had turned out there was no leaky pipe and he definitely wasn't a plumber. That was the only solid lead we had.

"Every little bit helps. Whoever is behind this thinks he can go around terrorizing the people I love." He squeezed me. "I'm not going to let that go unpunished. We'll find him."

"I know."

"In the meantime, you're safe here. With me." He squeezed me tighter.

I looked up at him. "And I love being here with you. I mean, what's not to love?"

His eyes narrowed. "But?"

Shit. He already knew me so well. I wanted to be honest, so I took a deep breath and blurted out, "But this is really way too soon for us to be living together. I mean, *really* living together. Plus, I miss my stuff, you know? I love my condo. I miss my bed, my desk, my darkroom. I really miss my darkroom."

William looked at me, his eyes a clear bright blue, that "take no prisoners" blue I was sure had stared down more than a few business rivals across the negotiating table. He wasn't going to give an inch. "What can I do to make you more comfortable here?" he asked.

I knew he was completely sincere and was willing to be accommodating, but that wouldn't change the fact that this was his place, his style, his domain or that this is where he wanted me to *stay*. "You can keep pushing for the authorities to resolve this whole thing so I can go home," I said.

William tensed. "Catherine, I don't think you quite understand what we're dealing with.

I pulled out of his arms. "What are you saying?"

"I'm saying that maybe you living here shouldn't be just temporary. Having you here is the only way I can truly protect you."

I shook my head. "I don't accept that. I'm not ready to give up my condo or my stuff." I crossed my arms over my chest. "I'm going home again, William. I'll be perfectly fine. And *we'll* be perfectly fine," I added.

William held up his hands. It was a gesture of surrender, though he'd never actually surrender. "You're still not safe. If there's something you need, security can retrieve it for you."

"I need to go home." I was suddenly desperate for my own space, away from William's paranoia about the whole situation. I'd been unnerved by the break-in too, but I'd found out there had been a string of similar incidents in my neighborhood. The cop that night had told me that burglary was the most common crime in Lincoln Park. Which meant I wasn't so certain the break-in and the pictures I'd been sent were related.

But William wouldn't even listen when I tried to tell him my thoughts. He was way overreacting to everything. And I'd gone along so far because I'd been scared and because it was hard for me to tell him no sometimes.

"Listen to me, Catherine." He took me by the arms. It was a gentle but firm hold. "Do not go to your condo without Asa or Anthony, and then only if it's absolutely necessary. Understand?"

"Okay, but if I'm going to be here longer, I'll need a few things."

"Like I said, security can retrieve whatever you need."

Like my independence? I thought, but said nothing.

*****

I washed my face and brushed my teeth before changing into a T-shirt and flannel pajama bottoms. When I came out of the bathroom, William was lying in bed with his head propped on his elbow, watching me. I knew that look, but I just couldn't believe he was interested in more sex. "I'm going to get some socks," I told him.

"I'm just going to take them off again." He crooked a finger at me. "Come here, Catherine. I promise I won't let you get cold."

I hesitated but I wasn't going to win the battle, so I padded over to stand before him. He gave me a long, hot look. "You know, I think I've made a miscalculation," he said.

"You? Never." I was teasing, but he didn't smile.

"I didn't realize how hot you look in T-shirts."

I laughed. "Right."

He sat up. "I'm being serious. I like how that shirt stretches across your tits. Nice pokies."

"That's because I'm cold." But it wasn't. It was because he was giving me that look, the one that made everything inside me churn with need.

"Take it off," he demanded.

"If you like it so much—"

"If *you* like it, take it off before I tear it off." His voice was little more than a growl, and I knew he meant it. Since the T-shirt was one I'd bought in Australia when I'd accompanied Jace to a big surfing event there, I wanted to keep it. But I wasn't going to let William rush me. Slowly, I tugged it up and pulled it over my stomach, revealing my breasts inch by inch, finally pulling it over my head and dropping it on the floor.

"Your nipples are rock hard," he observed. They were. A moment ago, I hadn't been thinking about sex. Now I couldn't wait for him to touch me. Just thinking about him sliding inside me made my nipples ache. I reached up to fondle them, something that drove him crazy, but he shook his head. "Take your pants off. Slowly."

I grinned. "I'm not sure I can make a flannel strip tease very sexy."

"You can make anything sexy," he said, and his eyes were so molten grey I believed him.

I tugged at the tie of the pants, loosening it, then dipping my fingers into the waist of the pajamas. Millimeter by millimeter I lowered them over my tanned skin. William hadn't forgotten to feed me on Tropos—he never forgot to feed me, so there might have been a little more of me to see than when I'd first met him. That didn't seem to faze him. He said he liked my curves. I hoped so, because it didn't seem likely that his love affair with food was going to end anytime soon, which meant mine wasn't going to end either.

The pants slid over my hips and down. I wiggled a little to help their progress, though they were loose enough that it wasn't necessary. But the way William leaned forward told me he liked it, so I slid the pants lower until they hugged the curve of my buttocks. With my thumbs hooked in the waistband, I could feel the heat coming from my body. I was already wet for him, and I dipped my hand lower and slid a finger through the dampness pooling on my sex. I moaned quietly, then trailed my fingers up my belly and between my breasts.

William's eyes were impossibly dark now. I could practically feel the pulse of his arousal radiating toward me from the bed. I sashayed around until my back was facing him and wriggled the pants off my hips.

"Nice ass," William murmured. His voice was low and husky. I glanced at him over my shoulder then allowed the pants to drop to the floor.

"Oops," I said, and bent over, very slowly, to retrieve them.

I heard William's quick intake of breath and was smiling to myself when he barreled into me and pinned me to the wall. He'd moved so fast my head was spinning. One minute he was lying in bed, looking like a hungry panther. Now he'd grabbed me about the waist and propelled me against the wall. His hands cupped my breasts and his knee kicked my legs apart. "Enough teasing," he murmured in my ear. "Put your hands against the wall."

"William—" I don't know what I intended to say, but William wasn't having any dissention.

"Hands on the wall. Palms flat."

I obeyed, pressing my hands against the wall. William took my hips in his hands, pressing down until I was bent and exposed. Holding me steady, he drove his hot cock into me. The savagery of it both surprised and exhilarated me. I loved it rough, and he was usually so gentle with me. He pounded into me, his hands sliding up to fondle my breasts, teasing my hard points until I was panting with pleasure and the promise of more to come. His balls slapped against me in a rhythm I couldn't resist. I rolled my hips against him, taking him deeper, pressing against him where I needed him most.

He drove into me again and filled me so deeply I had to dig my nails into the plaster. He slid out, every inch of him sending little frissons of pleasure through me. I sighed and closed my eyes, enjoying his hard member and the way he wielded it. Then he thrust into me again, and I threw my head back, biting my lip to keep my orgasm at bay.

"You're close," he said, his voice as ragged with desire as I felt.

"I'm there. William, please."

"Come for me, beautiful girl," he said, shocking me with his easy capitulation. Usually he made me wait until I was screaming with want. I let go, rocking back on him until I milked every last ounce of pleasure, until I was so sated that only William's hands on me and my palms against the wall kept me upright. Slowly, I opened my eyes and realized William hadn't finished with me.

There was only one reason he'd let me climax so quickly.

He had more in mind.

His teeth scraped against my shoulder and my skin pebbled in response. His breath was hot on my skin when he said, "Get in bed." He pulled out, and I was relieved his hands grasped my waist because otherwise I might have fallen over. I stood up, my legs wobbling under me, and William swept me into his arms.

"I could have made it," I protested, but the truth was I melted when William gave me what I called 'the princess treatment.'

"But I like carrying you," he said, kissing me and laying me down on the bed, which was still slightly warm from his body. "And you'll need your strength for what I have planned."

"And what's that?"

"I'm so glad you asked." He slid the door of the nightstand open, and I had to contain my surprise. William used a blindfold or handcuffs on me on occasion, but we'd never really gotten into sex toys. His cock was better than any vibrator, and he seemed to know it.

He pulled out a long silver container and flicked off the top. "Lube?" I asked. "I don't think we need it."

He eyed me wickedly as he cupped my sex and pressed his fingers between my damp swollen folds. "This, beautiful girl, isn't where I'm going to fuck you." He pressed the lever on the container and squirted a tiny amount of clear liquid onto his finger.

"It smells like…I don't know. Yummy."

"It's lightly scented with my personal fragrance."

I rolled my eyes and started to giggle. William's perfumers also made him scented lube? The ridiculous luxuries embraced by the super rich, the kinds of things I'd never imagine in a million years—like personally scented lube—constantly surprised me. And then William tilted the canister and squirted a thin line of the lubricant between my breasts. I gasped. The lube was cool but instantly began to warm to the temperature of my skin.

"Cold?" he asked, his gaze catching the way my nipples had puckered.

"Not anymore. It feels warm now. A little tingly."

He took a drop on his finger and rubbed it on one nipple and then the other. It was warm and pleasantly stimulating. "We'll have to try this somewhere else," I said.

"That's what I was thinking. But not tonight." He rose over me, his cock still jutting from between his legs. He was rock hard and unsatisfied. "Push your tits together for me, love. I want them wet and slippery."

I pushed my breasts together, barely resisting the urge to touch my nipples. The lube had begun to make them pulse and ache. I could only imagine how they'd feel if William used his skilled fingers on me. He'd given me a nipple orgasm before. I had no doubt he could do it again.

But now he clenched his legs on either side of my chest and slid his cock between my breasts. The lube warmed further when he glided through it, and at his movement I felt an answering pull in my sex.

"That feels good," he said, thrusting. I glanced down at his thick erection, the head of which glistened with lube as he worked it across my slick skin. I liked this position because I could look up at him and watch as he brought himself to orgasm. His thighs were taut, the muscles perfectly defined. His stormy eyes were intense as always, but when he looked at me I saw a ferocious love in their depths. I wanted to watch him climax, watch the way his throat worked to swallow and how his head fell back. I loved seeing when agony and ecstasy merged in that one powerful moment of release. But then his hands were on my breasts.

He didn't stop thrusting in the valley I'd made, but he plucked at my nipples, rolling them between his fingers. Something happened with the lube when he did that. It almost sizzled on my skin, making my already straining points even more responsive. William moved back and forth and his fingers worked my nipples until I was writhing beneath him. It was like he'd found a cord connected to my clit and he was tugging it gently, bringing me to closer and closer to the edge.

I moaned as the sensations he created with his hands reached a new height. William's cock was thick and the veins stood out. He moved fast, fucking my tits hungrily. Finally, he growled, "Oh God, I fucking love you, Catherine. I'm going to come."

"Yes." That was all the permission I needed to let go, and I felt the orgasm slam into me just as William pulled back and spilled himself all over my breasts. The hot liquid slid over my sensitive nipples, as my orgasm went on and on. William reached back, pressed a hand between my legs, and I shuddered the last of my release then closed my eyes and allowed myself to sink into oblivion.

*****

We snuggled in bed. I was dozing, but William still had plenty of energy. The light as he scrolled through his phone lit up his side of the bed.

"Anything interesting?" I asked with a yawn.

"Actually, yes." He moved to face me. "My aunt Abigail emailed."

I'd met William's aunt and uncle, his guardians after his parents' death, a couple of times. Most recently, William had taken me to dinner at their home in Lake Forest. I'd really liked his aunt. She'd given me a tour of the house, and in William's room she told me she'd never seen him as happy as he was with me. She also told me to be careful with him because he'd been hurt so many times.

"What's she up to?" I asked.

"She'd like you to call her."

I sat. "Why?"

In the glow from his phone, I saw the look of amusement on his face. "She's hosting a shower. I think she'd like you to come."

"Who's the shower for?" I asked, settling back down.

"Lauren, my middle cousin. You met her at The Peninsula."

I had an image of a tall, leggy blond. "Right. She's married. Her husband is Zach?"

"Good memory. Yeah. They're having a baby."

"You didn't tell me that."

He lowered the phone, dimming the light. "I'm telling you now."

"When is she due? She didn't look pregnant at The Peninsula."

"Um…June, I think?"

Wow. She must have been one of those women who never looked pregnant until they were eight months along and then only because they looked like they had a basketball under their dress.

"I don't know much about it. Abigail, Sarah, and Zoe are planning the whole baby thing."

That made sense. Sarah and Zoe were William's other cousins, and Abigail was the aunt who'd raised him.

"The whole baby thing?" I rolled my eyes. "This isn't a thing. You're going to have a new member of the family. A new little person!"

Silence.

"Is Lauren having a boy or a girl?"

"Yeah."

"William!" I smacked him lightly. "How am I supposed to buy her a gift if I don't know what she's having? Or maybe she isn't going to find out."

"I'm sure Abigail has all that info," he said, putting his phone on the nightstand and turning to pull me into the crook of his arm. I lay my head on this chest. He sighed. "She'll be happy to talk about it. She can't wait to be a grandmother. She's beside herself with joy."

"Aren't you excited to be a…what will you be? A second cousin? An uncle, really?" I raised my head and looked up but couldn't see his face in the dark.

"I'm excited that Abigail will finally get off my back. She's been riding me for years about having kids. But thanks to Lauren, she's eased up a bit." He pulled the blankets up over both of us and kissed the top of my head. "Abigail will give you all the details. Let's get some sleep." His voice trailed off.

I swallowed hard. He sounded so annoyed at the prospect of children. We hadn't talked about kids yet. Did William even want kids? I really wished I could have seen his face. Maybe then I could have read more into his words. Maybe this was something we should talk about—the two of us, having a family some day.

I yawned.

But not tonight.

FOUR

Monday morning I had a major vacation hangover. Watching William get ready for work had me missing our trip. We'd spent days alone together, just the two of us. I felt more connected to him than ever and I didn't want that feeling to end. But William had an empire to run and I had deadlines of my own. So after a quick workout, shower, and bowl of yummy granola prepared by William's cook, I headed to the study to get some work out of the way.

I couldn't complain. Photography was my passion, and it hardly even seemed like work. I took a moment with my mug of dark roast to admire the view from William's study. I really needed to get my camera out on the terrace. The frozen lake was an expanse of white and grey and in vivid contrast to the clear blue sky overhead. I knew that meant the air outside was crisp, but not too cold.

Look at me, I thought, *so in tune with Chicago's weather*. More and more this city was starting to feel like home, and I had William to thank for that. Despite my intense desire to get back to my condo, I had to admit that I could get used to the amazing view from my new workspace. William had gone out of his way to make me comfortable. My desk was outfitted with a top-of-the-line Mac, equipped with the latest photo-editing software. I had a printer, a scanner, and two monitors, one of which was giant—bigger than my TV.

I woke up the Mac. On the smaller screen, I had a document open with the proposal I'd written for Hutch Morrison for his digital cookbook project. I'd put it together almost immediately after our first meeting, and he'd barely looked it over before offering me the job.

I'd been so excited that I'd gushed about it to William for ten minutes before I'd realized he wasn't saying anything. "So what do you think?" I'd asked.

"Morrison is a great chef," William had replied coolly.

That was an understatement, although it was high praise coming from William, whose own culinary skills were right up there with some of the best chefs in the city—at least in my humble opinion. "This is such a fantastic opportunity for me. I really think a project like this could take me to the next level."

"I don't know. Are you sure that's what you want to do? A project like this might take you away from other opportunities."

"Of course, I'm sure. Hutch is at the top of his game and this project is innovative and unique. I would learn a lot and get some great exposure. I can't believe he thought of me for it."

That was when I'd caught the look on his face. He'd tried to hide it, but I knew him well enough to know when he didn't like something. His mouth had turned down slightly, and his eyes had iced to blue. It had hit me. William didn't want me working with Hutch Morrison.

"Wait, is it Hutch you're worried about?" I'd asked, but William had changed the subject.

He hadn't brought my working with Hutch up again, and since then, whenever I mentioned Hutch or his restaurant, Morrison Hotel, William found something else to talk about. I sighed heavily, turning my attention back to the proposal on the screen in front of me. Men and their egos—even if William was pretty cute when he was jealous.

I clicked to open a new window just as my cell rang. I didn't recognize the number, so I answered, "This is Catherine Kelly."

"Catherine, it's Abigail Smith. William's aunt."

I smiled. "Hi Abigail. William said you wanted me to call you."

"Well, I thought I'd better call you first thing since I'm giving you such short notice. It's unforgivably rude of me, I know. But I'd love for you to come to Lauren's baby shower on Saturday."

I didn't hesitate. "Thank you for inviting me. I'd love to come."

"I don't know why I didn't think of it sooner. I'm just not used to William having a...a woman in his life."

"Well, you're very sweet to think of me." I glanced at the image on the monitor and had an idea. "Do you have a photographer for the event?"

"No. Do you think I should hire a photographer?" Abigail sounded a little worried now. I could almost see her pulling out a pen and a pad of paper. "Who do you recommend?"

"Actually, I'd be happy to do it. That's if you want me to."

"Catherine, that would be lovely. Yes. Absolutely. Thank you so much for offering. But you must promise to enjoy yourself too."

"I will."

"Wonderful. I'll see you Saturday then. One o'clock at The Drake, which is just a short walk from William's, as you know."

After I hung up, I realized I'd forgotten to ask whether Lauren was having a girl or a boy. I'd have to call Abigail back later and ask.

I lost myself in my work for another hour and then my cell rang again, loud in the stark silence. I jumped and grabbed it. I didn't recognize this number either. "Catherine Kelly."

"Catherine, this is Lauren Matthews."

"Lauren, hi." I was a little thrown by Lauren calling me directly. We were hardly close, but I took it for what it was, a chance to get to know William's cousin—and to ask her first hand about the baby.

"I just talked to my mother, and she said you're coming to the shower. I'm so glad."

"Thanks. I'm happy to be included. It was sweet of you to think of me."

"And thank you so much for offering to take photos. I really appreciate it. Mom and I hadn't even thought to have the shower photographed. There's just so much to think about."

"I'm happy to. Congratulations, by the way. William says you're due in June."

"Yes! Can you believe it? I feel like I've been pregnant forever."

I hadn't had a lot of experience with friends being pregnant, so I didn't know what to say to that. "I'm sure it will go by faster than you think," I offered.

"You're probably right. Right now I'm just excited to see my sisters this weekend. Sarah and Zoe are both coming."

"I don't think I've met Zoe."

"Right. That's actually why I'm calling, sort of. Look, Catherine, I feel like I should warn you." Lauren's tone became hesitant. "Zoe can be, um, a bit of a handful."

What the hell did that mean? "Okay."

"She's really sweet. I love her to pieces, but when it comes to William, she gets a little intense."

Intense. Right. "Intense how?"

"They're so close, you know, and sometimes they just rub each other the wrong way and it can, well, escalate. They've always been like that. Ever since we were kids."

I was at a loss. William had never mentioned anything like this to me. Now I was getting nervous. "I'm sure we'll get along great."

"Yeah, that's the right attitude. Thanks, Catherine. And see you Saturday, okay?"

I hung up and stared at my cell for a long moment. That was a little odd. Now I was beyond curious and—if I were being honest—a little worried about meeting Zoe. What was the deal with her and William? And I still didn't know if Lauren was having a boy or a girl. *Shit*.

I closed my eyes and pressed my fingers to my temples. This was the part of a new boyfriend I wasn't ready for: getting to know the family. My experience with Jace's family had been less than stellar. I was determined my relationship with William's family wouldn't go the same way.

*****

A couple of hours later I was outside Beckett's apartment. Now that he was working baker's hours, he was home in the afternoon. Of course, Asa had had to drive me in the black SUV, and once we were out front, he insisted on going in first.

It was funny to think of someone lying in wait for me at Beckett's. I'd only been here a thousand times, and the most interesting thing I'd ever seen was a woman having a loud argument on her cell. But I got that this was part of Asa's job and that he took it seriously. And Asa in full commando mode was actually kind of entertaining. He insisted on walking in front of me into the courtyard of Beckett's building. He was trying to appear casual as he looked the place up and down, but everything about him screamed 'secret service.'

As we approached the outside door to the set of apartments where Beckett lived, a guy walked out and gave Asa a weird look. Then he looked at me, no doubt wondering what all the fuss was about. It hit me that I could really play this up. A big pair of sunglasses and people might think I was a celebrity.

After a quick look inside the building's entryway, Asa gave me the all clear.

"Thanks. I'll be at least an hour, Asa."

"I still think I should go up with you."

Yeah, that would be fun. "I'll text you when I'm ready to go."

"Okay, Miss Kelly."

Beckett opened the door as soon as I knocked and put a hand up to his eyes. "The light! My eyes!"

"Very funny." I pushed my way in, and Beckett closed the door. It might have been quitting time for Beckett, but he wasn't the kind of guy who lounged in sweatpants. He looked great in distressed jeans and a black T-shirt. I took off my coat and revealed my own black T-shirt. "Great minds," I said, giving him a kiss on the cheek.

"The glow is blinding."

"It's called a tan."

"Oh, this is more than a tan. This is an all-over"—he waved his hands up and down—"radiance."

"A few days in the Caribbean will do that."

"A few days of hot, no-holds-barred sex will do that, you mean. You look…shall we say, satisfied?"

I could feel the heat in my cheeks, but I couldn't stop the smile. The sex had been spectacular, but I wasn't going to discuss details with Beckett—at least not right now. He already thought that William and I were insatiable and I hated that he was right.

I tossed my bag on the table by the door and headed over to the couch. We'd had many long talks on this couch, and it was as familiar to me as my own couch in my condo. Maybe even more so now since my condo was off limits.

I took in Beckett's apartment—it was sleek, with a few bright accent pieces, including a bright green bench that Beckett placed below one of my photos. He had been an early and unconditional fan of my art, and I'd brought Beckett this piece when I moved to Chicago. It was a shot of the coastline in South Africa. I had followed Jace there on tour and loved that strip of pristine beach.

"So how's Alec?" I asked.

"Oh, Alec? We broke up." Beckett plopped down on the couch beside me.

I shot forward. "What? When? You didn't text me or call or anything! What happened?" I could not believe this.

He shrugged. "Valentine's Day wasn't that great for us. No private island, you know?"

I punched him lightly but felt a stab at the verbal jab. Private islands weren't my thing either. "Beckett, be serious. You don't give a shit about private islands."

He held up a finger. "Hey, I like private islands as much as the next guy." I glared at him. "Okay, *seriously*, what happened was we had a fight. A really big fight. And we both apologized and made up, but the next morning we both knew it was over. We agreed to remain friends. It's not like we hate each other or anything. It just didn't work out."

Holy shit. This was huge news. And I couldn't believe Beckett was being so casual about it. "Oh, Beckett." I hugged him hard. "I'm so sorry."

"Cat, I'm fine." He leaned back. "Really. I'm not heartbroken. At all. Look, no tears."

I could see that. It was strange. He almost seemed blasé about the whole thing. This was not like Beckett at all.

"Why not?"

"Cat, we were together for like a minute. Less than a minute. I mean, Alec is a great guy, but we barely know each other. Once we started to get to know each other better, we both realized it wasn't going to work. Our heads are just in different places."

"But…" I didn't even know what to say. Beckett and Alec were together only a couple of weeks less than William and me. I thought Beckett really liked Alec. Hell, I was sure he loved him. They'd seemed to get along so well and there was definitely tons of chemistry. What could have happened? And why wasn't Beckett upset at all?

"But," I said again, not sure what came next. What could I say to get him to tell me more?

"Oh, shit!" Beckett looked down at his watch. "I totally forgot I have to go meet the restaurant supply guy about loaf pans."

I stared at him, uncomprehending. Loaf pans? Seriously? He knew I was coming over. He chose the time for us to meet. I couldn't help but wonder if he was trying to get rid of me because he didn't want to talk about Alec. I was in shock. Was I supposed to argue? Maybe Beckett just needed his space? What was my job here as Beckett's bestie—let him throw me out or insist he talk to me?

"Beckett, I can come with you," I offered lamely.

"No, honey, I'm sorry. This whole new job thing has been a whirlwind. Things just keep popping up. I'm sorry to flake."

Left with no other choice, I followed Beckett out of the apartment, and when we stepped outside the building, Asa wasn't there. Of course, I told him I'd be an hour. He probably went to get a coffee or something and who could blame him. I weighed my options. I could stand here and wait, looking like an idiot, or I could try and find out more about what was up with Beckett.

"I'll walk with you."

Beckett arched a brow. "Think your hired muscle will like that?"

"It's a ten-minute walk from here to the bakery. I'll text him from the bakery, and he can pick me up there." I buttoned my coat and started walking, Beckett right beside me.

"So Tropos was really great?" Beckett asked. I was glad that he still wanted to keep talking, even if he was changing the subject from him and Alec.

"It was fabulous. I'm just sorry our trip meant we had to cancel dinner plans at William's penthouse. Maybe you and—maybe you can come over this week." God, I'd almost said *you and Alec*.

"Great."

I knew Beckett noticed my slip, but he didn't say anything. "Beckett, are you sure you don't want to talk about what happened—"

"Actually, I'm kind of glad you're coming to the bakery with me. I tried this new carrot cake recipe, and I wanted to tell you about it. Really, it's not the cake so much as the cream-cheese frosting." Beckett went on for the rest of our walk, talking about his special technique for whipping the cream cheese with confectioner's sugar, butter, and vanilla and then discussing some of his great new ideas for Patisserie LeClerc. They all sounded delicious.

My stomach was growling by the time we crossed Clark Street and headed down the block to where the bakery was located. It was right next door to The Webster, a new boutique hotel perched at the corner of Webster and Lincoln Park West that would be opening soon. The vintage building had been totally revamped and the entire block was about to become a hot destination in the neighborhood.

Once in front of the bakery, I covered my mouth in surprise. A huge *Coming Soon* sign stood in the window. It was flashy and totally professional, and they'd done a lot of work on the exterior. The whole thing looked hugely impressive.

"What do you think?" Beckett was watching me and smiling.

"Oh, Beckett." I grabbed his arm. "It's awesome. I can't wait to see the inside. Look at this window. It's almost the whole length of the shop! There'll be so much light." I was a photographer and I always thought about light.

"It's a great location, too."

"It's a perfect location." I hugged him. "I'm so happy for you. This is the big break you've been waiting for." I'd known it was going to be amazing, but I hadn't realized quite how amazing. The building, the location—right in the heart of Lincoln Park. I could just picture all the trendy, young moms stopping by for their morning coffee and all the neighborhood hipsters clamoring for a table to do whatever hipsters did on their days off. I couldn't help but wonder if William had more to do with this venture than he'd let on.

We said our goodbyes. I gave Beckett another hug and a quick kiss on the cheek, then pulled out my phone as he went inside. I really should have texted Asa then, but I knew I was going to get a lecture from him about not being where I said I would be. I glanced at the time, seeing that I still had some left before my hour was up.

And then I realized I was only a few blocks from my condo.

It felt like years since I'd been home and no way would Asa let me go. Which was stupid. I mean, what was going to happen? My condo was in a nice neighborhood where I had lived for a year, perfectly safe, until the random incident less than two weeks ago. A break-in where nothing was stolen. Besides, it was a gorgeous February day, one of those rare thirty-degree days without wind that offered the hope of spring. It was good to be outside, and I wanted to stretch my legs. So I started walking.

As I walked, my thoughts turned back to Beckett. I still couldn't believe he and Alec had broken up. I'd known him forever, and he was a total romantic. I mean, he'd gotten weepy when guys didn't call him after the first date. He had more ideas about his future wedding than I did. There was just no way he was as cool about this break-up as he acted. Why wouldn't he talk to me about it? Maybe he figured I couldn't relate. I met Jace my freshman year of college and then we got married right after I'd graduated. He'd died six months after the wedding, but that wasn't exactly the same thing as a break-up. It wasn't having someone voluntarily walk away from you.

William and I had had that big fight about the dossier I'd found on the women he'd dated. I'd been pretty miserable for a few days, but we hadn't broken up. When I thought about it, I'd never been dumped, and I'd never really dumped anyone—getting away from Jeremy didn't count. And Beckett had been—and still was— frustrated with me for complaining about my life. He had told me as much. Maybe I wasn't the person he wanted to confide in anymore. The thought broke my heart.

Still, I knew that there was more going on than Beckett was letting on, and I wanted to find out what.

FIVE

I smiled when I reached my building, which was as charming and welcoming as ever. I felt warm all over when I saw it, with no fear whatsoever. The converted old greystone mansion was my home, and I was thrilled I could have a few minutes alone here. I headed inside and stopped to check my mail in the foyer. I slipped my mail key in and pulled the door open, expecting envelopes to tumble onto the floor, but the box was empty.

Okay, that was odd. I'd been gone for almost two weeks. The box should have been full of junk mail and catalogues, at least. Was Minerva taking care of my mail? Or maybe William had had it held? On the way up to my condo, I stopped at the Himmlers and knocked on the door. Minerva opened it, her face breaking into a huge smile when she saw me. "Catherine! Darling!" She pulled me into her arms and hugged me tightly. "We've missed you," she said when she released me. "You look wonderful."

"So do you." She looked as trim and elegant as ever in a sweater and wool slacks. Her grey hair was swept up and back in an effortless twist.

"Come in, come in. I just made *bienenstich*. It will melt in your mouth."

"So that's what smells so good." The whole condo smelled like almonds and honey. "I can't really stay, but I wanted to stop by and check in." I spotted Hans sitting in his chair, reading a newspaper. He lowered it to smile at me. "Hi, Mr. Himmler."

"It's good to see you, Catherine. If you can't stay for cake, take some with you. We can't eat it all."

"Yes, take some to that handsome man of yours." Minerva motioned me into her kitchen, which was warm and homey as usual. It was full of vibrant colors that matched her personality. While she wrapped up two slices of the cake, we chitchatted about the neighborhood.

"No one has seen anything suspicious since the break-in?"

"Not a thing." Minerva slid open a drawer and pulled out aluminum foil. "And we've all been very careful not to buzz people in we don't know."

"Good. I worry about you and Hans. Call the police if you see anything that doesn't seem right."

Minerva laid a hand on my arm. "We're fine, Catherine, really. Besides, with the new security system, we will be safer than ever."

"You installed a security system? That sounds pricey"

"No, your William offered to have it installed. It's state of the art, with cameras and computer monitoring." She said more, something about keycards, but I wasn't listening. William was having a security system installed in my building? He'd never even mentioned it.

"Your William is very thorough, Catherine." She pressed the warm cake into my hands. "We're very grateful. You'll tell him?"

"Of course. Thanks again for the cake." I gave her a hug. "Oh, before I forget, I wanted to ask. Have you picking up my mail? My box was empty when I checked."

"No. But I have no doubt that man of yours took care of that for you, no?"

"I'm sure you're right," I said more to reassure myself than her. "I'll see you soon." I waved to Hans on the way out. "You too, Hans."

As I climbed the stairs, I could feel myself getting pissed. William hadn't said *one word* about the new security measures, even after I'd mentioned how much I wanted to go home. With a security system in place, my condo would be perfectly safe, so why was he insisting I stay at his penthouse indefinitely? William had promised to be open and honest with me but yet again, his version of that was still very different from mine.

I unlocked my door and walked in. The condo was so quiet and still, and it was weird not to have Laird bounding up to greet me. I almost felt like a visitor in my own home. I vowed that wouldn't last long. I'd be back soon.

I wanted to grab a few things, so I headed into the guest room and dug out a duffel bag. As I moved from room to room, I couldn't get over how eerie it was. It was the middle of the day, not dark at all, but my place seemed stale and different. I suddenly wanted to hurry and get out.

I grabbed some clothes from my bedroom and a few toiletry items, then on the way back to the kitchen, I spied the one picture of Jace I had displayed. It was of the two of us in Hawaii, the last time we'd been together. I had the urge to take it off the shelf and pack it, but how awkward would that be? Taking a picture of my dead husband to my new boyfriend's place? It was strange enough that William has a big Cat Ryder surfer print hanging in his living room. He definitely didn't need Jace staring him in the face every day. But this picture always felt like it belonged with me, just like Jace's memory, so I grabbed it and shoved it in my bag.

I headed into the kitchen. I tugged open the Sub-Zero thinking I'd clear out any spoiled items, but it was almost empty as always. Just a few condiments and my good bottle of champagne.

My arm started to hurt from all the stuff I was holding, so I placed the wrapped plate of Minerva's cake, my purse, and the duffel on the counter. Now unencumbered, I couldn't resist the lure of my darkroom. I'd converted the pantry of my condo into a darkroom right after I'd moved in. I just wanted to make sure it was in order, I told myself, and I headed in and shut the door out of habit.

I flicked on the red light and inhaled. Everything was right where I'd left it. There were prints still hanging on the line, long since dry, and I pulled them down, one by one, looking them over. A few shots of William and me, a few landscapes, a cute shot of Beckett. *I should take pictures at the bakery opening*, I thought. I could frame them and give them to Beckett as a gift. I thumbed through a stack of digital prints sitting on the table. These were my shots from the *nyotaimori* dinner—the naked sushi dinner—that William had staged for me. I'd been thinking about creating a series of small film prints based on the images as a gift for William. But I'd have to wait until I was home to start working on them. Just thinking about it made me excited and eager to get back to my art. I missed my darkroom and the way it relaxed me to work in here. There was something comforting about the process of developing film, watching the image materialize in the bath. I often lost track of time when I was in here and—shit, today was no different.

I checked my watch. I'd been in here for over half an hour just musing and looking around. Asa was definitely going to be looking for me and was probably worried. I turned the handle of the door and pushed, but the door didn't open. I pushed harder. It didn't even budge.

Okay, that was bizarre. Had I been gone so long that I couldn't even open the door to my own darkroom? I took a deep breath and tried again. Nothing. My heart raced. There wasn't a lock on the outside of the door. I didn't even have one on the inside. Something had to be holding it closed, somehow. I tried again, practically wrenching the knob off.

Tears welled up in my eyes and my palms started to sweat. "Calm down, Cat," I said out loud to myself. "Maybe the door is just stuck. Old buildings. Old doors. That happens."

Right? I wasn't so sure, but I needed to believe it. I took another deep breath and decided to try the door with more force. I moved back and slammed my shoulder into the door.

Nothing.

My heart thundered in my ears, and I started shaking. "Don't panic," I murmured to myself, but I was already doing just that. I checked my pockets, hoping I had miraculously brought my cell with me, but they were empty. My phone was in my purse, just like it always was. Shit.

I pounded on the door, slamming my fists into it. "Help! Help!" I screamed. Maybe somehow Hans and Minerva could hear me. Their kitchen was right under mine. Could I scream into a vent?

Impossible. This was a converted pantry, with no extra duct work. There was no way anyone could hear me.

Suddenly, the room seemed to close in on me, and all I wanted was to get out. I slammed against the door again and again, adrenaline surging through me, making me almost dizzy with fear and urgency.

Finally, I stood back and kicked the door. "Let!" Kick. "Me!" Kick. "Out!"

The door flew open, and I stumbled out as a screwdriver sailed across the kitchen floor. Instantly I realized the screwdriver had been wedged in the door frame, holding it shut until all my slamming and kicking dislodged it.

Someone had deliberately locked me in.

It seemed surreal. How was that even possible? I was sure I was alone in the condo.

A cold wind ruffled my hair, and I swung toward the back door, which was standing wide open. No way was that open before.

My gaze dropped to the counter and I saw the scattered contents of my purse and duffel. I stared at the evidence in disbelief, trembling, my heart racing. I was about to run for—I didn't even know where—when I heard, "Catherine? Miss Kelly?"

I practically crumpled onto the counter. I recognized Asa's voice and relief surged through me. "In here!" I yelled, my voice sounding hoarse and weak. I heard the front door bang open and the clump of Asa's boots as he raced to the kitchen. He took one look at me, surveyed the kitchen, and said, "Are you hurt?"

I shook my head then slid to the floor. I felt like I was going to throw up or pass out or both. Asa knelt down before me. "Tell me what happened."

Trying to hold back tears, I spilled the whole story. When I finished, Asa made no comment—nothing about how dumb I was or how I should have listened to him and William. Nothing about how much trouble he would be in when he explained to his employer that he had lost track of me. Instead, he pulled out his phone and started making calls. I closed my eyes and tried to stop shaking. I heard him tell whoever he was talking to that I was pale, shaken, and scared, but not hurt.

I just about had the nausea under control when Asa put a hand on my shoulder. I jumped, and he held his hands up in front of him. "Sorry. I'm taking you home now, Miss Kelly. We're to go to the penthouse immediately."

The penthouse. William. *Shit*. Asa carried me outside to the SUV, and I let him. I didn't think I could make it down three flights of stairs on my shaky legs anyway. He placed me in the backseat, handed me a bottle of water, and put the seatbelt into my hand. I managed to click it into place as he closed the door and walked around to the driver's side. Asa got in and quickly pulled the vehicle into traffic and I gripped the armrest, the pangs of fear I had felt in the darkroom still fresh in my mind.

On the way back to the penthouse, I stared out the window. Asa had picked up the screwdriver from my kitchen floor and placed it in a Ziploc bag and I'd watched him do it, staring in disbelief at the object. I didn't own a screwdriver, so whoever had come into my condo had brought it with them. Did they bring it just to lock me in? I shuddered at the thought of it being used as a weapon. As we approached William's, I started to calm down. I was safe. I also started to apologize to Asa. "I'm so sorry. I really don't want you to get in trouble."

"Don't worry about it, Miss Kelly."

"It was all my fault. I'll make sure he knows it."

Asa didn't answer, and we lapsed into silence. I was glad because I was still really nauseous. Wouldn't the day be perfect if I threw up in the back of William's SUV? I'd only ever felt this kind of fear once before and that was when Jace died. I never wanted to feel it again.

Finally we arrived at William's building. Asa opened the door for me and asked me if I was okay to walk. I said yes. He escorted me up to William's residence. He didn't exit the elevator when I did, leaving me alone in the foyer. Then William stepped into view.

He crossed to me in three steps and pulled me into his arms. He engulfed me in his warmth, his strong arms encircling me and holding me close. He put his head down and breathed in my ear, "Thank God." He wrapped his arms around me even tighter. I felt safe, loved, and oh so stupid. I lost it. I couldn't hold the tears back, and I started weeping and blubbering. "I am so sorry, William. I should have listened to you. I'm so sorry."

"Jesus, I'm not mad," he said against my temple. "I was so worried." He kissed the top of my head.

"I'm so sorry," I said again. I felt awful. I never meant to worry him. What a complete nightmare.

William pulled back and looked at my face. "I was so scared something happened to you. You have no idea what you mean to me."

His eyes were grey and as full of love as I had ever seen them. This man truly loved me. I had been a fool to put myself in danger. I burst into tears again, and William held me and rubbed my back until I was finally spent.

I was so tired by then that I allowed him to lead me to the bathroom, where he drew a bath, stripped me, and washed me. Everything was so tender. He touched me, as though I was some rare, priceless object. Then he dried me and took me to bed. He slid in next to me and pulled me against his chest.

"I love you more than I can say, Catherine. More than words. I can't lose you. Do you understand that? I can't."

I nodded and snuggled deeper into him. "I love you too, William." And I knew it was true. I had never felt safer or more whole than I did at that moment in William's arms.

He kept talking, telling me over and over how much I meant to him until I fell asleep.

SIX

I opened my eyes slowly, wiggling and writhing in William's expansive bed as spirals of pleasure wound through me. It was early and the room was still dark, but I could feel William's tousled curls softly brushing against the sensitive skin of my inner thighs. His tongue lapped leisurely at my sex, but he paused and raised his head when he realized I was awake.

"Good morning, beautiful girl."

"Yes, it is," I said with a moan as he gently thumbed my clit.

"It's about to get even better." His smile was wide, genuine, and a little bit devilish as he looked up at me from between my legs. I was barely awake, but I could feel myself yielding just from that look alone. God, how I loved playful William, even first thing in the morning and hours before my first cup of coffee.

William excelled at sex, but he really excelled at oral sex. William clearly loved it. He knew how to use his tongue, his lips, his whole mouth to keep me on the brink of coming for what seemed like forever, heightening my pleasure in tiny increments until I was insane with need. If he wanted to start the day with a little taste of me, who was I to say no?

I spread my legs wider.

William got right back to business. My hips bucked, and he pulled away, teasing me with darting little flicks and nibbles. When his tongue dipped lower, thrusting inside me, my moans intensified and echoed through the enormous master suite.

"You're so sweet, Catherine. Just like candy," William said, withdrawing and then licking me with long, luxurious strokes that threatened to shatter me.

"William, please," I begged. I could feel beads of sweat starting to break out across my forehead and chest. I hadn't even been up to pee yet and the building pressure was starting to get a little uncomfortable.

My pleas went unanswered as two and then three fingers were thrust inside me, filling me, pressing upward against my g-spot. It wasn't his cock, but it was enough to make me shudder and squirm.

"Oh fuck, oh fuck, oh fuck," I gasped. I was seriously uncomfortable now, but in the most delectable way.

He knew it, too.

"Do you want to come?" he asked innocently as his tongue continued its assault. My hips arched off the bed, and I struggled not to piston them.

"Uh-huh," I managed to say.

"Good." He pulled back, his lips and chin shiny with my arousal. His grey eyes caught and held mine just as he reared up and plunged his cock into me, then started to gently rock.

I spiraled up, feeling every nerve tightening and ready to explode until he withdrew, leaving just his wide swollen tip at my entrance.

"No," I choked out in anguish.

"What do you want? Tell me."

"You," I said hoarsely. "All of you."

Our eyes stayed locked as he slid into me, inch by delicious inch, and my muscles contracted around him, holding him in place. He rocked again, the tip of his penis angled perfectly, stroking me in that spot that drove me crazy. I could feel the tremors starting in my legs and I cried out, "I can't hold back."

"Almost there."

I could feel the contained power in him, the way he tensed before he said in a guttural shout, "Come with me, Catherine."

I did, grabbing his shoulder and holding on as he pumped into me, the climax ripping through us both.

We tumbled back, William rolling over and taking me into his arms. Usually I went back to sleep after we'd had morning sex, but not today. Memories of yesterday's incident started flooding back, even before William pulled out. The daybreak seduction might have been his attempt to keep my mind off of things, but—fabulous orgasm aside—it wasn't working. I could feel my chest tightening as flashes of being trapped in my darkroom and images of that screwdriver flying as I kicked my way out looped over and over again in my head.

I was still clasped in William's embrace, my head nestled under his chin and my ear pressed to his hard chest. He must have sensed my rising panic because he murmured, "I've got you, baby girl. I've got you. You're okay." He kissed the top of my head tenderly.

I nuzzled against William's neck and let his reassurances wash over me. I never wanted to leave right here, this moment. I closed my eyes and focused on my breathing, letting the steady thump of William's heart soothe me as his strong arms held me close.

I had just dozed off when William asked, "Feel like a workout?" His deep voice rumbled through me and he made the question sound way sexier than it was.

"Didn't we just have a workout?" I replied weakly.

"This one takes place in the gym, with our clothes on. Come on, it will do you wonders."

It was way too early to stand up, much less burn calories, but I agreed anyway.

On the way down to the building's private gym, I kept waiting for William to say something about me going to my condo. Even though he'd said he wasn't mad at me, I suspected he was actually pretty pissed that I'd made him worry and had put myself in danger. At the very least, he was entitled to an I-told-you-so, and I was ready to let him have his moment. Plus, we still needed to talk about the security system he was having installed in my building—the one he'd "forgotten" to mention.

But it didn't come.

We walked into the gym, which was empty except for us, and he gave my ass a squeeze, then hopped on one of the treadmills. He liked to watch the stock reports while he exercised, which had the potential to put me in coma, so I grabbed a couple of magazines and wandered over to an elliptical.

The magazines weren't half as interesting as watching William run on the treadmill. My man was in excellent physical condition. If not for the fine sheen of sweat on his body, you'd never know he was working hard. His breathing stayed level, even as the incline rose and his pace increased. He was like a fine-tuned machine, every sculpted muscle working in tandem with the others.

William glanced over at me and, when he saw I was ogling him, gave me a slow, smoldering smile. It was hard to exercise when I couldn't breathe, and I took a huge gulp of air when he looked back at the TV screen—and not just because he turned me on. I definitely needed to work out more. William never invited me to join him at the gym. Then it dawned on me: inviting me to this workout was another attempt to keep me busy and my mind off what had happened yesterday.

Okay, Cat, deep breath. I had to face it. What exactly *had* happened yesterday? I wasn't an idiot. There was no way another criminal had just randomly chosen to break into my condo, in broad daylight, at the exact moment I happened to be there, then spontaneously decided to lock me in my darkroom. I hadn't seen anyone and neither had Asa when he'd rescued me. I hadn't heard anyone come in.

Which meant whoever it was had either followed me there on my walk from Beckett's or…was already inside when I'd arrived.

Bile burned at the back of my throat. The possibility made sense. Someone could have hidden until I went in the darkroom and then come out and…

I didn't want to think about what could have happened or the fact that some creep might have been there, watching me, the entire time. Something bigger *was* going on and it was finally crystal clear to me that William was right. He'd had a lifetime of experience with threats and extortion attempts. What did I have? A stupid impulse to prove I knew better, which had backfired horribly.

I let out a huge sigh. I definitely didn't want to be alone until whoever was pulling this shit was caught. Which meant I'd be staying at the penthouse. That wasn't so awful, really. I sighed again.

William must have heard me exhaling because he looked over from his treadmill and gave me a thumb's up, like he was encouraging me to keep pushing myself in my workout. I smiled back.

But I wasn't working out very hard, and in fact, I was barely moving my arms and legs. I'd already expelled enough energy this morning. I really wished I was back upstairs in bed.

The latest issue of *Chicago Now* was open in front of me, and I was mindlessly flipping through pages filled with images of beautiful people at various events around the city—boutique openings, charity fashion shows, a debutante ball over the holidays—when something caught my attention. It was a picture of Hutch Morrison at some party, surrounded by about eight women, all sticking their chests out for the camera. I kept staring down at the image of smiling Hutch, whose grin looked a lot like the 'shit-eating' kind. Who could blame him, surrounded by a bevy of babes? My new boss—I guess I could call him that—was smoking hot and his ripped body and rock-star tattoos screamed "bad boy."

The good kind of bad boy.

No, really the *best* kind of bad boy. Judging by the looks of the ladies in the picture, Hutch's bed wasn't cold. I was just curious how many of those women had been in it.

I looked up just as William walked over. He'd finished his workout and had a towel around his neck. He glanced down at the open magazine in front me, and his gaze locked on the picture. Something flickered in his eyes and turned them stormy blue.

"Are you ready to go? I have an early meeting."

Shit.

*****

William didn't say anything until we were back upstairs, naked, and under the shower jets in the master bath.

"Keeping tabs on Morrison now?"

I let the water wash over my hair. "No. I just happened to see him in that picture. I don't see people I know on the pages of society magazines very often." I reached for my shower gel, but William already had it in his hands.

"Interesting that it was Morrison you happened to spot."

I wanted to roll my eyes. Did he really think I was interested in Hutch? "Just coincidence." I held out my hand. "Can I have my shower gel?" He started to hand it to me, and then seemed to think better of it.

He flicked it open and squirted a small amount into his palm. "Turn around."

Since this was the first time in the last fifteen minutes he'd lost that annoyed, pouty expression, I turned. William's hands started at my shoulders and worked their way down my back, leaving a trail of yummy smelling suds. I heard him squirt more into his palm, and then his hands were on my waist and working their way down my bottom. He moved lower, his hands caressing my thighs and my calves, then back up again to soap my backside.

"You have a sweet ass, Catherine."

I almost laughed. "Thanks." He didn't usually go for my butt. William was more of a breast guy, but his hands kneading me there felt pretty good. Then they slipped lower, between my legs. He ran his slick fingers over my sex, and I had a jolt of anticipation.

"You like this," he said, stroking me.

"You know I do."

His fingers slid higher, into the seam of my bottom, and he ran one finger up and down the cleft. "You're going to like it when I fuck your ass too."

It wasn't a question. It was a command.

Apparently, the tender William who'd bathed me, caressed me, and held me last night and then again this morning was gone, and possessive William had come to take his place and claim what he wanted. And maybe today, right now, we were going to do this. It would be a first for me.

William's fingers continued to slide up and down between my cheeks, and I reached out and braced my arms against the wall of the shower, lowering my head so the water could pound on my back and release some of my tension.

"That's right." William used a knee to spread my legs. "Let me see that sweet ass." His finger circled my anal opening lightly, and I shuddered. "Every part of you is mine, Catherine. You know that, don't you?"

I looked over my shoulder and met his hungry eyes with mine. "I'm yours. *You* know that."

His finger probed me gently. "I'm going to enjoy taking you here." His thick digit pressed more insistently at my opening, and I sucked in a breath and held it.

"Just breathe," William ordered. "Don't I always make you feel good? Trust me." His soapy finger circled and toyed with me, then gently pressed against my resistance. "Relax, baby. Take a breath and then push back against me."

I did as he instructed and pushed back against him, exhaling. I felt his thick finger slide in and go deeper than it had ever been in, past my tight ring of muscle and completely inside me.

Oh my God. My legs went weak and heat instantly shot to my core.

Slowly, William fingered my ass, gently stretching me and moving in and out of my most intimate place, filling me until I was arching myself toward him and meeting his finger with my own thrusts.

"You like that, don't you?" he asked with a growl.

I met his gaze again. With the water sluicing over his hard chest and plastering his dark hair back from his forehead, he looked like a Spartan warrior. His eyes were molten grey now, and his piercing stare was directed fully at me. Just a look from him when he was this intense, this aroused, reduced me to a quivering bundle of nerves.

"I love everything you do. I love you."

At that moment, with him looking at me with such raw desire in his eyes and me so thoroughly consumed with need, I would have done anything he wanted me to.

"Who do you belong to, Catherine?" His finger slid out of my ass and then his cock was moving up and down between my cheeks.

I panted with anticipation. "You, William. Only you." As the head of his penis pushed against me, I curled my hands into fists. Everything inside me was tightly coiled and ready.

"That's right. Only me."

There was a subtle pressure as that rounded head pressed harder to gain access. I rocked back, inviting, needing. William let out a harsh groan. "Fuck, you're so tight."

But then he pulled away.

What? I was ready. Why was he stopping?

"But not today. I don't want to hurt you."

Then I felt his hard member move down until it rested at the entrance to my sex. My body was screaming with need, and I pushed back to force him to penetrate me. He chuckled. "Not yet."

He slid his slick cock over my swollen sex. I dug my fingernails into my palms as I tried to slow my breathing and will the spasms in my legs to stop. The head of his cock pushed in and I braced for more, for the full, hard length of him to fill me completely. But he pulled out. Then he was inside me again, teasing then withdrawing to slide over my clit, and then pushing into my swollen sex again.

My head whipped back and forth under the warm spray of the shower. I wasn't going to beg. Not this time.

Finally William thrust fully into me, so deep I could feel him at my womb. I bit my lip to keep back a cry of pleasure. There was pain, too, but he felt so good inside me it was almost blinding. I whimpered.

"Wait, beautiful girl. I know what you need, and I'm going to give it to you."

He pressed harder, his cock hitting all my most sensitive places. His thumb stroked the cleft of my ass, penetrated the opening until he was inside me there, and both my passages were full.

My breathing was ragged and hot and I let myself soar. Just as the wave of my ecstasy was about to crest, William growled in my ear, "You wait until I tell you, Catherine." His thumb was still in my ass, moving in small circles.

"Now," I moaned as I thrust back against his hard length. "Please now." All my hot need coiled into a tight ball. I was so ready to explode, to let go, and then he withdrew.

I let out a scream of frustration. I knew why he was doing this. He was pissed about the picture of Hutch Morrison, and this was another way to remind me who I belonged to.

I didn't need a reminder.

He slid in again, his thumb going deeper into my ass as his cock thrust up and up, filling my sex and pressing against the thin membrane that separated his finger from his cock. Dark shivers raced through me as I struggled on tiptoes to take him all in. My sex held him in an iron grip, clenched around him tighter than ever, wanting to keep him in me, wanting each stroke to last forever.

My orgasm took me by surprise. William never stopped thrusting, and at the height of my coming, I felt him release hot and hard into my depths. He let out a harsh cry, and lowered his forehead to my shoulder, the unshaven stubble on his chin scratching my back as I slowly, very slowly, drifted down and my legs gave out.

*****

When we'd dressed—me in a slim, wool, plaid mini-skirt with brown boots and a pink Oxford shirt, and William in a grey pinstriped suit, a light blue shirt, and a purple tie with medallions—we sat in the kitchen over breakfast together. Laird was asleep in his dog bed in corner, his feet in the air and pleasant doggie snores coming from his mouth. The housekeeper had already fed him. She'd prepared a full breakfast for us too, but the buttons of my fitted shirt were straining over my breasts just enough that I'd thought twice about wearing it. I decided to stick to grapefruit and coffee. I either had to drop a couple of pounds or buy some minimizer bras.

I was more than a little sated this morning and the memory of William's thumb in my ass—and how much I'd liked it—made me blush. William glanced at me and lowered his tablet. "Are you free tomorrow afternoon?"

I was meeting Hutch at Morrison Hotel today, but I didn't have any appointments tomorrow. "Sure. Why?"

"Come to my office for a meeting."

My brow arched. "More stand-up sex against your office window?" The idea had appeal. William had a great view of the city.

He gave me a small smile. "Not this time. It's something else. Two o'clock work for you?"

"Sure."

William stood and leaned in to kiss me. He smelled wonderfully clean and slightly musky. "Asa will drive you today."

His lips lingered on mine and then he nibbled at my bottom lip before pulling away. "Be good, please."

"I will," I nodded without even the slightest protest. "I promise."

I watched William go and then glanced down at my grapefruit. I'd only eaten maybe half of it, but I pushed it away.

I spent the next five minutes searching for my purse. I had no memory of where I'd left it the night before, but I finally found it in the bedroom. I rummaged through it, looking for my phone so I could put the appointment with William in my calendar. I shifted the contents of the purse several times but I had so much crap stuffed in it, I couldn't see a thing. *Shit*. I started feeling around.

"Miss Kelly?" It was Asa. "I'm ready to go whenever you are."

I glanced at the clock. I'd have to look for my phone later or I was going to be late to meet Hutch. "Coming!"

SEVEN

Asa drove me to Morrison Hotel, Hutch Morrison's signature restaurant located in the South Loop. Morrison Hotel was probably one of the hottest restaurants in the entire country, if not the world, and I still had a hard time believing that Hutch had picked me to shoot the photos for his first cookbook. He was only in his thirties but he was already a legendary chef, like, Julia Child legendary. Beckett had just about passed out when Hutch first called me.

In spite of the delay as I had searched for my phone, which I still hadn't found, I actually arrived a couple minutes early. Hutch must have been excited to get started because he opened the door as I was walking up and ushered me in. I barely had time to say good morning and shrug off my coat before he marched me back to one of the booths and gestured for me to slide in. Coffee was waiting. It smelled rich and earthy, and I sipped it while Hutch went over the work he'd done so far on his cookbook project.

"Now sweetheart, you're the expert, so if anything I say doesn't meet your approval, let me know. I live to serve." He reached over and tucked a lock of my hair behind my ear. Hutch was a shameless flirt. I didn't think we'd ever had a conversation where he didn't touch me at least three or four times.

"I'm impressed," I said, leaning over to peruse the list he'd made of what dishes he'd prepare for me to shoot.

Hutch might have seemed like a casual, down-home kind of guy, but his food was exactly the opposite. His style was elevated—incredibly formal, totally precise, and perfectly crafted. I wasn't anything close to a foodie and even I recognized the guy was a genius. Morrison Hotel's entire menu and concept changed on the chef's whim every few months, and Hutch Morrison's inspirations tended to come from rock albums. It was global news when he announced his next theme—and *Sticky Fingers* was about to kick off. Hutch called it "foods from his youth," and said he wanted to explore simple, Southern fare. I didn't see anything close to simple on his list, though I spied the brown sugar beignets with blueberry compote I'd already sampled. *Tasso pork tenderloin with goat cheese grits, sugared blue bantam peas, smoked tomato and morel medley, and Jack Daniels reduction* caught my eye. I couldn't wait to try that dish.

"You've made a lot of progress on this." And now that I had a picture of some of the dishes in my mind, I could start to envision the digital cookbook the way Hutch did. It was a genius idea, really, combining his culinary skills with sexy pictures of his dishes and a bit of food history. He'd fully refined the concept with this proposal—it was fresh and new and soon the world would get a candid peek into *his* world. Hutch was going to be a household name when we were done. I was sure of it.

"I'm not in the habit of wasting anyone's time," Hutch said in that slow Southern drawl of his, which seemed to indicate he had all the time in the world. "Especially not someone like you. I imagine William Lambourne keeps you plenty busy."

I glanced up at him, feeling my cheeks heat. Was it that obvious I'd had sex twice this morning?

A slow smile spread over Hutch's face. "Well, now, that wasn't what I meant at all, but I'm sure he keeps you busy in bed too. I only meant you're more tan than when we last met."

"Oh. Valentine's Day trip." I smiled.

He sat back and crossed his tattooed arms. He was wearing black jeans and a charcoal grey T-shirt that showed off his pecs and biceps. "Let me guess. Private island? That seems like Lambourne's style."

I nodded. "Tropos. Four days. We had the entire island to ourselves."

"Always wanted to go there." He leaned close. "Tell me, Catherine, is that an all-over tan?"

I could flirt as shamelessly as him. "You'll just have to wonder."

He laughed. "That I will. Cold showers for me the rest of the week." He lifted a hand and motioned a woman over. I hadn't even noticed her, but obviously Hutch had. "Catherine Kelly, this is Angela Sylvester."

He made room for her, and she slid into the booth beside him. Angela looked like she was in her late thirties. She was short and curvy, and wore her straight auburn hair pulled tightly back into a no-nonsense chignon, highlighting her striking bone structure and her deep blue eyes.

She held out a hand. "Nice to finally meet you. Hutch hasn't shut up about you since you signed on."

I gave Hutch a teasing look. "Oh, really?"

"He's worse than one of my goddamn kids at a toy store. *Catherine this* and *Catherine that*. I can't tell you how many times I've wanted to tell him to just shut the fuck up already."

I laughed and liked her immediately. There wasn't going to be any pretention with Angela. She seemed straightforward and open.

"So you have kids?" I said, wondering how she managed to be a mom and work for someone like Hutch Morrison. I imagined he was a bit like William. He wanted everything his employees had to give and then more.

"Three. Two boys and a girl, ages eleven, eight, and five."

"Wow. You don't look old enough to have an eleven-year-old."

"Well, fuck me. I see why Hutch likes you so much. Keep this up, and you'll be my new BFF."

"Angela's husband is a fireman," Hutch added. "I've been trying to win him over from the dark side, but so far no luck."

"The dark side?" I asked.

Angela shrugged. "He likes burgers and pizza, pasta and gravy. Meatballs. He doesn't go for all the fancy-ass shit Hutch makes."

"You make the fancy-ass shit too, honey," Hutch reminded her. He looked at me and winked. "Angela is a self-taught cook, but don't let that fool you. She's one of the very best or she wouldn't be my sous chef. The three of us will be working together. I don't think I have to point out that with two beautiful women on either side of me, I'm getting the better end of the deal."

We worked out the shooting schedule, and more than once I wanted my phone so I could enter dates into my calendar app. I hopefully dug through my purse yet again, but still no luck.

Fortunately, the schedule was something I could remember pretty easily, as it basically worked out to me being at Morrison Hotel twice a week for the next month or so.

"And bring your appetite," Hutch told me when we'd finished. "I told you, pleasure before business. I'm going to insist on feeding you the next time you're in my restaurant, Miss Catherine Kelly."

"I'll see you soon, Cat," Angela said, heading back to the kitchen.

Hutch walked me to the door. I could see Asa parked in front through the glass, and it was comforting to know he'd been there the whole time.

"Thanks again for thinking of me," I told Hutch. "I'm really excited about this project."

"Honey, it's hard *not* to think of you." He gave me a kiss on the cheek. "But I'm not doing you any favors. You're the best. No doubt on that score."

"Thanks. See you soon."

"Yes, you will, and if you want to tell me any more about that all-over tan of yours, you know where to find me."

I laughed and left the restaurant. Asa was immediately out of the SUV and opening the door for me. I'd felt totally safe in Morrison Hotel, but I shivered a bit with fear out in the open. Which was ridiculous.

I slid in the back and didn't feel quite right again until Asa was behind the wheel and the doors were locked. I leaned my head against the back of the seat and took a deep breath. My mind went back to the darkroom and the helplessness of being locked inside. It reminded me of my recurring dream—the one I had where I was sinking in dark water and couldn't raise my arms. I shivered, hating feeling helpless and hating that the incident yesterday had scared me so much.

I reached for my phone, thinking I'd text Beckett and see what he was up to, but then I remembered I didn't know where it was. *Fuck!* When I got back to the penthouse, I was going to turn the place upside down until I found it. It was probably under the bed or in one of my suitcases.

It had to be.

EIGHT

Asa drove me to back to the penthouse, and as soon as I stepped out of the elevator, I heard voices. One was William's and the other was a female voice I didn't recognize. *Interesting*. William didn't usually have guests, and he hadn't told me he was expecting anyone. Laird's nails clicked on the floor as he bounded over, pausing for me to scratch his ears before giving Asa a hopeful look.

"Want to go for a walk, boy?" Asa asked.

Laird gave a soft *woof* and danced around with excitement.

"Thanks, Asa," I said, watching as he snapped the leash on and led my dog out. I felt a small pang of regret that I couldn't go with them. I supposed I could have, but by now William and his guest must have known I was home. If I walked out, it would be rude. Taking a deep breath, I followed the sound of the voices.

"Catherine." William crossed the living room with his long, confident strides and met me near a sleek modern corner table. He was still in the same clothes as this morning, but his tie was absent, his shirt was open at the neck, and his sleeves were rolled up. I guessed he'd been home for a while. I caught a quick impression of a young woman with blond hair before he pulled me into his arms. He smelled wonderful, as always, and he was warm when he embraced and then kissed me. On the cheek. I detected a hint of the woodsy, smoky scent of his favored bourbon on his breath, which meant he'd already had a cocktail.

Where were his lips, and why didn't he press them to mine? That wasn't like him. And who exactly was my boyfriend relaxing and having drinks with on a Tuesday without me, his girlfriend?

"I don't think you've met my cousin Zoe."

Well, that explained it. *So this is Cousin Zoe*, I thought as William pulled back and I could look squarely at the girl now standing next to an armchair that flanked the couch. I couldn't exactly get all territorial over his cousin.

Zoe Smith wasn't at all what I'd expected. She was really petite, maybe five foot two at most, with long, straight honey-blond hair pulled back in a ponytail. She could have been a model if she'd been taller. She was naturally very pretty, even with minimal makeup, and her bone structure was perfect. William or his aunt had told me she was twenty-six—we were about the same age—but in skinny jeans and a blue-and-white striped, scooped-neck, long-sleeve top, she looked younger. I would have pegged her at eighteen, tops.

The other thing I noticed right away was that Zoe carried herself like an athlete. The way she shifted to look at me as I walked in the room, the way she held a bottle of water in her hand spoke of a flexibility and grace that all the great athletes I'd known—mostly surfers—had carried. Another glance told me that under her clothes she was lithe and muscled. Maybe a gymnast? She was short enough but maybe a bit too willowy. Ballet dancer?

"Hi," I said smiling. I started to take a step forward to shake her hand, but paused when Zoe didn't move to respond and instead boldly looked me up and down. I noticed she had a tiny diamond stud in her nose and another in her eyebrow. *Edgy.* I wondered what the Lake Forest crowd thought of that.

Zoe nodded and gave me a tight smile, then sat in the armchair. If William noticed my aborted attempt at approaching her or the tension between us, he didn't show it.

Okay then.

William sat on the couch and pulled me down beside him. He tucked me against him and settled his arm around me. I could see the ice in Zoe's eyes as she watched us.

"So as I was saying before we were interrupted," Zoe said, with a look in my direction, "you can tell the Board to change the charter and the by-laws of the Foundation to admit directors under thirty."

"I'm not going to do that, Zoe." The tone of William's voice suggested they'd been over this before. "There's a reason the by-laws have an age stipulation."

"You're under thirty, so why can't anyone else on the Board be under thirty? That doesn't seem fair. "

"It's not about fair. I'm the head of the goddamned Foundation, Zoe. And I didn't make the rules, remember?" William spoke patiently, but his voice sounded strained. "Why are you suddenly so interested in the Lambourne Foundation anyway?"

The Lambourne Foundation? It sounded vaguely familiar, but I had no idea what it did. I felt like I should contribute to the conversation in some way—say something meaningful—but I had no clue where to jump in. Plus I didn't love how Zoe was glaring at William and me.

"Because I would like to become more involved. I know after this fall everything is going to change, and I thought it would make sense to have another family member on the Board. Someone you can trust."

William clenched his hand on my arm and blew out a breath. "Zoe, you have no idea what you're talking about."

"Yes, I—"

He cut her off with a curt wave of his hand. "Save your bullshit for Abigail and Charles. There's no way you're ready to dedicate yourself to a life of philanthropy and good works. I know you and you don't have a…"

Zoe cut him off. "Yeah, well, maybe I do. Maybe things are different for me now. How about that? And I do pay attention to things, William." Zoe narrowed her eyes and clearly wasn't going to back down.

I was shocked. I had never seen anyone interrupt William, especially when he was in a mood like this. Even *I* was intimidated by him. But Zoe had a slight smile on her lips, like she was enjoying this conversation and causing a reaction. It was the kind of thing I expected of siblings, or people raised as siblings, but it seemed like maybe she should have grown out of it by twenty-six.

She continued. "I don't see why the Foundation is spending nearly two million dollars on that school breakfast project, for example. Did you know there's a federally funded USDA program that provides assistance to low-income school systems? How do you know the Foundation's funds are actually being used for meals if schools are receiving federal aid for the same thing?"

"You haven't read even one of the executive summaries prepared by the consultants I hired," William countered, and I could tell he was almost ready to spiral into a full-on tirade. "Something like sixty percent of Chicago public schools have students on free or reduced lunch, which means—"

"Please. I've done my homework. Do you know what the Foundation should have spent that money on? Another proton therapy machine for the Lambourne Cancer Wing at Chicago Hospital."

William released my arm and sat forward, his shoulders tense. Now she was really hitting below the belt, and her smirk said she knew it. That wing was William's special project.

"Maybe..." I began, thinking I might diffuse some of the tension. But Zoe cut me a look that shut me up, and William didn't even seem to notice I'd spoken.

"What the *fuck*, Zoe? We already invested over twenty-five percent of this year's annual budget on new therapies for the cancer wing. That's *ten times* the amount we gave the school lunches program."

Zoe rolled her eyes.

"Almost twenty *million* dollars, Zoe, and that includes starting two new clinical trials using gene expression profiling. Which you would know if you actually read the Foundation's annual report. So, again, what the hell is this really about?"

I had no idea what any of this was about except that Zoe clearly wanted to piss William off.

And she'd succeeded.

She jumped up. "You *never* take me seriously. Any time I ask questions about the Foundation's investment strategies, you blow me off. I'm a member of the family, and I *should* have a seat on that Board. Waiting another four years is stupid, especially if you won't be as involved after this fall. I have great ideas now, better than Joe Saunders, your ancient outside director."

"Dr. Saunders is only sixty-two and is the former president of the Chicago University Medical Center. He knows a hell of a lot more about cancer research than you do. And furthermore—"

"Oh, save it." Zoe glanced at her phone, seeming completely oblivious to William's annoyance as she cut him off yet again. "I've got to go. Mom and Dad are expecting to see me before they go out tonight, and I'm supposed to meet them at Gibson's for a drink in like twenty minutes."

Thank God.

I thought William would cross the room and throttle Zoe if she stayed any longer. I could see why he didn't talk much about her. She was definitely as alpha a personality as he was. I couldn't see her backing down any more than I could see William giving way. Maybe it was because I'd just come from Morrison Hotel, but the image of Hutch popped into my head. I bet his Southern drawl and effortless flirting could diffuse some of her intensity.

William stood, and I rose too. William nodded to the foyer. "I'll walk you to the door."

"Sure thing." She glanced at the print displayed prominently on the wall. "Interesting choice." Her gaze drifted to me.

"Catherine's work," William said, with a smile at me.

"That's what I thought."

Guess she wasn't a fan of surfing shots. "Bye, Zoe," I said before she turned away. "I'll see you at the shower."

She gave me another tight smile. "Right. And you"—she gave William a nudge and he nudged her right back—"I'll talk with you later."

As William saw her out, I sank back down onto the couch. At least now I understood what Lauren had meant by her warning. *What a...* More than a few choice names came to mind.

*****

William came back a few minutes later, running a hand though his hair and looking both annoyed as hell and slightly shell-shocked. I could relate.

"So that was Zoe," I said. "You've never really told me much about her. I'm guessing you two don't get along very well."

"Not when she's talks about things she knows nothing about, which happens a lot. What do you want to know?"

I shrugged. "For starters, where does she live? What does she do?"

He sighed and threaded a hand through his hair again. She'd really gotten to him. No one ever got to William, and I was fascinated.

"Right now, she's living in Oklahoma City, and she's in training."

"Training? For what?"

"She's a coxswain."

"A *what*?" Knowing William, and seeing how much like him Cousin Zoe was, my mind jumped to all sorts of forbidden territory. I could just imagine Zoe in a dominatrix outfit, whip in hand, taming—swaining?—cocks. Did her mother know? Was there some sort of BDSM school in Oklahoma?

"A coxswain, Catherine. The US men's eight team training for the World Championships is in Oklahoma City."

There are championships? "Championships in what?" I sputtered.

William smiled for the first time since I'd seen him with Zoe. "Rowing. She's a rower. You know, crew."

"*Oh.*"

He shook his head slightly, obviously amused. "She rowed all four years in college, and then a few years ago, one of her former boyfriends convinced her to become a coxswain."

"And that is…?"

"It's the person who sits in the stern of the boat and steers. She's in charge of coordinating the rhythm of the rowers. That's the description anyway. In reality she yells out commands and tells the rowers to speed up, push harder, that kind of thing."

I nodded. "Interesting." Despite her diminutive size, I could see her yelling at a bunch of men with oars. And she obviously had the muscle to compete. There hadn't looked to be an ounce of fat on her.

"I've heard she's really good, which doesn't surprise me in the least. Her mouth has always gotten her into trouble, but now she's found the perfect outlet for all that bullshitting—yelling her head off at a boat full of guys."

"How has her mouth gotten her in trouble?"

The more William talked, the more interested I was in Zoe. I could see how all her arguing with William had annoyed him, but it seemed like there was more to her outspokenness than discussions about investments and foundations.

"How hasn't it?" William said curtly. "Anything else you want to know?"

The whole encounter with Zoe felt kind of like a bomb had gone off. I was struggling to piece together all that had just happened, but one thing Zoe had said stood out. "What exactly did she mean when she said everything is going to change in the fall?" I looked up at William and watched as he ran his hand through his hair yet again.

"I'll turn thirty this fall, Catherine. In September."

"And?" When William didn't reply, I asked, "Why is that a big deal?"

He looked at me and I could tell he was wrestling with how to answer, which started to freak me out. "William, what is it? Just tell me. It can't be that bad. Thirty's like the new twenty-five or something, right? It's not that old."

William stood up from the couch and begin to pace back and forth in front of the fireplace, the image of my lone surfer seeming to peer down at him from above.

"I told you about what happened after the plane crash, about how our house in the city was sold and I went to live with my aunt and uncle in Lake Forest, remember?"

Oh shit, this was serious. William wasn't comfortable talking about his parents and brother, but of course I remembered what he'd revealed to me so far. William telling me about his difficult childhood was one of the few highlights of our trip to his estate in Napa. I nodded up at him in acknowledgment and held my breath a little. I had no idea where this was going.

"When my parents were officially declared dead, I inherited all of their assets. I wasn't supposed to be their sole heir, but Wyatt was on the plane with them and I was the only one left. Charles was my father's attorney and the executor of the estate until I turned eighteen. Then I gained control of a good portion of it."

"Your inheritance." That much money and the responsibility that came with it must have been a huge burden at eighteen. William's Aunt Abigail had implied as much to me a few weeks ago. In that same conversation, she'd told me William had a tender heart and that I should be careful with him. I'd thought about that often and what losing his entire family when he was just a little boy had done to him.

"But not all of it," he said. "I told you my father was a gifted investor. And truly he was, because he used his inherited wealth and grew it into an enormous portfolio of holdings. So enormous, that I couldn't possibly have managed all of it until I spent years finishing my education, gaining experience, and learning his business. Charles realized that early on, so a large portion of my inheritance has been held in trust this entire time. When I turn thirty, it will all be released to me."

I sat in stunned silence. William was already very wealthy. I didn't exactly know how wealthy but he was probably far better off than my wildest guess. So what exactly did this mean? He was going to be even richer? I looked up at him and could see the hesitation and concern in his stormy eyes as he gazed at me. I'd never really cared about William's money—I didn't mind that he was rich, but I didn't love him because he was. I loved him for him, and the money didn't matter at all, except when his wealth complicated things.

Which it had.

I saw the look of anguish in his eyes as he waited for me to respond. And I didn't know what to say. How exactly was I supposed to react to his revelation? I didn't think William moving up a few places on the Forbes 400 list was going to be that big of a deal, but what did I know? Then it hit me: maybe everything *was* going to change, even what was between us, and he didn't want to tell me. I could feel my heart speeding up as a wave of panic started to wash over me. "William," I began, asking slowly and quietly, "how exactly are things going to change?"

He sighed, then walked over and sat next to me on the couch. He took my hand in his and looked directly at me, his expression solemn and his eyes a cool, steady blue. "It means more, Catherine. More money, more responsibility, more visibility. More everything." His shoulders seemed to slump as he said it, like the addition of a few more billions to his bank account was going to put an impossible weight upon him.

"And that's a bad thing because?" I asked softly.

His head bowed slightly and I could tell he was considering his answer. "Because I don't want it," he almost whispered. "It's never been what I wanted. Everything I've done in my life so far has been expected of me. I wasn't on that plane so I'm the one who has been expected to carry on the family legacy. Obligation is very different from doing something because you want to." His voice trailed off, and he cupped my face and softly stroked my cheek. "And I know what I want now."

He wanted me. I melted and crawled into his lap, needing to be as close to him as possible.

He continued on. "WML Capital Management was my father's company. Even the Lambourne Foundation isn't something I created, though finding ways to spend money to make a difference is much more gratifying than finding ways to make more of it. I like that."

"You like making things. You told me that on our first date."

William chuckled. I'd finally pulled him out of the melancholy that had set upon us so suddenly.

"I do. I like making champagne and chardonnay and the occasional rosé. And I like making you smile, beautiful girl." He softly kissed me.

We stayed like that for a few minutes. Me, warmly nestled in his lap and wrapped in his big muscular arms while he kissed me gently, his tongue urging mine to dance with his.

Finally we came up for air and he glanced at his watch. "We should get ready."

I thought for a moment. "For what?"

"For dinner tonight at The Peabody Club."

"What dinner?"

William set me off of his lap and gave me a questioning look. "The one I texted you about this morning. You replied OK." He gestured and went on, "It's an event for the Botanical Society, which is one of Abigail's favorite organizations. I know it's not going to be very entertaining, but I always go with her. She'll be happy if you're there with me, and I don't want to leave you alone. Even with Asa here."

I stared at him, my heart beginning to thump loudly.

He'd texted me.

And someone had texted him back.

William spread his hands. "You don't want to go now? I thought you were okay with it. *Are* you okay?" His gaze sharpened. "What's wrong?" His voice hardened, which I knew was from concern.

My throat was dry, and I tried to swallow before I spoke. "William, I didn't text you."

His eyebrows came together, and his body seemed to tense and shift. But he didn't speak.

"I… can't find my phone."

William's fists clenched and opened, clenched and opened. It was the only sign, other than his eyes, that he was not calm. His eyes had gone an icy blue. When he spoke, his voice was low and quiet. "What do you mean, you can't find your phone?"

"I don't know where it is. I've checked everywhere, and I can't find it."

"*What*?"

I started at his shout.

"You're just telling me this now?" His face had darkened, and he wasn't trying to hold back his fury any longer. It wasn't directed at me and I was sure that all the emotion Zoe had stirred up in him earlier was coming out now, but it was still terrifying.

"Catherine, who the fuck has your phone? Who the *fuck* texted me back?"

I shook my head, helpless.

William knelt in front of me, his movements quick and efficient. "When did you have it last?"

I looked away, toward the darkening sky visible through the large windows of the penthouse. "I know I had it at Beckett's yesterday. But then…"

William grabbed my arm and pulled me up. "Come with me." He moved so quickly he practically dragged me through the penthouse. He wasn't at all gentle, which wasn't like him, and so very different from the tender nurturing he'd shown me just moments ago when I was in his lap.

He yanked me into the study and thrust me into a chair in front of his large desk. "Sit." He held up a finger. "Don't move."

I felt sick as I watched him walk around the desk and lift the house phone. This was the phone that linked to the extensions for security, housekeeping, and the rest. Everything seemed to happen in slow motion, or maybe I was just too shocked to comprehend it all. My head pounded. It was like I'd swallowed something heavy and sickly sweet.

After a few moments, I realized William was on the phone with George Graham. Of course he was. George was head of security. I could hear William explaining, using words like "stalker" and "incident." It was all so surreal. Like it was happening to someone else. It *should* have been happening to someone else. This kind of thing never happened to me.

Why did everything keep going wrong? My eyes stung, but I blinked back the tears. William had enough to worry about without me crying. I took a deep breath, tried to stay calm.

I heard William set the phone down. "George is coming right now. We'll figure this out." His voice was level and controlled and so cold it made me shiver. I glanced up at him and saw his expression was the same, chiseled granite. He looked deadly, like a warrior going into battle.

And it was my fault. There was nothing I could do to fix this. My stomach churned and I closed my eyes. What the fuck was happening?

NINE

I stared out the window of the black SUV at the sea of red taillights up and down Michigan Avenue. For once, I was happy to be stuck in traffic. Despite the hot shower I had taken—alone—before heading out for our dinner, I was still tense from the discussion William and I had had over my missing phone. A dull ache was forming at my temples and I wished I'd had the foresight to take some Advil before we left. I usually got headaches after I'd been upset—especially if I cried—and this was no different. I hated that William was mad at me. Even though he was acting like everything was okay between us, I knew it wasn't.

For the millionth time I racked my brain, trying to figure out what could have happened to my phone. Maybe I'd dropped it on my walk from Beckett's to the bakery or somewhere along the way from the bakery to my condo. I really hoped that was what had happened. But I also remembered my purse lying open on my kitchen counter, its contents spilling out next to Minerva's wrapped slices of cake. At the time I'd thought it had been upturned in the commotion of my breaking out of the darkroom. But now I had to face the real possibility that the screwdriver-wielding intruder had taken it after locking me in my converted pantry.

We were stopped at a red light and the acidy taste of bile rose in my throat as I watched shoppers scurrying to escape the cold by heading into Water Tower Place. God, all of this would be so much easier if I had just not gone over to my condo. I was such an idiot. I looked over and caught William staring at me.

"You okay?" he asked.

"Fine. Just tired," I said and gave him a reassuring smile. I knew tonight was important to him, and I vowed to make up for my phone fumble by being a great girlfriend to William at Abigail's event.

William and I were on our way to The Peabody Club, one of Chicago's most elegant and exclusive private clubs. Of course it was—everything in William's world was elegant and exclusive and I'd be lying if I said I wasn't enjoying getting to know this side of life. So far my relationship with the Windy City's hottest bachelor had taken me to galas at the Art Institute and The Peninsula Chicago, to a Napa estate, and to a private island. Every day with this man was truly an adventure.

The club was only a short distance from William's penthouse and we should have arrived already, but the weather wasn't cooperating and we were at a standstill thanks to a rush-hour snow shower. These people spent half the year in snow, but it felt like every snowfall caught Chicago drivers by surprise. I was glad that it was Anthony behind the wheel since I had never been a fan of stop-and-go traffic.

Outside, the wind was fierce, rocking the car with every gust as the snow swirled silently to the ground. Even though the heat in the SUV was set to the perfect temperature, I shivered. This was the perfect kind of night for my beloved black cashmere turtleneck dress, but Beckett had banished it to the back of my closet, an area he'd dubbed "Never Never Land," as in never to be worn, ever. So tonight I was freezing my ass off for fashion. Beckett would be so proud.

I had on my warmest wool coat and under it, I wore a simple, red silk crepe Dior dress that tapered at the waist and was accented with a folded neckline. My hair was swept back in a messy up-do I'd copied from a post on one of my favorite blogs. It was hard to recreate the twists, but I thought I did okay. My makeup was pretty neutral with just a hint of lip gloss and mascara and some shimmery eye shadow. I was aiming for a funky-cool-chic vibe that would fit with Abigail's friends, but wouldn't be too stuffy. I'd know soon enough if I hit the mark.

I was also wearing new ankle-strap black Manolo Blahnik pumps. The dress and the shoes were courtesy of a little shopping excursion William and I had taken before Valentine's Day. I'd loved the shoes in the store, and had been excited to strut my stuff in them, but as I eyed the snow falling outside, I prayed I wouldn't slip when we exited. Maybe Anthony could carry me up the stairs to the club? I silently giggled at the thought. How did these society women do it, always dressed to the nines in sky-high heels? Maybe there was a trade secret I'd be let in on one day, but I doubted it involved a hidden pair of Nikes.

I shivered again and hoped The Peabody cranked the heat as well, since my silk dress was pretty flimsy. Looking over at William, I smiled at the dashing figure he cut even in the dimness of the streetlights. He wore a dark grey suit with a crisp white shirt and a pale blue tie. When he'd put it on, I couldn't help but notice how the tie made his stormy eyes look a dreamy blue.

The car was full of tension. I was determined not to let that get in the way of this evening's dinner. I wanted Abigail to like me and I wanted to make a good impression, which meant any strain between her nephew and me needed to be undetectable. I glanced at William for what was probably the hundredth time. He didn't seem pissed, more like he was on high alert. Our eyes met, and he stared at me, taking me in intently, like I might disappear at any second. He'd been looking at me that way for the past hour. His entire body was wound tight, almost vibrating. I think he'd said maybe three words to me since we got in the car.

I wished, again, that I hadn't lost my phone. William had acted like I'd intentionally kept the fact that it was missing from him, but people lost their phones every day. I was still so flustered by the darkroom incident—every time I thought about it too long that panicky feeling came flooding back, bringing me to the edge of tears—I wasn't even thinking of my phone. The fact that William had immediately jumped to the conclusion that whoever was in my condo had taken my phone terrified me. What if he was right and I was some sort of target? I just couldn't let my mind go there.

For once I was appreciative of George Graham and William's security team. They'd been able to calm him down about the lost phone and the thing that had really sent him over the edge—the mysterious "OK" text message he'd received. George had calmed me down too. He'd pointed out that the "OK" text could be a stupid prank from whoever had my phone. He'd said that the SIM card and the phone were probably long gone and gone for good, but they would trace the text and ping the phone, hoping to locate where the text was sent from. I'd seen covert ops like that on TV shows and marveled that the technology really existed. Apparently it did for business tycoons with private security teams. If anyone could trace a missing cell phone, it was William. By the time we'd left, his guys had tried calling my voicemail without much luck. Initially, William had suggested we stay home, but George had said there was nothing to be alarmed about. He'd practically pushed us out the door.

The throbbing in my head was getting worse as we inched forward in traffic. I All I wanted to do was turn the car around then crawl into William's bed and forget the mess my life had turned into. Some freak had sent creepy pictures. My condo was off-limits. My phone was gone. I'd been locked in my darkroom. What next? I didn't even want to think about it.

I needed a distraction, and another glance at William made me think he did too. I hated being at odds with him and I especially hated when we disagreed over things that were out of my control.

Maybe if I could get him talking, I could take the edge off of this tension between us. If that didn't work, I'd turn to the open bar to help. "Remind me what tonight is all about again?" I asked.

"It's the Chicago Botanical Society. Abigail has been on the women's board for years. Tonight is a dinner and a lecture on…some garden topic." He gestured vaguely. "They do these once a quarter for their corporate sponsors and most generous donors. The Board is always looking for money for some special project or another. But the real reason we're going is because Abigail wants to introduce you to some of her friends. She's excited I finally have a girlfriend."

With this last statement, William smiled at me, and warmth coursed through me, as I always did, when he referred to me as his girlfriend. It was good to see him smile. Maybe he was starting to get some perspective on the whole phone thing.

I needed some perspective on the event ahead of us, which loomed like a dark cloud. After all I'd been through the past few hours, smiling and making small talk with a room full of society matrons was not on my list of things to do. But it would be over in a few hours, and I really wanted Abigail to like me—I wanted all of William's family to like me—so I gave myself a mental pep talk to be my best, most charming self. If only my headache would go away, at least that would be something. I sighed softly, knowing I would get through it.

I guess I hadn't been quiet enough, because William squeezed my shoulder. "Don't worry, Catherine. We'll get out of there early if you want."

He bent and kissed me, and I leaned into him, giving his mouth better access to me. His lips grazed mine, brushing over them and nipping softly. He ignited a slow burn that flared hotter when his tongue traced the seam of my lips, seeking entrance. I loved that, no matter what was going on with us, our attraction was undeniable. I opened for him, and he entered, exploring slowly and thoroughly. My headache and my sense of everything around us faded away. There was only the two of us, our mouths pressed together and our bodies seeking each other's warmth.

William pulled back, his hand tilting my chin up as he looked deep into my eyes. "We'll definitely have to leave early."

I nodded, and he slid his hand to my nape, angling my neck so he could brush his lips against the sensitive skin. Thank goodness I opted for an up-do. His kisses fluttered against me, light as a butterfly's wings, and I squirmed in my seat as the heat he'd ignited pooled lower and lower. My coat slid from my shoulders, and William's hands moved up from my waist, lightly brushing over the fabric of my dress until he hit the underside of my breast. I moaned softly and my head fell back. His lips continued their gentle assault, caressing my jawline as his palm found my already hard nipple. The heat of his hand through the red silk only made the peak harder.

He palmed me, his breath warm on my neck and then sliding to my earlobe. I trembled as his lips pressed to my ear and his fingers closed on my nipple. "Soon you'll be back in my bed. Under me. Naked." His fingers worked my nipple, and I felt myself grow wet. My sex was moist and ready, and I was about to take his hand and move it between my legs when William pulled away.

I blinked, making contact with his stormy eyes for a second. I wanted more, but before I could pull William back, he tugged my coat back onto my shoulders and, looking out the window, said, "We're here."

"Oh." I shook my head, trying to clear the haze of arousal. Why was it that I couldn't get enough of this man?

He took my hand, kissed it lightly, and said, "Later." His grey eyes met mine. "That's a promise."

*****

We'd arrived at a large, three-story brick building with rectangular windows and a sweep of steps leading to the door. The footprint of The Peabody Club was impressive, given how tightly buildings were packed together in this neighborhood. A warm glow emanated from the large windows, and valets stood ready to park the stream of expensive vehicles pulling up outside.

Anthony jumped out of the SUV and opened the door for William and me. I pulled my coat close around me as William took my elbow and escorted me up the stairs. He held me tightly, as if aware of my shoe concern. Luckily, the club had taken great pains to make sure the steps were clear of snow. The doorman recognized William immediately. "Welcome back, Mr. Lambourne. The event is right upstairs."

At the top of a grand staircase, we entered what I could only describe as a ballroom, filled with about a hundred or so people. The cavernous space was all arches and dark, wood-paneled ceilings. It was old school Chicago at its absolute finest. The wood trim gleamed in the dimmed light and, with the snow swirling outside, the large windows that lined the room on one end made it feel like we had walked into a posh snow globe. Several people were lined up at a large mahogany bar not far from the windows, and tuxedoed waiters milled around with silver trays of *hors d'oeuvre* and glasses of wine. Round tables were scattered throughout, set with white tablecloths and tasteful centerpieces made up of white flowers. My stomach rumbled at the thought of dinner and I realized that it had been a while since I'd eaten. I was suddenly famished.

My gaze swept the room, and I spotted a photographer taking pictures. He was discreet as he mingled among the guests and paused to pose and then snap his willing subjects. I caught sight of Abigail, who quickly detached herself from a small group and headed toward us. Abigail looked poised and elegant in a classic black Chanel suit accented with a string of pearls, her grey hair swept up in a sleek French twist. Behind her, Charles, in a dark suit, followed.

Abigail smiled when she reached us. "William. Catherine. It's so wonderful to see you both. You look lovely, Catherine." She gave William and then me a quick kiss on the cheek.

Charles greeted us, holding out his hand to shake William's and then kissing on the cheek. William squeezed my hand tightly and smiled at me proudly. He looked so happy to see his aunt and uncle greet me warmly. I almost felt like part of the family, and my heart melted. This was what I'd wanted—to be part of William's world. I loved him, and his family's acceptance mattered to me.

Abigail had a flute of champagne and as a waiter with a silver tray passed by, I took a glass of white wine. After our disagreement about the phone and make-out session in the car, I was eager to relax with a drink. William declined, and I noted Charles had a short glass half-full of an amber liquid. Given the choice, I knew that William would have preferred bourbon to wine.

Charles slapped William on the back. "This man needs a real drink. Come on, William. I'll get you three fingers at the bar."

William squeezed my hand. "Maybe later."

"William, go," I urged him. After the evening we'd had so far, he could probably use a stiff drink. "I'll be fine. Really."

He looked at me with the same intensity he'd had in the car and nodded. "I know. I'll be back in a few minutes." He kissed me tenderly on the cheek and strode off with his uncle.

Almost immediately, Abigail smiled at an older couple who approached and introduced themselves as the Van Horns. I shook hands and kept myself busy with my glass of wine as Abigail caught up with them. Their conversation moved to something about the Lyric Opera and I tried hard to look interested and follow along, but between my headache and the few sips of wine on my empty stomach, I wasn't retaining much.

As the Van Horns continued to talk, I looked around again and realized that most of the attendees were of Abigail and Charles's vintage. I started to feel hopelessly out of place and wondered if it showed. Under the Dior dress and the Manolo pumps, I wasn't fashionable or important. Or sixty.

The Van Horns moved away, taking their chatter about opera with them, and Abigail said, "I heard you met Zoe this afternoon, Catherine."

"Yes, I did. I didn't know she lived in Oklahoma." I wasn't sure what to say about my initial meeting with Zoe. *Your daughter was intense and kind of freaked me out and was kind of a total bitch to me* seemed wrong. What had Zoe told Abigail about me?

"She's here for the shower, of course," Abigail continued, "but I convinced her to stay two weeks. Not that I'll see her much. Her training regimen means she keeps long hours at the gym."

"You must be proud of her. I'd never even heard of a coxswain—" But before I could finish sucking up to Zoe through her mom, I was interrupted.

"Abigail? Is that you?"

William's aunt turned, and I looked past her to see a young woman approaching. She was in her thirties; had dark, shoulder-length, straight hair; and was thin to the point of gauntness. Her brown eyes dominated her angular face, the muscles of which stretched tight when she smiled. Abigail glanced back at me. She was smiling, but her expression was puzzled. She obviously had no clue who this person was. I smiled too, confused.

"It's Elin. Elin Erickson," the woman said. "How nice to see you this evening."

"Oh, Elin." Abigail's eyes widened as recognition washed over her face. I couldn't tell if she was pleased or not, but was glad that she at least knew this person. The moment had been getting awkward.

"It's been too long. Look at you." She gestured to Elin's slight frame. Did Elin look better or worse than the last time they'd met? Abigail looked Elin up and down, taking in her dark, long-sleeve shift dress, which accented her skinny frame. "How wonderful to see you," Abigail continued, embracing Elin lightly. I wasn't sure what to do. It seemed like Elin and Abigail might want to catch up, but I didn't really have anywhere else to go. As if reading my mind, Elin turned to me and tilted her head in an *And who might you be?* way.

Catching Elin's pointed look in my direction, Abigail said, "Elin, this is Catherine Kelly, William's girlfriend. Catherine, this is Elin Erickson. Her late mother was a dear friend of mine and of my sister. We spent many summers together in Lake Geneva when our children were young."

"Nice to meet you," I said, holding my hand out. Elin looked at it for a moment then stretched her face into a smile that might have seemed genuine from afar, but up close came at me with lifeless eyes. Finally she took my hand and shook with a loose grip. Was she afraid of catching something?

"You too."

Silence descended, and we all gave awkward smiles. I searched for something to say and was relieved when Abigail finally said, "Had I known you were going to be here, Elin, I would have asked the girls to come. I'm sure they'd love to catch up with you."

"It's been so long since I've seen them. I ran into Lauren a couple of months ago, but I haven't seen Zoe or Sarah in so long."

"I have the perfect solution to that. Why don't you come to Lauren's baby shower? I know she would love to have you."

Suddenly my invitation to Saturday's festivities didn't seem so special. Apparently Abigail was inviting anyone and everyone.

Just then the photographer approached. "Can I take a picture, ladies? For *Chicago Now*."

"Oh, of course!" Abigail said. No one moved for a moment, and I was wondering if I should cozy up to Elin for the shot when Elin scooted to the other side of Abigail. It was as though she didn't want to stand next to me.

Okay then. I closed the space between Abigail and myself and smiled for the camera. This was definitely turning into a bizarre evening. Or maybe my hunger had me imagining things.

The camera flashed and I remembered seeing Hutch in the pages of *Chicago Now*. As the photographer moved away, I said, "Hey, if we make the pages of *Chicago Now*, I'll have to send the issue to my mother. She'll be thrilled." I laughed and, to my surprise, Elin laughed too.

"Kind of surreal to see your own face on the same page as a celebrity. Always makes me do a double take."

I couldn't help but wonder how often this happened to Elin, but appreciated that she'd contributed to the conversation. I nodded as the hostility I'd felt a few seconds ago vanished and I became sure I'd imagined it. Maybe Elin wasn't so bad after all. She might even make a good ally in this social world I kept being pulled into, courtesy of my relationship with William and his billions. Maybe we would be sitting together at dinner tonight.

My neck warmed and I turned to see William making his way toward us. I could always sense his presence. Our connection felt primal sometimes. I smiled at him, taking his hand when he held it out to me. "William, I just met a longtime friend of yours." I gestured to Elin, but she had already walked away. I frowned. That was weird. I totally thought she would want to say hi to William.

"Who was that?" William asked, following my gaze.

"That was Elin Erickson," Abigail said. "Jack Erickson's daughter. You remember her, of course."

I looked to William for confirmation, but before he could answer, a bell rung, signaling that everyone should take their seats for dinner.

*****

We had been standing off to one side of the big room, so William led me back to the tables I had noticed when we'd walked in. They were beautifully set with crystal and silver and illuminated by soft candlelight. On the ceiling, heavy antique chandeliers provided a warm glow, which was perfect for the more intimate setting. I wished I had my camera.

William led me to a table in the back, which surprised me. We weren't seated with Abigail and Charles, and I felt a pang of disappointment as I watched them move toward the front. I had been looking forward to chatting with Abigail more, but maybe this was for the best. I was starving—without the scrutiny of William's aunt and uncle, I might not feel as self-conscious as I inhaled my dinner.

Three older couples joined us, and I guessed they were about Hans and Minerva's age. We shook hands and smiled, making polite introductions. Yes, I was having a wonderful evening. No, I didn't have a garden. Everyone seemed very nice, but I had a feeling most of the table would be napping after dinner when the lecture started.

William pulled out my chair and we took our seats. Waiters came around offering wine and I chose another glass of white since that's what I had started the evening with. As the wine was being poured, William leaned toward me and murmured, "Dinner should be good, at least. Abigail and the Board went all out and hired Jane Remington to cater."

"Who's that?" I asked. William knew by now that as much as I was trying, I knew very little about the food scene in Chicago—or about fine cuisine in general for that matter. Though I was learning a lot from William, and from Hutch, you could hardly call my palate refined. If someone had come and plopped a plate of cheese fries in front of me, I would have thought I'd died and gone to heaven.

"She's old guard, but notable," William explained. "A James Beard winner years ago, and she never disappoints. I'll have to take you to dinner at her restaurant. It's out in the western suburbs, but it's worth the trip."

I loved to hear William talk about food. It was sweet that a man as busy and powerful as he was still got excited about things like sauces and wine pairings.

"It smells delicious," I said with a smile. Scents of garlic and spices filled the room and waiters served some neighboring tables with big, silver-domed plates. I watched as a team of eight waiters approached the table next to us and, in unison, put down the plates and removed the domes with dramatic flourish. Their grand service was met with excited *oohs* and *aahs*, which drowned out the loud growls of my stomach. I tried to get a peek at what was being served, but other than the orange of a squash or sweet potato, I wasn't able to see much. Luckily, it looked like our turn was next.

The waiters approached our table and when a plate was put before me and the dome dramatically lifted, I couldn't help but smile at the spectacle. I looked at William, eager to share my excitement at this cute production, but noticed that he was looking at my plate with a furrowed brow. I looked down and gasped.

Instead of the beautiful plate of food I was anticipating, my plate held a pile of raw, bloody meat or uncooked...organs. My stomach churned at the sight, and I gripped the table to remain upright.

What was I looking at? A quick glance at William's plate told me I was the only one with the unappetizing meal. I lifted my gaze to catch William's, but he was already on his feet, upsetting his own plate and sending his chair toppling over.

"Catherine, don't touch that," he said as he followed the waiter who had served me. In a flash, he grabbed the guy and turned him around "What did you do?" he demanded as he shook him hard. The waiter, who couldn't have been more than twenty—a kid really—was no match for William, with his powerful physique and barely controlled rage. William's eyes were blazing and he looked violent. The waiter looked ashen and terrified.

We were in the back of the room, but I could feel all eyes on us. My face grew hot, and I began to shake. The waiter held his hands up in defense and I could tell by the look on his face that he had no idea what William was talking about, but he was scared shitless nonetheless. Whatever happened here had not been the waiter's doing. William must have realized the same thing because he let go of the guy and came back toward me.

He pulled me from my chair, and I stood on wobbly legs. William held me close. "We need to get you out of here, now," he growled as he ushered me quickly away from the table and out the door.

Everything was a blur as I struggled to take a deep breath and push the nausea back down. Soon I was somehow sitting in a chair near the top of the grand staircase, then Anthony was beside me with a bottle of cool water. I took it from him and saw that my hands were still shaking.

William, his face red with rage, strode by with Asa. How had Asa arrived so quickly and what was going on?

I watched them—two brawny men, my protectors, my rescuers—take a few steps away from the small crowd and speak in hushed tones. I could only hear a little of their conversation, like "bag the plate" and "fingerprints." Asa nodded and William turned in my direction. When his eyes found mine, I felt tears well up. My headache was in full force now, and all I wanted to do was get as far away from here as possible.

Sensing my need, William took three steps toward me and slung his suit coat over my shoulder.

"Let's go home."

TEN

I woke alone, squinted, and glanced around. I was in the master suite in the penthouse. I remembered coming back here, then William helping me into bed and holding me close until I fell asleep. But he was gone now and I had no idea what time it was. Maybe it was still night. The room was dark, but that might have been because the blinds were closed. I rolled to my side and reached for my phone to check the time, but my hand touched empty space on the nightstand.

I groaned with frustration. I'd forgotten my cell was gone, but now it all came back to me. My phone, the dinner, all of the horribleness. I reached for the light, flicked it on, and checked my watch. The hands read ten minutes after eleven. In the morning.

Shit. I'd been sleeping for hours. Someone, probably William, had put a bottle of water on the nightstand, and I sipped from it. I felt like I'd been hit over the head. My limbs were so heavy I had to set the water down. My head was pounding, and the light was only making it worse, so I turned it off and fell back on the pillow.

I had a horrible migraine. I hadn't had one since right after Jace died. The vague thought that I should probably get up and take something for it crossed my mind, but I couldn't summon the energy. Instead, I whimpered a little, then rolled over and closed my eyes. I fell back asleep, but it wasn't a restful sleep. I dreamed of plates of bloody organs and of being trapped in a darkroom, unable to escape.

Hours later, I opened my eyes again and expected to feel my head throbbing. But the pain had finally, thankfully, dissipated. I turned on the light again and checked my watch. *Crap*. It was almost five. I'd slept the entire day, but at least I finally felt better. I obviously needed the rest. I mean, after the events of the last few days, who wouldn't? Jetting back and forth to the Caribbean for a sex marathon, being locked in my pantry by a mystery intruder, having all eyes on me at a society function thanks to the heaping helping of bloody organs someone decided to serve me for dinner, all the while being shadowed by security and living at my new boyfriend's multi-million dollar penthouse, kind of under protest.

It was all...exhausting. I threw my arm over my eyes and groaned. No wonder I'd slept for nearly twenty hours.

But I had to get up. I threw back the blankets and stood, then headed to the bathroom for a long, hot shower. I needed all of William's seven jet showerheads to rub away some of the aches from my limbs. After, I toweled off and threw on yoga pants and a long-sleeve T-shirt. I swiped my hair into a ponytail and padded out of the master suite. I doubted William was home, but I wanted to call him and let him know I was better, so I headed toward his study and the landline.

Laird must have heard me, because he came bounding down the hallway and excitedly slammed against me, almost knocking me over. "Hey, Laird, how's my good boy?" I scratched behind his ears while his tail thumped against my legs. Outside the huge windows lining the penthouse I could see it was dark and snow was still falling. I shivered and rubbed my hands up and down my arms. It was then that I caught the most amazing smell coming from the opposite end of the penthouse.

Maybe William was home after all.

I changed course and headed toward the kitchen, my stomach growling, registering its protest of my long hours in bed. I was famished.

I found William in front of his state-of-the-art, eight-burner stainless steel range. He was dressed in old jeans and a white T-shirt with a chef-style apron tied around his waist. He looked so cute. I loved seeing him so relaxed and casual.

He turned from the range and smiled at me. "There's my beautiful girl. You're finally up." He pulled me into his arms and held me close. I couldn't resist resting my head on his chest and reveling in being clasped by his big muscular biceps. I could feel his heart thumping softly, solidly. He was firm, not to mention warm. On top of that, he smelled delicious—a mixture of his usual scent and whatever he was cooking. "I didn't go into the office today," he said against my hair. "I wanted to make sure you were okay."

I glanced up at him. "Thank you." I hugged him again, hoping he could feel just how grateful I was for his taking care of me.

"Since I was home, Parker sent over some legal documents I needed to sign. I also asked her to bring your mail. It's on the desk in my study."

I'd totally forgotten about my empty mailbox after I'd been locked in my darkroom. "Why do you have my mail?"

"Security's been picking it up and then testing it for safety reasons. I'm afraid it's been opened, but I assure you, that wasn't intended as a violation of privacy. We're just trying to protect you."

"I know you are." And I did, but it didn't mean I didn't feel violated. When would all of this be over?

"How do you feel now that you're up?" he asked

"I'm fine, and thanks for letting me sleep. I haven't slept like that in forever. I just had this killer headache, and I couldn't seem to shake it."

"You clearly needed the rest. It's been a long week for all of us, Catherine. I guess it just finally caught up with you. But now you're awake, and just in time for dinner." He gave me one of his dazzling smiles.

As if on cue, my stomach growled. "What are you making, and can I help? I'm starving."

He chuckled. "I thought comfort food would go over well tonight." He stepped back and gestured to the oven. "The bread is about done, and I have Kalamata olives and an assortment of cheeses." He nodded at the platter on the counter. "There's salad in the fridge, and I have everything to go for a nice mushroom risotto.

Plus, I have fresh berries and whipped cream for dessert. And wine, of course."

I couldn't help it. I started laughing. William frowned. "What's so funny about mushroom risotto?"

"Nothing. It's just that your idea of comfort food and my idea of comfort food are vastly different." It was adorable how sensitive he could be about his food.

"What's your idea?"

"Mac and cheese or a big burrito smothered in cheese and salsa." Just thinking about food made my stomach rumble again. I was seriously hungry. I hadn't eaten since…lunch yesterday because dinner had been…

Oh my God. Dinner last night. It all came back. "William, I am so embarrassed about last night. Please tell me I didn't ruin Abigail's event. I don't know what happened, I—" Truth be told I didn't know how to finish that thought. What had happened?

But William didn't wait for me to finish. "Stop." He grasped my hand. "You don't have anything to apologize for, and don't worry about my aunt. She isn't upset. Just worried. We all are. George is already looking into it."

"George?" I blinked. And then I knew. "Oh no. You think this is all related, don't you? The break-in, my phone, last night. Is that possible? Couldn't last night just have been someone's idea of a sick joke or…or maybe it was a disgruntled waiter?"

Even as I said it I knew it wasn't true. There was coincidence and then…there was this. I couldn't explain away all the strange things that were happening lately. Not any more.

William was quiet for a long moment. His hand in mine was warm and comforting, and then he squeezed my palm and said pretty much exactly what I was thinking. "If it was just the break-in at your condo, Catherine, or just the darkroom, I'd be willing to chalk it up to a random occurrence. But those two events, plus the theft of your phone, the text, *and* the incident last night. This is all connected, most likely to the pictures we both received and the Wyatt situation."

He took my other hand. I was glad because I'd started shaking. When he laid it all out like that, it really frightened me. I had tried my best to keep it all at bay and to not lump everything together. I explained the break-in as random, tried to laugh off the security detail, had even managed to convince myself that my phone was in the possession of some klepto high schooler. But when William put it all together, I knew it was more than that.

William seemed to sense my fear because he said, "I don't want to scare you, but we have to take this seriously. George is working with the FBI, and until this is resolved to my satisfaction, I'm not taking any chances. *You're* not taking any chances."

"What does that mean? What exactly is going on?" If we were going to talk about this, I needed to know everything.

William nodded and released my hand, moving to the oven to stir the risotto. "We should discuss it all. I'll cook while I talk or the risotto will get clumpy."

"Okay." I hopped up on the counter, crossed my arms, and, needing something to do with my hands, popped an olive in my mouth. It was delicious, of course.

I watched William roll his shoulders the way a boxer does before entering the ring. I sincerely hoped he wasn't preparing for a fight because I didn't have one in me tonight.

His voice was steady and even. "The first time I learned about the plane wreckage in Alaska was the night of our date at the Art Institute. Our first date." He tasted the risotto and sprinkled some salt into the pot. "That was the call I received in the car. After that call, I was reeling and I know I was an asshole to you. When you left, I worried I'd completely blown my chances with you." He looked at me and grinned, clearly pleased I was in his kitchen, in his life, now.

I remembered how Minerva had let him in to my condo the next night and he'd surprised me with homemade bucatini with Bolognese sauce to make up for that disastrous first date. But this was the first time I'd heard about that phone call.

"About two weeks later, I received a package at my office with a letter stating that my brother Wyatt was alive, and that, for ten million dollars, I could be reunited with him."

My jaw dropped as William went back to stirring the risotto. I couldn't believe all of this had been going on behind the scenes and I had been so totally unaware.

"As I told you, we've received a lot of these over the years. They're usually just ploys to get money, and George makes them go away, but this one…this one was different." He shook his head as though he was remembering it. "Whoever sent this one knew about the plane wreckage that had been found in Canada. They knew a lot about it, actually."

He stopped stirring, his spoon resting in the risotto. "And they knew you and I were together. There were photos and clippings about us. The package arrived via courier, and until my security team could come up with something concrete, I wanted you out of Chicago." He lifted the spoon, tapped it, and reached for an oven mitt.

"So I took you to Napa," he said as he pulled the bread from the oven. The top was golden brown and the scent made me dizzy with hunger. "But coincidentally, just after we arrived at Casa di Rosabela, the CTSB finished their analysis of the wreckage in Alaska." He took a bread knife and began slicing the flaky loaf. "Those pieces had been transported to Whitehorse, and I had one chance to see what the investigators had discovered. I know it seems crazy, but I needed to see what was left of that plane. You understand, right?"

I nodded. Of course I did. At least I thought I did.

"That's when I went to Canada. I'd planned to fly in, view the pieces, and fly immediately back to California. But, of course, the weather didn't cooperate." He gave me a rueful look. "And then you left and went back to Chicago."

I could mostly fill in the rest, but I waited for him to continue. He didn't. He set the bread aside and stirred the risotto again. It seemed like I should say something, but I didn't know what. I'd been blindsided. I knew some of this already, but finally all the pieces were fitting together, and the full picture explained so much—about William and his behavior, his situation and mine. I'd always thought if I knew the whole story, I'd be relieved. Instead, I was scared. I hated that he was still been keeping things from me. Now that we were together, all of this impacted me, too. I hated that he didn't see it that way. It was a lie by omission, the sort of thing William excelled at.

But I could understand why he'd never put it all together for me before. It was… overwhelming and terrifying and… surreal.

I loved William. I really did. But this was fucked up. And now I felt guilty because at the heart of it all, he'd been worried about *me*, and I hadn't understood why. I'd thought he was some kind of control freak with a complicated billionaire lifestyle. But that wasn't it at all—well, that wasn't *all* of it.

"I've told you before," William said, adding more broth to the risotto. "I don't want my shit to fuck up your life. I hate that this is happening, and that despite my security team and all of my goddamned money"—he tossed the spoon down and braced his hands on the counter—"it *keeps fucking happening.*" He turned to me. "And I hate that you've been pulled into this."

He crossed to me, put his hands on my waist, and looked at me so earnestly. I could see the plea in the clear blue of his eyes.

"Please. I need you to trust me. Don't think the worst and run away again. Promise me that you'll give me a chance to explain before you jump to any conclusions. This *will* be over soon. I love you, and I'll do whatever is needed to make sure I don't lose you. To make sure we don't lose each other."

I swallowed. It was definitely my turn to say something, to tell him I understood and that I loved him too. To make him a promise. But I was too stunned to speak. He'd never told me so plainly how important I was to him, and even though he wasn't saying it directly, I understood what he was implying. My life was in danger. And as much as I didn't *want* to believe it, it was true. I started to open my mouth to say something, to promise him I would always give him a chance, but then he spoke again.

"That envelope you brought over with the proof sheets? That was the last communication we've received. There have been no more letters or packages, no more instructions about how to meet Wyatt or where to send the money. Nothing but silence. And the incidents. The incidents started happening to you and, Catherine, I know they're intentional. They're threats. My suspicion is that when I got involved in that wreckage and had the pieces sent to France for analysis, I got too close to something. Whoever is behind this isn't happy about it. But I'm not going to back down. I need to know the truth." There was anguish in his stormy eyes now, something I had seen too frequently of late, and he turned back to the range to stir the risotto again.

I didn't speak. Instead I tried to take it all in, to comprehend what it meant for me, for us. I knew how passionate William was and why he was so unrelenting in his efforts to find out what had happened to his brother and his parents in that plane crash almost twenty years ago. He wanted closure for so many reasons, and I understood that. We'd both experienced painful losses and, though it was a terrible commonality, it really did help me understand him sometimes.

But what I didn't understand, at all, was his refusal to back down now. If he truly believed someone wanted to hurt *me* because he was getting too close to the truth about the plane crash everyone thought was a terrible accident, then why wouldn't he call it all off? Why put us through this? Why risk *me*?

And then the answer hit me.

Because they meant more to him than I did. He was willing to continue to risk my safety to find the answers that had eluded him since he'd been eleven years old because they were more important than me.

I could feel my heart squeeze in my chest, feel it break just a little. I loved William, and I was certain we belonged together. But I was way less sure that I wanted to be in the middle of whatever this was. This was crazy. For the hundredth time, I wondered why we couldn't just have a normal relationship.

"Catherine, I know this is a lot to take in. I need to know you're okay. Are you okay?" William asked, shaking me out of my thoughts. The truth was I was numb, but I nodded. I needed to sit with all of this for a while.

"Good," he said and gave me a smile. "Can you open the wine?"

I nodded again and spotted the bottle of cabernet on the counter. It was from William's vineyard, which meant it would be delicious.

By the time I'd poured, the kitchen was filled with the heady aroma of mushrooms and garlic and the warm crusty bread cooling on the counter. William plated the risotto, tossed the salad, and set everything on the table. We sat down to eat. I still didn't know what to say. I wanted more time to think.

"This is really delicious," I began, trying to turn the conversation. "I love mushrooms."

"I thought you'd like it. Oh, before I forget, I have something for you." He rose and walked out of the room. I held my breath, uncertain whether to be excited or apprehensive. He returned with a small white shopping bag. "This is for you."

I peeked in the bag and pulled out a box with a new iPhone.

"It's already been set up with your old number, and your old contacts, email, and calendar have been restored. We turned on GPS, so we'll be able to find it if it goes missing."

I met his gaze. "And you'll be able to find me, too, right?" I smiled tightly. "You're kind of scaring me. You know that?"

"Yes, we'll be able to find you, Catherine. It is scary, but security is being stepped up, and you'll be fine. You will have to make some adjustments for the time being, but I'll make it as comfortable for you as possible." William's face hardened, and his eyes turned that icy shade of blue that signaled he was not willing to negotiate.

"What kind of adjustments?" I asked slowly.

"I'd like you to work out of the penthouse. Your workspace is already set up, but I'll get you whatever else you need. It's no problem."

I shook my head. *No, no, no.* This wasn't going to work at all. "I have to meet with my clients. I have a Fresh Market shoot coming up." I ticked it off on my finger. "And I have to be at Morrison Hotel twice a week until the cookbook project is finished. I signed a contract."

"We can get you out of that contract. I'll have Charles take a look at it."

I held up a hand, stopping him before he could say another word. "I'm not getting out of the contract, William. I want the job. You know how excited I am about it, and Hutch is counting on me. Not to mention, it's a huge career opportunity. I'm not just going to—to," I sputtered "walk away from that. Plus, why is my working a problem if Asa drives me and is nearby?"

Instead of answering, William set his fork carefully on the edge of his plate and ran his hands though his hair, tousling it. I loved it when his hair was rumpled like that, and right now I wanted to run my hands through it—then tug it hard and kiss him deeply. I wanted to force him to stop talking about all of this security stuff. I wanted him to make me forget.

I swallowed and sipped my wine. The quick surge of arousal surprised me. I was usually on the edge of coming undone around William, but I hadn't expected this hit of heat and not right now. I sipped the wine again and watched William thread his fingers through his hair, trying to take control of his frustration.

Finally, he dropped his hands and looked up at me, his eyes still steely but soft around the edges. "We can't control everyone who goes in and out of Morrison Hotel. Besides the staff, there are produce, liquor, wine, and linen deliverymen there almost every day, not to mention the patrons. It's a security nightmare. It would be better if you worked out of the penthouse until this is all resolved."

I bit back a retort, but I was not going to back down. "No," I said quietly, "No, William. This is my life. I want this job. Am I just supposed to stay here, all day every day, and never leave? What about seeing Beckett? Walking Laird?"

William sighed, sat back, and crossed his arms. "This building has every possible amenity you—or anyone—could want, and whatever it doesn't have, I'll get for you. There's no reason whatsoever to leave. *Hutch* will understand or be made to understand and can find another photographer. I'm sure you can recommend someone."

I refrained from throwing my glass of wine in his face, but just barely. My emotions were all over the place. I was scared, pissed, and, frustratingly, very turned on. I wanted to fight. I wanted to tell William to go fuck himself and storm out. I wanted to kiss him hard and force my tongue into his mouth. But I wasn't the same woman I'd been a month ago. I wasn't going to let my emotions get the better of me.

I took a few shallow breaths and focused. William was overreacting. I knew it, even if he didn't. He wasn't thinking clearly, and I could hardly blame him. He was worried for my safety. That was part of it. The other part was that he was jealous of Hutch. It was strangely charming, under the circumstances. It was also maddening, but how could I not love a man who cared about me this much?

So instead of throwing my wine in his face, I set my fork on the counter and pushed away. I walked to William, who had a wary look on his face, and moved between his legs. He was still on the stool so I was slightly taller than him at the moment. I wrapped my arms around him. "I love that you want to protect me, William. I understand that's what you're doing, but you can't keep me locked up in your tall tower. That's not realistic for either of us. But I promise we will figure this out. We'll work out a solution acceptable to both of us. A compromise. But know this, I am not giving up my work. I can't."

William pulled me closer and looked up at me. "I won't lose you, Catherine. I can't. I just found you."

I nodded. "You won't lose me." I bent and kissed him slowly and deeply. I let my mouth tell him how much I cared and make the promises I hadn't yet said aloud. "Let me show you. Let's go back to bed."

ELEVEN

I asked William to stay in the kitchen and finish his glass of wine so I could get ready. I was making this up as I went along, and when, before I exited the kitchen, I made a quick stop at the giant SubZero and grabbed the can of Reddi-Wip I'd spied on a lower shelf, the expression on William's face had been priceless. I didn't know what I was going to do with the whipped cream exactly, but I'd become pretty familiar with creative uses of food in foreplay thanks to Mr. *Pain au Chocolat*.

I raced to the master suite and into William's giant closet, pulling off my T-shirt and yoga pants. My pre–Valentine's Day lingerie shopping had yielded more than the just the red botanical lace ensemble I'd worn the other night. I opened one of my drawers and shook out a small bundle of tissue paper, which, given how much I'd paid for what was inside, should have been much bigger. I unwrapped the parcel, careful not to tear the layers of paper, and revealed probably the hottest lingerie I'd ever bought. I'd been saving it for something special, and tonight felt like the right night to take the plunge.

The Bordelle black open bra was basically an incredibly expensive holster for my breasts. The banding was trimmed in delicate lace and the front closure was made of eighteen-carat gold, but that's all there was. No cups, no support, just a beautiful frame that showcased William's favorite parts of me. I slipped it on, followed by the matching banded thong with eighteen-carat-gold accents, then a garter belt, black silk stockings, and black stilettos. I was trussed up in a way that I knew looked downright dangerous.

William rarely let me be in charge, and that worked for me because I liked submitting to him—in the bedroom. But for once, I wanted him to relinquish control to me. He'd shared all of the information about his family with me tonight and then asked me to trust him to keep me safe. And I did trust him. William would protect me no matter what, but I'd never felt more vulnerable. I didn't like feeling weak. I wanted us to be on more equal ground, which meant William had to yield to me sometimes. If he would let me take care of *him* and intuit his needs for once, maybe we'd both feel less like my life was spinning hopelessly out of control because of him. I was getting more and more turned on just thinking about it, and I prayed this was going to work.

I walked out of the closet with the can of whipped cream in my hand just as William strode into the master suite. He stopped dead in his tracks, his eyes widening when he saw me. "Whoa." He stared and took me in. "Where have you been hiding that?"

I smiled. "I still have a few secrets."

We stood silently for a moment, facing each other while William gave me a thorough head-to-toe perusal, pausing for a few extras seconds on my exposed breasts. His eyes traveled over every inch of me, and my nipples pulled tight as a warm heat built steadily between my legs.

I broke the silence first. "Take off your clothes," I said in a husky voice that didn't sound like mine. It was a direct order, and I watched as William's eyes narrowed. But they didn't turn icy blue. They stayed liquid grey. It was like I could see the inner battle going on in his head. Part of him definitely liked that I was calling the shots, but he was still debating whether or not to play along.

I sauntered a few steps toward him, allowing my stilettos to tap on the floor, then put my hands on my hips. We were close enough that I could smell a hint of cabernet on his breath as he exhaled.

"Clothes. Off," I purred. "And William? Do it slowly. I want to watch."

Our gazes met and held for what felt like five minutes but was probably more like twenty seconds. Giving up control was contrary to his every instinct. He *took* control. He didn't give an inch. Finally, as I watched, he reached for the hem of his T-shirt and drew it up. It slid over his taut abdomen and the ridges of muscle under his strong pecs, revealing his thick, corded arms when he pulled it over his head and tossed it on the floor.

I was practically panting. I didn't know if it was because he'd submitted to my request or because his body was so incredibly hot, but I was definitely turned on. I wanted to touch him, but I held back.

"Keep going," I said, my voice breathy with need. His gaze met mine, and I knew he saw how aroused I was. Maybe that was why he kept playing along. He reached for the top button on his jeans, flicked it open, followed by the others, then slid the jeans over his hips. My breath caught in my throat. He wasn't wearing any underwear.

His cock, already hard, sprang free. While he let the denim slide down his ripped thighs, I studied his jutting member. It was thick and veined, the head rounded. That ridge that often brought me so much pleasure when he teased me with it was smooth and silky. He kicked off the jeans. "You like what you see?"

"I didn't say you could speak."

His brows rose, and I held my breath. I'd never talked to him like that before. I half expected him to slam me up against the wall and make me pay for my insolence by pleasuring me until I couldn't see straight. Instead, I saw his throat move as he swallowed whatever he'd been about to say. And he waited.

I let him wait. I knew the way anticipation could heighten pleasure. It was working for me, too. His cock grew more rigid and he clenched his hands open then closed.

Finally, I stepped over to him. His hands moved toward me, but I shook my head. "You touch me when I say. Spread your legs."

He spread them, and I sank to my knees in front of him. I took my time, sliding my hands over his calves and his thighs, brushing my fingers over his tight ass. I moved to his front and cupped his balls, their heavy weight filling my hand, then leaned forward and slid my tongue over them. His breath came out in a whoosh, and he made a strangled sound of pleasure.

"Fuck, Catherine. You're killing me here," he groaned.

"No talking, remember," I said, then I slid my wet tongue up the shaft of his cock. It twitched where I stroked it, and he had to brace himself when I circled the head.

I teased him with my tongue in the same way he often teased me. He was panting hard by the time I finally took him fully into my mouth. He made a strangled moan as I sucked long and hard. My hands began stroking him, running up and down the length of his shaft.

I slid his cock in and out of my mouth. I paused at the sensitive tip and circled it with my tongue. As I did so, I looked up. His eyes were so dark I could have lost myself in them, and I could see a muscle in his jaw clench. He was exerting tremendous control, but I knew he was very close to breaking.

I rose. "Get on the bed." He hesitated, and I held my breath again. Even though I was making the rules, if William turned the tables on me, I wouldn't be able to resist.

Finally, he moved to the bed and lay down. The other day one of my stockings had had a run, so I'd tossed it in the nightstand drawer and worn another pair. Now I opened the drawer, lifted the stocking out, and held it in my hands. Then I climbed onto the bed, climbed on top of William, and settled myself over his cock. I wanted him to feel the heat from my damp sex.

"Raise your arms," I said. "Wrists together."

"Catherine." His eyes flashed a warning, but I wasn't backing down now.

"Arms up, William."

He didn't move.

"Trust me," I said, leaning forward and pressing my body against his, my hard nipples rubbing and chafing against his hot skin. "Let me show you I can take care of you. I know what you want, what you need. And no more talking."

His jaw clenched with the strain of the internal struggle. I knew I was asking a lot of him, but I also knew this was exactly what he and I needed in this moment.

Finally, he raised his arms and I leaned over, brushing my breasts in his face, as I bound his wrists together. I cinched them tightly until he hissed in a breath. Unlike William's huge four-poster bed at Casa di Rosabela, the bed in the penthouse's master suite was a modern platform bed, so there were no posts to tie his wrists to. He wasn't going to get loose, but he'd have to keep his arms above his head only because I told him to.

"Keep them raised. If you don't, I'll have to do something about that."

I watched as he tried not to smile. He recognized my words. He'd threatened me with the exact same thing on Valentine's Day, when he ordered me to keep my hands at my sides while he ravished me with his mouth on the living room couch.

"Now close your eyes."

William took one last look at me, his eyes a shining molten grey, then lowered them closed, his thick dark lashes like inky smudges against his cheeks.

I looked down at the big, handsome man stilled under me. With his hands tied together and his chiseled arms stretched above his head, his sculpted naked body taut and waiting for my touch, he was 100% male perfection. And he was all mine.

Now it was time for some fun.

I reached and grabbed the can of Reddi-Wip from the nightstand, shaking it up as I pulled off the top. "This might be a little cold," I warned.

"Catherine," he started, twisting to the side a bit and pulling against his tied wrists.

"Trust me, William," I cooed as I stilled him with my thighs.

I started by putting a dollop of whipped cream on my finger and tracing his lips with it. I bowed my head and gently licked his lips, lapping up the sweet cream with the soft point of my tongue. His mouth opened a little and I kissed him deeply, feeling him arch up beneath me as our tongues caressed. I pulled my mouth away and sprayed another cone of whipped cream on my finger, then pressed it against his lips. He opened and took my finger in my mouth and licked it clean. This was so fucking sexy. My little black thong was positively soaked with my arousal, and I was just getting started.

I decided to work my way down. I put whipped cream on William's nipples and licked it off slowly, pebbling him into hard little points. I took my time exploring his body, putting little dollops of whipped cream on just about every inch of him, then licking it off and kissing where I'd licked. I licked and kissed places I'd never had much time to explore before—the inside of his elbow, his hip, the indention near his shoulder.

By the time I returned to his cock, he was groaning with need. I coated his hard member with one final topping of whipped cream then took him into my mouth, pulling him in so deep I thought I might gag. I could feel the whipped cream squeezing out of the sides of my mouth as his hips rose and he pushed deeper. I pulled back, breathless, and swallowed. "Trust me," I said. "I'll take care of you."

I wiggled on top of him again, pushed my wet thong to the side, and took him slowly inside me. It tortured me as much as him. I was so swollen and wet, my body screaming for his. I let the head of his cock, only the head, slide in and out of me, through my folds and over my clit, and then back inside me. Inch by inch, I took more of him, rolling my hips from one side to the other. "You're so hard," I panted. "God, you feel good inside me."

I took him in fully then, letting him stretch and fill me to the hilt. When he was buried deep, I moved my hips up and down, sliding his thick hardness into my tight sheath. I could feel him swelling, and I opened my eyes and shook my head.

"Don't you dare come before me, William. I come first."

"Then fucking come already." It was the closest he would ever come to begging.

"Not yet." I settled him deep inside me again then bent and positioned my hands on his shoulders. "Open your eyes."

Our gazes locked, and I moved my hips slowly, feeling the stirrings of pleasure I had pushed down rising to the surface. I moved slowly now, my breathing harsh and rapid. William's breathing matched mine and his gaze was hot and dark as he looked into my eyes. His fingers were clenched tightly as he kept his arms raised above his head. He was helpless to take his own pleasure and he was helpless to give me mine with anything but his cock. He was mine, and his pleasure mine to give. Our gazes crashed together again, and I slid that big cock along my sensitive walls again. I could feel myself tightening and quickening as I clutched him in an iron grip. Just before I came, he whispered, "I love you, Catherine. I love you."

The world shattered around me as an orgasm slammed through me so hard it shook my whole body. William made a sound somewhere between ecstasy and pain, and I ground out, "Come. Come inside me."

He tumbled over the edge, and I felt the hard gush of his semen deep within me as our gazes remained locked. As many times as we'd come together like this, I'd never felt so close to him, never felt as much a part of him as I did at that moment. We were one, and if we stood together, nothing would ever come between us.

*****

The whipped cream had left a sticky sweet residue all over both of us and a long soak was definitely in order. William's huge tub was filled to the rim with bubbles, and I was nestled between William's legs, my head back on his shoulder. He stroked my arm absently and told me how Laird had kept him company in the study while he worked at home today. "But every hour, he'd check on you in the bedroom. He's very protective."

"He's the best," I said. Then I sat up. "William, I totally slept through the meeting you'd wanted to have with me this afternoon!"

"Yes, two o'clock came and went, and you didn't even roll over."

I laughed, and he bent forward and kissed my temple. "I was even planning on wearing a skirt," I said, "since your big windows offer such a...stimulating view of downtown."

He shifted slightly, and I smiled. He was remembering the exact same thing I was remembering—the hot sex we'd had in his office the first time I'd gone there. He'd pushed me up against the windows, raised my skirt, and fucked me standing up for all of Chicago to see. It had been seriously hot.

"Definitely wear a skirt for our next meeting," he murmured against my neck.

"I will. What did you want to meet about today?"

"I want to hire you."

"What is this, *Pretty Woman*? Know that I cost way more than three grand."

"Sorry to ruin your Julia Roberts fantasy, but I'm serious. I'd like to hire you. We're rolling out a national ad campaign for WML Champagne. I'd like you to shoot the images."

I sat straighter. I was paying attention now.

"We have several very specific shots in mind, and you're absolutely the right photographer for the job. I have an offer written up to present to you."

I turned to look at him. "You don't have to pay me."

His brows slashed together. "I'd never ask you to work for me for free," he practically growled. "My offer is generous but competitive for this kind of specialized work."

I nodded. He was in charge and all business now. No matter that we were in the bathtub and he was naked. He might as well have been in his three-piece suit, seated behind his desk.

"Who do I report to on this project, Mr. Lambourne?"

"To me. I personally oversee everything related to the winery. I plan to stay very involved in that endeavor."

I pressed my lips together, mulling it over. "I'd love to do it and I will…but I have a few conditions."

His eyes turned steely. "Such as?"

"I'm not giving up Hutch's project, and I'm not giving up Fresh Market. But"—I raised a finger before he could argue—"I'll back off on my other work for the time being."

"What else?" William, of course, knew that wasn't all.

"I'll continue to work out of the penthouse, but I need to go on location sometimes. I'll go with Asa or Anthony or whoever you want, and I promise I won't go anywhere without security. I'll stay in contact, and I'll be careful."

His eyes were icy blue and his gaze didn't waver as it met mine. "Anything else?"

"Just two more things." His look was cold and hard, so I spoke quickly. "I want to take Laird on walks. I don't care who goes with me, but I need to go outside. And…" I paused, taking a breath.

"And?"

"I want my darkroom. Is there any way we can get my stuff and set it up here? I don't know where, but I really miss it. It's not absolutely necessary, not a deal breaker, but if we could find a way—"

"Of course we can find a way. Consider it done." He sighed. "You drive a hard bargain, Miss Kelly."

"But?"

"I agree to your conditions."

"We have a deal then!" I settled back against him, excited to begin. But a small part of me was concerned too. I couldn't shake the nagging feeling that William had given me what I wanted too easily. Was he hiring me because I was really that good, or because I was his girlfriend and he wanted to make sure I had less time to spend on my other projects?

Specifically, less time to spend on Hutch's cookbook project?

TWELVE

The next week passed in a blur. The night of the Chicago Botanical Society event had been the first in a string of snowy days. The weather had been raw and shitty as February rolled to a close and the groundhog had been right all those weeks ago: winter wasn't letting up.

I longed for spring and couldn't help but think about Santa Cruz and the fact that I wouldn't be trudging through snow, ice, and slush if I were there. My favorite pair of Frye boots had developed stains from the salt on the sidewalks—and it's not like I was trekking to and from the L every day. It had been way too easy to stay in, just like William had wanted. Maybe billionaires could control the weather after all?

But I couldn't really complain. I relished spending my time indoors with my boyfriend, snuggling in front of the fire, cuddling under blankets, keeping each other warm in bed. William and I had settled into a comfortable routine, and I'd even found time to unpack and hang most of my stuff in a small section of William's massive closet. Maybe it was because I had taken these steps to "move in" that William had been keeping quiet about my work with Hutch. Whatever it was, I was happy that Hutch and Morrison Hotel were no longer a point of contention between us. I loved my new gig and I wanted William to be proud of me.

I had ventured out to begin shooting dishes at Morrison Hotel for the cookbook on Thursday, two days ago, and the day hadn't started out well. I'd been psyching myself up for the first shoot for the better part of a week. I'd been prepared. I'd had my gear. I'd had Asa in tow. I was comfortable around Hutch and I knew he trusted me. But when I'd arrived at the restaurant, something had felt off. I'd tried to get warmed up by taking a few test shots, but I'd had trouble focusing. Only when Hutch had brought out the first dish and one of the stylists I'd recommended had walked in had it hit me what was wrong: Beckett. I was missing Beckett. Faced with having to do a major shoot without him, I'd had an epiphany and realized just how important he'd been to my work as a food photographer.

Beckett and I would usually meet before a shoot to talk strategy and his ideas would often inspire me. Then on the day of, he'd always make me feel grounded with jokes, encouragement, and his snappy one-liners about his magic sprays and food having a perfect window, how to perk-up any food item that had wilted or dropped even the slightest bit. Shooting with him had always been fun and not like work at all and he gave me a confidence I didn't feel on my own.

Hutch's cookbook project was in an entirely different league for me, which was unnerving enough, but it also threw me into a working situation with a stylist I'd heard was great but whom I'd never met. It had taken a little while for me and Chris to find our groove, mostly because of me. He was fine, but he just wasn't Beckett. And that had sucked.

Thank God for Hutch. I think he'd sensed my nervousness and he'd had taken the edge off by being his charming—and I admit sexy—self. He'd started the morning with his mega-watt smile and his brown sugar beignets with blueberry compote and chicory coffee for those of us on set. It was a lethal combination, and I'd probably eaten ten beignets by the day's end, mostly at Hutch's urging. Good thing I'd picked that day to become a stress eater. Of course, I hadn't argued much. The beignets had been delicious and Hutch was a hard man to say no to.

Once he'd declared my beignet shots were perfect, I'd started to relax and finally got into my zone. The rest of the shoot had gone by in a blur. Hutch had brought out three more dishes, including a spectacular deconstructed gumbo with sugarcane, shrimp, crawfish, Louisiana Andouille sausage, and fried chicken that had been truly breathtaking. In between the plates, I'd gone back to the kitchen to shoot him and Angela in action. It had been inspiring to watch him work. He was so in love with what he did and I'd gotten great shots of the kitchen, its controlled chaos, and of Hutch and his staff. My favorite was a shot of Hutch forming tiny little finger-sized lobster and basil-infused hush puppies by hand. Hutch was looking up with this smile on his face that pretty much encompassed his total joy at cooking, and his muscular, tattooed arms were such a contrast to the delicate, perfectly shaped little ball of cornmeal batter in his hand. If that shot didn't make it into the book, I really wanted to do something for Hutch with it.

Just thinking about Hutch's food made my stomach rumble—loudly—and I rolled out of bed to the smell of coffee wafting into the master suite. I threw on leggings and a Lululemon savasanah wrap and headed to find William.

I found him in his favorite room in the penthouse standing at the range, flipping pancakes, my Saturday morning favorite. The beignet overload Thursday should have satisfied my craving for carbs, but I couldn't ever say no to pancakes.

William's dark hair was damp and curly, which meant he'd already worked out and showered. My breath hitched as I watched him, his muscled broad shoulders rippling under his tight, light blue T-shirt as he wielded his prowess with a spatula. God, he was so hot. I wondered for probably the millionth time how I ever got so lucky.

I came up behind him and put my arms around his waist, breathing in his clean, musky William smell and feeling the hard planes of his abs tense at my touch. "Are all of these for me?" I asked at the sight of the stack of cakes on the counter.

"If you want them to be, beautiful girl," William answered. His put his hand over mine and stroked it. I couldn't see his face, but I knew he was smiling.

I did want them all, but I promised myself I'd stick to one…*okay, maybe two*. This perpetual winter wasn't doing my waistline any favors. I'd been carb-loading like an athlete, except without a marathon to burn all the calories.

I slid onto one of the stools at the breakfast bar and William set a plate in front of me, the pancakes covered in whipped cream and strawberries, and then he bent and gently brushed his lips against mine. "Good morning, love," he said between maple syrup–sweetened kisses. "I hope you enjoy your breakfast."

"I'm sure I will," I replied between kisses. The pancakes smelled delicious and I really was starving, but I was hungrier for William.

We stayed like that for a while longer, making out as our kisses deepened and waves of pleasure began coursing through me. I could have spent all morning like that, wrapped in his arms, warm and satiated by his sugar-coated lips, but when my stomach rumbled audibly, the spell was broken. William pulled back and laughed. "Someone's hungry, I see. Eat up."

So I did.

*****

Lauren Smith Matthews's baby shower was being held at The Drake, the iconic hotel overlooking Lake Michigan. I'd never been because I'd never had a reason to go, so I was excited to check yet another Chicago landmark off my "must see" list. Like The Peabody Club, I was sure the Drake would impress with old Chicago flair. Standing in front of my closet, I was stumped. I couldn't decide what to wear. As I surveyed my wardrobe, I saw lots of black, great for photography gigs, but not really the right choice for a baby shower. This was a celebration, not a funeral.

I pulled down a winter-white sweater, still in its dry-cleaning bag from earlier in the season, took it out, and tugged it over my head. It didn't feel right, though, and I stared down at the way the fabric strained across my boobs.

"Damn it." The cleaners had done a number on this piece. I might as well have washed it myself if I was paying for the cleaners to shrink it.

I pulled it off and, as I did so, I caught a glimpse of myself in the mirror. As much as I wanted to deny it, my boobs spilled out of the cups of my favorite T-shirt bra. So maybe it wasn't the dry cleaners' fault after all. I had to acknowledge that the sweater wasn't the only article of clothing that had been clingy lately. Clearly, I'd gained a few pounds. *Damn it*. Factoring in William's sensational home-cooked meals, Hutch's beignets, and the non-stop winter, I was helpless. I was powerless against all those carbs, and my body seemed to hold onto them like a bear storing up for winter.

I'd been hitting the gym with William nearly every morning. I'd even come to appreciate those early workouts, though I was still far from liking them. But they weren't doing enough to counter the calories, and I knew I wasn't imagining the extra weight because Beckett had noticed it the last time I'd seen him. William was enjoying the way my tops clung to my breasts lately, however, and wasn't complaining. So I wouldn't dwell on it.

Since I wasn't going to lose five pounds in the next thirty minutes, I had to find another outfit to wear. I browsed through my section of the closet and settled on a pretty white blouse with a ruffled, plunging neckline. If I had cleavage, I reasoned, I might as well make the most of it. I paired the blouse with slim black pants and sleek, high-heeled Prada ankle boots. I looked chic, but the clothing was also functional. I was the photographer, as well as a guest, today. I had to be able to move around freely.

I wound my hair into a low, messy twist, a style I had spied while flipping through a magazine at the gym, threw on some mascara and lip gloss and a few spritzes of perfume, and headed out.

In the living room, William intercepted me, pulling me into his arms. "Lip gloss," I said, pointing to my lips. "No kisses unless you want to be covered in Sexy Vixen."

"Is that a proposition?"

"No, a color." I said and gave him a playful shove. As much as I wanted William's family to like me, I could have easily succumbed to his come hither tone and stayed in.

"I won't mess up your perfect lips," William said, ducking his head to kiss me on the neck. "I just wanted to tell you how pretty you look. I love you in white, Catherine."

"Thank you. I kind of threw this outfit together, so I'm glad it works"

"And I love your tits."

I rolled my eyes. So much for sweet William.

"That blouse is sexy as hell. If you didn't have to go, I'd enjoy taking it off you." His eyes were a shining, silvery grey and I knew what that meant.

"Tempting," I said, as William dipped his head to kiss the other side of my neck. "But I need to take a rain check. I don't want to disappoint your aunt."

William groaned in disappointment. Somehow he knew just how to boost my self-esteem. A few minutes ago, in front of my closet, I'd been feeling fat and bloated, but now I felt beautiful and desirable again.

"Oh, I almost forgot. Don't move." He took a few steps backward, holding up his index finger in a "one minute" sign, then turned and strolled off toward his study. I glanced at my watch and hoped whatever distraction William was plotting didn't take too long. He came back with a large shopping bag and handed it to me. It was heavier than it looked, and I peeked inside. A professionally wrapped gift, topped with an extravagant amount of ribbon, was nestled inside.

"Oh my God. I totally forgot to get a gift." I would have been mortified if I'd shown up empty-handed.

The door opened and Asa, leading Laird, came in. William took the bag from me, handed it to Asa, and said, "Don't worry about it, Catherine. Abigail gave me some hints. I had Parker pick something out."

Thank God for jack-of-all-trades assistants.

"There's a card too, and I signed both of our names."

I raised my eyebrows, "Oh really? Both of our names?" I couldn't help but smile. I loved how much of a couple William and I were becoming.

"Of course," he replied and gave me a kiss on my nose. "Now go. Do your baby thing." He gave my ass a pat as I headed to grab my coat.

*****

The Drake was only a few blocks from William's penthouse, but Anthony was driving me because I had my camera equipment and the gift as well. With all the safety measures in place, William would have probably insisted Anthony drive me anyway. Asa was with us, and he'd stay with me during the event, though William promised that my bodyguard would remain discreetly in the background. It still felt weird to have Asa go everywhere with me, but I had to admit, after recent events, having him close by did make me feel safe.

I smiled when we pulled in front of The Drake's awning and classic gold doors. I shouldered my equipment and Asa grabbed the bag with the gift. The doorman saw the baby shower bag and directed me to the Palm Court. The hotel's dark wood accents and cream crown moldings were perfectly accented by the brilliant chandeliers and plush carpets. Large gilded mirrors and fresh flowers spoke to the understated elegance of the iconic building.

The Palm Court's central feature was a limestone fountain with a gorgeous bronze urn. The room had been beautifully styled for Lauren's shower with flowers, pink and blue balloons, and a draped gift table. As with all things William's family, the décor was refined, but it was also whimsical. I noticed that each of the luncheon tables had a pair of booties worked into the centerpiece. Cute. I immediately grabbed my camera to get a few shots of the light, airy space before the room was too full of guests.

I caught sight of Asa in the camera lens and giggled as I watched my big, burly security guard—in a tight black suit that barely contained his brawn—deliver the gift bag to the table filled with similarly beribboned presents. More than a couple of the guests were also following his progress, turning back to look at the direction he'd come from and at me. I was relieved when Abigail and Lauren approached, and I smiled warmly and greeted both of them. "Lauren, this is so nice. Thank you so much for inviting me."

As clichéd as it sounded, Lauren really was glowing. She wore a cute polka-dotted wrap dress that accented her baby bump and looked like she should be a model for a high-end maternity site, especially as she confidently walked over on sky-high heels. I was impressed that she could walk in them at all, let alone at nearly seven months pregnant. Abigail also looked chic in classic pantsuit.

"We're so happy you're here, Catherine. And thank you again for offering to take pictures," Lauren said.

"I'm happy to."

"Thank you, also, for providing the eye candy," she said looking at Asa, "He'll take some of the attention off me, which I appreciate. There's only so much belly rubbing I can stand."

I laughed. It must be so crazy to have people touching you because you were pregnant. But before I could say as much, Lauren was whisked away by one of the staff, and Abigail ushered me into the center of the room. Sarah, William's oldest cousin, gave me a quick hug.

"I'm so glad you could make it." Sarah was in a navy shift dress with three-quarter length sleeves, her hair back in a knot.

"Thanks. Did you just get in from D.C.?" I asked. "I hear the airports have been horrible."

"Luckily I came in a few days early to help Mom get everything ready so I missed the really bad storms."

Abigail smiled. "The museum can spare you for a few days, Sarah. And we're so happy to have you. Catherine, I know you've met Zoe." She gestured to her youngest daughter, and Zoe made her way over.

"I have." I held out my hand, and Zoe took it. "Good to see you again."

"You too. You look great. Can I get you a glass of wine?" Zoe looked good, too, in a white, long-sleeve sweater tucked into a cute high-waisted mini-skirt that showed off her toned legs.

"I'm fine right now, but thanks."

Zoe was a lot warmer than she'd been the first time I met her, but I was still skeptical. I had a feeling that if her mom hadn't been standing beside her she would have ignored me. But these sisters were William's family, more like his siblings than his cousins, so it was up to me to make an effort. If Zoe genuinely didn't like me, at least I could know it wasn't for lack of trying on my part. The three of us chatted about the weather and the décor and their excitement over welcoming a new member to the family. I was a little relieved when Abigail introduced me to Joanna Matthews, Lauren's mother-in-law, and Danielle Fitzgerald, Zach's sister. I learned that the grandmothers were at odds over the sex of the baby. Abigail was sure Lauren was having a boy, whereas Joanna had her money on a girl. I snapped a few pics of the doting grandmothers-to-be and sneaked away to get some photos of the other guests.

Through my lens, I spotted Elin Erickson across the room. After those first weird minutes at the Botanical Society event, I'd liked her, so I made my way to her. "Hi, Elin. I'm Catherine Kelly. We met the other night at The Peabody Club."

She smiled. "Of course. Good to see you again." She looked as gaunt and wan as she had the first time we'd met, today wearing a plum blouse and black pants, but she chatted brightly about the last event she'd attended at The Drake and how much she liked Lauren's choices for the shower.

I nodded and agreed, and, as Elin moved away to chat with someone else she knew, I was never so glad to have a job to do. Of the fifty or so guests, I only knew Abigail and William's cousins—and I didn't even know them that well. I glanced around the room, feeling out of place and conspicuous. Of course, that was when I spotted Lara Kendall. My heart sank into my belly. She was the last person I ever wanted to see again. The first time I'd met her was at the Art Institute event I'd attended with William, our first real date. When she'd found out I was with William, she had accosted me in the ladies room and basically called me a whore to my face. I had nothing to say to her now, so I went back to my bag and busied myself with replacing the battery in my camera.

I moved around the court, taking various shots of the room and the guests. I wanted a shot of the gift table, the place settings, the centerpieces, and the adorable cake made of cloth diapers. Everything was in cool pink and blue pastels, more icy than Easter egg-y, which I appreciated.

I started taking candid pictures of a radiant Lauren talking with her friends. She looked so happy. As I snapped away, capturing her smiling and laughing and stroking her belly, it was hard not to think about babies. What girl didn't think about babies at a baby shower? Jace and I had talked about kids a few times, but it had been sort of a joke between us, something to think about for the distant future. We were so young and carefree when we got married, and Jace's surfing career had been most important to us then. But that future wasn't so distant any more. So much had changed since I was married to Jace and since he'd died. *I'd* changed. I was more settled now, more mature. But what about William? He was the wild card. I knew he loved me, but I had no idea if we were we heading down the path toward marriage and children or not.

I lifted my camera to capture another image of Lauren and caught sight of Asa lingering near the door. I loved William, and I wanted to be with him—today, tomorrow, forever. But I needed answers from him about our future. When was the right time to have that conversation? Between discussions of stalkers and what was for dinner? How could I even be thinking about having babies with William when I required round-the-clock security?

$$*****$$

Abigail finally called us all to lunch. I was thrilled to be invited and to spend time with William's family, but being the outsider got old quickly. I found my place card and made my way toward my table. I passed Lara Kendall on the way—thankfully going in another direction—but she just smiled her ice-princess smile and kept walking. *Bitch*. I'd been at the shower less than an hour and had already begun wondering how long it would last.

And then it couldn't end soon enough when I saw Zoe and Elin were seated at my table, Elin on my left and Zoe to my right. Elin would hopefully be okay, but I hadn't trusted Zoe's show in front of her mother earlier. Hopefully we'd be too busy eating to have to talk much. We started with a light salad of mixed greens with strawberries and blue cheese. I was starving and ate every bite in between polite chitchat with my tablemates.

The rest of the table was made up of Lauren's friends, a few from college who already knew one another and were dying to catch up, and a pair of girls from Lauren's work. It was easy to talk about the food—how light the dressing was, the merits of blue cheese versus goat cheese—and then the waiters brought out an assortment of small sandwiches: egg salad on brioche, salmon on pumpernickel, cucumber on white bread. An afternoon tea theme struck me as genius because ladies like these wouldn't eat much more than a few bites of anything.

Zoe and I both reached for our water glasses at the same time, and the sleeve of her sweater slid up slightly, revealing the edge of an inky tattoo. I'd seen something peeking out from the neckline of her sweater, and now I wondered if the tattoo wound its way from her arm to her chest. I would have loved to ask her about it, but with how icy she'd been during our last meeting, I wasn't sure I wanted to bother. Maybe William had some insights?

Zoe caught my eye. My cheeks burned at being caught looking at her arm so intently, so when Elin said something about the petite sandwiches in front of us, I quickly turned away and pretended to be interested. But Zoe wasn't having any of it.

"So you're living with William now?"

I turned back and shrugged, trying to play it cool. "It's temporary. I have my own place."

"How long have you been dating?" Zoe asked, taking a bite of her cucumber sandwich. "A couple weeks?"

"Longer than that," I said. *But not much longer*. I knew where she was going. My relationship with William had seemed to progress quickly, and she didn't like it.

"Looked like you were pretty settled when I was over there, but I'm sure it's helpful to have William's staff drive you around and walk your dog."

Her words stung and my first instinct was to defend myself, but this wasn't the place and I wasn't going to give Zoe the satisfaction. Besides, her thoughtless comment made me think that Zoe didn't know about the threats. If that was the case, then I wasn't going to tell her. Besides, it wasn't any of her business what I did. If she wanted answers, she could ask William.

"How did you two meet?" she asked. She was not letting the subject drop "Did you manage to con someone into giving you an invite to some exclusive event where you knew he'd be?" Evidently she was intent on getting in a few punches no matter what. Well, if she wanted to hear the story, I was happy to oblige.

"No," I said quietly and met her eyes before continuing. "We met when I was doing a photo shoot for Willowgrass, a new restaurant. William is one of the investors."

"That's right," Elin said, surprising me by jumping in. "I'd heard you were a talented food photographer. Wasn't your work in *Chicago Now*?"

"That was the Willowgrass shoot," I told her, happy to talk about my work instead of my love life.

"It was gorgeous. I guess I'd never thought much about that sort of work. Clearly, you have the eye for it," Elin added.

"It all just seems really fast," Zoe remarked, preventing me from responding to Elin's comment and taking the conversation in a different direction.

Elin shrugged. "I saw them together at The Peabody Club the other night, and William seemed really happy. Besides, people fall in love fast for lots of reasons."

I nodded, not sure what to say. Who would have thought Elin, as awkward and aloof as she was, would have been my defender?

"We should all be so lucky to find that kind of happiness," Elin added. Then she looked directly at Zoe. "I imagine pickings are kind of slim for you in Oklahoma City, Zoe."

I glanced down at my plate to hide my smile. *Nice one, Elin.* Not only was it the perfect zinger, it shut Zoe up. She turned to the lady on her other side and didn't speak to me again. I turned to Elin and gave her a wobbly smile. She'd saved me from a really awkward, really uncomfortable situation, but Elin, too, was talking to the woman seated next to her as if nothing had happened. I picked up my water glass and just about drained it in one long gulp. Fortunately, Abigail announced Lauren would open gifts shortly thereafter, so I excused myself to take more photos. I'd never been so happy to leave a table in my life.

*****

As the shower wound down, I gathered my camera equipment and packed it away. I had taken some really great shots. I was particularly hopeful about one of all the Smith women together— even Zoe was all smiles now that her family was around. I'd look at them all later, but when I'd scanned the images I was pleased. I was almost done stowing my camera stuff when Lauren approached. "Catherine, thank you so much for coming and for the Baby Bullet. I can't wait to make my own baby food. And the cloth diaper delivery service too. Really, it's too much!"

I smiled. "Well, you know how William is. I'm glad you like it."

"I love it, and now I think I need to go home and take a nap." She stroked her belly and smiled. "Everyone keeps telling me to get sleep while I can."

I almost laughed. "Lauren, you look amazing. I didn't even know you were pregnant until a week ago. Congratulations."

"I'm lucky I'm tall. The best thing is these boobs. I've never had boobs like these. That's definitely one of the perks." She laid her hand on my arm. "I'm sorry we didn't get to chat much."

"That's okay," I reassured her. "It was your shower. You had so many friends here."

"I hope you and Zoe got to know each other a little better. I asked Abigail to seat you next to her. She doesn't get to town much and she is so important to William."

There she went with that "important to William business." *How could that be possible?* They were so close yet she wouldn't give me a chance.

I forced a smile. "Yes, we did." It was the truth. Zoe made it clear she didn't like me with William.

"I'm sure," Lauren said with a knowing look.

Only, I imagined, she didn't know the half of it. It was obvious that Zoe was an old hand at being one way in front of her family. No matter what bond she and William had, I doubted Lauren was in on all of it.

"I told you she's a handful, but she always means well. You know, I keep telling William that the four of us need to get together for dinner soon. Zach is game for it, so I'll stay on William."

"That sounds great. Thanks again for having me, Lauren."

Asa intercepted me as soon as I left the Palm Court. The black sedan was waiting, and Asa helped me inside, then climbed into the front with Anthony. "Hello, Miss Cat. Back to the penthouse?"

I glanced at my watch. It was just before two o'clock, too early to return to the gilded cage.

Then I had an idea. "Actually, Anthony, I'd like to go to Morrison Hotel."

He nodded and put the car in gear. "Morrison Hotel it is." I watched as we pulled out and headed down Michigan Avenue.

Hutch wasn't expecting me, but he had told me he wanted candid shots of pre-service prep for the cookbook, and I did happen to have all my gear. So technically this *was* work, but it helped that I needed an escape. I didn't want to go back to lockdown at the penthouse at the moment and a visit to Morrison Hotel seemed like the perfect way to reconnect with my own life. Zoe had rattled me, and I felt like I had forgotten who Catherine Kelly really was, outside of William.

Asa had probably given George our itinerary as soon as I mentioned my change of plans, but I texted William anyway and told him I had some work to do. I didn't mention Hutch or where I was going. He'd know soon enough and I figured we could talk about it later.

I'm with Asa and Anthony, I texted to finish. *So don't worry. See you for dinner.*

XOXO

THIRTEEN

My car arrived at Morrison Hotel, and Asa opened the door for me and helped me pull my camera bags out of the back. The minute my feet hit the sidewalk, a surprisingly brisk gust of wind ripped right through me. "Shit, that's cold," I said through nearly chattering teeth.

"That's March in Chicago for you," Asa chuckled. "We better get you inside and warmed up before you blow away." His cheeks were red and his eyes watered in the wind. It wasn't sunny, but thankfully it wasn't snowing either. I shivered as the wind kicked up again. A return trip to Tropos sounded like a good idea right about now.

I took a deep breath and tried to shake off the lingering effects of my luncheon conversation with Zoe as I headed into the restaurant. I hated that William's cousin—ostensibly the cousin he was closest to—didn't like me. I had no idea why, and it stung. Admittedly, I was sensitive, but how could I not be? I had been unfairly vilified after Jace's death by his family, some of his friends, and lots of his fans. I walked away from all that hate, but what was I supposed to do about Zoe? How does one say, "Hey, I think your cousin hates me for no reason" to one's boyfriend? And would said boyfriend side with his girlfriend over his favorite family member?

Mindy, one of the hostesses, was on the phone when I walked in but gave me a smile and pointed to the back. I felt totally comfortable here now, which was all Hutch's doing. He'd introduced me to his entire staff and told them to give me whatever I wanted. The man truly had a talent for making people feel welcome. No wonder Morrison Hotel had a waitlist a mile long.

Asa took a seat in the booth closest to the kitchen, and I set down my gear just as Hutch came through the kitchen doors. His serious expression turned into a warm smile the instant he saw me, and he changed course from wherever he was initially heading to turn toward me. He wiped his hands on the white apron tired around his waist, covering distressed jeans. His black T-shirt molded to his chest and his tattooed arms popped with color against it.

"This is what I love about you, Miss Catherine." He took me by the shoulders and kissed me on both cheeks. He smelled like spices and wood smoke. "You keep me on my toes, and you're certainly never predictable."

"Predictability is very overrated, don't you think?" Being so warmly welcomed by a gorgeous man was exactly what I needed to snap me out of the funk of Lauren's shower.

Hutch always seemed thrilled to see me, and with that wide, infectious smile, how could I help but feel a little fluttery inside? He was off-limits for so many reasons, but there was just something about him. If I was being honest, I knew what it was: he reminded me a little of Jace. His confidence. His blond hair. His easygoing, laid-back attitude. All of these connected powerfully with who I used to be in California. Cat Ryder, surf photographer, would have had a major crush on Hutch. And maybe Catherine Kelly, Chicago food photographer, did too.

I cleared my throat, smiled, and tried to focus on why I was here. "I thought today might be a good time to do the candid pre-service prep shots you wanted for the book. I happened to have my equipment with me, and I was already out. But if this is a bad time, I can come back."

"I'd never send you away, Kitty Cat. Not now that I have you here." He grinned like a mischievous child. "Come on back and you can get started. The *mise en place* is done, and Angie's already staging," he said over his shoulder as he led me into the kitchen. He lowered his voice. "She's a ballbreaker, that one. She's the secret to my success, you know."

"I doubt that," I said, dropping my bag and reaching for my camera and a lens. My hands were shaking a little. 'Kitty Cat' was what Jace had called me—intimately, *in bed.* Hearing Hutch call me that was unexpected, to say the least. But he didn't need to know. I plastered on a smile.

"Don't doubt it," Hutch said, oblivious to my internal drama and sounding serious. "My grandmother always said, 'Behind every successful man there's a good woman.' You wouldn't argue with my grandmother, would you?"

"I wouldn't dream of it."

"Smart move because you'd lose." He winked, then headed over to where Angie was working.

I took in the activity of the kitchen, then got quickly immersed in my work. The food was gorgeous, and the staff didn't seem to mind that I was present. The shots really did look candid and not at all stiff. Maybe it was the dynamic between Hutch and Angie. He was clever with the innuendo, and she brought him back down to size with her sarcasm. Watching them work was fun, and I was having a great time. Mostly, though, I enjoyed watching Hutch's genius realized. The way he cooked was intense and wild and free all at the same time. It would have been easy to get caught up in looking at him, in witnessing him create his art on a plate, but I remembered to watch through the lens of the camera and take what I hoped were great shots.

The entire time I watched Hutch, I kept thinking about Beckett. I wished he was here, witnessing what I was. He would love it. I pulled out my new phone and snapped a quick pic of Hutch as he julienned carrots with both remarkable ease and precision.

I thought you'd appreciate this, I typed.

I knew he admired Hutch as a chef—what chef didn't? —but I bet the two of them would actually hit it off, too.

Call you later to give you the deets. Overdue 4 cocktails, yes?? XOXO.

I hit send. I still worried Beckett secretly nursed a broken heart. With all the drama going on in my life, I hadn't been a very good friend lately, and I needed to change that. ASAP.

*****

I was so focused on getting a variety of shots that when Hutch appeared in front of me with two large bowls of something that smelled like butter, bacon, and cheese, I was totally surprised. My stomach gave a little leap of joy, and I wondered how long I'd been there. Surely I couldn't be hungry again. I'd eaten at Lauren's shower. Of course, that had been light fare, and what I'd learned about Hutch was that nothing he made was light on calories.

"That's a wrap, Cat. Isn't that what they say?"

I smiled and tried not to stare at the food. I didn't want to start salivating. "I think that's in movies, but I get your point. I got some great pictures. I think you'll be pleased."

"I know I will be, and I like that you aim to please." Hutch was definitely ramping up his flirtiness. "Now, you come eat with me. I always chow before the first seating, and I don't like to eat alone."

"Oh, um…" I vaguely remembered that I'd promised William I'd be home for dinner.

"Don't tell me no, sweetie. The staff has already been served." He jerked his head toward a rectangular stainless steel table. Angie and the line cooks were seated around it, eating bowls of whatever Hutch had brought me.

"But you and me," Hutch said, "we're going to sit out here." He pushed through the kitchen doors and into the main dining area. Asa still sat in his booth, and I was ashamed that I'd totally forgotten him.

But Hutch hadn't. Asa had a steaming bowl of food in front of him and a bottle of sparkling water. Hutch really was the sweetest man. He seemed to read my mind. "A man's got to keep up his strength. Keeping an eye on you can't be easy."

He gave me a smirk, and immediately diffused the embarrassment that threatened to turn my cheeks red. There were few employers, I reasoned, who would be okay with their employees coming to work flanked by a bodyguard, let alone be so okay with it that they would feed him. Asa's constant presence sometimes made me uncomfortable—or at least explaining his constant presence to other people did—but Hutch acted like he didn't mind and I appreciated it.

Hutch led me to a booth where Asa could see us and put one of the steaming bowls in front of me. Still in his apron, he sat and looked at me. I looked back. His blue eyes sparkled, his hair was gorgeously messy, and his hands, which he'd placed flat on the table, were strong. I couldn't help but be drawn to the tattoos on his arms. I had never gotten a good look at them and I found myself wondering what he had on there. As my gaze traveled up over a spindly branch and some black lettering, Hutch cleared his throat and I realized I was staring. I also realized that I wasn't eating, which was obviously what he was expecting—and wanting—me to do.

I quickly grabbed my spoon and looked down at my plate. I recognized the shrimp and the chopped bacon, but I wasn't sure about the rest. "Polenta?" I asked.

"Oh, honey." Hutch shook his head. "You kill me. This, darlin', is shrimp and grits. It's a Southern staple. Of course, I fancied it up a bit." He grinned knowingly, and I smothered a laugh in response. Hutch saying he'd just 'fancied up' some grits was the understatement of the century. He was one of the most inventive and talented chefs *in the world* and any dish he fancied up was bound to be beyond spectacular.

Still, I played along as I found his modesty disarmingly charming. "I thought grits were for breakfast."

Hutch gave me a look that said stop-while-you're-ahead. I lifted my spoon and tasted the dish. My eyes popped open and Hutch threw his head back and laughed. My reaction was, apparently, spot-on. I'd expected something like a savory oatmeal or cream of wheat, but this was wonderful—creamy, buttery, cheesy. The flavors exploded in my mouth. "Oh my God," I said around the spoon. "This is absolutely to die for."

"You didn't even taste the shrimp yet. They've got a kick." He watched as I loaded my spoon with grits and shrimp. He had the same look I'd seen on William's face when he was enjoying watching me eat.

"So good," I said, spooning up more. "And probably ten thousand calories."

Hutch stirred the grits in his bowl. "Honey, calories don't exist at Morrison Hotel."

I laughed and scooped up another helping. "Tell that to my clothes."

"It's not the clothes that get me in trouble, Cat," he said softly "It's the body underneath." His eyes dipped slightly, and I remembered the way the blouse I had chosen showed off my cleavage. *Holy shit.* Our little flirt-a-thon this afternoon had just crossed a big line and I could feel the heat rising to my cheeks. So Hutch had noticed my cleavage, and a part of me definitely liked that he'd noticed. But I loved William, I reminded myself—I was in love with William—and nothing was going to happen between me and Hutch. Ever.

"So tell me about your shadow," Hutch said, his eyes back on my face. I glanced at Asa.

"It's complicated," I said, torn between not wanting to reveal any of William's personal issues to Hutch and trying to steer our discussion away from more sexy banter.

"It always is," he said with a note of seriousness in his voice. He wasn't flirting now. I waited for him to probe, but he seemed to let it go. That was probably what I liked most about Hutch. It was easy to talk to him, to just be with him.

"I remember back when I was in the band. I couldn't go anywhere without security. Couldn't go to the damn bathroom by myself. The security was necessary, but that didn't mean it wasn't a drag."

"I forgot you were in a band. You must have been popular if you needed security."

Hutch shrugged. "We did alright, but mainly we needed bodyguards to keep all the adoring women at bay."

He probably wasn't joking, but I laughed anyway. "And what about now? Are you seeing anyone? Every time I open *Chicago Now*, you're pictured surrounded by adoring women."

"*Chicago Now* would have me engaged to half a dozen socialites. The truth is I'm blissfully available."

That was what I'd figured, but it didn't really make sense. Hutch was sweet and funny and handsome as sin. The first time we'd met he'd told me no one could cook, play guitar, or fuck better than he could. No wonder he had women lining up, but why no one serious? "Is it the chef's hours?" I asked. "Because—"

The door to the restaurant opened, and I turned to see who was entering. It was still too early for the first seating. I couldn't see, but I heard footsteps and then: "Hello."

My jaw must have dropped because the last person I expected to see was William.

"What are you doing here?" I sputtered. That was probably a bad way to greet him, but I was completely taken off guard. Hutch was more poised. He stood, wiped his palms on his jeans, and offered a hand. As the two men stood facing each other, the stark difference between them came into focus. Hutch was the epitome of effortless hipster chic with his blond hair, his casual dress, his tattoos, his Chuck Taylors. William, by contrast, screamed mogul in his suit and overcoat, with his thick dark hair neatly combed back. Both were hot as hell and evenly matched in height.

"Hello, William."

The two shook hands, and William glanced down, taking in the food and the table for two. "Morrison. Catherine."

God, everything was so awkward. The easy atmosphere between Hutch and me was gone, replaced by a stress I could see William also held in his shoulders. He wore a tense expression, his face like chiseled granite, his jaw tight, and his eyes a hard, cold blue

"We were just having a bite to eat before the first seating," Hutch said, still standing. I wondered if I should stand, but what I really wanted to do was sink onto the floor and crawl under the table. "Care for some shrimp and grits?"

"It's really good," I offered lamely. *Way to go, Cat.* Maybe it was better to stay quiet.

"No, I'll take a rain check. I'm just here to pick up my girlfriend. How much longer will she be?"

I felt like I'd just been caught stealing and the guilt washed over me again. I glanced at my watch. *Shit.* It was already after five. How had I so easily lost track of the time?

Hutch picked up on William's meaning and took his question as a cue. "We were just finishing up," he said easily. "In fact, my first service is in an hour, and I still have some prep to take care of."

I rose awkwardly. "Thanks for the meal, Hutch," I said.

"Anytime, Cat. I'll see you soon. William." Hutch gave us a nod then was back through the doors of the kitchen. He knew how to make a quick exit, and I was happy he was gone.

I walked past William and fumbled for all of my equipment. I took way longer than I wanted packing it up. William stood silently, watching me with his dark-lashed, turbulent blue eyes. Was I in trouble? I felt like I was being put in place by my boyfriend, which I did not appreciate at all…though maybe I did deserve it a little.

By the time I was done, Asa had the restaurant door open. William led me to a waiting black SUV and still hadn't said a word. The sedan I had arrived in had apparently been replaced by the SUV while I was working. I slid into the back, catching Anthony's eyes in the rearview mirror. A moment later, William slid in beside me.

*****

I wasn't quite sure how to act on the ride back to the penthouse. Was William pissed or just reminding Hutch that I was *his* girlfriend? I might have asked him about it if Asa and Anthony hadn't been within earshot in the front seat. The SUV was spacious, but with three hot, muscled men in it, it was like I was drowning in testosterone.

"Sorry I lost track of time. I was working," I finally said when Anthony had us underway. "You didn't have to come to the restaurant. You could have called."

William took my hand. "True, but I wanted to see you." He pulled me close and kissed me lightly. My frustration melted away. Maybe William didn't have any ulterior motive for coming to get me. "I missed you." He kissed me again, and I wished Anthony and Asa could disappear. If William and I kept kissing, things would be even more awkward. William must have read my mind because he reached into the center console and the privacy divider came up. We were alone now, and William resumed kissing me,

Finally, he pulled back. "How was the baby shower?"

"It was lovely. Absolutely perfect. They had it in the Palm Court, and the decorations were just adorable." I reached in my bag for my digital camera. "I'll show you."

William leaned close as I clicked through shots of the décor. "Aren't these little booties cute? They had them on all the tables. And this is the diaper cake."

William frowned. "A diaper cake?"

"Not those kind of diapers. Cloth. It's so Lauren will have a slew of cloth diapers on hand. They're good for whatever." I glanced at William. "She loved our presents, by the way. She really appreciated the diaper service and the food processor."

"Uh-huh."

"Oh, and here's Lauren. She hardly even looks pregnant. And she was glowing the whole time. Here's another shot."

"Mmmhmm."

I realized William probably didn't really care about pictures of onesie cookies or baby-rattle centerpieces, but it was sweet that he was taking an interest for me. I knew this was kind of a chick thing, but it was also his family, and I wanted him to be a part of it. "These are some shots of Lauren opening the gifts. That's a breast pump."

"Just what I needed to see."

"Hey, Zach got some stuff too. This is a baby carrier just for men." I tilted the camera. "See, he can carry the baby snuggled against his chest, or when he or she gets older, on his back."

"I can't wait to see Zach in that." William laughed. "I can't imagine wearing one of those, much less having a kid."

I froze. My finger kept clicking to bring up new pictures, but I was remembering the last time William and I had talked about Lauren and the baby. He'd said something similar

My heart sank a little bit more.

William was saying something, obviously clueless about how his random comment had affected me, and I tuned back in just as I slid to another picture. This one was of Zoe.

"She looks almost respectable," William joked.

I hesitated for a second, then decide to tell him about Zoe. "We were actually seated next to each other," I said." I don't think she likes me, but I can't figure out why."

"Don't take it personally," William said, putting an arm around my shoulders. "She doesn't like anybody."

Traffic was at a standstill, and I really didn't want to talk anymore about Zoe, so I changed the subject and asked William what he'd been up to all day. He elaborated on projects he'd been working on and then asked about Hutch. I clearly wasn't getting out of talking about my afternoon. "I didn't realize you were making a stop at Morrison Hotel today."

"It was sort of unplanned. Hutch wanted some candid behind-the-scenes shots. I had my stuff with me, so I figured, why not?"

"I'm not comfortable with you being there." His gorgeous face was expressionless but his voice was tight and clipped, which belied the turmoil I knew he was feeling.

"William," I pleaded softly, "we talked about this already. Asa was there the entire time and nothing could have happened. And I was there to work, nothing more."

"And did you get the shots you needed?"

I leaned back into my plush, heated leather seat. "I think so. I'll have to take a look in the morning."

"Are they all shots of the man himself?"

I raised a brow. "No. Some are of him and some are of the line chefs and the sous chef. Angie is the sous chef, and she's really great."

"So you did spend time with someone other than Morrison today. When I arrived you looked pretty cozy."

I glanced over at William and saw that his eyes were a stormy grey. He was worked up, and it was over me spending time with another man. I felt instantly guilty. Yes, Hutch had shamelessly flirted with me, and I had flirted right back until I knew we had taken it too far. William never needed to know about that, and I would make sure it never happened again. I loved *him* and I wanted to be with him—only him.

I responded carefully. "Hutch had to eat before the first serving. And we weren't cozy. Asa was right there. William," I asked quietly, "are you worried about me working with Hutch?"

"No." He answered a bit too quickly.

I shifted and moved closer to him. "Are you sure?"

"Very sure."

I slid my hand in his hair and leaned in. "Because if you were jealous, I'd probably think that was pretty cute."

"Catherine, I'm not cute, and I'm not jealous." His voice was still tight and controlled, and I didn't hear a bit of playfulness in his response.

I needed to make this right. I stroked a hand down his chest. "Oh, I don't know about that. I think you're a little of both, and that makes me pretty hot."

William looked down at my hand and then into my face. "Does it?"

"Yes," I cooed. "It makes me want to show you that you have nothing to be worried about." My hand slid lower, wrapping around the hardening bulge in his trousers.

"I'm not jealous," he said, his voice gritty.

"Of course not." I flicked the button on his trousers open. "Because there's nothing to be jealous about." I slid his zipper down and freed his erection from his black boxer briefs. "There's only one man I want to be with." I stroked his cock, admiring the way the veins stood out, the way it seemed to pulse in my hand. "Only one man I think about. Only one man I belong to."

I slid out of my seat and onto the floor, then made my way over to William. I knelt in front of him and pushed his legs apart, settling between them. My hand never stopped sliding up and down that hard flesh.

"One man who makes me wet." I licked the tip of his cock, and he groaned. I swirled my tongue around the tip again.

William watched me, his gaze hungry.

"Only one man I want inside me. One man I want to do this to. Only one man I love. And that's you."

With that, I swirled my tongue around his tip then slowly, deliberately slowly, I took the rest of him in my mouth and sucked. William groaned again. By the time he'd filled my mouth, William's head had fallen back against the headrest. His hands were clenched at his sides, and his breathing was rapid.

I slid him in and out of my mouth, finding a slow rhythm I liked. I pulled and sucked, pulled and sucked, and when he tensed, ready to come, I pulled back, lightly scraping my teeth along the sensitive underside of his member.

"I love you, William." I had my hand wrapped around him now, sliding up and down.

His hot grey eyes locked on my face. "And I love you, beautiful girl."

I took him in my mouth again. This time there wasn't any tenderness or slowness. I gorged on him, taking him to the hilt, working his flesh with my hand and my tongue. He liked it fast and tight.

William's response was immediate. He grabbed my hair and pushed me down, and I let him control my movements, let him bob my head up and down in the rhythm he wanted. I loved that I could pleasure him this way. Shivers ran down my back as his fingers tangled in my hair and his whole body tensed in response, poised for pleasure based on what I would do next. Finally, I gripped William's hips and sucked hard, moving my mouth up and down over his swelling flesh until he pulsed against my tongue.

"Yes," William rasped. His hips arched, pushing him to the back of my throat, and his hot, sweet release threatened to choke me. I quickly swallowed and swallowed, milking him and sucking until he had nothing left to give me.

From under heavy eyelids, William gazed at me. "You're mine, Catherine. Only mine."

FOURTEEN

Monday morning I lay sprawled in bed in the penthouse's master suite. I was naked, alone, and trying to psych myself up to get ready for work. Easier said than done.

William and I had spent all day Sunday in bed. We'd woken up to a cloudy morning and a forecast for more snow, so when William had peeled off my T-shirt and panties and suggested we not even bother getting up, I'd been happy to comply. Maybe he'd still been feeling the effects of Saturday's meeting with Hutch or maybe my actions in the back of the SUV had inspired him. Whatever the reason, to say William had been particularly *creative* in his ministrations was an understatement. Another all-day sex-travaganza had ensued and by lunchtime, I'd lost count of how many orgasms William had given me.

William had left for the office early this morning, so I had the big bed all to myself. I stretched wantonly and all of my muscles ached, like I'd worked out too hard. I *had* worked out too hard—the kind of sex we'd had qualified as strength, endurance, *and* cardio training, I was certain. My nipples felt permanently erect, chafed even, from William's continuous attention yesterday. And yet I still wanted more. I couldn't stop thinking about the man I loved, about his body over mine, his tongue and his hands on me everywhere. If he were here now, I'd try to convince him to call-in sick—if billionaire business moguls ever did such things.

Saturday replayed over and over in my head and I couldn't believe I had actually gone down on William while Anthony and Asa were mere inches away, separated from us by only the privacy divider. Did they have any idea what we were doing back there? Did they hear William moan as he writhed under me and then came in my mouth? I started to blush at the memory. It just went to show the effect my gorgeous man had on me. When I was with him, I couldn't think straight. I wanted him so much, I would do *anything*, including giving him a blow job in the backseat of his chauffeured SUV in rush-hour traffic with his security team at the wheel.

I looked at the clock. It was just past nine and I had a meeting at eleven with the creative executives at Fresh Market about the summer campaign. I needed to get moving. I forced myself out of bed and into the shower, then hurriedly dressed in a dark grey, long-sleeve wrap dress with black opaque thigh-highs and cute ankle boots, then grabbed a quick bite and a huge mug of coffee. I was ready to head out by ten-fifteen.

"Good morning, Miss Cat." Anthony was all smiles when he met me at the elevator and traveled down to the building's garage with me where Asa waited by the car. "I'll be driving you today, and Asa will be accompanying you."

"Sounds great," I said. "I have a meeting at eleven at Fresh Market's corporate offices at Franklin and Wells."

"I know," he replied. "We'll get you there on time, I promise."

"Punctuality has never been my strong suit, Anthony. Thanks for making me look good." Asa held open the door for me and I slid in the back of the car. I was relieved we'd be riding in the black Mercedes sedan today.

On the drive over, I tried to get my thoughts straight about the next Fresh Market campaign, which made me miss Beckett again. I checked my phone and he hadn't responded to my text from Morrison Hotel on Saturday, which was not like him. I shot him another quick one: *Miss you. Drinks soon?* We'd had so much fun putting together our shots of phallic asparagus and glistening cherries for the 'Fresh for Spring' campaign, which had been a big success. The plan now was for strawberries and peaches for the summer campaign.

It should have been an easy job, but I was more than a little nervous. I wouldn't have my bestie by my side on this one. How was I ever going to make peaches and strawberries look erotic without Beckett's help? And, I'd be working with Alec again. I liked Alec, a lot, but he was Beckett's ex now and that was just plain weird. I had no idea how he was taking the break-up. I didn't want things between us to be awkward, but I knew they might be.

Alec greeted me as soon as Asa escorted me inside the building and up to Fresh Market's suite. He was as warm and easy-going as always and gave me a big hug and gushed about how glad he was to see me. I relaxed right away. Of course this wasn't going to be awkward. Alec was a pro and no matter what was going on with him and Beckett, this was work.

"Everyone is thrilled you're on board for the summer campaign, Cat," Alec said as he led me down a corridor toward the conference room. He looked super cute as always in slim black pants, a button-down, and a color-blocked cardigan. I looked over my shoulder and saw Asa settling into a chair in the small waiting area as the receptionist handed him a steaming cup of coffee. Waiting for me seemed to be his life. I wondered if he read. Maybe I should get him a book?

"They're all ready for you." And with that my attention snapped back to Alec.

I grabbed Alec's arm as we paused outside the door to the conference room. "Before we go in, I just want to make sure you're okay, and that we're okay."

He furrowed his brow. "What do you—*oh*, because of the Beckett thing?"

"Right. I hope seeing me…" I wasn't sure how to finish the sentence exactly. It wasn't like I was a staple in Alec and Beckett's relationship.

"No way." Alec waved a hand, as though my comment was the silliest thing ever.

Interesting. Alec seemed as unaffected and casual about the break-up as Beckett had been. Had I totally misread their relationship? I'd thought they really liked each other.

"In fact," Alec continued, "Beckett and I are still friends. He texted me about your little trip to Tropos over Valentine's Day."

"He did?"

"Yes, and I'm uber-jealous. Your life is fabulous. Not only did you go to your own private island, you landed a gig with Hutch Morrison. He's totally gorgeous. More importantly, his food is to die for."

"You have no idea. And he's a nice guy too," I added, still a little thrown by how *okay* both Beckett and Alec seemed to be.

"Morrison Hotel is major, Cat. Fresh Market would wet its pants if we could work with Morrison on a campaign—any campaign. Seriously, can you just Photoshop him into some of our ads? But really, congrats."

"Thanks."

Alec opened the door to the conference room, and I strolled in, giving the execs my biggest smile. There was a lot to discuss and concentrate on, but I couldn't stop myself from glancing at Alec every once in a while during all the presentations and brainstorming. What was wrong with me? Did I expect him to break down in the conference room? If he said he was fine, then he was fine, right? No matter how much I told myself this, I couldn't shake the idea that there was more to the Valentine's Day break-up than either of them was letting on.

*****

I had peaches and strawberries on the brain when I met Asa in the reception area a few hours later. The meeting had gone really well. We'd discussed the look and feel that Fresh Market was going for—refreshing meets healthy meets sweet, with a sexy twist, of course—and I was confident that I could deliver what they wanted. The shoot was scheduled for Friday and I entered the time and location of the studio into my calendar on the ride over to William's office.

William had requested that I come by today so we could discuss the WML Champagne photo shoot, since I'd slept through our first meeting on my migraine day and he was very eager for this little project to get started. I loved that he personally oversaw everything to do with his winery. The vineyard and making wine were his real passions and he became so animated and genuine when he talked about it. And, as excited as I was to add the pictures to my portfolio, I was more excited to see my boyfriend. I still ached for him—and because of him, literally—and I was very aware of my tender nipples deliciously rubbing against the fabric of my bra.

When we arrived, Asa escorted me to the private elevator bank and used a key card to gain access. We bulleted to the executive floor so quickly it made me queasy. The doors slid open and there was Parker, who was waiting for me with a smile.

"Good afternoon, Miss Kelly. It's a pleasure to see you again."

Parker was William's executive assistant. She looked chic in a black tailored suit, but I noticed that her shoes were red patent leather. The idea of Parker with a wild side made me smile. Her brown hair was subtly highlighted and pulled back into a sleek ponytail. She was in her mid-thirties and had worked for William for several years. I kept meaning to ask him about her—things like her last name, for instance—but it always seemed to slip my mind.

"Thanks, Parker. How have you been?" I watched Asa stride toward one of the couches in the seating area. Poor guy would be waiting for me again.

"I've been well, thank you. Just trying to stay warm and dry. The snow has been unbelievable this past week, hasn't it?" She chattered away about the weather and then gestured for me to follow her through the luxurious reception area and past the sign that read WML Capital Management, LLC. Soft music floated through the cream, brown, and beige office as Parker led me along the quiet executive floor.

"Mr. Lambourne is expecting you," Parker said. "I'm glad you were able to reschedule."

I gave her a curious glance. Did she know the reason we'd rescheduled, or was she just making small talk?

"Me too. I'm ready to talk champagne," I told Parker as we reached William's office. His door was open, and when he heard my voice he turned from his window and smiled.

For an instant, I froze.

The sight of him in his impeccable—and no doubt incredibly expensive—suit, one hand in his pocket, all that tousled dark hair and those stormy eyes, made me lose my breath. He was so incredibly handsome and I loved that every time I saw him it was like I was seeing him for the first time. Added to the image of William himself was the view from this lofty height. All of downtown Chicago, from the river to the lake, was spread out below his windows and it was breathtaking.

I'd grown used to the starkness of William's city design preferences. Like his penthouse, this room was clean and modern. The office was a stark white with black accents—a black leather couch, leather chairs, a settee, and a coffee table. Parker arranged coffee and water on the coffee table for us, then said, "Anything else, Mr. Lambourne?"

His gaze drifted toward her as though he'd forgotten she was even present. "That's all for now, Parker."

She nodded and gave me a smile as she moved past me to exit. I scooted inside, and William came to me, reaching around me to key a code into a panel that locked the office door. His heated grey eyes lingered on my face.

"That's better." His arm wrapped around my waist, and he pulled me close into the musky scent of him.

I loved the way he smelled, the way he felt when he held me. His mouth met mine with gentle insistence, and I immediately opened for him. He kissed me thoroughly, pressing me against the wall until I could feel the hardness of his erection against my belly. His hands stroked up and down my back, cupping my ass, molding my hips.

He pulled away and smiled down at me. He caressed my cheek, pushing a strand of hair behind my ear. "Hello, beautiful girl.

I've been thinking about you all day. I'm so glad you're finally here."

"I'm not late, am I?" I said, my voice breathless. Since William's security team had started driving me, I was almost never late to anything anymore, but I had also stopped checking the time as often.

"No, you're not. I'm just not a patient man." He took my hand and led me to the black leather couch. "How was the meeting with Fresh Market?" He sat down, but before I could sit beside him, he pulled me into his lap. Fortunately the skirt of my dress wasn't narrow, and I was able to straddle him, just barely.

"Is this how you conduct all your business meetings?" I teased.

"Yes, I always have my business partners sit on my lap. It's a negotiating technique."

"I bet it works in your favor every time."

His hand wandered down my back to settle on my waist. "And what does Fresh Market want you to shoot for summer?"

"Strawberries and peaches."

His hand slid down my thigh until he reached the hem of my skirt. And then he inched underneath. "Peaches. One of my favorite fruits," he said, sliding his hand higher up my leg to the tender flesh past the top of my thigh-high. "So ripe and juicy and," his hand brushed against my naked sex and his eyes widened, "naughty."

"Oops," I said with a smile. "I may have forgotten something this morning when I got dressed."

His hand pushed against me gently, his fingers tickling in a way that made my toes curl. "You haven't been wearing panties all day?"

I shook my head.

"Catherine," he said, sliding two fingers against me, teasing. "You are a very bad girl." One finger gently pressed inside me and then another. "And you're also very, very wet." His thumb swirled around my clit, and I arched my neck. I was still a little sore from yesterday, but whatever he was doing with his fingers made all the hurt instantly disappear. My body was starved for him, craving the pleasure only he could give. I rocked against his nimble fingers, feeling the pressure build inside me.

"William," I gasped.

But he stopped. He withdrew his fingers and removed his hand from under my dress. I stared at him through a haze of desire until I realized he was holding an envelope out to me.

"What's that?" I asked.

"My offer. Open it, Catherine."

I took a deep breath and grasped the envelope with shaky fingers. It wasn't sealed, so I lifted the flap and peeked inside. I cleared my throat as I skimmed the contract for my services. The offer was generous, to say the least. It was too generous. I tried to hand the envelope back, but he wouldn't take it. "It's too much," I said, explaining. "This is at least triple my normal rate. I can't accept it."

William's eyes went from grey to blue. "But you will accept it," he said in a tone that told me any argument would be futile. "Because you're worth it and because it will make me very happy."

I sighed. "I'm not going to win this one, am I?"

"No." He leveled his gaze on me.

"Ok," I said with a shrug. If he wanted to pay me a ridiculous amount, that was his deal. He had the money to spare. "So let's talk about the campaign. I usually do this with paper and pen at a conference table, so I can take notes, but I suppose if I forget anything, you can remind me."

"I have all the details in a proposal that I'll have Parker email to you this afternoon. You won't have to remember anything. As for the shots, that's up to you. You're the expert."

"But you must have some idea of what you want, of the look or the feel of the pictures."

"Of course. I was thinking of several images. My idea is that the main one will be a champagne bottle with its cork popping, fizz, bubbles, and cork flying up and out."

"So a fun, energetic vibe," I recapped.

"Yes." He nodded, but I could tell by the look on his face that I didn't quite have it yet. "But sexy too. This champagne is very sexy. Focus on the spurting of the champagne and that flying cork. Maybe the bottle is tilted at just the right angle."

"A phallic look."

He smiled. "I knew you were the right woman for the job."

I nodded. I had plenty of experience making food look phallic. For whatever reason, food that suggested sex—or sexy body parts—seemed to sell. But I felt concerned about William's suggested shot. I'd never done a shoot so technical before. The popping of the cork and the spray of the champagne would have to be timed just perfectly.

"What's wrong?' William asked, sensing my mood.

"This shoot is going to require some special effects, I think."

"I'll get you whatever you need."

"I know, but I've never done anything like this before. What if I can't deliver what you want? Maybe you should hire someone with more experience in this sort of photography. I really don't want to disappoint you."

William waved a hand, dismissing my concerns. "You are a fantastic photographer, Catherine. You're so smart about your craft and I know you're fearless. You used to put yourself in danger to capture the right shot. Photographing world-class surfers was way more difficult than this will be and you were amazing at that. Look at this as a challenge, an opportunity to learn something new."

"You're paying me an awful lot of money to learn on the job."

"I'm paying you a lot of money because you're damned good at what you do. No one can make food sexier on film that you can, and I have complete faith in you. And as I said, I'll get you whatever you need—equipment, assistants, you name it."

I turned my head from the heat of his eyes and stared out the window. I still wasn't sure. Could I could pull it off?

"Catherine," William said, drawing my gaze back to him. "You are brilliant. You will figure this out. Trust me. I have no doubts."

How could I say no to that? His belief in me made *me* believe in me, so I nodded. "OK. I'll do it." I decided I would make this shoot work, and I'd do a damn fine job too. I never disappointed. My job was to make sure the client—who in this case was also the man I loved—was completely satisfied.

"Good." William took the envelope from my hands. "Now that that's settled, we can discuss what's really important."

"I thought that *was* the important discussion."

William's hand trailed over my chin and down my neck "Not every discussion requires words," he said, outlining my breasts through the fabric of my dress. My nipples immediately tightened into hard, almost painful points.

"So all that talk of exploding champagne corks and spurts of effervescent golden liquid didn't turn you on?"

William reached for the tie at my waist and pulled. The material parted to reveal my pink lace bra. "Nice touch," he said. "And you should know by now that you don't have to say anything." His hand snaked inside my dress to tease the lace over one breast. "I'm turned on just by the sight of you." His finger trailed over my taut nipple, and I gasped in sweet agony. The heat I had felt at his earlier play between my legs started again. I could hardly wait to have him, but I didn't want to rush this, especially since I was currently on top.

William pressed his mouth over the lace covering my sensitive point. He sucked and bit until I was squirming in his lap. And then, when I thought I couldn't take any more, he repeated the gesture on my other breast. I was in a frenzy of wanting him, and I showed him how much by grinding my pelvis against his hardness.

"What were you hoping for when you came in here not wearing any panties?" William asked, his breath hot against my skin.

"I was hoping for a continuation of yesterday. Now I'm also hoping we might make a few of our own explosions."

"I like that idea." His hand slid under my dress again, his fingers slow and teasing as they traced a path up my thigh. I reached between us and pushed his tie to the side. I unfastened his belt and undid the button of his trousers. I could feel his erection, hot and hard, beneath the expensive wool. His two fingers entered me slowly, curving up to press against that most sensitive spot inside me. I moaned and pushed, increasing the pressure. I was already at a fever pitch, and we'd just begun.

"You're so ready for me, Catherine," he said. "So plush and slick. I can't wait to sink myself into your tight, hot little pussy."

Oh my God, I loved it when he talked dirty to me. When he said *pussy* like that, my impatience grew to explosive proportions. I slid the zipper of his trousers down and spread the material, revealing his navy blue boxer briefs. I pushed the band down, freeing his hard erection. The thick flesh pulsed in my hand. My gaze met his, and we stared at each other as I slid my hand up and down the length of him. I leaned forward, kissing him urgently. He kissed me back, his fingers teasing me in imitation of his lips. His tongue licked out to taste my lips as his fingers tapped against my clit.

I moaned into his mouth, tormented, and rubbed myself against those extraordinarily skilled fingers. He was driving me wild in exactly the way I loved. I knew I was driving him wild too. I could feel how the muscles in his thighs strained under me. He wanted to toss me back on the couch and thrust into me.

"You're ready for me," I said, moving to nibble on his neck, taking my time on the sensitive lobe of his ear, allowing my mouth to caress his smoothly shaven jawline. "You like it when I don't wear panties."

"I *love* it when you don't wear panties. It makes it so much easier to fuck you."

"Then why don't you? Fuck me."

"With pleasure." His hand slid away, and I rose on my knees slightly to poise above him. He looked up at me, his eyes burning with need as I lowered myself onto his rigid cock. I saw the flicker of pleasure in his eyes, the need, and I reveled in it. No man had ever wanted me so much. I slid over him, sheathing him in all my slick heat. I moved slowly, rocking back and forth, taking him deep and then all but releasing him before I took him to the hilt again.

Our eyes stayed locked, his gaze so intense on me that it seemed like we were the only two people in the world. If I'd listened

I might have heard the soft sound of phones ringing or music playing outside of his office, but all I could hear was William's harsh breathing and the sound of our bodies moving together. I did fit him like a glove. It was like we were fated to come together in this way.

William's hands cupped my face and I bent close, resting my forehead on his as I moved my hips up and down, rocking into his heat until both of us were panting with need. "I love you," I said as the spirals of pleasure coalesced into a hot, pulsing knot that was quickly unraveling. How could I have ever doubted we were meant to be? Whatever our differences, we'd work them out. At this moment, with our bodies and our gazes connected, we were invincible. "I love you," I gasped as pleasure rippled through me in twirling ribbons.

"And I love you, beautiful girl," he said, thrusting deep inside me and coming apart.

FIFTEEN

The next day I stood in the doorway of my condo and gave a small sigh. Asa, Anthony, two movers William had hired, and I had just spent the better part of the morning and early afternoon disassembling and packing up all of my darkroom equipment. The bevy of brawny men had made easy work of taking apart what had been, up until recently, probably the most important room in my condo and maybe even in my life. Everything was now carefully loaded in the small moving truck parked in front of my building and would be on its way to William's penthouse as soon as I gave the go-ahead.

"Miss Kelly?"

I looked up and Asa stood in front of me, wearing a gentle but questioning expression. I forced a smile as I gazed at my hired protector. His usual *Men in Black* suit had been replaced by clothes more suitable for moving day: faded jeans and a tight grey T-shirt with "Gold's Gym" blazoned across the front, which clung to his muscled shoulders and sculpted pecs. Standing this close, I was reminded again of just how big a man he was—nearly six and half feet of hard muscle and tightly-coiled power. *He's licensed to kill, too*, I thought and my stomach roiled in response.

Asa spoke again before I had a chance to say anything. "We're all packed up here and Anthony is pulling the SUV around. Are you ready to go?"

"Thanks, Asa," I replied. "Yeah, I'm ready. Just give me a minute."

There was no reason for me to procrastinate. I had agreed to this step, and I was going to take it. William had found the perfect space in the penthouse for my new darkroom, just as he'd said he would. It was a little-used utility closet that was much bigger than the pantry I'd reconfigured, and it would definitely accommodate all of my stuff. It didn't have any windows to board up, and William had already brought in an electrician to install extra outlets and a contractor to build counters for my baths and cabinets for storage. I was essentially getting a custom-made darkroom-slash-art-studio and I should have been excited to set everything up and try it out. And I was, mostly. But as I looked around at my condo, which now held even less of my life, a wave of melancholy washed over me.

This was a good thing, I reminded myself. I had been jittery when Anthony and Asa walked in with me this morning and glad to have them beside me. After the break-in and the screwdriver-in-the-door incident, my home didn't feel like a sanctuary to me anymore. Even so, I wasn't quite ready to let it go. I sighed again. This push-pull was becoming the rhythm of my life.

Behind me, Asa, who had been standing a little off to the side to give me a moment, cleared his throat. He was right. It was time to go.

"Alright, let's get going," I said. I closed and locked the door, then headed down to the waiting sedan. The moving truck would follow us to William's.

*****

Once we were on the road, Anthony behind the wheel and Asa beside him in the frontseat, I leaned my head back and closed my eyes. I would have laid down in the backseat if I hadn't known that it would invite twenty questions from Asa about how I was feeling.

How *was* I feeling?

Stressed. Confused. Overwhelmed. I was in love, goddamn it, *in love*, which was so very major. I should be feeling like *that*, not like my nerves were shot and like I might puke at every turn. I was so fucking tired of the constant upheavals thanks to the ongoing threats and, clearly, it was all catching up with me. Aside from our trip to Tropos, William and I hadn't had enough time to just *be*. And that's really what I wanted—just to be with him, in love. I was ready to get off the rollercoaster and get back to normal, whatever our normal was now. Maybe then I would stop feeling like I was always at one extreme or another. Just in the past few hours, I'd felt both totally energetic and then completely exhausted, eager to get the packing up of my darkroom started, then unable to get my bearings when we did start. This morning I'd been totally ravenous, but then I'd barely touched my meal, oatmeal with cinnamon seeming not that appetizing after all.

Poor William didn't know what to think. I'd been blissfully happy about the new darkroom when he showed me the space, and then had practically burst into tears at the thought of dismantling my old one.

I decided what I needed—what William and I both needed—was stability. No more drama for a while, if ever. I needed to calm down and get centered and for that, I needed my man, my Leica, and a little inspiration. Maybe I could convince William to go on a road trip somewhere out of the city, so I could take some shots and get back to making art, in my new darkroom? Maybe I should get rid of my condo?

Or maybe we could have Beckett over for an impromptu dinner party? Beckett had practically lived at my condo, but he hadn't been to William's penthouse once. He would be excited to see my new darkroom.

By the time we arrived at William's building and Asa and I were being whisked up to the 56th floor in the private elevator, I felt better and my mind was racing with ideas about how I was going to organize my new space and what to unpack first. When the elevator doors opened, Asa stepped out, then ushered me to follow and wait. It was relatively dark, but I could hear the low notes of a piece of classical music playing somewhere.

Asa returned from his security sweep, Laird trailing behind him. Why hadn't Laird raced to the foyer to greet me? I gave him a pat on the head, and Asa said, "Mr. Lambourne's in the living room. You can let me know when to send the movers up."

"If the movers are here, shouldn't we...?" I'd thought we were going to unpack everything now but something in Asa's eyes made me stop me midsentence. "Okay," I said.

He left, and I walked cautiously toward the sound of the music. It was barely four, a little early for William to be home on a Wednesday. I stepped into the living room and froze.

William reclined on the couch in the darkened room with his feet on the coffee table, his tie loose, and his hair wildly tousled. It looked as though he'd run his hands through it a million times. My gaze tracked back to the table, where a half-empty bottle of bourbon sat near his feet. As I watched, he raised a glass with about two fingers still in it and drank deeply.

"William?" I called softly.

He didn't look at me, didn't even seem to know I was there. Instead, he sat forward, grabbed the bottle, refilled his glass, and downed the contents in one gulp.

My heart started pounding and my throat went dry. So much for a life free of drama and my wished-for stability. I'd never seen William like this. Something was wrong—terribly wrong.

A feeling of dread settled over me, and I moved toward William and sat on a chair near the couch. Something told me not to sit beside him, not to touch him. "Hey there," I tried again.

No response.

I cleared my throat and tried for a third time. "William, what's going on? Are you okay?"

He laughed softly, which wasn't quite the reaction I'd anticipated. It was a dark, angry laugh, and it made the hair on the nape of my neck stand up. Finally, he looked at me, and I took a slow breath. His eyes were bloodshot, their color a dark, steely blue. "Do I *look* okay?"

I recoiled as though hit and I could already feel tears threatening. He'd never used that tone of voice when speaking to me, when speaking to anyone—at least not in my presence. I was *not* going to cry and I had to keep cool. If he was looking for a fight, I wasn't going to give it to him. "Actually, you don't. What happened?"

He didn't answer.

I tried again. "Do you want to talk about it?" My voice faltered. "Please talk to me. You're scaring me."

At my words, William tried to sit straighter, tried to right himself. He moved slowly and deliberately, the way a person would move if they were hammered but didn't want to look it. He must have drunk half the bottle of bourbon, or at least a great deal of it, before I got there. He was really drunk, and I'd never seen him drunk. On his jet to Napa, he'd taken a Xanax and had two glasses of bourbon. That had slowed him down, but he was much more affected now. He cleared his throat and the sudden sound in the silence made me jump.

"Come over here." His words were slurred, but the tone in them was unmistakable. Commanding.

"What?" I asked, not because I hadn't heard him but because I didn't know what to do. Everything about him was so foreign right now.

"I said, come over here, Catherine." He patted the sofa cushion. "Here. Right here. Next to me."

I stared at him for a long minute, uncertain what to do. Finally, I conceded, rose, and sat beside him. I could smell the bourbon on his breath, see the unfocused look in his eyes. But even this drunk, he had a controlled tension about him.

"Where were you?" He was drunk enough that he couldn't disguise the demand with his usual finesse. "Were you at Morrison Hotel?"

Fuck. I took a deep breath. I really hoped this wasn't something about Hutch. "No, I was at my condo with Asa, Anthony, and the movers you hired. Remember? We took my darkroom apart and packed it up today."

He laughed again, a dark gritty laugh that was so unlike him. "You didn't try to give them the slip, did you? You're good at sneaking around when you want to. Aren't you, Catherine?" His look was accusatory, and I all but recoiled. What the fuck was going on? This was not my William. Was he suggesting I was cheating on him? Doing something behind his back?

Drunk or not, William was acting like a complete asshole, and I didn't deserve his accusations. But I managed to keep control of my tongue. I stood, intending to walk away before it got ugly. Keeping my voice level, I said, "I don't know what's going on, but

I'm not going to talk to you when you're like this." I moved away, but he grabbed my wrist and pulled me back down.

"Stay."

His grip hadn't been rough, just unexpected. I yanked my arm away. "Stop it! What the fuck is wrong with you?"

And finally I saw it, the flash of pleading in his eyes, the snatch of vulnerability he'd been trying so hard to hide.

"I'm sorry," he said. "I know I'm being an asshole, and you don't deserve this, any of this." The music swelled to a crescendo around us as I considered his words, his look. Finally, I swallowed and settled back down next to him.

"What's wrong?" I asked again. "Just tell me. Maybe I can help." I had no idea if I could do anything to help, but I had to offer. I had to do something to take that pain out of his eyes.

William took another deep drink from his glass then set it on the table. I hoped it would stay there. "I got a phone call today. From France."

Oh shit. The plane wreckage they'd found in Alaska had been sent to France to be analyzed and he'd been waiting to hear the results for the past five weeks. This couldn't be good.

"It's not their plane," he said flatly.

It all made sense now: the bourbon, the dark mood. He'd been so convinced the wreckage was from his parents' plane and so hopeful he'd finally have closure. But, it wasn't, which meant he was back to square one on…everything.

"The paint's not right," he was saying. "The color is similar, but the pigments don't match the model."

I nodded. He spoke so matter-of-factly. There was no emotion in his voice, though I knew he must be devastated.

"The paint found on the pieces wasn't even used in production for another nine years. Isn't that just my fucking luck? It's not their plane. It's just…not."

"Oh, William." I moved closer, still not touching him, but trying to lend some comfort by my presence. "I'm so, so sorry. I know how much you wanted this. I know how much you want to know what happened."

William lowered his head, his dark hair falling over his forehead so I couldn't see his eyes. "I've spent eighteen years wanting this more than anything else. This time I thought—" His voice broke. "I really thought this was going to be it. I thought I'd finally be able to—" His voice became garbled, too choked with emotion.

I waited for him to regain control. Finally, he raked a hand through his hair again. "I know…I know they're dead. I've known that for years. But I want to *know*." He looked up, his eyes brimming with grief. "I want to know what happened to them. I've always thought if I knew…if I knew the facts, they would end…this."

I could feel the pain radiating from him, and I wanted to take it all away. But there was nothing I could do, nothing. "I'm so sorry. I'm so, so sorry." It seemed like such a lame thing to say, but I didn't have anything else. I felt entirely helpless.

William raised his head and looked at me, his gaze intense. "There's something else."

I held my breath, afraid of what he might say next. What more could there be?

"That bullshit letter, the photos, the threats?"

I nodded, a lump in my throat.

"They're not connected to this. We all thought they were— George, me, hell, even the FBI believed that the investigation of the wreckage triggered everything. But apparently that's not the case. We were wrong."

I was confused. What exactly was he saying? "Wrong about what?" I asked quietly, not really wanting to hear the answer, but I had to know.

"It means that there's some sick fuck out there who wants to hurt you for no other reason than I'm William fucking Lambourne the Third."

He buried his head in his hands again. "You'd think I would have learned my lesson." He looked up at me, regret in his eyes. "But obviously, I haven't. And now I've pulled you into this mess, into my life, and I don't know how to stop it." Anger and something else—fear, maybe—burned in his gaze. "I don't fucking know how to stop it."

His voice grew louder, probably an effect of all the bourbon running through his veins. He was losing control. He swore again then yanked me toward him, crushing his lips to mine. His kiss was hotly possessive, bruising and overwhelming. My body went molten, responding to him immediately. My head, however, protested. I pushed him back, something I'd rarely, if ever, done. "Stop. What are you doing?"

"I won't let anyone take you from me, Catherine." His voice was dark and almost feral. He sounded dangerous, and he scared me. He also aroused a hidden part of me, the part that responded to William no matter what, the part that always did what he wanted, the part that couldn't say no to him.

"I won't," he said again. His voice was rough, as was his grip on my arm. "I don't care what it costs me or if I have to keep you locked in this building for the next year for your own safety. I love you, damn it. I can't lose you. I *won't* lose you."

Sixteen

William's words resonated through me like a low hum that traveled straight to my core. I'd never seen him like this, never seen him so primal and so uninhibited about his feelings. I'd always known he was possessive, but he'd never laid it out like this before.

I won't lose you.

He pulled me into his lap, and I immediately felt his thick erection pushing against me. He was aroused and so was I. A part of me was intoxicated by his swell of possessiveness, bourbon or no bourbon.

There were pieces of William's sexuality still untapped, dark alleys I hadn't yet explored, and I had the feeling we'd just turned into one now. Grief and pain and fear were powerful aphrodisiacs. I understood that better than anyone.

William needed me. And I needed him. I wasn't going to abandon him this time. I was going to be the girlfriend I should have been in Napa. The girlfriend who gave her man what he needed, when he needed it most.

I looked up at him through lowered lashes. "What do you want from me, William?" I kept my voice low and careful. I knew exactly what I was offering him: me. If he wanted me, he could have me—anyway he wanted—as an outlet for his angst, for his pain, for his pleasure.

That night by the pool at Casa di Rosabela came back to me again. I'd been swimming laps, wearing a red bikini. I'd been so angry with William for leaving me alone, but when I'd emerged from the water, the pain in his gaze had washed all that away. I'd fucked him on the deck chair, taking his body and, with it, all of him. At the same time, I'd showed him how I'd felt—my anger and hurt, my love for him—with my body. I would do the same tonight.

I gasped when William gripped my upper arms tightly. His breathing was heavy now and as my eyes widened I saw the color of his—molten grey.

"Go to the master suite and get undressed." His voice was soft but commanding, and I shivered with anticipation. "I want you naked, in the bed, waiting for me. Go. Now." He released me, and his hot gaze never left my face.

I stumbled to my feet, struggling to free myself from the pull of desire between us. This was a desire unlike any I'd ever experienced, one that crackled and sparked with dark temptation.

I would submit to him. There was no question of it. I wasn't certain I could have resisted if I'd wanted. I was too turned on, too trapped in this web of wanting. And when my fear at the raw sensuality on his face rippled, I pushed it down and reminded myself this was what William needed. I loved him. I would be there for him. I would give him what he needed, and maybe it would be just what I needed too. Maybe this was what we'd been building to all these weeks, what William had slowly been pushing me toward: a total and complete surrender.

My knees wobbled, but I managed to walk toward the stairs. I could feel William's impatience, and I yanked my shirt over my head and dropped it on the first step. Still peeling off my clothes piece by piece, I kept walking, and I didn't look back.

*****

I lay on the bed, naked, when William pushed the door open. He didn't say a word, but his gaze was predatory, animalistic as he shrugged out of his shirt. He stood beside the bed and said, "On your knees. Here." He pointed to the floor in front of him. I rose, but not fast enough, because William barked, "Now. On your knees."

My breathing hitched and a delicious warmth began smoldering in my lower belly. I fell to my knees before him and watched as he slid the zipper of his trousers down and kicked them off. His thick hardness was clearly outlined in his black boxer briefs. My mouth went instantly dry, and I licked my lips. William chuckled low. "That's right. Get your mouth ready for me."

He lowered the shorts, revealing his enormous erection. I reached for him, but William stepped away. "Hands behind your back."

I looked up at him, confused.

"Hands behind your back," he repeated softly. "And hold them there. No matter what. Don't make me bind you, Catherine. I don't trust myself tonight."

I pulled my shaking hands behind my back and locked my fingers together.

William nodded. "That's right. That's the image I want. Open for me." He stroked his shaft and moved to position himself in my mouth. I opened for him, watching his eyes darken to almost black as his engorged cook slid slowly past my lips.

"God, you feel so good," he said, rolling his head back as he entered me. He slid out then in again. "Lick me," he demanded. "Get me nice and slick."

I licked him, sucked him, all the while keeping my hands behind me. I let him control my movements, control my mouth, and there was something heady and erotic about that. Finally, he looked down at me, his eyes so hooded I couldn't read them. "Do you think you can take me?" He braced his legs apart and put his hands in my hair. "All of me?"

I nodded, unable to speak with my mouth full of his hot flesh.

"Good." He pushed himself in deeper and deeper until he hit the back of my throat and I gagged, and then he pulled out. His cock was glistening and throbbing. I clutched my fingers tightly as he entered my mouth again, moving faster now, until my eyes started to water. Then his hands were in my hair, holding my head as he fucked my mouth deeper and deeper. My face was wet with the mixture of my tears and my spit, but I didn't try to move away.

"That's it, Catherine." His voice was hoarse and strained as though he was barely holding on to his control. "Let me fuck that sexy mouth of yours."

He seemed to swell as he talked, telling me how good I felt around him, how much he needed me. I didn't know how much more I could take, and then he thrust hard, making me lose my breath and gag.

Suddenly he stopped and withdrew.

I sat back on my heels, my heart racing as I bowed my head and waited for William to tell me what to do next. The tears I'd been holding back trickled from behind my eyes, but I willed myself not to breakdown, not to say "rosé" and bring everything to a screeching halt.

"Catherine, look at me." William's voice was barely a whisper.

I looked up at him and watched as his face, which had been so fierce and so controlled just moments ago, completely crumbled.

"Oh fuck. I'm sorry. I'm so fucking sorry."

My tears started falling in earnest then, and before I could say anything, he was bending down and pulling me off of my knees and into his arms.

"I'm sorry. I'm so sorry," he said over and over again as he pulled me tightly to him, stroking me, nuzzling me, kissing me. "Oh fuck, I love you. I love you. I don't know why the fuck I did that. Please, tell me I didn't hurt you. Are you okay, baby? Please, tell me that I didn't hurt you." His voice was raw and desperate, which just made me cry harder.

"I'm okay," I managed to say.

"Thank Christ," William replied. "Wrap yourself around me, baby."

I put my arms around his neck and wrapped my legs tightly around his waist. He was standing and we stayed like that for a while, me pretzeled around him and both of us trembling.

Finally, I looked up at him through my wet lashes. I was still shaking and my throat felt raw and used, my arms ached, and my knees burned from the hard wood of the floor. And despite it all, I still wanted him. I still wanted more.

I could feel his erection pressed against my sex and I was certain he could feel the heat radiating from my center in response.

"Let me love you, Catherine," he begged hoarsely. "Please, let me love you." He kissed me deeply then, using his soft lips and tongue to soothe away the hurt. He was remarkably gentle for a man who'd just had me so violently. He set me down on the bed and directed me to lay on my stomach.

"Stay down and be still, baby. Let me take care of you."

I nodded, although it was doubtful he could see the gesture. And then there were feathery kisses and tender caresses everywhere, as William made his way down my body. He reached my lower back and covered it with hot kisses, then gave me a few playful nips on my ass. It tickled, and I laughed a little and that seemed to encourage him.

"There's my beautiful girl."

I couldn't see his face, but I could hear the smile in his voice.

He widened my legs, the heat of his body warming the skin of my thighs. His hands stroked my cheeks up and down, up and down, then he gently parted the seam of my ass. His finger traced the cleft, lightly caressing my opening. I couldn't stop myself from tensing.

"Shh," he said. "Relax. Just try to open for me."

I tried to relax, but when he touched me again, I jumped. He didn't press his finger in, but instead moved it in slow, steady circles. I'd never before felt the sensations he was giving me, and I spread my legs further, giving him more access. I must have moaned because he said softly. "Hang on, love."

I felt the scratch of stubble on my bottom then as he kissed each cheek. His finger never stopped rimming me. A thin sheen of perspiration had broken out all over me and my clit was throbbing, though he hadn't yet touched me there. Everything inside me was tightening and pulling in and I was going to come.

And then his finger was gone.

"Oh fuck, William," I hissed. "Please, don't stop."

He parted my ass cheeks and licked down.

At first I was so surprised, that I made no sound, but when he licked up again, I couldn't stop a moan from escaping. I moaned louder when I felt his tongue right on my tight opening. His touch was light and tentative at first, and then it was gone. But he was right there. I could feel him blowing on me, then his tongue was there, moving around in a slow, moist circle, then entering me just enough to give me a taste of pleasure before withdrawing to lick me again.

He went around and around until I was crying out for more, and then his tongue was replaced by a finger gently pressing against me. I opened for him immediately, and his finger slipped inside. When he straightened, his thick erection brushed against my thigh.

"Christ, baby, you are so beautiful right now. I want you so much." His finger moved in and out, filling me and causing me to rock back to keep him inside me.

"Please," I panted. "Please."

I felt another thick finger probing and then it was inside me too. My thighs were wet with my arousal as his thick fingers just kept sliding in and out, in and out. I could feel myself edging closer and closer to completely shattering.

"Fuuuuuuckkk," I called out. My cry was guttural and ragged as the head of his cock slid through my folds to my slick entrance and he pushed into me with tantalizing slowness.

"Breathe, baby. Just breathe and push back against me."

I did what William said and raised my hips a little, pushing back against him until he was fully seated inside me. I wondered for a split second if he could feel his own hot hardness. Both of my channels were full and even while we remained perfectly still, the waves of pleasure coursing through every part of my body were incredible, like nothing I'd ever felt before.

"You are so wet and hot, baby" William murmured. "I'm going to start to move now," he groaned, sliding his cock in and out. "So fucking hot."

He thrust a little harder, first with his cock, then with his fingers in my ass, alternating one with the other. I was pinned under him and there was nothing gentle about the way he was fucking me, yet I knew he loved me, knew the intensity that existed between us at this moment wouldn't have been possible without that love.

I surrendered to it completely.

I couldn't hold back my orgasm for much longer and William growled, "Not yet," and thrust harder and deeper. Every pump moved my whole body, pounding me into the bed as he pounded my body. If he'd touched my clit or my nipples, I would have exploded, but he ignored them both. His whole effort was on my ass, on his fingers' exploration alternating with the driving rhythm of his cock inside me. And then finally, finally, he swelled and his thick fingers pushed deep into my ass "Come, Catherine. Clench those muscles around me until it hurts."

I came. I came so hard I screamed. And I kept coming, waves of pleasure crashing down on me until I didn't know where one began and another ended. His fingers kept working me, bringing me higher and higher even as he emptied himself inside me.

Finally, William gently withdrew his fingers and his cock, then rolled me onto my back. "I so fucking love you. God, I don't know what I'd do without you."

He kissed me and pressed his forehead against mine, closing his eyes, his breathing ragged. Mine was ragged too, and the muscles of my legs were weak and trembling. We lay like that for a long time, my body still tingling, my mind still trying to wrap around what had just happened. T

Finally, I opened my eyes to look at William and saw his eyes were still closed, his chest steadily rising and falling. "William?"

No response. He was heavy on top of me and his breathing was thick. I pushed at his arm and squirmed out from under him. His head hit the pillow and then he turned on his side. He'd either passed out or was deeply asleep.

I stared down at him, and my stomach clenched. Now that we were no longer connected, I didn't feel so good. My tears started again and I put my hands over my eyes. I didn't know why I was crying, but I was wracked by sobs. My emotions were all over the place. I felt so vulnerable, so completely bare in a way I'd never been before. William was right next to me, yet I was trembling and so cold.

William murmured and stirred. His hand found mine, and he pulled me down beside him. His arms came around me, holding me close, wrapping me in the scent of him, the scent of us. His breath was warm on my ear. "I love you, Catherine," he mumbled. My hair rustled as he spoke. "Please don't leave me."

I shook my head. I could never leave him. I snuggled into his warmth, into the safety of his arms, closed my eyes, and fell into a dreamless sleep.

Seventeen

"I keep asking Hutch to let me borrow this baby for the Fourth of July," Angela said, gesturing to the huge stainless steel box in front of us, which was billowing delicious-smelling plumes of smoke out its top. "I'd be the queen of the neighborhood."

"This isn't a grill. One wrong move, and you'd blow the entire block," Hutch quipped.

Angela just smiled. "That's when it's helpful to have a husband who's a firefighter. Your man like to grill, Catherine?"

"I'm sure he does," I said. William loved to cook, but since I'd met him in January and our entire relationship had taken place in the winter months, I hadn't had any opportunities to see him flipping burgers or cooking steaks on an open flame al fresco.

After the emotional turmoil of last night, it felt good to spend time with Hutch and Angela, making jokes and acting like my life was actually normal. I'd been smoking with them most of the afternoon in the cold back alley behind Morrison Hotel. That was, Hutch and Angela were using Hutch's commercial-grade smoker to make Tasso, a spicy, peppery, pork shoulder that was a specialty of Southern Louisiana cuisine. Hutch was featuring Tasso in several of his dishes on the *Sticky Fingers* menu and, as he did with most things, he'd "fancied up" the dry rub he applied to the meat before it went into the smoker. I was thankful for the buffer all my layers provided against the noise of my rumbling belly. Even though he enjoyed feeding me, Hutch always seemed to leave me starving.

I lifted my camera and took a few shots of Hutch adjusting the smoker's settings. It was about the size of a large refrigerator and had to be monitored carefully. Hutch had thrown a Canada Goose parka with a fur-trimmed hood over his usual uniform of jeans and a T-shirt. If it weren't for the smoker, this could easily have been mistaken for a fashion shoot. Hot, tattooed model in designer garb? Hutch definitely looked the part. Edgy, industrial setting? Yes.

I liked taking shots of Hutch and Angela working together. The sous chef was decked in restaurant black-and-white checked pants, a puffy, purple Patagonia parka, and a warm winter hat. The two of them in their winter coats gave the shots a more personal look than those when they were inside and in uniform. This was Hutch and Angie having fun.

"It's too bad I can't capture the smell with the lens," I said, lowering the camera. "I'm pretty sure my mouth has been watering for the past two hours." A heady mixture of burning pecan wood chips and roasting meat permeated the air around us. If the Tasso tasted half as good as it smelled, Morrison Hotel would be sold out for months.

"I know," Angela said. "Hutch has really outdone himself this time. I'm going to try and sneak a bit of this home for Nick. Can't go wrong with smoked pork. He'll be all over me the second I walk in the house. Him and the dog."

Hutch and I laughed. I'd finished my work about thirty minutes earlier, but I'd hung around, taking extra shots here and there because it was fun to be with these two. After offering myself for service to William last night—and the manic results—my head was still reeling and I wasn't sure I was ready to go back to the penthouse just yet. Hutch and I had an easy relationship. Things were simple and uncomplicated with him, and I genuinely liked him. Angela was a riot—I never knew what she'd say next. Plus, I loved taking "in the wild" shots and capturing the cooks' joy as they did what they loved. So much of the past year had been filled with shots of inanimate apples or pears or asparagus. It was nice to capture people and action for a change. Or again.

"I'd better head in and whip the line cooks into shape. There's still lots of prep work that needs to happen before we seat." Angela glanced at Hutch. "Holler if you need me."

He nodded and turned back to the smoker and adjusted the controls. I shoved my hands in my pockets and burrowed into my scarf. The shoot today had been fun, but I couldn't stop thinking about William and last night. He'd been so completely devastated and he'd surprised me by the way he'd wanted to be consoled.

I won't lose you.

My cheeks still heated when I thought about everything he'd done to make me his. I wished we'd talked about it this morning, but when he'd woken me up early to say goodbye, it had been obvious that he hadn't wanted to talk—at all. I couldn't decide if he'd been withdrawn or hung over. Or something else.

"You okay, Miss Catherine?" Hutch asked.

I blinked. "Oh, yeah." I shook my head and tried to give Hutch a confident smile. Instead, I felt myself blush again.

"Yeah? You seem a million miles away."

"Oh. Just…thinking." I shrugged. It wasn't like I could tell Hutch about the crazy sex William and I had had last night or how I was kind of weirded out by it.

"Uh-huh. Well, for the record, Mr. Lambourne should be putting a smile on your face, honey, not a scowl."

"What?" I started. "He does. How did you know I was thinking about him?" I seriously hoped I wasn't that transparent.

"Oh, I can always tell. I've had a lot of practice with that look."

"What look?"

"The *love* look. The questioning look."

"Really," I said, folding my arms and leaning a hip against the table holding platters, various bottles of sauce, and tongs. Now I was intrigued—not to mention eager to turn the conversation away from me. I may have been confused, but Hutch was not the person I was ready to talk to about my relationship. "So, Mr. Morrison, are you the heartbreaker or the heartbreakee?"

He smiled, that easy smile that lit up his eyes. "I've been both."

My brows shot up. "I'm surprised. It's hard to see you as the one who gets hurt."

"How do you see me then?" He'd stopped tending the meat and was looking directly at me. He was flirting, but there was also a hint of a challenge in his voice. I met his eyes.

"I bet you charm your way into a different girl's panties every weekend. I know your type: total player."

Hutch's brows rose. "Player? I'm crushed."

"Are you saying you're not?"

"Well…" He grinned his little boy, mischievous grin. "Maybe in another life I was, Miss Catherine, but I left the band a long time ago. I'm reformed."

"What reformed you?"

He turned back to the smoker. "I suppose I fell in love. Head over heels." He glanced at me, his eyes serious. "I would have done anything for her, but she broke my heart," he said softly. "And there hasn't been anyone since."

I gaped at him for a long moment. I think I was waiting for the punch line. When it didn't come, I said, "Seriously, Hutch?"

"Cross my heart." He made a little X on his chest.

"No one?"

"No one. Is it that hard to believe?"

"Maybe I'll believe no serious relationships, but you *have* to have gone on dates or had hook-ups. I mean, nothing?"

He shook his head.

"Have you sworn off women? Hey, if you have, I know a really great guy I could fix you up with."

Hutch guffawed loudly, the laughter echoing off the building. "I haven't switched teams, don't you worry. I've just directed my energies elsewhere."

But I still didn't get it. "So what are you saying? You haven't been with anyone? No one?"

He spread his hands.

I pointed my finger at him. "I don't believe you, I mean," I gestured toward him, "look at you."

He looked down at himself, his mouth curved in a grin. "You like, Kitty Cat?" Hutch asked in a seductive tone. "I'm glad to hear it."

I knew he was just playing around but God, when he called me Kitty Cat like that he reminded me so much of Jace...of Jace *and me* having sex. I'm sure my face was positively beet red as I smiled and shook my head. "Women must throw themselves at you all the time. I'd throw myself at you, if it wasn't for..." I closed my mouth. What the hell was I saying that for?

"Well, I'm flattered you'd even considered me. A woman like you might be exactly what I need. But really, it's not about opportunities. You're right about that. There's no shortage." He looked away as though he was considering his next words carefully. Finally, he looked back at me, his voice low. "It's a conscious choice. Today is day 817, actually."

My voice wouldn't even work. I couldn't wrap my head around this. "800...you mean days? That you haven't..."

"It's been 817 days since I've been with a woman, and yes, I count."

I didn't know what to say. Hutch, this gorgeous specimen of a man, hadn't had sex in over 800 days? On purpose? I figured I should say something, but my mind was completely blown. *800 days*? That must have been some break-up. I wanted to ask him about it. When Jace had died, I'd been heartbroken, at my lowest point ever, and I'd sought comfort with Jeremy. That hadn't been the best choice, no question, but I hadn't denied my sexual needs. But I had learned from that mistake. There hadn't been anyone else until I'd met William.

I glanced at Hutch again. Maybe it hadn't been a break-up that devastated Hutch. Maybe he'd lost someone too.

"Why?" I asked finally. It seemed the most straightforward question.

"Well, that's a story to tell over cocktails. But let's just say I thought I had it all, and it turned out I couldn't have been more wrong."

While I puzzled over that, he checked the Tasso again. "This is about done. I'll grab some help so we can get this unloaded and ready to cure." He walked inside and left me standing beside the smoker completely dumbfounded.

Had he intentionally left me curious and wanting to know more? What drives a man to become celibate for over two years? What the hell had happened to Hutch?

✶✶✶✶✶

George had been tapped to drive me home from Morrison Hotel. Five minutes with him made me miss Anthony. George and I never talked much, and I always had the impression he didn't like me. I would have been perfectly happy to stare out the window, but the silence inside the car felt too deafening.

I cleared my throat, and in the rearview mirror I saw George's eyes land on mine. "Is William home yet?"

"No. Mr. Lambourne is still at his office. He said to expect him about seven."

I checked my phone. It was almost five now. William typically worked until seven and sometimes later, so that wasn't anything strange. What had been strange was coming home yesterday and finding him drunk. And then we'd had some of the most intense sex of my life, and this morning he'd barely said a word to me. I had no idea how to interpret any of this.

I scrolled through my emails. Nothing from William. No texts or missed calls either. I didn't expect him to check in with me throughout the day, but he usually did. This was weird.

Disappointed, I was about to stash my phone back in my purse when it buzzed. *Mom* and her number displayed across the screen. I sighed—I wasn't sure I was in the best state of mind for a long chat with my mom, but I answered anyway. "Hi, Mom."

"Hi, honey. How are you?"

We went through the usual small talk and questions about work. I told her about Hutch and Morrison Hotel and the cookbook and she seemed genuinely impressed. And then my mom said, "I called your landline a few times, but it just kept going to voicemail. Where have you been? I was starting to get worried."

Oh shit. I hadn't even thought about the phone at my condo. I should have had it disconnected or at least forwarded to avoid pointed questions from people I wasn't ready to tell about William and me living together and why. "Oh, probably seeing a client," I told her, hoping that would be enough for her to drop the subject.

"On a Sunday afternoon?"

"Maybe I was walking Laird."

"You never called me back. I left three messages, honey."

Shit, shit, shit, and more shit. Most of my calls, including work calls, went to my cell. I couldn't remember the last time I checked the voicemail on my home phone—since my parents and a hoard of telemarketers were the only ones who ever called that number.

It was on the tip of my tongue to say I was just really busy, and then I figured, *screw it.* There was no reason to be evasive with my mother, plus I was too tired to lie anymore. She had the right to know what was going on with me and maybe it would do me some good to talk to her about it. I took a deep breath. "I didn't get the messages," I said. "I've actually been staying at my boyfriend's place."

"*Boyfriend*?"

I had to hold the phone away from my ear. *Good thing I hadn't mentioned the billionaire part.*

"The last I heard it was casual, and you were just going out on a date."

"Well, that date turned into another, and..." There was no turning back now. She was going to hammer me with questions until I told her everything anyway. I gave her the highlights of my relationship with William, leaving out the drama. I played it up as a whirlwind romance, which it was, and I didn't mention threats or bodyguards. I wanted to be honest, but I didn't want to worry her.

"Honey, I'm so happy for you! Now, when am I going to meet him?"

I should have seen that coming, but then I realized that I hadn't seen my mom since New Year's. Hell, she didn't even know that I had been in California a few weeks ago. "I don't know. I guess that depends on when you're coming to visit."

Now that she knew about the boyfriend, I half expected her to say *tomorrow*. Instead, she said, "I had been thinking about coming for Easter. Would that work for you?"

"Sure. I'd love for you to come. And you know Beckett is going to die when I tell him you're coming to town. He'll be so excited. Patisserie LeClerc will be open by then, and he'll want to show it off. Get ready for a sugar rush."

My mom laughed and I found myself happily looking forward to her visit.

"I have some news too," she said.

This was the part I'd been waiting for, the part where she told me about *her* new boyfriend. It must be the third in the last six months.

"I'm seeing someone new."

I tried not to roll my eyes while my mom described the new man she'd met and how perfect he was. Finally, we were at William's building, and I said goodbye as George pulled up in front. Asa was waiting, and he stepped forward to open the car door for me and escort me upstairs. I could only hope all the security would be unnecessary by Easter. How was I going to explain bodyguards to my mother?

*****

Since I had almost two hours until William would be home, I decided to organize my new darkroom. Everything had been moved inside and mostly unpacked. I changed into my ratty darkroom gear—stained cargo pants, a ratty sweatshirt, thick socks, an old pair of Converse—and went to finish the job.

I started by unloading my bag from today, putting away my gear and plugging in my back-up batteries. As I did so, my mind drifted back to Hutch.

800 days. 800 days without sex. It didn't seem possible for a man as jaw-droppingly hot as he was. Was there seriously no woman gorgeous enough to break his resolve? No drunken night that ended with a supermodel in his bed? How could he manage it? And more importantly, why? As I ran through the possible scenarios, I organized. I knew where I wanted everything, and the darkroom was spacious enough that I could spread out.

By the time I was done, I was eager to use some of the equipment. Now would be the perfect time to work on the *nyotaimori* prints for William. *William.* He was such a contrast from Hutch. I wondered if William would ever do anything as drastic as deny himself physical pleasure to heal a broken heart—if that was, in fact, what Hutch was doing.

I found one of the rolls of film I was looking for. I had actually used my best digital camera, the one I used for work, on the night of the sushi dinner. But I had decided to try a new technique for this project. Before the break-in, I'd printed the digital images and then photographed them with my vintage Leica. Lots of photographers were wed to digital and didn't like the hassle and expense of real film. But I loved the dynamic range of film, how it retained details in highlights and shadows, how I could manipulate the print process. I liked to *make* prints—just like William liked to make wine.

As I began processing the roll, I thought about that night, which had only been about a month ago. William had insisted I bring my camera and he'd been right. For a food photographer, the *nyotaimori* had been fascinating. The marriage between the nude models' bodies and the placement of the food was so artistic and so, so sensual. I remembered how caught up I'd been in capturing all the angles and colors and designs, studying the curve of a model's breast and the way the sushi seemed to caress and enhance the most beautiful elements of the female form.

William had watched me react that night, knowing that photographing the models would turn me on. How could it not have? It had been one of the most sexually charged, erotic displays I'd ever seen. He'd done his part too, feeding me sushi still slightly warm from a model's body while his eyes devoured me. I remembered the feel of his mouth on my neck, his hand on my back, the anticipation I'd felt as I'd snapped pictures, knowing he would soon strip me naked and feast on my body.

And he had.

Just looking at the pictures and thinking about William brought it all back and put me into a state of low arousal. I wasn't wearing a bra, and my breasts were tingly and achy as my now-hard nipples brushed against my old sweatshirt. I felt a familiar heat between my legs and knew I was swollen and wet and ready. I let out a long, frustrated sigh.

Fuck. Just thinking about him did this to me. There was no way to deny how hot we were for each other. Which made me wonder again how could Hutch do—or *not* do—it? Wasn't there someone out there who elicited this primal reaction from him? I was lost in thought about Hutch, again, when I heard a light knock.

"Catherine?"

I blinked, William's voice snapping me back to the task at hand. "I'm in here. I'm developing film, so don't come in."

"I'll be in my study."

"Okay. I'll come find you in a few minutes." I made sure all the prints were stable on the drying racks, cleaned up the supplies, and washed my hands, then headed back into the light.

I found William in his study with his laptop and a glass of red wine. There was a second glass waiting for me. I took a sip, nodded my approval, and perched on the edge of the desk, facing him. He didn't look up from his laptop or even lean in for a kiss, which was very unlike him.

Last night, William had been more upset—and more dominating—than I'd ever seen him. Which was understandable, as was his needing more time to let everything sink in. Having his hopes of finding answers about his family dashed with just a phone call was fucked up on so many levels, but I was determined to not let him go through it alone this time.

"Hey baby," he said, finally looking up from the laptop. "Love the outfit." He didn't smile at me, but there was a hint of amusement in his voice, which gave me hope that the sweet and thoughtful man I loved hadn't completely left the building. Maybe we were okay after all.

I'd forgotten I was still wearing my darkroom clothes. The old cargo pants and sweatshirt, now with several new stains, weren't exactly sexy, but I was still a little flushed with arousal. I smiled. "I was working. What's your excuse?"

William laughed, then grinned at me. Of course, he looked gorgeous as usual, and even though he'd probably put in twelve hours at the office, his suit was pressed enough that he could have stepped right off a fashion-show runway. It was good to see him laugh, and I relaxed slightly, relieved to fall into our easy banter. I was even more relieved that he seemed back to normal. The pain and grief that had been in his eyes last night wasn't there and I wasn't going to ask him about it now. I knew William well enough to know that we'd talk about it again only when he was ready to, no matter how many questions I might have.

He turned in his chair and pulled my foot toward him. "What were you working on?"

He flipped my shoe off, rolled my sock down and off, and began to massage my foot. I shouldn't have been surprised that William knew exactly where to touch me, even on my foot, and heat shot straight to my core as he kneaded and pressed. Another one of his hidden talents.

"I was developing some prints for Lauren," I said quickly, trying not to squirm as waves of arousal spiraled through me. "You know, the baby thing?" Hopefully, he wouldn't remember I'd taken my digital camera to the baby shower. "How was work?" I asked, changing the subject.

"Oh, the same. I'm working on a deal with a German firm and had a late conference call with them." His fingers continued to massage my foot, taking all the day's stresses and strains away.

"The Germans now, huh? I guess you'll have to move on to another continent, now that you own most of this one and part of Asia."

He grinned at me. "Something like that. Where were you today? Morrison Hotel?"

I nodded and told him about the smoker. I didn't mention Hutch's revelation about his sex life. I knew William didn't want to spend the evening talking about Hutch.

I slid closer to William and moved the foot he'd been rubbing onto his thigh. He glanced at it, and asked me about my plans for tomorrow. I answered, reminding him I had a Fresh Market Shoot as I moved my foot slowly toward his fly. When I was close enough to caress his hardening flesh through the material of his trousers, he couldn't ignore it any longer. In one motion, he pulled me onto his lap and kissed me. I wrapped my arms around his neck, loving the way his hot mouth moved over mine. We explored each other, our mouths meeting and parting. It was delicious just to sit and kiss him like that, my soft curves rocking against his hard angles.

He slowly moved his lips to my throat and placed burning kisses there. "Are you sore from last night?" he murmured against my flesh.

I'd begun to think what happened last night was either a dream or something totally off-limits for discussion. It was nice to hear him a little worried.

"I'm fine," I said, reassuring him. And I was. Now. Last night had been intense but it was a relief to see him in good spirits today.

"Good," he growled, kissing my ear. And then his mouth met mine again, and our conversation once again became lips and tongues and soft moans.

EIGHTEEN

I had to see Beckett. After an abominable shoot for Fresh Market this morning, I needed my best friend. As soon as I'd finished at the studio in River North, I'd called Beckett, then told Anthony and Asa to take me to Patisserie LeClerc. I needed coffee or a sugary treat or just a hug from the other most significant man in my life.

I waited in the SUV with Anthony while Asa did his usual security sweep of the property. Its windows were still papered over, but the bakery would be opening in just about a week. I couldn't believe how quickly all of this had happened for Beckett. Asa emerged from the bakery and waved me inside. Beckett was waiting and gave me a big embrace.

"What's wrong, sweetie?" he asked with obvious concern, eyeing Asa. "You sounded so depressed on the phone."

"I am depressed," I whined. Then I glanced around. "But it can wait for a minute. Look at this place!" The inside of the bakery looked incredible. Everything was bright and white and crisp and chic. It was like a quaint Parisian neighborhood *patisserie* had been transported right to Lincoln Park.

On one side was a huge glass display case built to hold Beckett's creations. Beside it was a professional-looking coffee bar.

Café tables made of what looked like antique wood were clustered around the room with adorable little chairs.

"This is amazing. Do you love it?"

Beckett grinned from ear to ear. "I adore it. But look at you. You look great. I love that you're eating again. You look like…well, *you*."

"Thanks a lot." Leave it to Beckett to notice the extra pounds I'd put on since I last saw him—that awful day almost three weeks ago when I'd been locked in my darkroom and had my phone stolen. I couldn't believe I hadn't seen Beckett in the flesh for nearly three weeks. With the exception of when he was living in Chicago and I was living in Santa Cruz, this had to be some kind of record for us. "What's that supposed to mean, I look like me?"

"It means," Beckett said, leading me deeper into the café, "you look healthy and beautiful and happy. You don't have that underfed, waify look any more. Love suits you."

I instantly forgave him. "Yes, it does. And so does William's cooking. And Hutch's. I've lost all willpower."

"Sweetie, willpower is so fucking overrated."

I laughed. "Yeah, I know. And they're both really great cooks. And now this," I waved my hand around. "Seriously, I'm doomed."

Beckett chortled. "Want the grand tour?" he asked. He hadn't stopped smiling since I walked in and I knew he was excited. I was so happy for him. I reminded myself to thank William, again, for recommending Beckett for the job.

"Absolutely."

Beckett showed me the whole place. I loved the white walls, the dark, hardwood floors, and the accent of the rustic wood tables and chairs. The designer had gone for a quaint kitchen look behind the counter, with glass cabinets stocked with white mugs and plates, a farmhouse sink with vintage fixtures, and a small stainless steel refrigerator. A big chalkboard, which would display the menu and the daily specials, was on the wall behind the register. Beckett also showed me the kitchen, but it wasn't as interesting as the front—lots of mixers and ovens and stainless steel prep tables. But Beckett would spend most of his time there, and I could tell he'd made it comfortable and homey with small touches.

"How about a latte?" he finally asked.

"Yes, please. Are you going to act as barista?"

"I'm a man of many talents, Cat."

We headed back to the seating area, and Beckett stopped in front of an enormous chrome espresso maker. At least I thought it was an espresso maker. It looked more like a spaceship.

"Ta-da," Beckett chimed, showcasing the coffee maker with his hands like he was on a game show. "I am pretty sure that Patisserie LeClerc will soon be making the best coffee drinks in Chicago. I had to get trained on how to use this and my entire staff will have to too."

"Really?" Beckett was going to have a staff? I kind of assumed there would be other employees, but this was the first time it hit me that Beckett was going to be the boss. I took another look at the coffee set-up. The machine did look pretty sophisticated, but it was still just coffee, right?

Beckett pointed to the gleaming chrome ensemble again. "This, Cat, is a nearly $30,000 espresso maker," he said, putting heavy emphasis on the dollar amount. "It's handmade and considered the holy grail of espresso makers. The designer is some guy from Belgium. LeClerc knows him and he uses *only* these machines in all of his restaurants. And it makes fucking incredible coffee." Beckett was smiling wickedly now.

A $30,000 coffee maker? This I had to try. "Who am I to say no to that? Bring it on," I grinned.

"A latte it is," Beckett replied and got to work.

He handled it as though he'd made coffee in the Rolls Royce of espresso makers all his life. I watched as the machine whirred and steamed and the aroma of fresh-brewed coffee filled the air. God, I had missed Beckett, but it was so nice to see him here. He was really proud and seemed like he'd finally found his place, although he looked more tired than I remembered ever seeing him.

When the frothing and foaming was complete, Beckett handed me two plates and placed a beautiful chocolate cream–filled éclair on each. He carried the lattes and I followed him to a small table. While Beckett had been showing me around, Asa had come in and taken a seat by the window. Beckett had given him a bottle of water, and I watched as he sampled a cookie from a small plate in front of him. I wondered if Asa had put on a few pounds since he started accompanying me to Morrison Hotel and now to Patisserie LeClerc—everyone was feeding him non-stop too.

I sat, then took a sip of my latte. "Oh. My. God. This is phenomenal. I don't know what it is, but it's, it's…" I was at a loss for words. About a latte.

Beckett's smile grew even wider. "I told you. Fucking incredible coffee."

"Yes, incredible," I managed to say before taking another long, perfect sip.

Beckett got down to business. "So, tell me about the shoot today."

I paused, considering how to discuss it without mentioning Alec. Beckett said he was okay with their break-up, but I wasn't sure I believed that. "The shoot sucked. I missed you so much. They had me paired with this woman named Anna Feinstein. Do you know her?"

"Name sounds familiar, but I can't place her."

"Perpetual scowl on her face, the personality of a chair, and completely humorless. I mean, she didn't crack a smile the whole time."

"That *must* have sucked."

"Well, she aced the mechanics. Her only crime was that she wasn't you. The whole day was a slog."

"How did the shots turn out?"

I bit into the éclair and when a little blob of the chocolate filling oozed out, flashes of William licking warm chocolate off my thighs and…elsewhere flooded my mind and I shifted in my seat. *Fuck.* I needed to stay focused, so I nodded my head appreciatively at Beckett. "The shots were fine. I got some great ones of the strawberries. Think peak of perfect ripeness, glistening with sweet juices."

"Sexy."

"Except every time I'd get excited, I'd look up and see Anna's sour expression. I'd ask you to come back, but you obviously have a way better gig here."

"You don't need me, but if I had time, you know I'd help you."

I sighed, wishing Beckett *could* help me. Sexing up peaches and strawberries without him wasn't nearly fun as doing it with him. I watched as he sipped his latte. He looked great—Beckett always looked great—but he couldn't camouflage the dark circles under his eyes.

"I know you would, and I can see you don't have time. Are you getting any sleep at all?" The concern in my voice was genuine.

"I'm exhausted, if you want the truth. Happy but exhausted." He took another sip of his latte. "This is the hardest thing I've ever done, Cat. I mean, it's been awesome, but fuck, the schedule is killing me. I can barely keep my eyes open, and I never know what time it is anymore. Promise you'll prop me up if I fall asleep at my own party."

"What party?" I asked.

Beckett gaped at me. "What do you mean, *what party*? The opening party!"

I shook my head in confusion. "When is it?"

"*When is it*? Cat, it's a week from tomorrow, next Saturday. At The Webster. It's for the bakery, the restaurant, and the hotel. It's the launch party for all of it, and it's going to be big. How do you not know this?"

I had no idea. From the way Beckett was reacting to my confusion, I was clearly at the very top of his guest list and I *should* have known about this. "Well, why am I just hearing about it from you now? I've been staying at William's, but my phone still works."

"I figured you already knew," Beckett said slowly. "So you tell me—why don't you know about it when your boyfriend is the one throwing it? Okay, not just him, the whole investment group."

"Seriously?" I asked, wide-eyed as my heart sank a little. William hadn't mentioned it, which didn't make any sense at all. Yes, he'd been a bit preoccupied lately, but Beckett was my best friend.

Beckett's eyes sharpened. "He didn't tell you, did he? What's with that?"

I didn't reply and looked down at the foam that topped my latte.

"Are you guys okay? Don't tell me there's trouble in billionaire land."

My face heated, and I looked up and met Beckett's eyes. "Not trouble exactly, but William has been…distracted." I lifted my hair off my neck, which suddenly felt warm. "He has a lot on his mind."

"Like what? Business stuff?"

I shook my head, and Beckett leaned closer.

"What is it, Cat? Now I'm worried."

I could never keep things from Beckett and really, I needed to tell somebody what was going on, or at least most it. So I took a deep breath and said, "Well, for starters, William just found out that the wreckage in Alaska wasn't from his parents' plane and that crushed him."

I filled Beckett in on the details of the analysis of the plane wreckage, updated him on the threats, including my dinner plate of bloody organs at The Peabody Club, on the extortion situation and the crazy increased security, and topped it all off by sharing that William was going to inherit a few more billions on his birthday in September—billions he didn't want. And I added that his cousin Zoe was a total bitch and seemed to hate me for no reason.

We'd finished our coffee and our éclairs by the time I was done. Beckett shook his head. "Jesus, Cat. It's like *Scandal* and *Revenge* had a baby, and it's William's life—and yours by default. I actually feel really bad for the guy, and for you. You have a secret admirer and not the good kind." He glanced at Asa, who was pretending to ignore us. "Sorry. I'm not trying to be funny."

I let out a deep sigh. "I know. It's over-the-top drama and not what I was expecting at all. I thought it was bad after Jace died, but this is worse, actually."

Beckett stared at me. He'd seen me through that dark time after the car accident that had claimed Jace's life. I had walked away from the scene while Jace—a handsome favorite on the pro surfing circuit with several big endorsement deals and a huge, mostly female, fan following—hadn't. Even though we'd been hit dead-on by a very drunk driver, once it had come out that I had been behind the wheel with an expired license and alcohol in my system—not enough to be impaired but some nonetheless—things had gotten bad. Lots of Jace's fans had thought it should have been me that had died that night, not Jace, and they'd found creative ways to tell me. The cyber-bullying had gotten serious enough that I'd had to hire an internet security company to remove as many online mentions of me as they could. It had been a horrible, horrible time and I knew sometimes Beckett and I both thought it was a miracle that I'd survived it at all.

"So let's talk about something else," I said with forced gaiety. "Who are you bringing to the party?"

Beckett brightened at the mention of the party. "Who am I *not* bringing? I've invited everybody, and you should too. Tell Allison and Dana to come. And Hutch. Oh my God, Cat. I would die if Hutch Morrison graced me with his presence. Please make him come."

"I'll try. But who are you taking?"

He shrugged. "I'll go solo."

"Why? You should bring a date."

"Hello? I just broke up with someone. I don't feel like ever dating again right now. Plus, I'll be awful company. I'll be asleep by nine and muttering about fondant."

"I'm sure you'll be fabulous, Beckett. You always are." I paused and then went for it. "When are you going to tell me what really happened with Alec? I saw him at the shoot this morning, and he's not talking either."

"How did he look?"

"Really cute, as always."

"Did he like the shots?" Beckett asked, and I didn't fail to notice he was switching topics. Okay, so he didn't want to talk about Alec right now. I could understand that. He had a lot going on. He'd talk when he was ready.

"He said he did."

"Then he did. You're a fantastic photographer, Cat."

"Thanks. No more compliments, though. Unless you just can't stop yourself." I grinned.

We chatted a while longer, and then I mentioned my mom was coming at Easter. Beckett perked right up. "Jill! Oh, I can't wait to see her. Please tell me she has a new man."

"Of course she has a new man. This is my mother we're talking about." I checked my watch then stood. "I better go."

"Me too. Maybe we could get together for something soon, but just know that if I'm up past my bedtime I might cry."

"Ok, I'll call you. And I will see you at your party in a week, I guess."

"Right. It's on St. Patrick's Day, and trust me, I'm going to need the luck of the Irish to pull all this off in time."

"St. Patrick's Day? Already?" It seemed like we'd just had Valentine's Day. "I can't believe it's the middle of March." I pulled out my new phone and glanced at the lock screen. *Yep.* It was March. "I can't figure out this new phone, and I don't have the calendar set up yet. I just need to sit down and take some time with it. I totally forgot Laird's birthday last week. He's seven now. I'm the worst mommy ever."

"He's a dog, Catherine. I'm sure he didn't notice. But get your calendar up and running and put in a reminder for the party. You can *not* miss it. And straighten this all out with your man. I like you two together. Plus, you give the rest of us hope." He smiled knowingly.

"I'll figure it out, I promise. And I'll be there." I gave him a kiss on the cheek.

He hugged me tightly. "Stay safe, Cat."

"I will."

*****

I asked Anthony and Asa to take me to the library next. I'd deal with William and Beckett's party later. Right now I needed to figure out the special effects for the cork-popping shot for the WML Champagne campaign. I had a few reference books at my condo, but I didn't know if they covered what I wanted, plus I really didn't feel like going back there, even with security. Rather than spending hours searching online, I decided to do the old-school thing and go to the library.

It was only three-thirty and already traffic was at a standstill. The SUV crawled along, and I pulled out my phone to pass the time. I had an email from my mom confirming Easter, and I replied that we were still on and that Beckett wanted to hear all about…what was the new boyfriend's name? I couldn't remember. I typed, *Beckett wants to hear all about the new man,* and hit send. I also had two texts. One was from my dad. I'd loved knock-knock jokes when I was a kid, and we had a tradition of texting each other the worst ones we could find.

Knock, Knock

Who's there?

Cows go.

Cows go who?

No! Cows go moo.

I laughed and texted back, *Good one.* I shared the joke with Asa because I figured anyone could appreciate a stupid knock-knock joke. His eyes sort of crinkled, which I took to mean he was amused.

I also had a text from William.

Client sent me a gift basket with gourmet jelly beans. Eating them and thinking of you. I'll save you the root beer and banana.

My body tingled as I remembered the night we'd spent at The Peninsula, lounging in each other's arms and eating jelly beans. I loved that he remembered that I liked the exotic flavors. That had been the night I realized I loved William, and the first night he had truly opened up to me. I stared at my phone and exhaled loudly. I hated it when he kept things from me. The "two steps forward, ten steps back" thing with us was getting ridiculous. It wasn't mysterious when he neglected to tell me about a party he was throwing for my best friend—it was intentional, and that hurt. What was the big deal? How could he keep something like this from me and, more importantly, *why* would he? It didn't make any sense.

As tempted as I was to tell Anthony to forget the library and take me to William's office so I could confront him about Beckett's party, I glanced up and saw traffic was at a stop. We weren't going anywhere in a hurry and besides, barging in to his office unannounced and demanding answers probably wasn't the best idea anyway. So I'd wait. I texted him back. *Save me the pink ones, too. XOXO.* When I didn't get an immediate response, I figured William had gone back to doing whatever it was he did all day as a global business tycoon.

The Loop was like a parking lot and as the SUV inched along, I had time to mess around with the calendar app on my phone. I opened the app and studied it for a long moment. Even though William said all my emails, contacts, and calendar entries migrated to the new phone, it hadn't been a perfect sync. I'd had an old Android, and this was my first iPhone. Not all of my contacts or the calendar entries had moved. Case in point, Laird's birthday hadn't shown up. I tapped March and spent a few minutes figuring out how to add Beckett's party to the seventeenth. I even added a reminder but just to practice. This was one event I wouldn't forget since William and I would be going together.

I tapped my fingers on the screen. What else should I add? Oh, my mom's visit on Easter. "When is Easter, Asa?" I asked.

"No idea, Miss Kelly. April?"

"Let me check." I Googled Easter and the year and reported back. "You're right. Third Sunday in April this year." I added my mom's visit and then went back to March and typed Laird's birthday on March 1. My dad's birthday, which was also in March, had transferred over. *Weird.* What else did I need to add?

Oh, my period. I scrolled back to see if the asterisk I used to track my cycle had transferred over. Nothing.

I reminded myself this was a new phone. I closed my eyes and tried to remember when I'd last had my period. I got it on the plane coming back from California. That was the end of January. I scrolled there and saw a little star on January 30 and the following three days. So it *had* transferred.

So January 30 and then I'd had it...I scrolled through February and my hand started to tremble. No asterisk in February. My heart started racing, but I refused to allow myself to panic. Had I skipped it in February? I really couldn't remember. And now it was March. I scrolled through March and did a quick calculation.

Deep breaths, deep breaths.

Could I be almost two weeks late?

I closed my eyes and tried not to hyperventilate, mainly because I didn't want to alarm Anthony and Asa. I cycled through all the logical reasons why I might be off. Stress was the likely cause. I had way more stress than usual and more than enough to mess my body up. I mean, I was living at my boyfriend's penthouse and being guarded around the clock because someone was trying to hurt me. That would mess up any girl's cycle.

Finally we made it to the Harold Washington Library, the main branch of the Chicago Public Library, and I pulled myself together enough to make a good show of meandering through the stacks. I was still shell-shocked, and Asa probably wondered if I even knew what I was looking for. He trailed me discreetly, but he never let me out of his sight.

My head slowly cleared enough that I figured out where to find the section that housed books on lighting techniques and special effects photography. I stopped in the photography section and began to read the book titles. Asa loitered nearby. I supposed something nefarious *could* happen in the Russian history section or maybe in the deserted aisles with the volumes on building codes. I was done taking chances, and I was glad Asa was ready for any eventuality.

I pulled out a book on photography techniques and started paging through it. Nothing. I shelved it and grabbed another. I flipped pages, then replaced it too. I flipped through at least five books before I found a promising chapter heading in one of the technical books. I paged to the chapter and smiled. This was exactly what I was looking for—a detailed description of how one photographer pulled off the very shoot I'd been tasked with achieving. I scanned the account of the photographer's experience with the elusive champagne cork pop and realized I was going to need all sorts of props. I thought about digging in my bag for a pen and paper to jot them down and then decided I could use my neglected library card and just check the book out. I made a mental note to let William know that I'd need, at minimum, a plastic tarp, PVC pipe, and a laser timer.

"Would you like me to carry that for you, Miss Kelly?" Asa asked, nodding toward the book in my hand. It wasn't a particularly big book, but it was a sweet gesture.

"Okay, I guess," I said. I handed the book over and watched him tuck it under his massive, muscled arm. "Thanks," I added.

"No problem. Which way now?"

"The circulation desk? I need to check out."

"Lead the way. I'll follow you."

I headed back through the tall stacks and toward the stairs to the first floor and the check-out desk. On the way, I spotted a bank of computers. Asa was right behind me, and since I wanted a moment of privacy, I said, "I just need to check one thing, Asa. Could you give me a sec?"

He nodded and moved to the opposite side of the room, enough space to give me breathing room. I sat at one of the available computers and logged in using my library card number. I clicked out of the card catalog and onto the internet, then pulled up Google. I glanced over my shoulder. Asa was still standing in the same spot. I took a breath and typed in: *Can I be pregnant with an IUD?*

Bile rose in my throat, and my belly churned. I pressed my lips together, hit Search, and watched the results come up on the screen.

*****

Once I'd checked out my book and was settled again the back of the SUV, I heard myself say, "Asa, can we make a quick stop at Walgreens before we go back to the penthouse?"

"Of course, Miss Kelly."

NINETEEN

At the last minute, I talked myself out of it. The closer we got to Walgreens, the clearer it was that I was majorly overreacting. My life had literally become a crazy mess lately so no wonder Aunt Flo was a little delayed. Being supervised 24/7 by my boyfriend's armed guards was more than a little stress inducing.

What I really needed was to stop panicking, start taking care of myself, and get my life back to normal. So I told Asa to skip the drugstore and take me directly home. Then I pulled out my phone and texted Beckett.

How about hot yoga tomorrow? Know it's a longshot…

It had been weeks since Beckett and I had gone to hot yoga and an hour or so of Saturday morning sweaty centeredness was exactly what I needed. What *we* needed.

He responded immediately. *Can't in the am + too tired. Lunch @ noon instead?*

Ok, I texted. *I'll yoga and meet you after. Spanglish? Need a taco fix.*

Spanglish Mexican Kitchen was a casual little taqueria in the South Loop, and I loved their tacos. I loved tacos, period.

Done. See you manana. XO

I put my phone back in my purse then pulled off my scarf and opened my coat. It was freezing outside, but I was suddenly too warm. I could feel beads of perspiration breaking out on my forehead, so I pressed the button on the door to open the window. It didn't budge. *Shit.* I was sure child locks in the backseat were another of William's security measures.

"Asa, can you turn the heat down back here? I'm roasting."

"Sure thing, Miss Kelly. Sorry about that."

I watched as he leaned forward and adjusted a dial on the center console.

"It should cool down in a minute."

A refreshing blast of air washed over me, and I leaned my head back and closed my eyes. I knew that getting my butt up and out of bed tomorrow morning for yoga was going to suck, especially since William would be in that bed. Even if I was pissed at him about the party, one look from him was all it would take to derail my plans, but I'd have to stand my ground. I needed some me time.

"Are you more comfortable now, Miss Kelly?" Asa's question startled me out of my thoughts.

"Much better. Thanks."

I wondered if I should bring an extra mat for Asa tomorrow. An image of my big, burly protector going through the Bikram posture sequence alongside me popped into my head. *This was getting ridiculous.* I hoped Asa liked tacos, because he would inevitably be joining Beckett and me for lunch too.

*****

George Graham walked out of William's building just as I was walking up. His coat was slung over his arm, and he had car keys in his hand.

"Hi George."

"Hi Miss Kelly." George's granite expression looked even more stony than usual.

"Is everything alright?"

"Just fine, Miss Kelly."

Something about George's extra-steeliness didn't feel right at all, and my heart started racing in response. So much for my moment of calm in the car.

"Is William home?"

"He is, Miss Kelly."

Once upstairs, I strode through the penthouse's oversized rooms, a little panicked and looking for William. I finally found him in his enormous closet in the master suite. He turned as I walked in, as though he'd been expecting me.

"Hey, love," he said, coming over to greet me with a kiss. Circumstances aside, I loved that I got to come home to this man every day.

"Hi." I leaned against the door after William released me. I eyed him suspiciously. He was in workout clothes—a black compression T-shirt with tight black gym shorts. His hair was messy and damp in the back and curling, and his face flushed. "Slow day at the office or something?" I asked.

"Not exactly," he replied.

I continued to look at him. William regularly hit the gym in the early morning—in fact I was pretty sure he'd hit the gym *this* morning. Not that I minded seeing him like this. God, I was so fucking lucky. His body was pure muscled perfection, proportioned and ripped in just the right places. I loved his big shoulders and defined biceps. He was in incredible shape, so how was it that all his fine wining and dining didn't seem to effect his physique at all? I wished I was so lucky.

I watched as he flipped through a row of neatly hung suits that were organized by color. Maybe he was going back to the office.

"Counting your Tom Fords? You have at least a dozen."

"Is that so?"

Whatever strange vibe I had picked up from George was coming from William too. He looked casual and relaxed, but he was acting weird.

"Which one are you going to wear to Beckett's party?" I asked. That might have been a low blow, but it got his attention and I could feel my temper flaring.

His back was to me, and I watched as he hung his head and exhaled loudly. "Shit." He turned around and our gazes met. His eyes were hooded and he looked tired. "I hadn't thought that far ahead."

I folded my arms across my chest. "I saw Beckett today and made an ass of myself. Why didn't you tell me?"

William's jaw tensed. "I've been meaning to tell you, Catherine, but we're still sorting out the security and it is, like everything else, totally fucking complicated."

His eyes were that clear icy blue, but I sighed with frustration. Even going to a party wasn't fun or simple anymore, but I wasn't going to let him off the hook just because he liked to censor things.

"If it's any consolation, I just ripped George a new asshole about twenty minutes ago."

Well, that explained George.

"I'm sure the security is a pain in the ass. But that doesn't explain why you didn't just tell me. Beckett is my *best friend*, and it seems like everyone else has known about this for weeks. I know we've both been busy, but really? I thought we were past this kind of secretive bullshit."

He took two steps toward me until we were only inches apart. I could feel the heat radiating off of him and smell his musky, post-workout scent. He looked down at me.

"We are. And I had every intention of telling you, but I simply forgot. I have a lot on my mind right now."

"You're not the only one with a lot on your mind, William." I answered softly. I lowered my eyes and caught sight of a carry-on bag lying open on a leather bench at the back of the closet. I stared at it. His evasiveness made sense now. "You're leaving?"

"I have to," he answered.

"Where?" My stomach sunk like it was weighted with stones, and I suddenly felt abandoned. All of my anger about the party instantly dissipated. I couldn't believe he was leaving and that he hadn't told me. "Where?" I asked again.

"Japan," he said quietly. "For a week."

I looked up at him. "That's the other side of the world." It seemed like such a silly thing to say. Obviously it was thousands of miles away, but *there was going to be an ocean between us for an entire week*. I suddenly had to blink back tears.

"Come with me." He pulled my hands into his.

"What do you mean come with you? To Japan?" I pulled against his hands, but he held them firm.

"Why not? I hate being apart from you. So come with me."

"When would we leave?" I sputtered. I'd always wanted to go to Japan and I always wanted to be with William, but my head was spinning. This was too much.

"The jet's being prepped now. We should be in the air by," William released my hands and glanced down at the big Rolex on his wrist, "eight o'clock or so."

That was in just over two hours.

"I…can't just pick up and go to Japan. I have deadlines and work, and the champagne shoot to get ready for. Plus I'm meeting Beckett for lunch tomorrow." I looked up at him, his face impassive as I rattled off my reasons for not accepting his invitation. "If you'd asked me a few days ago, I maybe could have rearranged things. But I can't just drop everything and leave tonight. I can't. Why didn't you ask me earlier this week?" I tried not to sound whiny, but my heart was breaking as I asked.

William ran one of his hands through his hair, mussing it wildly. "I didn't know until this afternoon, Catherine. That's why. I was hoping to avoid going at all, but we're closing on a major deal and there was a last-minute change in plans. I need to be there in person."

"You're buying something in Japan?"

"No, they're buying. I'm selling one of my companies to a group in Kyoto. I been working on this deal for months, and I'll be damned if I let it fall through when I'm this close. I've done everything I could to avoid leaving you for this trip, but now it can't be avoided."

A lump that felt like a tennis ball lodged in my throat. I was a grown woman who had lived alone for years. I wouldn't even be alone with all of the security William had assigned to me. But I needed William more than ever now. Everything had been so strained and different between us since he'd found out about the plane wreckage. We needed time to find our footing again.

"I wish you could join me, but I'll be back before you know it. You have a full schedule and so will I. I'll only be a phone call away." He squeezed my shoulder.

I shook my head, not wanting him to worry, or to see the tears that were ready to spill down my cheeks. "I'll be fine."

He notched my chin up with his thumb. "I know you will. But I love you, beautiful girl." His voice was low and serious now.

"And I'll miss you." He pulled me into his arms then leaned down and kissed me softly. His lips were warm and sweet and I sighed into his mouth, which only made him pull me tighter to him. Being wrapped in his strong arms, our hearts literally pressed together, was all I needed to remind me that William was mine and I was his.

"If we keep this up, I'm going be late." William smiled down at me softly. "Come on, I need to get in the shower." With that, he grabbed my hand and pulled me along from the closet into the nearby master bath. I wasn't in need of a shower, so I hopped up on the counter of the giant Carrera marble–topped vanity that ran the length of one wall.

"You're not joining me?" he asked, as he pulled his shirt up over his head and revealed his sculpted chest and washboard abs. He dropped his shorts next and stood in front of me magnificently naked. He wasn't fully erect yet, but he was clearly getting excited to see me.

"I'm not the one who just worked out. Why did you, by the way? I thought you went to the gym this morning."

He walked to me, pushed my legs apart, and moved to stand between them.

"I did work out this morning, while you, my love, were still sleeping." He leaned in and started planting tender kisses along my neck. "But I'll be on the jet for about sixteen hours and I need to sleep for as much of the flight as I can. It helps if I'm actually tired."

My poor, sweet man hated to fly and who could blame him? William had told me as much on our trip to Napa, right before he'd downed some anti-anxiety medication with a big swig of bourbon.

"Kyoto is fifteen hours ahead of Chicago," he said as he switched to the other side of my neck. I tilted my head to give him better access. "Which means I'll arrive there at about three am on Sunday."

All his feather-light, hot kisses and nips were taking effect and a full-body shiver unleashed in me just as his lips reached that sensitive spot under my ear.

"My first meeting isn't until Monday, so I'll have most of Sunday to get acclimated."

"William," I mewled softly. I didn't need a shower, but if my boyfriend was going to be gone for a week, fighting a fifteen-hour time-zone adjustment, not to mention all the stress related to closing a big business deal, he deserved a proper send off.

I hopped off the vanity and pulled my shirt over my head. My breasts felt heavy, straining to be released from my lacy bra. William was in front of me before I finished with my shirt.

"Let me help you," he said, reaching behind me for my bra clasp. He flicked it open and pulled the bra down my arms and tossed it on the floor. He made quick work of my jeans and panties until I was naked before him.

"I want to look at you, Catherine."

I stood perfectly still as his hot grey eyes raked over me and paused on my breasts. "Fuck, your tits are amazing," he said wistfully before palming my left breast and starting to massage it gently.

I hissed in a breath as my breast seemed to swell in his hand, my nipple instantly pulling into a tight, hard peak. Then his mouth was on my other breast, skillfully drawing my nipple between his lips and coaxing gently.

"Oh God," I moaned breathlessly. Every pull with his lips shot straight to my core.

He lifted me, seating me back on the vanity, then returned to my breast. I ran my hands through his thick, dark curls as he pleasured one side, then the other, then switched back again. We stayed like that for a while, William adoring me with his mouth as tendrils of pleasure rocked through me with every gentle suckle of my nipples. So much for *me* giving *him* a proper send off.

Finally, he raised his head from my breast, my red swollen point popping from his mouth. "I really am going to be late if I don't get in the shower. Come on, love." He stood and swiftly pulled me off the counter. I wrapped my arms around his neck and my legs around his waist, and he walked us like that into the large shower.

Like just about everything in the penthouse, the shower was massive and opulent. Over the past few weeks, I'd come to deeply appreciate the seven jets that were placed so powerful streams of water could simultaneously hit just the right spots. But today William didn't turn on the jets. Instead he turned on the two huge rectangular showerheads in the ceiling. The effect was like being in a gentle summer rainstorm, waves of warm mist and steam curling around us.

With the water sleeking our skin and our hair, William maneuvered over to the built-in bench and sat down, keeping me nestled securely on his lap. My legs splayed to either side of his, and I could feel his hard cock pressing firmly against my belly. He didn't hesitate and began kissing me hard until we were both breathless.

Words weren't needed now. I lifted up and carefully slid him into me, his thick hardness filling me completely. I started to move slowly, rocking and lifting, then sliding down the length of him over and over again. I cupped his face, the stubble of his beard soft and wet under my fingers, and pressed my lips to his. Our mouths stayed connected as our bodies moved together, me taking him into my very center while completely surrendering to him, to us. There was no punishing pace this time, no denial, no urgency, just the innate rhythm of us, of our love, of becoming one.

I could feel myself quickening and tightening around him, flutters and tremors that urged him deeper.

"Let go for me, baby," he whispered.

So I did, my climax unfurling like a wave, rising higher and higher to a glorious peak before crashing down.

"William," I cried, my calls echoing in the shower as my walls gripped him tighter.

He groaned, pulled me impossibly closer to him, and spilled himself completely into me. We stayed connected like that, my head resting on his shoulder, until our breathing slowed.

"Catherine, look at me," he said quietly. My eyes met his again. I smiled, and felt him twitch inside me. "I'm yours," he whispered.

TWENTY

Rather than haul all the way to Lincoln Park, I'd found a hot yoga studio right around the corner from William's penthouse. Gold Coast Yoga was the poshest yoga studio I'd ever been in, and my hot pink Lululemon boogie shorts and crop top—which I'd bought only about six months ago—made me feel hopelessly last season amongst the better-dressed regulars. I really didn't care that much about what I was wearing, given that I was there to sweat my ass off and find my Zen, but girls will be girls.

Asa, smart man that he was, had opted out of joining me for Bikram, but he had come in to case the place and had drawn the usual hungry stares from the ladies waiting for the ten am class to start. No doubt everybody here thought he was my overprotective boyfriend or something, which made me laugh. He wasn't wearing his usual black suit—it *was* Saturday—but Asa's concept of casual still had a recognizable military precision. So while I was stretching and posing and sweating in the 105-degree studio, Asa sat in a metal folding chair just outside the door, probably warding off probing questions from the bubbly receptionist.

William had called from San Francisco just before one o'clock in the morning. They'd stopped to refuel and he'd wanted to check in before the next leg of his journey. He'd sounded sleepy and nervous.

"I'll be home by next Friday. Let Asa and Anthony do their jobs, Catherine. No going off alone."

I promised I wouldn't. I'd learned my lesson on that front. But I worried about his safety too. He had been the target of threats, too, not to mention the extortion attempts. "George is with you, right?" I'd asked.

"I thought it was best. You seem to get on with Asa and Anthony better."

We'd said our goodbyes, then I'd instantly grabbed one his pillows from the bed and wrapped my arms around it, hugging it closely and inhaling the lingering hints of the fragrance that was uniquely William. I'd shed a few tears then fallen back to sleep.

I leaned into Half Moon Pose, still thinking about William. He really did hate to fly—I knew that—and I couldn't imagine the mental resolve it required from him to get on that plane and fly nearly 7,000 miles to the other side of the world essentially by himself. I felt guilty for a second and regretted not going with him. *God, I missed him.*

Our rain-shower lovemaking had been as close to perfect as any sex we'd ever had. As mad as I'd been at him for not telling me about Beckett's party, all of my anger had instantly dissipated at his touch. It wasn't like I'd lost my head because he took his shirt off— which had happened before, I'd admit. Last night, we had really connected, deeply and emotionally. It wasn't always like that with us, but when it was, it was spectacular. I loved him so much that just the thought of us ever not being together was painful. And I was certain he felt exactly the same way about me.

We'll make this work, William, I thought, as I moved into Triangle Pose. *Somehow*.

*****

I was determined to fill my next few William-free days with the "me time" I craved, which was ironic given that I already missed William like crazy and wished he were home. Before meeting Beckett, I showered and changed then called my friends Allison McIntyre and Dana Sullivan. I'd met them in a grief support group when I'd first moved to Chicago. All three of us were widows, and we'd lost our husbands about the same time. Dana, who was a bit older, still attended the group, but Allison and I had moved on. The three of us liked to catch up every month or so over dinner and I hadn't seen either of them for a few weeks.

As luck would have it, Allison's kids were staying at their grandparents' house tonight, and Dana was free. So I invited them over for cocktails and said I'd send a car to pick each of them up—and that I would make all the arrangements for dinner. Both of them readily agreed, and I refused to answer any questions about what the special occasion was. There wasn't one, really, other than if my billionaire boyfriend was out of town, I was going to live it up a little and enjoy the perks of our relationship with my friends. Which meant using his driver, entertaining at his penthouse, and picking up the tab for dinner.

My next call was to Hutch.

"Hello, sweetheart," he drawled. "This is an unexpected surprise."

"I have a favor to ask you."

"Anything you want, darlin'."

"I want a table for three—no, four." I'd ask Beckett to join us. "For tonight."

Hutch hissed quietly, and I winced.

"I know. I know. It's a big favor, especially for a Saturday."

"No, no. I can do it. What's the point of having a restaurant if your friends can't come?"

I heard a tapping sound and figured he was checking availability.

"Are you going to starve if I can't get you in until the second seating?"

"Of course not. I'll take anything you have."

"Only the best for you, sugar."

I could almost see him winking.

"There. Done. I'll see you tonight."

"Really?"

"Really. And tell Mr. Lambourne the meal is on me."

"You don't have to do that, Hutch. Besides, William isn't coming."

"Even better. See you tonight, Miss Catherine."

*****

Beckett and I decided to meet up at Central Camera Company, since it was on South Wabash and close to Spanglish. Asa waited in the car.

Central Camera was the oldest camera store in Chicago and one of the only places where I could still find actual film for my Leica, plus whatever high-tech photography supplies I might need for work. And what I needed right now were props for the champagne shoot, starting with a laser timer. In fact, I had a whole list for the shoot, which was scheduled for the week after Beckett's party. I felt like I didn't know what I was doing, so having Beckett with me to ask questions and choose the best brands helped.

Once I'd finished loading my cart, then checking out, I handed off all of my purchases to Asa, who put them in the back of the SUV. It was only four blocks or so to the restaurant, so Asa agreed that we could walk. He would trail behind us in the car, ready to leap from the frontseat and tackle any interloper that might get too close to me.

"Thanks for doing this with me, Beckett. Lunch is on me, 'kay?

"Yes, *'kay*," Beckett said. "When you said you needed the best of everything for this shoot, I didn't realize that meant spare no expense. How much money did you just drop in there?"

We were walking underneath the El tracks on Wabash, enjoying the milder weather, which hinted that spring might actually come. I wasn't getting my hopes up, especially since there was still snow on the ground.

"Seriously, Cat," Beckett said as we waited for the light to change at Congress. "What did that cost? Five thou? Six?"

"I didn't look," I admitted. "I just signed the receipt. I'm charging it to the client."

"Who just so happens to be your rich boyfriend."

"So he shouldn't argue about the expense. I want this shoot to be perfect. I'm so nervous about it. I really don't want to mess it up."

"You won't," Beckett said with his characteristic confidence. "You're perfect for the job. You know you are."

"Except I've never done a shot like this before."

Beckett waved his hand. "Minor point. I've never been the chef at a patisserie before either, and I'm opening one next week."

"I know! So exciting. I can't wait for the party. I'm going to invite Hutch Morrison."

"Be still my heart." Beckett put a hand to his chest. "If he comes, I'll faint."

"No, you won't. But seriously, thanks for taking time away to shop with me. I know you're super busy right now."

"I am. You probably owe me dinner for this too."

"Exactly. Which is why I want you to come to William's penthouse tonight for cocktails and then to dinner with us at Morrison Hotel."

"Who's *us*? I don't want to be a third wheel with you and Mr. Stormy Eyes."

That made me laugh. I was glad Beckett remembered my secret nickname for William. "He's in Japan. I invited Dana and Allison."

Beckett groaned. "The widows? Cat…"

"What? I'm a widow too. Come on, Beckett. It'll be fun."

"It'll be three women talking about their dead husbands. I hate to miss at dinner at Morrison Hotel, but widow talk isn't enticing enough to make me miss my bedtime."

"I can't believe you just said that." I punched him lightly in the arm. "Okay, don't come. But you're missing out on a chance to meet Hutch Morrison."

"As much as that pains me—and it's a lot—it doesn't pain me as much as listening to widow-talk. No thanks, Cat."

"Fine," I rolled my eyes. "Don't say I never invited you."

I wanted to be annoyed with Beckett, but he had a point. Allison, Dana, and I did talk a lot about our dead husbands. Even though we'd all become good friends, we had widowhood in common. But I didn't want to talk about Jace tonight. The last time I'd had dinner with Allison and Dana, I had just started seeing William. I'd felt weird about dating a new guy and a little unfaithful to Jace. I hadn't told them much about William then, just the bare essentials. But I wanted to tell them everything tonight—and show them too.

We'd been walking while talking and had made it to the taqueria. The aroma of fresh corn tortillas and the smoke from the wood-fired grill wafted through the door as someone walked out with a takeout order. My stomach rumbled. I couldn't wait for tacos.

Just as we were about to head inside, my cell buzzed. I pulled my phone out of my coat pocket and glanced at the number. "Speak of the devil. That's Hutch. Give me a second."

"Remind him about the party!" Beckett hissed before I slid my finger to answer.

"Hello again, Mr. Morrison. I was just talking about you," I said with a laugh.

"You don't know how happy that makes me, Miss Catherine. And by sheer coincidence, I was just talking about you."

"Do you need me to come by? I'm in your neighborhood, actually, so I'm close."

"No. I need you to go to Paris with me."

"Excuse me?"

Beckett leaned forward. "What did he say?"

I shook my head. There was no way I'd heard Hutch correctly.

Hutch chuckled. "I need you to go to Paris with me, darlin'. For Fashion Week, in about two weeks."

"Fashion Week? What does that have to do with me?"

Beckett's eyes were wide now. "Fashion Week?" he mouthed.

"I happen to be friends with Fiona Joy. You heard of her?"

Holy fuck. Fiona Joy was only the daughter of Brian Joy, one of the most famous rock stars on the entire planet, right up there with members of the Beatles and the Rolling Stones. I think he was Sir Brian Joy now, thanks to his being knighted by the Queen. Of England. His daughter Fiona was decidedly American and had been tabloid fodder since about grade school. Tall, leggy, and with a famous mane of wild red hair, she was now a very serious fashion designer. Of course I knew who she was.

"Cat? Are you there? Did you lose your cell signal or something?"

"Yeah, I'm here. Sorry," I replied.

"So do you know who she is? Fiona, I mean?" Hutch asked again.

"Yes, Hutch, I know who Fiona Joy is."

Beckett's mouth gaped open at that. I smiled and signaled that I was trying to listen.

"I've known Fiona for a couple of years. She's a fan of my work and she heard about my cookbook project. Well, one thing led to another, and she wants me to put on her aftershow dinner. And she suggested that I include images of it in my book. The famous chef on location, that kind of thing. If she likes the images, she may want to license some of them to use in her next advertising campaign. I sent her some of the pictures you've taken for the book so far. She saw how good you are, Catherine. She was impressed."

Shit. I was trembling a little now. This was too much.

"No way. Hutch, I can't do this. Food is not the same thing as fashion or runways, or models. I photograph food and yours is the first cookbook I've ever worked on. I'm flattered, but this is so out of my league."

"You can too do it," Beckett whispered, shaking my arm. "Tell him yes."

"Well, I'll disagree with you on that," Hutch drawled. "And I might have hesitated to call you, if you didn't have all that experience shooting surfers. If you can catch an athlete in motion, you can catch a few amazing shots of me and my dishes while some skinny-ass models pout in the background. My food is always the star, honey. I wouldn't have it any other way. And you are a sensational food photographer."

"I-I don't know what to say."

"You're also *my* photographer. So say yes, darlin'."

"I have to think about it."

"You do that. And think about this: a trip to Paris, with me, hobnobbing with the rich and famous. A fucking kick-ass opportunity for you. Doesn't get any better than that."

"I'll think about it," I promised.

"Think *yes*. *Au revoir*, darlin'."

I slipped my phone into my pocket and looked at Beckett. "I need a taco or I might pass out."

"Fine, let's grab a table and order. But you have to tell me everything, Cat." Beckett held open the door and ushered me inside.

Once we were seated and both of us had heaping plates of tacos and rice and beans in front of us, I repeated the conversation with Hutch to Beckett. "He wants me to go to Paris for Fashion Week, so I can the shoot the dinner he's putting on for Fiona Joy, after her show, for his book. And she might want to license some of the images for her next advertising campaign. I don't even know what to say."

"Paris in spring. Your answer is yes."

"My answer is I don't know anything about shooting models and fashion shows."

"I heard him, Cat. It isn't going to be about the models running around. It's going to be all about Hutch running around and making his incredible food. In Paris. For Fiona fucking Joy and her fabulous, famous friends. How hard will it be to photograph that?"

I let my forehead thud on the table. "Even if I was up for that, how can I take off for Paris with all the shit that's going on with William? He wants me to stay close to home. To his home."

"So take security." He nodded to Asa who loitered by the door. "Are you going to live your whole life holed up in William's penthouse?"

It was a good question. The answer was no, but I wasn't sure Paris and Fashion Week was the right way to make my move. Not to mention that my taking a trip to Paris with Hutch was not going to go over well with William, even it was for work.

Fuck. What was I going to do?

Twenty-One

I hadn't gotten any closer to a decision about what to do by that evening, so I put Paris out of my mind and focused on what to wear to Morrison Hotel. I wanted to look good for our girls' night out at Chicago's best restaurant, so I wore a pair of really dark jeans with wide flared legs that flattered my butt and made my legs look a mile long. My favorite Manolo black stilettos helped too. On top I had on a tissue silk, black tank with sequin edging and a cute black tweed, fitted jacket with sparkly buttons that looked like vintage Chanel but wasn't.

My outfit reminded me a little of the ensemble Beckett had put together for me for the Willowgrass opening party so many weeks ago. That had been the night William and I had first kissed. I smiled, remembering William pinning me in the walk-in freezer and kissing me senseless. Maybe my outfit that night had helped get his attention. Beckett would be so proud of my styling this evening, as I'd even accessorized with a tangle of long, chunky necklaces and beads and a funky cuff bracelet. With my hair pulled back into a sleek ponytail and just a bit of dark eyeliner, mascara, and lip-gloss, I thought I looked trendy and pretty sophisticated.

I heard Allison and Dana before I saw them. I was in the kitchen of the penthouse, opening a bottle of champagne, readying the *hors d'oeuvre*, and trying hard not to make a mess on the pristine white stone counters. I might have lacked William's culinary skills, but I did know how to use a phone. I'd called Rajesh, the building's concierge, earlier and now I had a beautiful *antipasti* platter with assorted olives, meats, cheeses, and fresh-baked crostini from a nearby high-end Italian gourmet shop. It looked delicious.

"Holy fuck. Did she win the lottery or something? This place is unreal." Allison's voice carried into the kitchen from the entry hall by the elevator. I couldn't make out Dana's response, but I heard them both giggling, then Laird barking with excitement. Squaring my shoulders, I headed out toward the foyer to greet them.

And to blow their minds.

Thirty minutes later, I was gesturing to the tall glass windows that led to William's elegantly furnished outdoor space. "And this is the terrace," I said. "It's heated, but it's probably too cold to be out there tonight. But if you want to check out the view, we can." There were six inches of snow on the ground outside, yet the terrace was remarkably snow free. I wondered for a second how exactly it got cleared. Sky-high billionaire snow removal seemed right up William's alley.

I had just finished giving Dana and Allison my quick tour of William's penthouse, which hadn't been quick at all. It took a while to show them all 12,000 square feet of the residence, which spanned the entire 56th and 57th floors of this impressive skyscraper.

Dana and Allison had barely spoken the entire time, just nodding and smiling every time I opened the door to another room or pointed out some fancy feature. Who could blame them? From the floor–to-ceiling windows with the iconic Chicago skyline glittering just outside, to William's museum-worthy art collection and his minimalist modern furnishings, it was a breathtaking and spectacular space. It was also so very not like me, and I was surprised how comfortable I felt here now. The first time I'd stepped foot in William's home, my reaction had been pretty much the same and Allison's and Dana's: total awe.

Once the grand tour was done and we had settled in the living room, I fetched the *hors d'oeuvre* and freshened our glasses of champagne, then settled in for some girl time. The *antipasti* platter was on the coffee table along with a beautiful arrangement of fragrant pink roses. Rajesh had taken care of the flowers too. I'd turned on the fireplace and a few lamps around the room. I'd figured out the penthouse's central sound system and strains of Coldplay's latest were playing from some hidden speakers. I'd even rearranged the books on the console table and grabbed a grey cashmere throw from William's study to drape artfully on the back of one of the chairs. The overall effect was of a warm and comfortable salon, a perfect place for sharing drinks and conversation with my friends. Laird was curled up in front of the fireplace, no doubt enjoying the warmth.

"Let me get this straight. You're dating William Lambourne? The guy in the magazines? The billionaire? That's *your* William?" Dana's questions were coming fast and furious now that the initial shock of my new digs had lessened.

"The one and the same," I replied. "But he only likes me to call him a billionaire when we're in bed." I put on my best serious face, but I doubted I was fooling anybody.

Dana's mouth hung open as she stared at me, but Allison let out a huge guffaw.

"You're hilarious, Cat. I bet you guys do it on huge piles of hundred dollar bills too," Allison chuckled.

"That doesn't sound very comfortable," Dana said, which only made us all erupt into a huge fit of laughter.

We hadn't even finished the first bottle of champagne— WML, of course—but already we were giggly and giddy. I couldn't stop smiling and I was so happy I'd decided to invite them over.

"Seriously, Cat. Why didn't you say something about him and about all of this? You love him, right?" Allison always understood me, and it felt so good to finally let her and Dana in on my life. It reminded me, too, that there was happiness underneath all the drama.

"I do love him. And he loves me. It's all pretty new, but so far, so good. Though it has been a little…overwhelming." I could feel the blush rising in my cheeks.

Yes, I did love William. Truly. Madly. Deeply. Somehow, telling my girlfriends made it sink in in a new way and I felt like shouting it from the rooftops. *Catherine Kelly loves William Lambourne.* I glanced down at my Patek Philippe and tried to do the quick math to figure out what time it was in Japan. I hadn't heard from William all day and I couldn't remember how many hours ahead or behind or whatever Kyoto was. The champagne wasn't helping. I missed him terribly and wished he was here so I could finally introduce him to my friends.

"It must be going pretty well if you're already living together," Dana observed.

"Technically I'm just staying here for a little while. We're not *officially* living together."

"What are you *officially* doing then? From the look of the closet in that amazing master suite, you're living here."

Dana wasn't going to let this go, but before I could answer, Allison shot her a look and chimed in reassuringly. "It's okay, Cat. There's no rulebook for falling in love or for moving in together. If it feels right, it feels right. We're just so happy you're happy."

I took a deep breath and exhaled, then gulped down a big swig of champagne. I *was* happy, but I needed to tell them the truth. Holding it all in was one of the reasons I'd been feeling so out of control lately. I'd told Beckett everything and that had felt good. Allison and Dana were my other closest friends in Chicago and now I wanted their support too.

"I'm staying here for security reasons," I blurted out.

Allison and Dana both looked at me, totally dumbstruck, like I had just dropped a bomb. I had, I guessed.

So then I explained everything and they did exactly what good friends were supposed to do and exactly what I needed: they listened. They didn't judge or ask too many questions or demand explanations. Fueled by a refill of champagne and by missing my man, I became more emotional as my story of how I came to be the princess in William's castle went on, and more protective of William too. He had asked me early on to trust him and I realized, as I described our whirlwind relationship and then the threats, how much I did trust him now—implicitly. I liked him taking care of me and though I knew we still struggled over his controlling ways, I'd never doubted his intentions. Ever.

Just as I was finishing recounting the dinner incident at The Peabody Club, Asa appeared in the living room. "Excuse me, Miss Kelly? The car has been pulled around. We should get going if you're going to make your reservation." Asa, in his black suit, looked tall and more formidable than ever against the backdrop of the stark white walls.

"Okay, we'll just finish up here. We'll be ready in a sec," I replied.

"Very good. I'll meet you ladies in the foyer with your coats." He gave us a dazzling smile then turned and walked away.

"What was that?" Allison asked. I noticed her face was flushed and she was alternating between taking little swigs of champagne and glancing at the doorway where Asa had just stood.

"You mean who," I replied. "That's Asa Singer. He's my bodyguard and he goes pretty much everywhere with me these days." That included going to Morrison Hotel with us tonight. Anthony had picked up Dana, then Allison, in the SUV and brought them to the penthouse. He'd be behind the wheel again to take us to the restaurant, but Asa would be standing guard inside Morrison Hotel throughout our meal.

"I wouldn't mind having a man like that follow me everywhere. God, those shoulders," Allison said longingly. Then she turned to me, a concerned expression on her face. "It's that bad, Cat? You really need personal protection?" She looked genuinely worried for my safety.

I didn't want to admit that, yes, it was that bad or that I was incredibly grateful for all of William's security measures. I didn't want to think about why the security was needed in the first place. I tapped down the panicky feeling that started to rise in my throat. I was not going to lose my shit tonight, so I plastered on a big smile and grabbed Allison's hand. "Let me tell you some more about Asa," I said teasingly. "He might be just your type. For starters, he's single."

"Where are we going anyway? You never told us!" Dana broke in before I had a chance to start filling Allison in on all of Asa's attributes.

"Morrison Hotel. It's in the South Loop and you're going to love it, I promise."

*****

While we were in the car, William called. Allison and Dana watched as I slid my finger across the screen of my phone and held it to my ear.

"Hey, baby," I said. "What time is it there?"

"Eleven in the morning. Tomorrow. What are you up to?" William sounded tired and jetlagged. I wondered how many Xanax he'd had to take to make it through the long flight. Hopefully he'd been able to sleep.

"I'm in the back of your SUV with Allison and Dana and we're going to dinner. And don't worry. Anthony and Asa are with us." I deliberately didn't mentioned Morrison Hotel. The last thing I needed was William getting jealous and paranoid on the other side of the world.

"I'm glad you're getting some time with your girlfriends."

"Me too. I still miss you, though."

"I miss you too. I'll see you soon, beautiful girl. Be good tonight, okay?"

"I will. I love you," I said quietly.

"I love you too, Catherine. I'll call you tomorrow between meetings."

"Okay. Bye."

Just hearing his voice made me feel warm and tingly inside. He'd barely been gone a day and I missed him so much already. He was such a huge part of my life now and it scared me to realize how large the hole was that he left when we weren't together. And then I couldn't help but be reminded of Jace.

*****

Leave it to Hutch to elevate cocktails to the same level as his incredible food. I'd eaten at Morrison Hotel plenty of times—in fact, it seemed like I was always eating at Morrison Hotel these days, which was part of the reason I was ready to graduate up a D cup. But this was the first time I'd actually *dined* at Hutch's signature restaurant and it was a totally new experience. It really was cooking as theater, just like Hutch had explained at our first meeting. I looked around at the tables filled with diners. Everyone was excitedly waiting for the show to begin.

Once we were seated, Shane, Hutch's blond and very tall head bartender (who I'd dubbed Eric Northman's twin), personally presented us with the cocktail menu and then went into his spiel about freshly sourced organic ingredients and Hutch's philosophy of "mixology" that played out in his state-of-the-art kitchen night after night.

Dana, Allison, and I were more than impressed and I was reminded again of how lucky I was to land the gig photographing Hutch's cookbook. Morrison Hotel was a world-renowned temple of culinary exceptionalness, where every cocktail flavor and every garnish was hand-selected by Hutch as a part of his overall vision. His attention to detail was staggering and I loved that he equally valued tradition and innovation. And rock-and-roll.

Allison immediately ordered a Faithfull, which was made with tea, fresh ginger, and bourbon. Dana decided to try the Silk Upholstered Chair, a vodka drink with muddled cucumber, orange, and ginger. Despite the crazy names and the over-the-top presentations, the cocktails were delicious.

"So, what should we celebrate?" I asked Allison when she had sipped her cocktail then raised the glass for a toast.

"To a night without children."

We clinked glasses and all started talking at once. With a laugh, Dana said, "Allison, you go first. Tell us how you've been."

We'd finished the first course, a jambalaya featuring the Tasso I had watched Hutch and Angie smoke in the alley, and Dana was telling us about a roof leak she'd had to deal with when I spotted Hutch making his way toward us. He stopped at every table to greet his customers, but his gaze was on me.

"Who is that?" Allison whispered.

"Hutch Morrison. The *Morrison* of Morrison Hotel."

"You didn't tell us he was hot."

I grinned and shushed her just as Hutch reached us.

"Miss Catherine."

I rose and gave him a hug. Hutch hugged me back and sat down next to me in the booth, slinging his arm across the back of the banquette. "And who are these beautiful ladies? I think you've been holding out on me, darlin'. You didn't tell me you had such gorgeous friends."

"This is Allison, and Dana." I pointed to each in turn.

"Welcome to Morrison Hotel. How'd you like everything so far?"

"Delicious," Dana said, giggling. I gaped at her. Matronly, serious Dana was *giggling*?

"Good." Hutch turned his sparkling, thick-lashed, blue eyes on me. "Did Catherine tell you she's working on a book for me?"

Allison nodded. "Yes. It sounds like it's a fabulous project."

"That's because I have a fabulous photographer." His fingers stroked my shoulder, and even though his flirting didn't mean anything, I had to take a deep breath. "Catherine is fucking amazing."

"Hardly." I sipped my cocktail, a little uncomfortable with his attention. I wanted to think that Hutch's interest was harmless, but I knew better. He was charming and great for my ego, but a little dangerous too. I'd promised myself I wouldn't let this get out of hand. "But Hutch is definitely the best chef in Chicago. He's responsible for at least five of the extra pounds I'm carrying around."

Hutch shrugged. "No hardship to cook for a beautiful woman, and it looks like my beignets are going to all the right places." That shit-eating grin that no woman could resist spread across his face.

"Sounds like your relationship is a regular love fest," Allison said, raising her brows and giving me a *he-so-likes-you* look that reminded me of high school.

"If only." Hutch's fingers stroked down my arm. "Catherine is impervious to my charms."

I shrugged. "If only I was impervious to your beignets."

Hutch laughed and rose, placing both of his warm hands on my shoulders. "Ladies, if there's anything you need, don't hesitate to ask. Enjoy the rest of your dinner." He bent down and kissed me on the cheek, then whispered in my ear. "You look hot tonight, Kitty Cat." The heat instantly rose to my face.

"Thank you," Allison and Dana chorused.

Hutch had barely moved to the next table when Dana leaned forward. "Where have you been hiding him? He's smokin'!"

"I agree," Allison said, sipping more of her cocktail. "And he's totally into you."

I laughed uneasily. "Hutch is fun, but I work for him. And I already have a boyfriend, remember?"

"I wish I had your man problems, Cat." Allison said. "Maybe someday I'll find a guy as great as William sounds. Either that or one as hot as Hutch. Or Asa. Seriously, you need to hook me up."

We all laughed again. She might have been joking around, but I knew Allison was lonely. She'd been widowed for as long as I had, but she was raising two young children on her own and barely had any time for herself, let alone for pursuing a new relationship. "You'll find someone, Allison," I said. "When you're ready." Allison was wonderful. She'd fall in love again one day.

"And on that note," Allison raised her cocktail, "let's toast."

I raised my glass and Dana followed. "To love," Dana said. "Past and future." We clinked our glasses together.

"Catherine?" I paused in the middle of sipping my drink and turned at the voice behind me. For a moment, I didn't recognize the woman standing next to our table.

Oh. "Elin!"

"I thought that was you. How are you?"

"I'm good. How are you?" I indicated the empty space in the booth. "Join us." I didn't really want Elin Erickson to join us, but I hadn't forgotten that she'd been my defender at Lauren's baby shower. I wanted to be nice to her.

She smiled at me. "Oh no, I wouldn't think of interrupting your...celebration? Plus, my friends are waiting for me." She gestured behind her, and I craned my neck to look behind me. I didn't see any group that looked like it was missing a member of its party, but I really didn't know Elin or who her friends were.

"I saw you and just wanted to say hi. This is some restaurant, isn't it? The food is spectacular."

"Yes, it is. We're really enjoying it." If she needed to get back to her friends, I wondered why she was drawing out our conversation. Allison and Dana were patiently waiting for Elin to move along so we could continue our meal.

"I heard you're working with Hutch Morrison on his new cookbook. That's impressive. How's that going?"

"It's going fine." How did she know I was working on Hutch's project?

"That's good to hear. I'm sure you'll do a great job. Anyway, I'll let you get back to eating. I'll see you soon." She turned and strolled away on high heels and stick-thin legs.

"Who was that?" Allison asked. "She seemed a little nervous."

"Childhood friend of William's family. She kind of intense, but she's nice."

"Well, someone should teach her some manners," Dana said. "She didn't even ask our names. Now, I believe we were in the middle of a toast."

"Yes!" We raised our glasses again. "We were toasting to love."

We took sips of our drinks and Dana's eyes widened. "Perfect timing. Unless I'm wrong, here comes the next course!"

Twenty-Two

The Webster, in Lincoln Park, was decked out in green for St. Patrick's Day. William led me through the lobby, past exposed-brick walls, funky round windows, and wrought iron chandeliers. The hotel was a perfect mix of Craftsman chic and classic vintage. Perfectly distressed reclaimed-wood floors lined the lobby, while the check-in desk was made of old dresser fronts. The concierge sported a long hipster beard, in contrast to his slim-fit black suit. No doubt he was moonlighting in a bluegrass band.

"What's the vibe here? Roaring Twenties or art school studio?" I asked William.

"Yes."

I laughed as he led me to the staircase at the back of the lobby. He'd returned home the night before, weary but flushed with success. The Kyoto deal had closed without much trouble and we'd celebrated with a bottle of WML Champagne, then by falling into bed. William had made love to me with a passion and tenderness that showed he'd missed me as much as I'd missed him. Maybe the break had been good for us. Absence made the heart grow fonder, but, in William's case, it also made him hungrier for me. I didn't mind.

Tonight he looked gorgeous in one of his black Tom Ford suits, *sans* tie, with a white button-down open at the neck. The slim fit hugged his broad shoulders and the muscles of his chest. An Irish-green pocket square, with a crisp fold and a straight line, was his only festive slash of color. He looked relaxed, but powerful. His hair was longer than usual—he needed a haircut—and he'd swept the waves back off his forehead. I actually liked that dark, tousled look. I couldn't wait until later, when I could run my fingers through his thick curls and pull his mouth to mine.

Since it was St. Patrick's Day, I'd opted for a Carolina Herrera cocktail dress—one that had been included in the wardrobe William had given me in Napa. The top layer was black and gauzy with a splattering of sequins, and it had an emerald green silk chiffon underlay. It was sleeveless, swingy, and sexy, and it fit me beautifully. I'd left my hair down in soft, shiny waves and played up my lips with my favorite scarlet shade.

I could hear the murmur of voices at the top of the stairs, where the private launch party was being held. I was so thrilled that Beckett was part of this. William opened one side of a rustic-looking double-door and ushered me into a large but cozy room. Like the lobby below, it had vintage details. The floors were dark wood and long, farmhouse tables were scattered throughout. The lighting looked a bit industrial—bare bulbs hanging from brushed bronze pendants—and the tap on the bar appeared to be straight out of an English pub.

I didn't have much time to gawk because I immediately saw half a dozen people I knew, including one of the guests of honor. Beckett stood across the room, looking gorgeous in his Paul Smith

London three-piece suit. Beneath the waistcoat he wore a geometric-print shirt in shades of green, and he had a small green Gerbera daisy pinned to his lapel. He was speaking with a tall, grey-haired man who looked to be in his late forties. Something about his face told me he was European. "Is that Chef LeClerc with Beckett?" I asked William.

"That's him. I'll introduce you." With his hand in mine, he started to lead me across the room. We didn't get far before we had to stop because I'd spotted Ben Lee.

"You look stunning as always," Ben said, embracing me. Ever since I'd photographed his food at Willowgrass, Ben had been very kind to me, and I was always thrilled to see him. Ben gave William a wary look—probably wondering if he was still as territorial and possessive of me as the last time we'd met—and held out his hand.

William shook it. "Good to see you, Ben. Thank you for coming."

The two men exchanged pleasantries, and then Ben turned to me. "I know you want to say hi to Beckett right now, but I want to introduce you to my girlfriend later."

"I'd love that," I said.

We moved away, and I heard a loud, raucous laugh. Only one person I knew laughed like that: Angela. She was talking with, of all people, Zoe. I couldn't imagine what the two of them had to say to each other. Curious, I pulled William toward them.

"Hi Zoe," I said with a polite nod. I hugged Angela and introduced her to William.

"No wonder you keep him all to yourself," Angela quipped. "He looks good enough to eat."

"Is Hutch here?" I asked. William's hand in mine tightened slightly.

"He'll be coming if he can get away."

"Good. Beckett wants to meet him. Speaking of, I need to give him a hug. Excuse us."

I grabbed William and we headed toward Beckett again. Finally, after saying hello to about a million more people along the way, we reached my best friend.

"Cat!" Beckett exclaimed and threw his arms around me.

I laughed, hugging him back. "Congratulations, Chef. I'm so proud of you!"

A waiter circled with champagne and Beckett grabbed two glasses, handing one to me and one to William, then reaching back for a third for himself.

William shook hands with Emil LeClerc, and turned to introduce us. "Catherine, this one of the best chefs I know, Emil LeClerc. Emil, this is my girlfriend, Catherine Kelly."

"A pleasure to finally meet you," LeClerc said, bending to kiss my hand. He had a French accent with a touch of New York and looked like a cross between Eric Ripert and George Clooney. "I have heard so much about you from Beckett and from William, of course."

"Uh-oh," I said.

He smiled. "All of it good, I assure you. He's a very lucky man."

"This calls for a toast," William said, holding his glass high. "To Beckett and a sweet future."

"To Beckett," we echoed, clinking glasses.

William and LeClerc began a discussion about food, and I turned to Beckett. "This is it," I said, practically bubbling with joy at his success. "Can you believe it?"

"I'm pinching myself. I've never been so happy." He looked it too. His face practically glowed.

"It's no dream. All these people are here to celebrate *you*. I'm so proud of you, Beckett. You totally deserve this." I squeezed his arm. I took a sip of my champagne and looked around the room, for the first time noticing the big video screens on various walls flashing pictures. I thought they were just showing hotel guest rooms and amenities, but then saw that interspersed between were images of the bakery and lots of delicious dessert items, just like the ones Beckett would be serving at Patisserie LeClerc.

"Nice pictures." I raised my glass toward the screens. "Thanks for hiring me."

"Cat." Beckett made a face. "I had no say in those. They're photos from corporate. LeClerc's people manage all the branding."

"I'm just teasing." *Mostly.*

The steady stream of William's friends and business acquaintances stopping by to chat soon had me relaxed and laughing.

The party was bustling. It was nice to just focus on having a good time, and since I was certain William's security team was lurking everywhere, I felt safe and protected. I didn't even mind when Zoe came up and asked to meet Beckett. I had to admit, she looked edgy and hot in slim leather pants, a grey sequin tank and sky-high stilettoes.

I'd finished my introductions and Beckett, bless him, had just given me a knowing *I now totally know what you mean* look when I saw him stiffen. Zoe was acting human for once, so I followed Beckett's gaze and sucked in a breath.

Alec.

Alec had just walked through the door, and one look at Beckett's face told me everything.

Beckett wasn't over Alec, and the break-up hadn't meant nothing to him. Beckett looked, just for an instant, absolutely devastated. And then he swallowed the rest of his champagne, said something that made Zoe laugh, and did what he always did so well—covered the pain.

How could I have forgotten Beckett's gift for concealing his hurts? Maybe because he'd never bothered to do it with me before. He'd always shared everything with me—good and bad. *So why hadn't he told me the truth about his break-up with Alec?*

"Do you need another drink?" William asked.

I turned to find him at my elbow, and I had my answer. I'd been way too wrapped up in my relationship with William—again.

Which is why I hadn't seen how much my best friend was hurting. Beckett deserved better from me.

"My throat is parched," I told William. "Could you find me a glass of water?"

"Of course." He kissed my cheek. "Be right back."

"Who is that?" Zoe asked, bringing my attention back to her and Beckett. I glanced across the room and spotted Hutch.

I nudged Beckett with my elbow. "Guess what? Hutch Morrison is here!"

"Cat!" Beckett squeezed my hand with excitement, but I was more interested in Zoe's response. Her eyes were glued on Hutch, her expression dazed. I waved, and Hutch made his way across the room to us, stopping to joke with Angela for a moment. Lots of interested and admiring glances were thrown his way, but he seemed oblivious to the excitement his arrival created.

Hutch wore boots, tight-fitting dark jeans, and a band collar, black leather biker jacket with his trademark plain black T-shirt beneath. No green for him on this holiday. His blond hair was carefully disheveled and he looked every inch the bad-boy-rock-star-turned-famous-chef he was. His gaze was on me as he neared, but the moment he caught sight of Zoe, interest flickered in his eyes and he looked startled and raw. I felt a jab in my gut. *Was I jealous?*

And then he blinked and smooth, charming Hutch was back. "Miss Catherine," he purred in that slow Southern drawl as he pulled me into a hug. "This is some party."

"It's all for Beckett." I gestured to my friend, who was staring as openly as Zoe. "Beckett Altieri, meet Hutch Morrison."

Beckett held out a hand. "Mr. Morrison, I'm honored. I love your work."

Hutch took Beckett's hand. "And I know I'm going to love yours. But Mr. Morrison is my daddy. Call me Hutch."

"Hutch." Beckett said the word reverently.

Hutch's eyes slid to Zoe.

"This is Zoe Smith." I gestured to her. "She's William's cousin."

"A pleasure, Miss Zoe," he said, taking her hand. He didn't so much shake it as hold it in his.

"Likewise," she said. If I wasn't mistaken, she was all but drooling while looking at him intently.

Something was definitely going on there. I could practically see the sparks between the two of them, but I didn't see what Hutch would be so drawn to—and he was drawn. He couldn't take his eyes off of her.

"Hutch owns Morrison Hotel," I told Zoe.

She frowned. "I thought you were a chef."

"It's only called *hotel*," Beckett chimed in. "It a restaurant, the best in Chicago. One of the best in the world, in fact."

"You'll have to come in for dinner sometime," Hutch told her. He still hadn't let go of her hand.

Zoe was transfixed by Hutch, her head titled to one side and her eyes locked on his face, questioning. "Yes, I will," she said quietly. "Have we met before? I could swear that I know you."

Beckett said something then that caught Hutch's attention, but I missed it. I felt a tingle on the back of my neck and glanced around the room. The music had gotten louder but I didn't see anything to alarm me, just the crowd mingling and flashes of images on the video screens. William was making his way toward me with a glass of water. Maybe that was the tingle I'd felt.

I smiled at him as he drew up to our group, but he didn't return it. He'd obviously seen Hutch. William handed me the water and wrapped his arm around my waist, pulling me hard against him. I saw his gaze lock on Hutch's hand holding Zoe's and the two of them talking intently. I was glad to have something to sip so I could look busy.

Finally, Hutch dropped Zoe's hand and held his palm out to William. There was a long pause, where I worried William might not hold his hand out at all, then they shook.

"Morrison."

"Lambourne. How was Japan?"

William's stormy eyes landed on me. They were steely blue.

"Dana and Allison and I had dinner at Morrison Hotel last Saturday," I said. "I told you."

I hadn't mentioned the venue, but that was beside the point. Hutch and I were working together, nothing more. I could mention that my boyfriend was out of town to a friend without it meaning anything.

"Japan was busy," William said. "I'm glad to be back." He squeezed my waist, and I smiled.

"I guess it's Catherine's turn to travel now."

I tensed and flashed Hutch a *shut up* look, but he wasn't looking at me. His attention was back on Zoe. "Did she tell you I'm taking her to Fashion Week in Paris? Fiona Joy asked me to put on her after-show dinner and I need Catherine to photograph it. It's going to be quite the event."

William's arm had gone rigid, his fingers like stone against my waist. "Absolutely not," he said, his voice so low I wasn't sure anyone but me could hear it.

"William—"

"Catherine's not going to Paris," he said loudly enough for half the room to hear.

Beckett took a step back, Hutch raised a brow, and Zoe smirked. *Great.* We were causing a scene at my best friend's party, in front of my boss and the one woman who would jump for joy over any discord between William and me.

"We'll talk about it later," I said quietly, pulling away from him.

"There's nothing to talk about. There's no fucking way I'm letting you go."

Our gazes met and clashed. I narrowed my eyes. Did he really want to do this here and now, with half the room watching us? He didn't blink, so I could only assume he did.

"The last time I checked, I was quite capable of making my own decisions. I don't need you to tell me what to do."

"Then don't do stupid things."

"*Excuse me*?"

The moment was tense, but our voices weren't raised. Only Hutch, Beckett, and Zoe could hear us, but I sensed something rippling throughout the room. People were murmuring and looking around. William must have noticed it too. He broke off and scanned the room, probably looking for Asa.

As I followed his eyes, I noticed some of the guests were staring at me.

The music, which had been a fun big-band mix, went dead and was replaced by some sort of audio montage of people talking.

I looked at Beckett, hoping this was something he'd planned, but he looked as clueless as I felt. And then he grabbed my arm. "Cat."

He nodded to the video screens. Weird images had replaced the pictures of hotel rooms and pastries on all the screens. *What the hell was going on?* I caught the flash of an image of me and gasped. A shot from an online news site, one I recognized instantly, filled the screen.

Next was a screenshot of a surfer website with an image of Jace doing an aerial on a wave. I'd taken that shot. And next was a clip from TMZ. I'd never seen it air, but the headline screamed, "Surfer Killed in Car Accident with Wife behind the Wheel," and another one "Jace Ryder Dead. Wife Responsible?" The video was of flashing lights and a scene of an accident.

Somewhere a glass shattered, and I realized it was my water glass. I'd let go of it, my fingers going slack.

"Oh my God." I swayed, but William was right there to steady me.

"What the fuck is this?" he barked at Beckett.

"I don't know," Beckett said, looking around frantically. "This isn't supposed to be happening."

I couldn't look away. Another headline flashed on the screen—"Wife Drinking, Pro Surfer Jace Ryder Dead."

"No," I whispered. I'd told William about Jace and the accident and about the reaction from Jace's fans. But I'd never told him about all the negative online stuff or about Jace's angry groupies. I thought Jeremy was the biggest secret I'd kept from William, but apparently I was wrong. This was.

Someone had put a lot of work into making this video. Fake blood splashed on the screen next, and there was a shot of me and Jace on a beach in Santa Cruz. I looked so young, standing with the water at my back and Jace at my side. We were grinning at the camera. As I watched, blood ran down, obscuring our faces.

"Where's the AV system?" Hutch asked. "I'm shutting this down."

Beckett gestured vaguely, and Hutch took off across the room.

I shook violently, my teeth chattering. Sweat dampened my back until my dress stuck to it. All the Cat Ryder mistakes I thought I'd left behind in Santa Cruz were splashed on the screen for everyone to see. William's family and friends, people he did business with—they all had a front-row seat to the biggest tragedy of my life. And I feared William, the man I loved with all my heart, would never look at me the same way after this.

Ever since that day in January when I'd met William I'd worried that my past, my baggage, would ruin us. I was a liability for a public person like William, and I hadn't wanted my mistakes to hurt his reputation.

A light flashed, shocking me out of my thoughts. More than a few people in the crowd of party guests were holding up their cell phones, snapping pictures or taking videos of me. No one looked away when I met their eyes, or lowered their phones. The embarrassment I would inevitably cause my prominent boyfriend was just seconds away from exploding across the Twitter-sphere and Instagram.

"We're getting out of here." William grabbed my arm and tugged me. I stumbled, my gaze still fixed on the images on the screen.

Jace. My poor dead Jace.

He didn't deserve to have his memory treated like this.

And then it was all gone. William was on one side of me and Asa was on the other, and they pulled me down the steps of The Webster and into a waiting car. I cowered in the corner of the SUV, my body still shaking. William sat beside me, ranting and cursing into his phone.

I closed my eyes and willed it all to go away.

*****

I didn't remember arriving back at the penthouse. I must have stepped out of the car, walked through the lobby, gotten on the elevator. I didn't remember any of it. I finally came out of my trance when William pushed a glass of cold water into my hand.

I sipped the water, grateful to have something to do. We were in the living room. I sat on the couch, while William paced back and forth, glanced at the photo I'd taken of the surfer in Santa Cruz. I finally knew why it had always bothered me that William had it. I hadn't wanted Cat Ryder's past and Catherine Kelly's present to mix.

Too late for that now.

Suddenly, William hurled his glass across the room. It shattered in the fireplace, spraying water all over the floor. I peered up at him, the stony look on his face, the stormy eyes. He looked haunted and…broken.

He pulled his cell from his pocket, ignoring the glass on the floor. "Why the fuck hasn't he called me back?"

"Who?"

He stood and paced again. "I'm so fucking frustrated." He raked a hand through his hair. "I'm the one who's causing all of this."

"You? I don't understand."

"While I was away in Japan, there wasn't a single incident. Asa told me they didn't see anything or anyone suspicious. Now I'm back, and this happens. It's me. I'm the one causing this, and I. Can't. Fucking. Stop. It."

"William." I rose and grabbed his hands. "This isn't your fault. You're doing all you can."

"It's not enough, Catherine. It's not enough."

I sank down on the couch. He was right. It wasn't enough, and I couldn't take this anymore. I wanted to escape him, my past, the humiliation of the video. I wanted to be alone, to wallow, but I couldn't even have that. I couldn't go to my own house because home wasn't safe.

All I'd ever wanted with William was a normal relationship. We'd tried and tried, but it was time I realized it wasn't ever going to happen. I kept waiting for us to get past all of the fucked up shit, but every time I turned around our lives became more fucked up.

"I'm sorry," I said. "I'm so sorry."

He was by my side in an instant. "There's nothing to be sorry for." As if reading my negative, wallowing thoughts, he pulled me into his arms and stroked my hair. "This wasn't aimed at you. It's me he wants, and he gets to me through you. You didn't do anything wrong."

"This is my worst nightmare. They all saw. Everyone knows about me now. I never wanted this for you."

"Shh." He moved his hand down to stroke my back. "Do you think I care about that? I love you, Catherine. No one can do anything to change that. I love you." He pulled me tighter against him and just like that, being in his arms, I felt the knot of guilt and fear in my chest start to slip.

TWENTY-THREE

"Do you want to blow or do you want me to?" Beckett asked.

I giggled and took another sip of champagne. "You do it. You're so good at blowing."

Beckett toasted me, clinking his champagne flute against mine. "That's right. Watch and learn, Cat. It's all in the lips." He puckered, and we dissolved into laughter again.

When I could catch my breath, I sighed. The studio William had booked was outstanding, a state-of-the-art space with the best equipment. The techs William had hired to assist me probably thought I was an idiot right about now, but I didn't care. Beckett had been able to swing this Monday afternoon off, and I'd jumped at the opportunity to have him work with me on the WML Champagne shoot. It was just like old times.

Except we'd never worked in a space like this.

I didn't think I could have pulled off such a complicated shoot without this perfect studio. I'd rigged a tarp over the camera and around the champagne bottle. The lens of the camera was protected by a clear glass panel. Beckett and I suspended the cork above the lip of the bottle with fishing line, which would look invisible on film—and which was easy to tinker with postproduction. We'd put the techs to work drilling a hole in the bottom of the champagne bottle—that was where the glasses of champagne had come from; we couldn't allow all that good champagne to go to waste—and installed PVC tubes. Beckett blew compressed air through the pipe to set off an explosion of golden liquid.

I put the laser timer I'd bought to good use coordinating the spray and the click of the camera. The set-up was time consuming, so each shot was crucial, and while the first few shots looked good, there'd been something missing.

Then it hit me: Vapor. We needed a little vapor in the shot. Beckett sent one of the techs to find a can of Dust-Off. The tech sprayed a shot of that into the bottle lip, Beckett released the compressed air, and I snapped the shot. The last few stills looked *amazing*, so we started celebrating.

As always, Beckett and I were a fabulous team. Why shouldn't we toast to another successful photo shoot?

I'd had so much fun working with Beckett in Chicago. After Jace's death, I hadn't known where to go or what to do, and Beckett had given me a new career and a new purpose.

He'd given me a new life.

"I have to say we have definitely *blown* this *job*," Beckett quipped.

I almost fell out of my chair laughing. It was the champagne. Beckett and I had…*sampled* several glasses of William's excellent vintage. It was mostly in the name of research, though I also hadn't passed up the opportunity to self-medicate a little bit. I'd skipped lunch, so I was more than a little tipsy. Beckett was too. But who cared? The shots I'd taken so far were great, and Beckett and I were having fun. Plus, it helped me forget for a little while the complete fucking mess my life had become.

This was how my life in Chicago used to be.

Fun.

Before the security guards, the threats, the entrails on my dinner plate...

Before William.

Before my ancient history became a Google news item and before I became infamous, again. Since the party at The Webster on Saturday night, I'd received countless emails and texts from "old friends" forwarding me pictures of myself from that night asking, "Is that you?"

Yes, it was me. Now leave me alone.

I swallowed the contents of my champagne flute and sobered.

"Uh-oh." Beckett raised his brows in concern. "I know that look. What's wrong now? You want to do the blow job this time?"

My lips quirked ruefully.

"No, you do it." I lifted the tarp. "Come on. One more shot for the win."

"You got it. *Garçon!*" Beckett flicked his finger at the tech with the Dust-Off. The poor tech came running.

We set up for the shot again. I knelt under the tarp and looked through the lens, focusing the image of the neck of the bottle and the cork.

Behind me, I heard the door open and someone speak, but I ignored it. I concentrated on what I was doing. I wanted one last perfect shot. *The* shot.

"Places," I said without moving away from the camera.

"Start the timer," Beckett said.

In my peripheral vision, I could see the blinking numbers. *3-2-1.*

Click, click, click.

I let out a whoop. "One of those had to be it. I can feel it!"

"Cat—"

I held up a finger and went to the monitor to view the shot. "Hold on, Beckett. Just let me…"

"Cat, William is here."

"William is going to," I swung around, "love this. William?"

He stood by the studio door, George at his side. The techs stared at him as though he were Ryan Gosling. What was William doing here? Checking up on me? Wasn't it enough that Asa had been outside the whole time?

"Catherine, I'm sorry to interrupt."

Of course, he had every right to interrupt and to stop by. I had to remember he was the client on this shoot, not the overprotective boyfriend I loved with all my heart but who just couldn't let me into his life the way I wanted. William had been pretending that everything was fine between us, but we hadn't spoken much since the party—since the video—and I could tell he was bothered more than he was letting on. He'd spent most of yesterday in his study with the door closed, presumably on the phone. I'd heard raised voices a few times, but when he'd emerged, he was tightlipped and told me nothing. He'd gone to bed early and offered me just a chaste kiss before rolling over and going to sleep.

"You're not interrupting," I said. "It's your studio. If you step over to the monitor, I'll shhhow…" I stumbled. Maybe I'd had a little more champagne than I realized. I tried to pull myself together. "I mean, I'll *show* you the shots."

Beckett applauded. "Way to recover, Cat."

"Fuck you," I shot back.

"Sorry, you're not my type."

It was an old joke and shouldn't have been funny to either of us, except we'd been drinking, so Beckett dissolved into giggles. I glanced at William and motioned to Beckett to stop. William looked stone-faced and not amused in the least.

Beckett immediately straightened. "Sorry."

William put an arm around me. "It's fine. Catherine, I need you to come with me."

"Let me show you some of the shots first, *Mr.* Lambourne," I said. "I promise we really were working."

William squeezed me. "I'll look later. Right now I need you to come with me."

I squinted up at him. I'd taken his tight-lipped expression as disapproval at my antics with Beckett. The strain around his eyes indicated more than disapproval. He was upset and concerned.

"What's wrong?"

"I'll tell you when we get there." He gave a pointed look toward the techs who pretended to rearrange equipment that didn't need rearranging. They hadn't been drinking and had probably noticed his tension long before I had.

"Okay, but I'm in the middle of this." I gestured to the tarp and the champagne bottle that Beckett and I had spent hours rigging at exactly the right angle. It had taken us forever to form an airtight seal on the hole in the bottom of the bottle. "I'll just finish up and meet you—"

"No. I need you to come *now*."

I didn't like to be summoned. My face must have shown my annoyance because William's expression softened.

"Catherine, this is important. Please. Leave everything and come with me now."

My heart thudded hard in my chest. I'd rarely heard William use that tone of voice before. It freaked me out, and a pallor beneath his gorgeous face scared me. I nodded and then fumbled, not sure what to leave and what to grab.

"Leave everything," William said. His hand fit perfectly on the small of my back, and he ushered me toward the door. I glanced at Beckett over my shoulder. My friend was wide-eyed and slack-jawed. Belatedly, he handed me my purse.

"Here, Cat. Call me later, okay?"

"Thanks. Beckett..." I gestured to the studio.

He understood without me saying a word. "I got it, Cat."

And then William whisked me into the SUV, and Anthony hit the gas before George had even closed his door.

In front of us, George and Anthony stared hard at the growing traffic on the downtown streets. In the backseat, William pressed a cold bottle of water into my hands. "Drink."

I sipped the water. I wasn't really thirsty, but I understood William wanted me to sober up. His look back in the studio—fury mixed with panic—killed my buzz faster than any water would. But I sipped anyway, my gaze on William.

"Where are we going?" I asked.

"My office." He didn't look at me, just stared out the window.

"What's this about? The thing at Beckett's party?"

William nodded and my heart sank. This was not good.

The car pulled to the front of William's building, and he ushered me inside. His warm hand on my back gave me some comfort, but all of the secrecy made me jumpy. When George, William, and I stepped into the private elevator, I started at the quiet ping it made when George pressed the button to close the doors.

He took a key from his pocket, inserted it into the panel, and pushed a button labeled *S. S floor?*

"Where are we going?"

I might as well have been speaking to myself. No one answered me. The elevator slid downward silently.

I hadn't spent a lot of time at William's office or in his private elevator. I did have fond memories of the first time I'd ridden in it—the way William had kissed me until I was breathless. There was none of that warmth in here now. My belly was a cold lump of fear. I'd only ridden the elevator a half dozen times, but I didn't remember ever seeing an S floor. I'd never taken the elevator down either. I'd always gone up to the top floor of the building.

Was this a basement level? What could the S stand for?

Secret?

I almost giggled, but it wasn't the champagne this time. It was nervous laughter. Finally, the door slid open revealing a large open area. The walls and floor were the silvery grey of metal and the ceilings were low, making the place feel like a bunker.

Maybe that's what it was. Video screens displayed images from cameras all around the building. Some screens even showed the exterior and interior of William's residential building. The video feed flickered in the dim light and several laptops sat around a center circular pillar, their screens lit by a scroll of numbers and letters that made no sense to me.

The soft hum of voices silenced as soon as we stepped into the room. I looked away from the cameras and the computers and blinked in surprise at Charles Smith.

"Mr. Smith." I sort of waved then lowered my hand, feeling awkward. What was William's uncle doing here? George moved to stand beside Asa, who was next to one of the large screens projecting a view of the lobby. People filed in and out, unaware they were being watched from below.

Charles gave me a wan smile. "Hello, Catherine."

He looked tired. They all did. William's hand still rested in the small of my back, and I was grateful for the reassuring contact. His expression was granite—nothing reassuring about that.

Behind me, the elevator whooshed again, and Anthony stepped off.

"That's everyone," George said curtly. "Secure the elevator."

"Yes, sir." Anthony punched a code into the panel and the hum of the elevator ceased. The room was silent except for the whir of the machines.

I knew what the S on the elevator panel meant now. *Security.* This was William's security room. George was in charge here. He cleared his throat and addressed the gathering. "As some of you know, the authorities finally apprehended the man who broke into Catherine's condo."

"What?" I gasped. "When?"

George ignored me, as usual. He looked at the tablet he held in his hand, consulting notes. "His name is Lance Reilly. He's a known perp." He nodded to Asa, who tapped the screen of one of the laptops. An image of a guy in his early thirties popped up. He had dark hair and light blue eyes, a handsome face marred by a cocky smile.

"Is this the man you saw enter your building, posing as a plumber, Miss Kelly?" George asked.

"I...yes. I think so." I took a step closer. I remembered that the guy had reminded me of William, and this man had the same dark hair, light eyes, and handsome features. I tried to picture him with a baseball cap. "That might be him."

"He has a record." George consulted his tablet again. "Minor infractions, mostly—petty theft, breaking and entering, vandalism. Enough for him to see some jail time when we press charges. We offered to go easy on him if he gave us information."

"What sort of information?" Charles asked. I was glad I wasn't the only one who didn't have all the facts.

"We wanted to know who hired him."

"And did he tell you?"

"He gave us a description of the woman."

"Woman?" I looked at William. His expression told me nothing. I had no idea if this information was new or if he'd heard it a hundred times before.

"He didn't know her name, but he gave a detailed description. She's in her late twenties or early thirties, petite, brown hair." George looked up at me. "Those weren't the exact words he used, but that's what we put together."

I shook my head. Why would a woman hire someone to break into my condo? The description didn't sound like anyone I knew. For some strange reason, the moment George had said it was a woman, an image of Jace's mother popped into my head. She was the only woman I could think of who hated me. *Ridiculous*. She was in California and probably glad to have nothing to do with me.

And the description didn't match Mrs. Ryder's.

"We also obtained this footage from The Webster." George nodded at Asa, who brought a grainy black-and-white film onto the screen beside the picture of Lance Reilly. I narrowed my eyes, trying to figure out what I was seeing. Finally, I saw a man in a white shirt and black pants step into the shot. He reached into his pocket, took out his phone, and scrolled through it. Behind him were stacks of boxes and something…a wine rack?

"Move ahead to the incident," George said.

Asa tapped the laptop and the video seemed to fast-forward.

"This is footage of a storage room behind the bar," George explained. "It's staff-only. You can see the boxes of beer and spirits and the wine selection."

"And that waiter?" Charles asked.

"Just taking a break to check his phone," George said. "He wasn't supposed to be back there, but he leaves without incident. What we're interested in is the AV set-up."

"It's in that room," William said. It was the first time he'd spoken, and I wasn't certain it was a question. George nodded.

"Yes, that's where the video and music are piped in. It's not hard to gain access to, if you know where it is. Initially, we suspected that one of the staff was responsible for the incident Saturday night. But then we saw this." He nodded to Asa, who slowed the video back down to normal speed.

I stared at the grainy image of the empty room. A woman stepped into the frame. She looked over her shoulder, then moved to the far edge of the shot. She bent and seemed to be working on something.

"That's the media interface." George pointed to an area just out of the camera's range. "Note the time." He tapped the screen. In the corner it read 10:32:27.

"At exactly 10:32:33, the music changes and the unauthorized images and video appear."

I stared at the screen, watching as the seconds advanced. At 10:32:33, the woman stood straight and nodded to herself. Then she turned and left the room.

"And this is the same woman who paid to have Catherine's condo broken into?" Charles asked.

"We believe so. She matches the description," George said.

I hadn't been able to see her very well in the grainy footage, but I'd made out that she was probably in the age range.

"I think it will become clear when Asa cleans up the feed." George nodded to Asa.

Asa pressed another button and we had the image of the woman leaving the room again. He paused the video right when she passed directly in front of the camera. He tapped the screen, and a square appeared around the grainy image of her face. The square enlarged until it was just her face on the screen. Asa tapped again, refining the image. Another tap.

I gasped.

The final tap and the image was crystal clear.

The woman was Elin Erickson.

*****

For a few minutes I didn't hear anything anyone said. I had an impression that the room erupted into angry shouts, but I was too confused to process it. One thought cycled through my mind: *Why?*

Why would Elin Erickson do that to me? Why would she want to hurt me?

And she did want to hurt me. If she was the mastermind behind all of this, she hadn't just made these videos or paid a man to break into my condo—she'd had me photographed, locked in my darkroom, and served that unappetizing plate at the Botanical Society dinner.

Why?

I'd never done anything to her. I hadn't even *known* her until a few weeks ago.

"—been taken into custody."

George's words caught my attention. "She's being held for questioning, and we will press charges."

This was crazy. Elin had been a friend of William's since they were kids. Was this some sort of crush gone wrong? Had William not told me the truth about their relationship?

"What the hell is going on here?" William's voice startled me. I could feel the tension reverberating through his entire body. Everyone turned to look at him, but he glared at Charles, his gaze never wavering.

Charles shook his head. A sign of confusion or an unwillingness to say what he knew?

"Don't shake your fucking head at me. You know something. You have to."

"William—" Charles didn't need to finish the thought. His expression gave everything away. The lines in his face grew deeper with regret and pain flickered in his eyes.

"Tell me what you know," William demanded.

Charles gave a deep sigh. "Maybe we should discuss this in private."

"There's nowhere more private than this," William said. "And as soon as the media gets wind of her arrest, everyone is going to know."

I reached for William's hand, but he drew it away. He didn't want my comfort right now, and I could tell from Charles's defeated expression that he wasn't going to give William comfort either.

"You know that Elin's father, Jack, worked for your father at WML Capital Management for several years. Your parents were close with the Ericksons, to Jack and his wife, Lisa," Charles began. "They socialized together, traveled together. You remember summers with them in Lake Geneva, I'm sure. Perhaps…" He looked directly into William's face, his eyes full of pain. "Perhaps your father became too close to Lisa Erickson."

William didn't move. I wasn't even certain he'd heard.

"He had a…relationship with Lisa. And there was a child born from that relationship."

The room was quiet except for the sound of William roughly exhaling now and again. His eyes—a cold, icy blue—were locked on Charles's face.

Charles broke away first, his gaze dropping to William's hands, which were clenched together, the knuckles white with rage.

"Lisa had a son, William. His name was Wesley, and he was your half-brother."

The silence hung around us. William clenched his jaw again and again and a vein pulsed at the side of his neck, but his stare never wavered. "Go on," he finally said.

"That last spring, Jack found out about Lisa's affair with your father, and all hell broke loose. Jack left WML Capital Management and he and Lisa separated shortly after that. Relationships were damaged, friendships lost, business affected. It was not an easy time and your father struggled a great deal with all of it."

"And so later, those letters from the woman who claimed to be my father's mistress," William said, his voice cold. "Those were legitimate, weren't they?"

"You were still just a child. You were never supposed to know. But yes, the letters were from Lisa."

"She did have a son with my father?"

Charles nodded, his throat working. "But your father never knew. He never even knew she was pregnant. The accident happened and…" Charles's voice trailed off. There was no need to say more. William's father had died in plane crash later that summer.

"But her story wasn't discredited, was it? And then she died in a car accident. That really happened, right?"

"Lisa's drinking got out of hand. She was killed in a car accident in which she was clearly at fault. Her blood alcohol level was off the charts." Charles closed his eyes. "Wesley was with Lisa and was also killed. She slid off the road into a retention pond. Wesley was strapped in his car seat in the back. He was just a toddler and never had a chance."

The story was tragic and gruesome and so incredibly sad. William didn't seem to move or breathe for a long moment. I wanted to go to him, to put my arms around him, but I didn't. I could see the anguish on his face, and imagined the turmoil inside him must have been a thousand times worse.

He idolized his father, and now his father had fallen from grace. Fallen hard.

"How long have you known?" William asked. "Elin grew up with us. She and Lauren played Barbies together." Though he tried to keep his voice even, I could tell William was close to losing it.

Charles couldn't seem to bring himself to look William in the eye. He looked at the floor, his hands, William's shoes. "I've always known," he said finally. "I knew when the relationship began. I didn't know about Wesley's paternity until the letters. No one really did. Jack maybe…and maybe Elin knew."

"My mother…" William's voice broke on the words. He slammed his hand down on the table in front of him and I jumped.

So did Charles. "Did she know about his affair?" William asked quietly, the anger building in his voice.

Charles covered his eyes with his hand. "I don't see how she couldn't have, William. She loved your father, but I suspect she stayed with him for you and for Wyatt."

There was a long pause, then William gave a curt nod. "It's over now."

He abruptly turned and tapped the elevator panel. The doors slid open. Without another word, he stepped inside.

I caught his gaze as the doors closed. His eyes were hard and empty.

TWENTY-FOUR

It took a beat for me to make sense of what I'd just heard. William's father had had an affair with Elin's mother. Elin was responsible for all the horror of the last few weeks. I blinked. William was gone. I needed to go after him. I grabbed my coat, ready to follow him, but when I jabbed the elevator button, nothing happened.

"Let me out," I said to the room of men behind me. Charles had buried his head in his hands, and Anthony and Asa directed their attention on anything but me. I was sure they would have rather been anywhere else. Only George met my gaze directly and nodded.

I thought about the way William had reacted when he'd received the news that the wreckage couldn't have been that of his parents' plane—drunk, angry, dangerous. "He shouldn't be alone right now." My voice sounded small and desperate

"I'll go with you," George said. He inclined his head toward a door in the back of the room I hadn't noticed. "This way, Miss Kelly. It's faster than waiting for the elevator."

He keyed in a code on the panel beside the door, and it slid open. Grey metal stairs led up and into a stairwell lit by greenish lights. I followed George, running to keep up with the older man. By the time we reached the lobby level, I panted and gasped for air. George keyed in yet another code, and the door slid open. The hallway into which we emerged was completely unfamiliar to me. George motioned me around a corner. Ahead, light slanted through a glass door to the outside.

We pushed it open and stumbled into the bright and sunny March day. A breeze ruffled my hair and not a single cloud dared mar the perfect sky. The snow on the ground looked out of place against the bright blue sky. Ironic that today, of all days, would be so perfect, with a hint of thaw in the air. I couldn't appreciate the lovely weather when everything inside me felt black and desolate. I needed to find William.

"This way, Miss Kelly. We're on the side of the building. William probably exited the front."

"Unless he went to the parking garage for one of the cars."

"Let me check." George pulled out his phone and tapped the screen. "GPS tracking," he said, in answer to my unasked question. He slid the phone back into his pocket. "All cars are stationary. Most likely he'll take a cab or walk."

I pictured William in my mind's eye. "He'll walk." He'd have his head down against the wind, hands in his pockets, long legs striding quickly away. No particular direction. Just away. "Hurry!"

George ran toward the front of the building, which faced Michigan Avenue. He looked left and then right. I followed, careful not to slide on any slippery spots on the sidewalk, and did the same.

"There!" I pointed to a lone figure moving toward the Michigan Avenue Bridge. "That's him." I could spot William anywhere, even on a crowded street he stood out. He walked with purpose.

"Good eye, Catherine. Let's go."

I stood rooted in place for a moment even as George ran after William. That might have been the first time George had ever called me Catherine. I shook my head in wonder and raced after them.

When I caught up to William, George already had a hand on William's arm. "Let me call for the car," he was saying. "Anthony can take you and Catherine home."

William's stormy eyes, a mixture of blue and grey lanced through with pain, met mine. "I don't want to go home," he said in that flat, unemotional voice that frightened me. He didn't reach for me and that frightened me more.

"Then I'll have him take you somewhere else."

William's gaze shifted to George. "I want to see her. I want to hear explanations from her own mouth, George."

He didn't have to say her name: Elin Erickson.

George pulled out his vibrating phone, glanced at the screen. Whoever was calling didn't merit his attention at the moment. "That's not possible, William. Even if you could see her, there's no reason for her to talk to you. She has a lawyer, who will certainly advise her to say nothing."

"Let's just go home," I said, moving closer to William. I wanted to touch him, but I didn't know what he needed and I held back. Whatever happened next, I wasn't going to leave his side.

"She'll talk to me," William said. "She wants someone to listen to her or she wouldn't have done all of this. Make it happen, George." He raised his hand and flagged a cab. As the driver pulled to the curb, I took William's hand. It was cold and dry and didn't clasp mine back.

But he didn't pull away either. I wanted to show him that I was with him no matter what. I hoped he understood that.

"Are you sure you want to do this now? Today? You can go tomorrow." My voice was pleading.

"I'm going now."

"Where to?" The driver yelled out the window.

William looked at George.

George closed his eyes in defeat. "Cook County Jail. 27th and California."

William climbed in, and I slid in after him as George got into the front passenger seat.

"You don't have to come, Catherine."

I took his hand again and squeezed it. "Where you go, I go."

I don't know how George did it. He muttered into his phone for most of the cab ride that took us to the South Side. I don't know who he called or what sort of power he had, but the few snatches I heard made me cringe.

When the cab pulled to the front of the imposing correctional complex, William handed the cab driver a hundred dollar bill without even asking the cost of the fare. I climbed out last, listening to George murmur, "Just do it, or I'll have your fucking head on a platter."

William never seemed to doubt that George would work his magic. He held the door for the two of us and gestured for George to take the lead. George seemed to know where to go, so we walked quickly and I had only fleeting glimpses of old buildings with stately architecture but definitely in need of renovation. Cops were everywhere.

I swallowed the bile in my throat. Champagne and nerves didn't mix well. This was the last place I'd imagined I'd be today when I'd dressed in my studio shoot outfit of indigo jeans and a navy sweater this morning. I'd expected to spend the day behind my camera, not with criminals and police officers. The atmosphere here was so full of resignation and anger and fear that it was like a stench choking me. I was terrified and I almost felt sorry for Elin, that she was being held in this awful place. Almost, but not quite. I grasped for William's hand, and he took mine in his larger one. I had to be strong for him.

Finally, a uniformed officer emerged from behind a heavy security door, spotted George, and motioned for us to follow him. He led us inside, through an area filled with cops and desks. Some typed on computer screens, others spoke quietly into phones hooked between ear and shoulder. Almost all of them glanced at us curiously as we walked by.

We didn't belong.

When we reached an office with *Lieutenant Danford* stenciled on the door, George opened the door without knocking. A middle-aged man with short brown hair and a lean body beneath a button-down shirt and tan pants looked up from where he stood before a fax machine. I hadn't seen one of those in about a decade.

The man I took to be Lieutenant Danford frowned when he spotted George. "The authorization papers are coming through now. You can pull all the strings you want, but I can't make her talk to you."

"Let me worry about that," William said.

Danford glanced at William and then me. The officer held out a hand. "Mr. Lambourne, I'm sorry for all the trouble you've been through."

"Thank you."

"Ma'am." He nodded at me. "Can I get either of you something to drink? Water? Coffee?"

"No, thank you," William answered.

I didn't want anything either.

"Listen, Mr. Lambourne. I understand why you're here, but Miss Erickson does not have to speak with you. In fact, this is highly irregular."

"Where is she?"

"I'm having her brought to one of the rooms we use for questioning. I can't allow you to be alone with her, so I'll be behind the two-way mirror. We'll have to Miranda her again. Anything she says can be used against her, even what she says to you."

"Fine."

Danford looked at me. "Ma'am, you can wait here."

The hell I would. I was not going to let William face Elin alone. "I'm going with William," I said.

William didn't say anything, so Danford looked at George for confirmation. George gave a curt nod.

"Alright, but I'm not sure that's wise," Danford said slowly. "Miss Erickson is a bit unpredictable."

"You'll be a few steps away," George pointed out.

"Fine," Danford replied. "Let me see if she's been brought out of holding."

We waited in tense silence in the cramped office for almost an hour. Even George couldn't cut through police bureaucracy that quickly. I sat in the chair in front of the beat-up desk, trying to wrap my head around the events of the day and willing William to look at me. I wanted so badly to say the right thing, but didn't know where to even start.

He paced back and forth, unable to stand still for more than a moment or two at a time. His phone rang constantly the first fifteen minutes, and then he just turned it off. George spent the entire hour on his. At one point I thought he was speaking to Elin's lawyer. Another time he seemed to be talking to the FBI.

Finally, Danford came back. "This way." He gestured and stepped out of the office to wait for us. He led us down a narrow hallway lined with white walls and white doors. The paint was scuffed and yellowed in places. We stopped at a door marked with the number 3.

"She's inside," Danford said. "I'll be just on the other side of the mirror you'll see on your right when you walk in the door. Graham, you're with me?"

George grunted assent.

"Don't touch her, spit on her—"

William gave him a dark look.

Danford held his hands up in surrender. "Hey, I have to say these things. If you threaten her, be aware that the threat could be used against you if anything happens to her."

William's eyes narrowed. "Despite what you're implying, I'm not going to fucking touch her."

Finally, Danford turned to me.

"Are you sure you want to go in there? She's pretty pissed off."

I nodded, though I wasn't sure at all. My stomach sank and did a slow flop. I was suddenly glad I hadn't had any coffee because I wasn't sure I could have kept it down.

"Let's get this over with," William said. I took a deep breath and followed him into the room.

*****

I didn't see Elin right away. I was too busy looking around and comparing the room to the ones I'd seen on *Law & Order*. It was small with a rectangular metal table in the center and chairs on either side. I'd expected a single naked bulb to hang above the table, but fluorescent lights lit the room. As Danford had promised, a mirror ran the length of the right side of the room. I could see my reflection in it. I looked windblown and wan. The sleek ponytail I'd pulled my hair into this morning was coming loose.

My gaze met Elin's in the mirror, and I quickly looked away.

"Hello, William. Hello, Catherine," Elin said. "How are you?" She sat with one leg crossed over the other in the chair on the other side of the table. Her hands rested on the table, handcuffs large and clunky on her thin wrists. Her hair looked thinner than it had before. I sat down across from her and William did the same. It was weird seeing her like this. When we had run into each other at Morrison Hotel, she'd seemed so normal. Nice, even, when in truth she was the reason for the hell in which William and I had been living.

"Now that you're behind bars?" William said, his voice filled with anger. "I'm doing very well indeed."

Elin's fingers closed as she clenched her hands until they turned white with strain. "You're a bastard, William. Do you know that? I never liked you. And I loved watching you suffer."

William, for his part, kept calm. I had a million questions running through my head, a hundred different things I wanted to say to Elin, but William only asked one thing. "Why?" He stared at Elin intently, his cold blue eyes not leaving her face.

Elin stared back, then she broke out into a huge grin, a crazy grin, and laughed. "I wanted you to pay. I wanted you to suffer, the way I suffered." She slammed the cuffs on the table, the sound echoing through the room. I pressed my hands to my belly, trying to calm my stomach.

"And how have you suffered?" William asked. He was calm and seemed unruffled by her outburst or by the events of the day. I knew inside he must have been furious and even more upset than I, but he didn't show it. In the mirror, he looked every inch the powerful businessman.

"Was it money you needed? Was that was this was about?"

She sneered at him. "I don't want your fucking money. It has your asshole father's stink all over it. That was just the easiest way to get your attention. Initially, at least. Poor dead Wyatt..."

William's pinky twitched slightly, the only sign she'd hit a nerve. "You'll want to watch what you say about my family."

"Why? Because William Lambourne was such a fine, upstanding man? He destroyed my life and my family. Did your uncle Charles finally tell you the truth about Daddy Lambourne or did the coward leave that to me too?"

Her face contorted into an ugly smirk. Hot red dots of color stood out on her cheeks, and her scrawny body vibrated with anger.

"There's nothing you know about him that I don't."

She cackled. "I hardly believe that." She sat again and leaned her forearms onto the table so she could look William in the eye. "Where should I start?" She tapped her nails on the table. "How about the first time I saw your father cheating on your mother with my mom?"

William's pinky jerked again, but he said nothing.

"I was about twelve, and my father was away on a business trip. I came home from a friend's house early and caught your father bringing my mother home in that vintage Porsche convertible he used to drive around. When I walked up, he was kissing her. My mother told me it was nothing. But I knew then something was going on." Her eyes had turned hazy, as though she was reliving those days so long ago.

"Then that summer we were all at the house in Lake Geneva. I saw a thousand little signs, signs no one else seemed to see. Certainly not you or your brother or any of the Smiths—except your uncle. He saw. I could tell he knew what was going on. He'd seen the way your father looked at my mother. The touches, the smiles, the way the two of them disappeared together sometimes." Her mouth turned down in an expression of disgust.

"I'd hoped it ended that summer. I didn't see your father as much after school started, but I didn't know that was because my father had his own suspicions about what was going on. My parents started fighting all the time and I remember being woken up by their late night screaming matches. Then one day right before school ended the next spring, my parents got into a huge fight, and my father stormed out and didn't come home. A week later, they sat me down and told me they were getting divorced. And later that summer my mother told me she was going to have a baby. She admitted she was pregnant with *your* father's child and everything was going to change for us. We were going to be a family, just as soon he got back from Alaska."

My gaze shot to William. His pinky jerked at the mention of Alaska. "Except he never returned."

"No. He never knew he'd knocked my mother up or wrecked her life. And mine. My father wouldn't even speak to her once he found out she was going to continue the pregnancy. He was so angry and so embarrassed. After Wesley was born, my mom was broken. Something changed in her." She stopped abruptly.

Elin looked up then, a faraway look washing over her face "He was the best baby, William. I used to play with him for hours, making him laugh and giggle. It's too bad you never knew our little brother. He looked a lot like you, you know. "

William's breathing remained controlled and steady, though I could see his pulse beating rapidly in the vein at the side of his neck. "I'm sure he did," he said tightly. "Is there more?"

"Yes," Elin snapped. "There's more. She started drinking, okay? She'd lost everything. Once my father saw what was happening, he took me to live with him. I suppose I should have been grateful, but he'd met someone else by then. He didn't have time for me. I was sent away to school or pawned off on relatives while he built a new family with his new wife."

Elin's face contorted into a look of pure hate, but despite that, I wanted to go to her and hug her. She'd been a child torn apart by the poor decisions of adults. That didn't justify what she'd done to William and me, but it helped me understand.

"You act as though your mother was some sort of saint. She blackmailed my uncle."

"And she deserved every penny she got," Elin said with a satisfied smile. "He paid her to stay quiet because she told him about Wesley. He didn't want half the Lambourne fortune going to a bastard son."

I hadn't known Charles paid Lisa Erikson to keep quiet and it was obvious that this was news to William. He would hate Charles for keeping that from him.

"Your mother and the baby died in a car accident. She was driving drunk." William's steely gaze was fixed on Elin's gaunt face.

Elin jumped to her feet. "Your father ruined her life! She never got over what he did to her. It was *his* fault she started drinking. He killed her and Wesley. And he took away everything from me. I had nothing after they died. Nothing."

I could imagine how those losses had felt and I was sure William could too. He'd suffered after his family died, but he'd channeled the pain into becoming the man he was. Elin had allowed it to fester and build, and I was pretty sure it had made her not entirely sane. The more she talked, the more I realized she had planned to hurt William for years.

"That must have been terrible for you," I said.

Elin's eyes narrowed on me, her gaze full of suspicion. She couldn't even accept sympathy without questioning it.

"But William had nothing to do with what happened between your mother and his father. Neither did I."

"Don't you get it?" Elin said, spittle flying from her lips. "He's just as culpable as his namesake, maybe more so. I've watched him for years, waiting for my chance to punish him, to punish them. And then he met you, and I finally knew where I could hit him. You were the chink in his armor, *Cat*. I knew I could hurt him by hurting you. Finally, I could make him suffer, the way we'd suffered, by taking away something he loves."

William cut in. "I've heard enough."

"No!" Elin screamed. "I'm not done yet."

"I am." William pushed his chair back and stood up.

Elin moved quickly around the table, lunging toward him. In one swift turn, he grasped her shoulders and held her at arm's length. I pushed into the corner and watched, feeling helpless while she tried to claw him. "I hate you!" she screamed. "I hate you!"

The door flew open and two officers rushed in and pulled her off William. George yanked the two of us out of the room and ushered us away from the door. We turned the corner and William gathered me into his arms.

"Are you alright, Catherine?"

"Me? I'm fine." I was trembling and nauseous, but I determined not to make this about me. I buried my head in his shirt. "Are you okay?"

"No," he answered simply. "No, I'm not."

TWENTY-FIVE

William didn't say a word on the ride back to the penthouse. Anthony had been waiting at the curb in the SUV, so at least we weren't crammed into the back of a cab again. George sat up front, and since the privacy screen wasn't in place, I could see his stony expression. No one spoke and other than the occasional clicking of a turn signal, the car was eerily silent.

My mind worked and worked to conjure the perfect thing to say to comfort William, but nothing came to me. My eyes bore into him, but he wouldn't look at me and instead just stared out the window, his jaw flexing with tension every now and again. He seemed beyond my reach, lost in the devastating events of this afternoon.

I remembered when he'd first pursued me, the stunningly handsome man with the arresting turbulent blue-grey eyes. I'd never met a man as physically beautiful as William Lambourne but, looks aside, he had often seemed like two different people—funny and charming one minute, sullen and uncommunicative the next. The William sitting next to me in the SUV, the one who was refusing to meet my gaze and who was lost so deep in thought, was eerily reminiscent of that early version of him. The mercurial man who'd maddeningly kept me at an arm's length when it had suited him.

As much as it hurt, I couldn't blame him this time. What he'd been through today, learning about his father's affair and a secret half-brother who'd died, and now the confrontation with Elin—he needed time to sort through it all and process it, and to grieve. I just wished he would let me help him.

I inched my hand across the span of seat between us and nudged gently against him, seeking his warmth and a connection. His palm opened in response and I pressed my hand into his. He flexed his fingers, intertwining them with mine, then closed our hands into a fist, pulled it toward him, and leaned and kissed it. He still didn't look at me. I wanted to crawl into his lap, cup his face, and smother him with soothing kisses to take away his hurt. But for now I'd settle for holding hands.

The tense silence continued all the way to the penthouse and on the elevator ride up to the 56th floor. As soon as the doors slid open, William strode into the foyer and headed toward the master suite without looking back or saying a word to me. George and Asa scattered instantly, leaving me alone in the empty entrance hall.

"Crap," I muttered aloud as I knelt to pet Laird, who'd come walking up, tail wagging. William needed space, but I couldn't let him close the door on me, literally or figuratively. I loved him and he loved me, and I knew he needed me now whether he knew it or not. We belonged together and I wouldn't abandon him, no matter what.

Fuck Elin Erickson and her crazy threats. Fuck William's philandering father. Fuck everything. None of it mattered.

I finally found him in the bedroom closet. He sat on one of the leather benches, a photo album in his hands. At his feet was a box, neatly packed with what looked like Little League trophies, award ribbons, Power Ranger action figures, and a small baseball card collection.

He didn't look up when I sat beside him. He stared at a photo in the album of his young self and his family in front of a lake. When I leaned closer, he didn't close the book. I took that as a good sign. It wasn't just William in the picture. His aunt and uncle and cousins had squeezed in too. And then I saw why William had turned to this page. Next to Lauren was a young Elin. She'd been thin as a child too. Her parents stood beside her. The kids made funny faces and all of the parents smiled indulgently.

Not quite all, actually. Lisa and Jack Erickson's smiles were faint and strained. Lisa's eyes were not on Elin, who had her tongue out, or on the photographer. Her gaze cut to the far side of the group.

To William's father.

"I never saw it before," William said. "And it was right in front of me all along."

"You were a kid." I put my hand on his arm. "How could you have seen it? They kept it a secret. From everyone."

"My mom saw it." He traced her face in the photo. She smiled openly and didn't look as though she had a single worry in the world. She was a lovely woman, slim and elegant, with beautiful blue-grey eyes. One of her hands was on Wyatt's shoulder and the other was around her husband's waist.

"He betrayed us," William said, moving his hand to his father's face. "All of us."

"William—"

"I hate him for this. I hate that he did this to us. I hate Elin for tainting my entire childhood. But in a weird way, I understand why she did it."

I sucked in a breath. "A horrible thing happened to her, yes, but she's crazy, William. She did it because there's something wrong with her."

"And because I should be the one to pay for my father's mistakes. After all, I'm the one who's benefitted from his successes. I wouldn't be where I am now if my father hadn't started WML Capital Management or if he hadn't left it all to me."

"William, no."

"Yes." He looked at me, and his eyes were so sad. I'd never seen them that shade of grey-blue.

I took the album and closed it firmly. Before he could take it back, I set it on the floor and took his hands in mine. "Your father messed up. He was human. That doesn't have to change how you see him. It doesn't make him any less your father or make his love for you any less strong. You had a happy childhood. You were loved. He loved you." I gave him a tentative smile. "I've rarely seen you as happy as you were the night we went to dinner in Lake Forest, and you showed me your family albums and told me about your childhood. Your parents loved you. You had a good life. Nothing your father did all those years ago will ever change that."

William didn't speak for a long time. His hands rested in mine and he stared at the floor. Finally, he looked at me. "Thank you," he said.

He rose and walked away. And I wondered if he'd ever come back to me.

*****

William locked himself in his study, and as hard as it was, I respected his need to be alone. I waited for him to come to me, to talk more or tell me what he was feeling, but after a few hours, I accepted that it wasn't going to happen. I forced myself to eat dinner, but the leftover pasta was bland tasting, so after a few bites I opted for a pint of Americone Dream instead. I texted Beckett to let him know that I was OK and to ask about the studio clean up. He had taken care of everything and told me that he was up and could talk if I wanted. I didn't know what to tell him and didn't want to risk William emerging right as I was telling Beckett about Elin. So I texted back, *Thanks. I think I need to clear my head first. Love you.*

By midnight, I could barely keep my eyes open. I put on a T-shirt and a pair of boy shorts, and crawled alone into bed. I grabbed one of William's pillows and clutched it to me, just like I'd done when he was in Japan. I inhaled deeply, breathing in traces of his unique scent that clung to it, and missed him terribly. He was just steps away this time, but there might as well have been an ocean between us again. Tears welled up in my eyes as I drifted off to sleep.

My body was heavy and pleasantly warm. My breasts ached, the peaks taut and tingling with need. I gasped as my legs parted and pleasure pooled between them.

I should have known it wasn't a dream. I opened my eyes with effort. The room was dark, but I knew William's shape and smell. His hands slid up my arms lightly, raising them above my head. Then his lips were on my neck, making their way lower, while his hand teased my legs open and stroked me lightly.

"William?" I murmured. I was barely awake and sleep was drawing me back in.

"It's me, beautiful girl." His voice was low and sexy. The timbre resonated through me.

I moved my arms to embrace him, to pull him close to me, and felt restraints holding them in place. "What is this?" I asked, my mind still not fully awake.

"Shh," he said. His mouth teased the hollow at my throat, making my breath quicken. "You'll like this."

I had no doubt of that, but why had he bound me? My heart beat wildly as I stretched my fingers and felt the soft silk rope he'd used to secure my wrists. I wasn't sure what the rope was tied *to* since William's platform bed lacked a headboard. I pulled against it and was met with firm resistance, so it was anchored somewhere. There would be no escaping until he untied me.

"William." I was fully awake now and my voice faltered as he dipped his tongue lower and his hand palmed my breast. "Untie me. I want to touch you."

"No."

I stiffened. "What do you mean, *no*?"

He lifted his head, his eyes glittering in the darkness. "I'll stop if you tell me to, Catherine, but don't make me beg you to say yes. I need you like this." His hand caressed the bindings, and he slid his fingers down to my wrist.

I moaned softly as his mouth moved to tease my ear lobe, and I closed my eyes, trying to shut out the desire building inside me.

I wanted gentle and tender and loving William, and sex that would heal. I wanted to touch him and show him that I loved him. But he needed to be in control, to be able to do anything he liked to me without me stopping him. His life must have felt so chaotic at the moment, and I was what he could control right now, if I surrendered to him. "Ok," I whispered. "Don't stop."

The hand between my legs coaxed them open, and I moaned when his fingers brushed my sensitive sex. We hadn't been together since the night he'd returned from Japan, and I'd missed him. Even as I tried not to panic and my mind fought against being taken this way, my body welcomed him.

His mouth reached the top of my boatneck T-shirt and he yanked it down to expose my breasts. The rip of the material was loud amidst the sounds of our labored breathing. "William!"

"I'll buy you another," he growled. "I'll buy you a hundred."

He hadn't shaved, and the stubble on his cheek brushed over the tender skin at the curve of my breast. I withdrew from the pain even as he deliberately chafed my skin. His mouth soothed the hurt with light kisses. He repeated the action on my other breast—pain then pleasure, working his way closer and closer to my hard nipples.

When he brushed his stubbled skin over my aching point, I cried out in anguish.

"Shh," he said softly, though there was an unmistakable dark tone in his voice. "This is always about pleasure, Catherine, never about pain. I won't hurt you, but I am going to push your limits. Trust me. I'll take care you. I'll always take care of you." He raked my nipple then, and the hand between my legs brushed over my sex. I tensed in arousal as his fingers found my clit and then abandoned it, found it and abandoned it.

"You're wet for me," he said, his tone accusing. "So fucking wet. You like this. Sometimes you like it rough, don't you?"

"Yes," I moaned. "But please," I begged again. "Untie me. I want to touch you." I might have protested further, but his lips closed on my nipple, taking it into the warm heat of his mouth. His tongue lashed the abused skin, and two fingers delved inside my slick channel.

He was right. I was wet for him. But it wasn't playing on the edge that aroused me. It was him. It was always him. Pleasure or pain, I would take either because I loved him.

His mouth worked my nipple hard as his hand worked inside me. He thrust in and out, his fingertips pressing against all the most sensitive places inside me. I was on the verge of coming in seconds, my walls clenching around him.

"That's right, beautiful girl. Give it up for me. Let me hear you."

I climaxed fast and hard, reveling in the release and crying out. I closed my eyes and sank back, sated. I'd barely come down when his cheek brushed my other nipple. I hissed in a breath at the abrasive movement on the tender skin, and his fingers moved inside me again.

"No," I moaned as he stroked rhythmically. "William, I want *you*."

"You have me."

Did I? Or did I have pieces of him here and there but never the whole?

His lips closed over my tight peak, relieving the hurt. Between my legs, the heel of his hand pressed firmly against my clit. His fingers slid into me, finding my G-spot and stroking.

Pleasure and pain, pleasure and pain even as I spiraled into another climax that was almost uncomfortable, following so closely on the first.

"Enough," I panted when the waves of pleasure subsided and I was able to speak. "William, untie my wrists. I need to touch you."

"I'm not done touching you."

"Please." My voice trailed off into a moan when his damp fingers circled my clit. "Let me touch you."

"Not yet."

Not yet. Hadn't it always been *not yet* with him? He held himself apart, stripping me bare to the core while he kept himself at a distance. Even now, after the revelations about his father, he wouldn't let me comfort him. He wouldn't allow me in to witness his raw pain, his hurt, or his weakness. He shut me out, and I didn't know how to reach him. I didn't think he'd ever *let* me reach him.

And if he never allowed himself to be truly vulnerable with me then how could *we* ever survive? How could we get through every trial and tribulation bound to come into our lives over the years? I wanted to be his partner, but I couldn't hold his hand if he kept me bound.

Something happened then. I shut down. William continued to stroke and play with my body, but for the first time, I didn't respond to his demands. When his fingers couldn't bring me to climax, he put his mouth on me. His tongue flicked and sucked, and I should have been arching as orgasms slammed through me. But I didn't feel anything except a coldness where the bonds, literal and figurative, held my wrists.

He knew me so well and could tell something was wrong, but he only worked me harder. When his mouth failed to get me off, he slid his cock over my raw skin.

My breath caught when he spread my legs wide to stroke my clit with the head of his hard member. And then slowly, slowly, he filled me.

I tensed against the invasion. This wasn't how I wanted him.

"Let me in, Catherine," he demanded.

"You let me in, William."

He made no reply, and I didn't know if he understood or not. I was soaked with arousal, and he thrust inside me, burying himself to the hilt. His hands lifted my hips so I was more exposed as he thrust in and out, his pubic bone grinding against me with his every inward push.

I didn't fight the first stirrings of pleasure, but I didn't welcome them either. He fucked me relentlessly, and still I didn't come. He positioned me roughly, his hands shifting my hips and then raising my legs so my ankles were locked on his shoulders.

The new angle allowed him to penetrate me even deeper. He stretched me, stroking every tight muscle and ridge inside me. He knew the rhythms I responded to, and he moved his hips in motions I couldn't resist. A bead of sweat from his brow dripped on my breast.

"Fuck it," he said, voice hoarse. "Come. Let go and come."

There was no pleasure in his voice and no pleasure in the orgasm that wracked my body. There was only the peak and the fall and then feel of him spilling himself into me.

When it was over, he pulled out and wordlessly untied me. I reached for him, but he was already out of the bed and leaving the room.

TWENTY-SIX

My phone chimed the next morning as I tried to force down a piece of toast. I felt like shit. William hadn't been in bed when I woke up. I'd looked for him throughout the penthouse but came up empty. I'd tried his cell, which went straight to voicemail. I'd even called down to Rajesh and asked him to check if William was in the gym working out. He hadn't been.

Rajesh had told me the doorman had pulled the Range Rover out front for William just before five a.m. I had no idea where he was, and I hated that he'd left without saying goodbye. We'd talked about that once upon a time, but maybe it didn't matter now. Hell, I didn't even know where William had slept last night, and visions of being alone at Casa di Rosabela came flooding back. I hadn't handled being alone, being kept in the dark, very well in Napa in January, and I wasn't doing much better this time around.

It was lonely and scary not knowing where William had gone, given his state of mind. And how could he leave me after what he'd done to me in the middle of the night? Tying me up while I was sleeping? Fucking me senseless, then leaving? Things hadn't been right between us since The Webster, and we were on the verge of spiraling out of control. I could feel it, and I knew he could too. So how could he leave me now?

I grabbed my phone, hoping the chime was William calling me. Only Beckett's phone call would have been more welcome at the moment. I needed my best friend, but I didn't want him to come over if William was going to come home at any minute, so I hadn't called him yet.

The caller ID read *Hutch Morrison.* I leaned a hip against one of the barstools and stared, unseeing, at the stark kitchen. "Hey," I answered, trying my best to sound normal.

"Hey, yourself. How's my favorite girl?" Hutch asked in his familiar drawl.

"Hanging in there. How's my favorite chef?"

"Pretty good. I just finished up a helping of coconut brioche donut holes with Tahitian

Vanilla jam that would make your eyes cross."

"Coconut, huh?" I sipped my coffee, but it tasted particularly bitter this morning and my stomach roiled.

"Not your favorite?"

"If you'd said peaches, I might have swooned."

"You might swoon anyway. There was white chocolate banana bread French toast too. Delicious."

I had to admit, that did sound heavenly. "And did you share this feast with anyone?"

"As a matter of fact, I did."

"Really?" I leaned forward, resting my elbows on the counter. Had Hutch finally broken his celibacy streak? "Tell me everything."

"I shared it with Fiona Joy."

Fiona. The designer who'd asked Hutch to come to Paris to cater her Fashion Week dinner. I knew where this conversation was headed. I still hadn't given Hutch an answer about going with him to photograph his role in the event. I tried to deflect as my stomach tightened.

"Isn't she already in Paris?" With everything that had happened with Elin, I wasn't sure if Fashion Week had started or not. Hell, I didn't even know what day it was.

"She is. We had to have breakfast on different continents. But she was double checking that everything was set for the dinner, and she reassured me that you were welcome to photograph any part of it. She's very much looking forward to meeting you."

Hutch paused, and I knew he was waiting for me to speak. "That's your cue, darlin'."

"I don't know, Hutch. Paris is a big trip." I was stalling and we both knew it. This opportunity had come at the worst possible time. I wanted to be here with William. *But where was William?* On the other hand, I'd agreed to do the cookbook project for Hutch. I signed on for the job—the job of a lifetime—and going to Paris was part of that job. Plus, I did want to go. I'd be crazy not to.

But wasn't my place here with William? He needed me now more than ever, and I needed to be here for him.

I closed my eyes, readying myself to tell Hutch *No*, when the hairs on the back of my neck stood up. I sensed without looking that William was behind me

"I'd like to give you more time," Hutch said, breaking the silence, "but we fly out tomorrow. This is clutch time, Miss Catherine. Are you in or out?"

I turned around and looked at William. His stormy eyes were a brilliant ice blue. On first glance I would have said that he was pissed, but the longer I looked at him the more I realized that his eyes looked vacant and sad.

"I need an hour," I told Hutch. "Please."

On the other end of the line Hutch let out a disappointed breath and I knew I was trying his patience. No matter how much he liked me, this man was my boss and here I was acting like a millennial intern.

"I'll call you back in an hour. That's how much I want you on this trip with me."

I managed a "thanks" before hanging up, never breaking eye contact with William. As I took the phone away from my ear, I prepared myself for the fight of a lifetime with the man I loved.

Except it never came.

"You should go," William said.

I stared at him in disbelief, all the things I was prepared to say to him evaporating out of my head.

"William, I'm not going to Paris with everything that's going on here. I would never…"

But he cut me off. "There's no reason for you to stay. After yesterday, we both know where this is headed."

"What do you mean 'where this is headed'?" My voice was breathy and tight, belying the panic that was about to overtake me. *William wanted me to go.*

He lifted his hand and absently ran it through his hair. "My father, Catherine. You saw it for yourself, you heard Charles tell me what type of man he was. And look what he attracted. Even from the grave his mistakes have ruined my life and they've almost ruined yours. That's my family's legacy. I will ruin your life. I want you to leave."

"No."

"Catherine…"

"No," I said again, cutting him off. "I won't leave you now."

"I'm telling you to go. We shouldn't be together. Go to Paris. Stay away from me."

Suddenly the room felt too warm. A wave of dizziness washed over me as the acid started to rise in the back of my throat. William's words were like a punch to the gut from a prize fighter, and I felt physically ill. This was the man who'd told me that I was his and that he never wanted to lose me. Yet here he was pushing me away and shattering me into a million pieces in the process.

"William." His name was barely louder than a whisper when I said it, tears clouding my vision. "You said we would get past this."

"That was before I knew what being with me would mean for you." His voice was flat and dull and emotionless. A shiver ran through me, and the tips of my fingers started to tingle. I couldn't believe this was happening. I was the one who ran away when things got bad. I never expected to be the one who was told to leave.

"I thought you were going to protect me," I pleaded.

"This is me protecting you." His resigned response was almost cruel because it was so totally and utterly wrong.

"I thought you loved me…" My voice trailed off. I looked at him then, willing the tears not to spill down my cheeks. *Please, please, please*, I begged silently. *Don't do this.*

I waited for him to say something, but he didn't. He wouldn't meet my eyes, and I watched as his head bowed forward as if he was in deep thought or simply defeated. I didn't know which, but the silence that loomed between us was heavy and ugly and awful. He loved me. I wasn't wrong about that. But what more could I do to convince him to stop shutting me out, to let me in?

And then suddenly the answer presented itself as clear as the light of day: *nothing*. If after everything we'd been through William didn't love me enough to open himself up to me, there was nothing I could do. He'd asked, no, *demanded*, that I trust him until finally, I did. I trusted him implicitly and I'd opened myself to him completely because I loved him. And I loved him now with every fiber of my being. He knew the worst about me—about Jace and the accident and maybe even about Jeremy—but he'd told me none of it mattered because he loved me and I'd believed him. That he wouldn't open himself up to me in the same way was devastating. If right now he didn't trust me to love him no matter what, he never would. And nothing else really mattered.

"You should pack," he finally managed to say.

"Fine," I choked.

I moved past him, heading into the bedroom to start. There was no way I'd actually be able to choose anything appropriate for Paris, but I didn't know what else to do. My head spun, and my cheeks were wet with tears. I pulled my suitcase out of the cubby in the closet where I'd stowed it. I grabbed a handful of clothes and threw them in. Shoes followed next, then underwear and toiletries. I had no idea what I packed, and I didn't care. I spied the framed picture of Jace and me in Hawaii that I'd brought to William's from my condo. I'd never felt comfortable displaying it, so I'd kept nestled among my folded sweaters. I tossed it into my bag.

Laird had followed me into the closet, concern in his doggy eyes. He never liked suitcases because it meant either he or I were going. *Oh fuck, what was I going to do about Laird?* I gave him a hug. He'd be okay here for now. Asa and Anthony would look after him for me. I'd have to figure out the rest when I got back.

I stood up too fast and another wave of dizziness hit me, making my stomach churn and rise. Beads of sweat broke out on my forehead, and I had to lean against the wall and close my eyes until the room stopped spinning.

I headed to the darkroom next. Beckett had my cameras and most of my location stuff since I'd left it all at the studio for the WML Champagne shoot, but there was still some equipment here I'd need in Paris. William's thoughtful hand was all over this room, and my tears started in earnest as I looked at the beautiful space he'd made for me. I quickly shoved what I thought I needed into various bags and got out of there as quickly as possible.

Finally, I emerged with two overstuffed camera bags on one shoulder, my laptop bag and my purse on the other, and my suitcase rolling behind me, ready to leave. William stood in the living room, my surfer photograph above the fireplace staring down at us, looking so wild and out of place in the stark room. William had tried to act like the Cat Ryder photograph fit right in with his museum-quality collection of modern art gracing the walls throughout the penthouse. But it never had. Just like I had never really fit right into his life. Believing it to be true didn't mean it was true, as much as we both might have wished it did.

William watched me with cold eyes and made no move to stop me. I couldn't believe this was happening. The man I loved wasn't just letting me go without a fight—he was pushing me out the door, all because he was convinced I couldn't handle being a part of his life. My heart broke into a million pieces, and I was so fucking mad that he was being such a complete idiot.

I tried to walk past him, but the pull was too strong. When my arm brushed his, the spark was palpable, like I'd been stung.

"Why are you doing this?" My voice cracked as I spoke. I was still standing next to him, our arms still touching. "I can't believe you're telling me to go." I hiccupped, unable to hold my tears back any longer. I turned my head to look at him, but he stood staring straight ahead, the windows behind him showcasing the falling spring snow.

I set down my bags and let go of my suitcase and stepped in front of him. "Look at me, God damn it."

He dropped his chin and our eyes met.

"If you can't see that I love you, that I want to be with you and a part of your life, that I don't care about what your father did or Elin Erickson or all of your money, then I don't know how to change your mind. I love you, William. I really fucking love you. Why isn't that enough?"

In my desperation to get across to him, I did the only thing I could think of: I kissed him. My trembling lips found his, but he stayed perfectly still and didn't respond. He didn't kiss me back or reach for me. And that was all the answer I needed.

I lost it then, the pain coursing through me like a virus. "It's all been a big fucking lie, hasn't it?" I sobbed up at him. "You said you'd never hurt me and now you're tearing me apart. You're killing me," I wailed. "Why are you doing this?"

No response.

I backed away and wiped at my eyes and my running nose with my sleeve and tried to regain a shred of my composure. I look a deep breath. "I was ready to be with you no matter what, William. But if you can't see that, if we're over because you can't let me into your life, then that decision is yours."

I gathered up my bags and my suitcase and managed to walk down the hall without looking back, but I knew my trembling legs betrayed my resolve. I kept hoping William would stop me.

He didn't.

I stepped into the elevator, dropped my stuff, turned, and hit the button for the lobby. I looked up to see William, framed by the huge windows of his penthouse. His head was down again. Then he looked up and my breath caught. His inky dark hair was wildly disheveled and there was so much anguish in the stormy eyes I had grown to love. I wanted, desperately, to run to him, but before I could, the doors closed on my last look of him.

*****

No one waited for me when I stepped into the lobby. For the first time in weeks, I was free to come and go without a shadow. It was strange and exhilarating all at the same time.

I reassembled my bags and started to pull my suitcase across the wide expanse of polished marble floor when yet another wave of dizziness hit me along with a powerful surge of nausea. "Oh no," I muttered. I dropped everything with a loud clatter and ran toward an elegant silver wastebasket near a couch in the sitting area, into which I very inelegantly threw up.

I retched a few times, hating that it was happening but completely powerless to make it stop. My throat burned and my eyes watered. Finally, when the contents of my stomach were all out of me, I lowered the wastebasket, ready to find a place where I could dispose of the mess. I was met with a sympathetic look from Rajesh, the building concierge, who was standing just a few feet from me. At that moment, I just wanted to curl up in a ball and disappear.

"Miss Catherine, please come and sit down and let me bring you some water. I'll call up to Mr. Lambourne right away. I'm sorry you're not feeling well."

"Don't do that," I replied.

"But, Miss Catherine, you're not well. Surely Mr. Lambourne should…"

"I'm fine, Rajesh. Thank you. And I'm really sorry about this." I held up the soiled wastebasket. "Just a little upset stomach." I wiped my mouth and my sweaty forehead with the back of my hand. This was so not my finest hour, and I was pretty certain I looked positively green. "I'm on my way out, actually." I looked over at my pile of assorted bags lying in the middle of the lobby. "Could you call me a cab?"

Outside the entrance to William's building, the cool air washed over me as I waited for my taxi. I took another sip from the bottle of water Rajesh insisted I take, the cold liquid doing little to soothe my raw throat. I pulled my phone out of my coat pocked, dialed, then pressed it to my ear.

"I'm in," I said quietly.

"What was that? It sounded like you said, *I'm in*." Hutch answered on the other end.

"I did. I'm going to Paris with you."

He let out a whoop. "If I'm dreaming, don't wake me up. I'll have my people email you all the information. You won't regret this, Catherine."

I sincerely hoped I wouldn't, because it felt like I already did.

My next call was to Beckett. I'd need a place to crash for the night.

TWENTY-SEVEN

I managed to keep it together on the cab ride to Beckett's apartment. Rajesh hadn't said much as he'd loaded my bags into the taxi. He hadn't accepted the tip I'd offered to him, either. Talk about wearing your heart on your sleeve. Besides unceremoniously puking in a garbage can in the middle of the elegant lobby, I was sure I had "Just Dumped" splayed across my face too. I wonder what gave it away—my bloodshot, swollen eyes or my tear-streaked, blotchy face?

Rajesh hadn't mentioned calling William again, so he clearly had an idea that something was up. I'd gotten into the cab and he'd offered me a sympathetic look as he'd closed the rear door.

"Goodbye, Miss Catherine. I hope you feel better soon. And I hope I'll see you again." He must have known I might be leaving William for good. Then he'd given the cab two pats on the roof and the driver had pulled away. I'd watched out the window as William's tall, stately building, the place I'd come to think of as home for a short time, faded into the distance and became just another tower in downtown Chicago's forest of skyscrapers.

I let myself into Beckett's apartment with the spare key he'd given me for emergencies. If being kicked to the curb by your boyfriend wasn't an emergency, I didn't know what was. Beckett had been at Patisserie LeClerc when I'd called and couldn't get away. I'd told him I was fine and not to hurry home. I'd already taken him away from work yesterday for the photo shoot.

God, yesterday. How could so much change in one day? Yesterday I'd been William's girlfriend, today I was…I didn't know anymore. The knife in my heart twisted yet again.

Beckett's apartment was quiet and empty. I dropped my bags in the living room, grabbed a cold bottle of water from the fridge, and slid down to the kitchen floor before allowing the great wracking sobs that I'd been holding in to escape.

I would have been mortified if anyone had been there to see me cry like that. But I was alone, so I didn't hold back. I didn't know what hurt more, the fact that William and I were over or that he'd let me walk out of his life without a fight. Our relationship played out like a movie in my head, a highlight reel of mind-blowing kisses, intense intimacy, and soaring love juxtaposed with feelings of isolation, the fear that I had never truly known him, and the gnawing thought that no matter how much I tried, I wasn't enough for him, that I was somehow too damaged from losing Jace and all that had followed, that I would never be whole for him.

I don't know how long I stayed like that, a pathetic lump on Beckett's floor. Maybe an hour, maybe four. It had turned dark outside, but that wasn't much to go by since it was Chicago in March. My ass was sore and cold, and I felt stiff when I heard Beckett's key turn in the lock. I also had a killer headache—partly from dehydration and partly the result of more missed meals over the last few days than I could remember. I hoped Beckett had brought carbs, as I needed a truly grand break-up cocktail of junk food.

Beckett found me in the kitchen, sank down beside me, and hugged me. I started crying again. Crying wasn't really the right word. More like moaning in agony and sobbing at the same time. I hurt everywhere.

"Oh, Cat." He stroked my hair and pulled me close. "I'm so sorry." When my bawling had faded to whimpering with hiccups, he notched my chin up. "Is it really over?"

I nodded.

"What happened?"

"He told me to leave. He pushed me away, just like he always does." I told Beckett then about everything since I'd left him at the photo shoot, ending with how William decided to let his past destroy our future, how he had chosen his grief over me. "He thinks his father's mistakes have ruined his life and that he'll ruin mine, that it would be better if I stayed away from him."

"Oh, Cat, that doesn't make any sense at all. He loves you, I know he does."

"I know," I sniveled in response as I looked at Beckett with my watery eyes.

"It's so fucked up, Cat. I'm so sorry."

"It is. I always thought *my* shit would ruin us, you know? Everything with Jace and the accident and then with Jeremy." I swallowed hard and wiped my eyes again. "Then I thought maybe we'd be okay. Remember our fight? You were right. Once I finally accepted I could be happy again, I really believed I'd found true love. I found him. We found each other. God, I love him, Beckett. What am I going to do?" More great, wracking sobs erupted from me.

"I know, baby, I know," Beckett soothed me as he stroked my back.

"He told me once that he knew everything he needed to know about me the moment we bumped into each other outside of Willowgrass. All the stuff I tortured myself about for so long really didn't fucking matter to him, even after that stupid video at The Webster." I paused to catch my breath amidst more sobs.

"He said he loved me anyway. He told me he knew what it was like to feel guilty for surviving too. But now," my tears were flowing steadily. "Now, it's like this twisted resignation that he can't be happy and he'll ruin anything he touches. How could he send me away, Beckett? I don't even know if he ever really loved me. Maybe he didn't."

Just saying that aloud was like stabbing myself in the heart. It was too painful to think that everything William and I had shared since we met wasn't what I thought it had been.

"I told him I would stay," I finished lamely. "I don't really care about Paris and I would have stayed here in a heartbeat if he had asked me to, but instead he told me to go. For good."

There were more tears as I recalled how cold William had been toward me earlier. When I looked up, though, I saw that I wasn't the only one crying.

I was so lost in my rambling, I hadn't realized that Beckett was shaking beside me. I drew back and stared at his hunched shoulders, his face in his hands.

"Oh my God. Beckett!" I grabbed his wrists. "Shit. What's wrong?"

"I'm sorry," he said, his voice thick with emotion. "This isn't about me."

And then it hit me. I was unloading everything about my break-up with William, and my best friend was sobbing along with me, but definitely not because *my* heart was broken. Because *his* was. I'd known for weeks that there was something else going on with Beckett, and I'd run right over his break-up with my own. I had never heard the truth about what had happened between him and Alec, but now I needed to know.

I drew his hands away from his face and met his gaze. "Beckett, please tell me what's wrong. Please tell me. It's about what happened with Alec, isn't it? Just tell me.

He shook his head. "No. This is about you."

"You've been pretending you're fine since Valentine's Day. You're not fine. I know you're not. Please talk to me."

Now Beckett was the one trying to speak between sobs. "I tried to be fine. I tried to work so much so I wouldn't think about him and wouldn't miss him."

"Why didn't you tell me?"

"Because you had William, and I wanted to believe that there was a relationship in this world that could work out. I wanted you to be happy."

"And I want you to be happy. I thought you were with Alec. I saw the way you looked at him at the launch party."

He gave me a sad look and blew out a breath in defeat. "Remember I told you Alec said he had something special planned for Valentine's Day?"

"Yes."

"I got to his place, and he had everything set up. Flowers, chocolate, champagne, a gorgeous meal. It was amazing, Cat. No one has ever done anything like that for me. We ate, we talked, and over dessert he proposed a toast. And that's when he said it." His voice broke and he buried his face again.

I waited for Beckett to elaborate.

"Said what?" I finally prompted.

"'I love you.'" He glared at me with red-rimmed eyes. "He fucking told me he loved me, and I couldn't say it back."

"Oh, no." My heart sank. *Poor Beckett*. Alec had been ready for the next step, and Beckett hadn't. I knew my best friend. He was generous and affectionate and open, but he did not give his love easily.

"Oh, yes."

"And that was a deal-breaker for him?" I asked gently.

"I told him I cared about him. I told him I wasn't sure if I loved him, but he said if I didn't know then, that was all the answer he needed."

"Oh fuck, Beckett." I hugged him, squeezing him tight. "I'm so sorry."

"He wasn't even angry, Cat." He buried his face against my shoulder. "It was like he knew I wouldn't be able to say it. He said he wanted to stay friends. But how the fuck do you stay friends with someone you care about like that? Am I just supposed to forget my feelings for him when I bump into him on the street?"

I pulled back. "So you do love him?"

"Of course I do. I did then too, I just didn't know it."

I held Beckett and he held me and we cried together. For our broken hearts, for our lost loves, for all the heartache and pain and suffering that we were both feeling with the men we loved gone from our lives.

We stayed on the floor for a long time. Long enough that I felt like I didn't have any more tears left. Then we ordered Chinese food and ate the cupcakes Beckett had brought home from the bakery. And when that was done, we raided his freezer for ice cream.

We'd moved from the less-than-comfortable kitchen floor to the sofa, we'd changed into lounge-appropriate clothes, and Beckett had turned on a cooking show. Cooking shows always made him feel better. He liked to add his own soundtrack, commenting on whatever was happening on screen, rolling his eyes when he thought the chefs were skimping or making some kind of wrong food choice. The show he had on now was, ironically, dessert-themed, and Beckett was dissing the host's choice of crystallized ginger for his cookie recipe when my phone buzzed.

I looked at the screen, hoping it was William, but it was Emmy Schmidt, Hutch's assistant. I answered and she gave me the details about the flight tomorrow. Apparently Fiona Joy was sending a private plane for Hutch and me. For a moment, as Emmy briefed me on departure and flight times, I tried to focus on the positives. I was going to Paris. Tomorrow. Sure, it was the most romantic city in the world, but it also had crepes, and I could drown my sorrow in crepes.

As I hung up, I had a great idea. I grabbed the remote and powered off the TV.

"What the fuck, Cat?" Beckett tossed me an annoyed glare. "He was just getting ready to pull those out of the oven."

"I know what you need to do."

Beckett groaned. "If you say call Alec, I swear to God I'll throw this candle at you." He gestured to one of the decorative candles on the table beside the couch.

"Come to Paris with me."

He frowned, and his fingers paused above the candle. "What?"

"You heard me. Come to Paris with me. You love Paris." I grabbed Beckett's shoulders and pulled him up. "Beckett, you *need* Paris. You've been working like a maniac. You need a break. You need distance. We both need distance. Paris is distance. And it has crepes."

"Um, hello, Cat? Restaurant opening? There's a reason I'm working so hard." He removed my hands from his shoulders slowly, as though he were dealing with a lunatic.

"That's the beauty of a trip to Paris. It's work. And there's crepes!"

He started to protest but then closed his mouth and tried not to smile.

I pointed my finger at him. "Got you."

Beckett started to grin, then shook his head. "No. I can't leave now."

"Why not? You have good people working for you, and LeClerc's flagship restaurant is in Paris. He'll understand a quick trip for inspiration. It's only for a few days. I'm surprised he hasn't suggested it. I mean, think about all the baked goods you can sample in Paris. You can…" I stumbled, but recovered quickly. "You can see what the locals are eating, what's trending, and make your bakery even more cutting edge."

Beckett rolled his eyes and smiled. "Oh, you're good, Cat. Very good."

I grabbed his hands in mine. "Beckett, in all seriousness, you need a couple of days away. The break-up with Alec, the opening—everything has been crazy. This trip will be so good for you. You can get your head on straight. We need each other right now. And we can eat crepes."

"Enough with the crepes, seriously. Gaining crepe weight is not the way I want to get over Alec."

I held my phone aloft. "Say the word, and I text Hutch to tell him you'll be joining us."

"A trip to Paris with Hutch Morrison?" Beckett clutched his heart. "You're killing me."

"So the answer is yes?"

He closed his eyes tightly. "Paris. In springtime. Hutch Morrison. Crepes. And Fiona fucking Joy. *Yes*," he squeaked.

I fired off a text to Hutch.

"How much do I owe the man for the ticket?" Beckett asked.

"Nothing." I replied.

"Cat, I know Morrison Hotel has taken off, but I'm not letting Hutch pay my way to Paris."

"He's not paying your way. He's not paying anyone's way. Fiona Joy is picking us up in her private jet."

"What?" Beckett's expression of surprise was priceless. "A private plane?"

I nodded.

"I love your job. I can't believe I'm going to be on a private plane with Hutch Morrison for eight hours. Do you think I'll be able to get him to spill all his culinary secrets?"

"I don't know. Depends how liquored up he is on the flight."

"We should celebrate with more cupcakes," Beckett said as he reached for another one of his creations.

"Ugh. I can't. I'm stuffed. Too much stress eating."

"Hey, you have every right. Your life has been a shit show lately, Cat."

I gave him a look.

"What? It has. I'd be reaching for the carbs too."

"It's not just the carbs. I feel like I've had PMS for weeks."

I settled back on the couch, looked around for the remote, and found it under a throw pillow. But before I could turn the TV back on, Beckett grabbed the remote out of my hand.

"What?" I asked.

"Did you just say what I think you said?"

"I don't know. What do you think I said?"

"You've had PMS for weeks."

"Oh." I waved a hand dismissively. "I'm a little off, that's all. You said it yourself, I've been living in a shit show."

Beckett's eyes went wide. "Are you fucking kidding me?"

"About what?"

"Oh my God, Cat. Now it all makes sense."

"What makes sense?"

"The extra pounds—"

"Hey!"

"Your boobs are bigger too."

"Next you're going to say I'm glowing. I'm not pregnant, Beckett."

"So you admit it's crossed your mind?" He looked at me expectantly.

Seriously, this was getting out of hand. "I have an IUD. There's like a one percent chance I can get pregnant."

"*You looked it up?* Come on, Cat. That means you think it's possible."

Now that Beckett was really hung up on this, I didn't know what to think. It would be the cruelest of cruel jokes if I was in that one percent. For a split second I wondered how it would go over with William. A family with me clearly hadn't ever been part of his plan. I remembered how he had reacted to Lauren's pregnancy—his aversion to children had been plain as day. We'd never even had a chance to talk about a future together or what we both wanted, thanks to the extortion attempts, Elin's crazy threats, and William's commitment to being cryptic and keeping secrets. And just like that, I was hit with another wave of sadness and was on verge of tears again. I had to stop thinking about him.

"It's not possible. Stop it, alright? This isn't funny anymore."

"Cat, have you taken a pregnancy test?" Beckett asked earnestly.

"No. I've just been eating too much." I gestured to the cupcake wrappers on the coffee table. "See? Oh, and thanks for calling me fat." I plopped back on the couch, arms crossed over my evidently expanding middle.

He moved closer to me. "You're not fat. I told you before, it looks good on you. But tomorrow, before we leave for Paris, we're getting you a pregnancy test. I'm serious, Cat. You need to know."

"Um, yeah, whatever, Beckett." I hoped my response sounded convincing, especially since Beckett's arguments managed to plant a huge seed of doubt in my mind. "I'm not pregnant."

"Fine. If you're so sure, then take the test."

"Fine!"

But I wasn't sure. I wasn't sure of anything.

Twenty-Eight

I didn't take the test the next morning. Beckett and I slept in and then spent a few hours packing and getting ready. Rushing around was a relief, actually, since it didn't give me much time to dwell on William and our break-up. We had to scramble to make it to the airport on time. Not that the plane would leave without us, but I didn't want to keep Hutch waiting.

I had scrutinized the clothes I'd managed to grab from William's penthouse and was pleasantly surprised to see that even in my haste, I had selected some perfect items for the role I'd be playing in Paris. Lots of black. A few pairs of darkwash skinny jeans. I would be able to blend in with the background and take pictures, no problem. If by some miracle I was invited to any swanky parties, well then, I guess I'd have to go shopping…in Paris. I was pretty sure I could make room on my credit cards for that.

Beckett had more trouble, asking me, of all people, to help him decide between shirts and accessories. Finally, we hopped in a cab and were at O'Hare in less than an hour. When the cab pulled into the same section of the airport that housed William's plane— where we'd met to depart for Napa—my breath caught and I had to bite back tears. The plane waiting for us looked similar to William's jet, and I reminded myself that he wouldn't be waiting for me inside. *Wouldn't he?*

I closed my eyes and let the fantasy play out: me getting out of the cab, and William meeting me in the plane, taking me into his arms, and telling me how sorry he was.

"Cash or credit?" The cabbie's question bounced me out of my thoughts, and I lost it. Tears rolled down my cheeks, and I reached up to wipe at my eyes clumsily. There would be no William, no apologies. I couldn't believe that part of my life was over and the shock of it was almost too painful to bear. Beckett looked over at me, grabbed my hand, and squeezed.

"Credit," he said, sliding his card through the machine attached to the cab's Plexiglas divider. "Here," he said, handing me a pair of oversized sunglasses. "These will make you look *très* mysterious."

I managed a shaky smile and put the glasses on. I didn't need them on this grey day, but they would hide my red-rimmed eyes and for that I was thankful.

We had arrived so close to our five pm scheduled take-off that we didn't have time for small talk. Hutch and Emmy greeted us both and almost immediately the pilot asked us to take our seats. I took out my phone, thinking that I should text William to let him know I was OK, but stopped. He hadn't been in touch. Nothing made our break-up feel more final than that. All the times that we had ever fought, he'd always checked up on me. The messaging folder on my phone was empty. There was nothing from William. I sighed, set the phone to airplane mode, and buckled my seat belt. The four of us settled in, and in no time we were up in the air.

As soon as we were given the all clear to move around the cabin, I grabbed my purse and headed for the bathroom. I looked awful, puffy and blotchy, but I did my best to downplay my sadness with concealer and lip balm. I didn't dare reach for my MAC mascara. Waterproof or not, I couldn't risk raccoon eyes. When I came out, Hutch asked that I join him and Emmy at the larger table to go over the schedule. This was good. I could sink my teeth into work and keep from thinking about William, about the last time I was on a private jet.

Emmy had a folder for me and Hutch quickly went over the game plan for when we landed. We'd check in to the hotel and have some time to freshen up, then Hutch and I would head over to the venue where Fiona's dinner would be held, to check it out and go through a test run, which Hutch wanted me to photograph. I'd need the time to scope out the room and figure out the lighting and what equipment I'd need for the actual event. Hutch had the dishes all planned, and I recognized a few from his *Sticky Fingers* menu. At Hutch's instruction, Fiona had staffed the kitchen. The prep work was already underway, but it was going to require Hutch's direct supervision as soon as possible. This was going to be a major and intense undertaking and I needed to get on my game as soon as possible.

When our meeting wrapped up, Hutch called Beckett over and suggested we eat.

"It won't be my best work since I made it a few hours ago, but I thought we'd do something French in anticipation of our adventure," he said.

Emmy got up and came back with wine glasses and a bottle of wine.

"Voila!" Hutch said in his accented French. He presented us a plate full of bread and cheese and fruit and cured meats. There were pastries too, some of which I immediately recognized as *pain au chocolat*.

Keep it together, Cat. No one needs you crying over chocolate croissants.

"I hope the sweets meet your very high standards, Beckett," Hutch said, glancing at Beckett and throwing him one of his signature smiles.

"I'm sure you did fine," Beckett joked, taking a big piece of *jambon* and a few grapes.

"And for you, Miss Catherine" Hutch asked, noticing that I wasn't reaching for anything.

"Um, sorry." I looked back at the plate, knowing I should eat but feeling completely uninspired to do so. I didn't feel hungry. I didn't feel anything. "I just need water for now, thanks." And with that I stood and headed back to my seat. I was being rude, but better that then breaking down in front of Hutch and Emmy.

Before I could get back to staring out the window, however, Hutch was beside me. He sat in the recliner-esque chair next to mine and swiveled to face me. "Want to talk about it?"

"Not particularly." I took a beat. Hutch was just trying to be nice and here I was being bitchy. "I'm sorry about sneaking away, but my mind is elsewhere," I said lamely.

"I just wanted to make sure everything was all right."

"Fine. I'm absolutely fine."

"You suck at lying, sweetheart."

"And you're a good friend. But right now I want to focus on work."

"Okay," Hutch said. "I'll leave you alone. I hear there's a bedroom in the back somewhere if you need to lie down."

I winced when he mentioned the plane's bedroom. Images of William sleeping in his black T-shirt and boxer briefs on our way to Napa flooded my mind. He had been my perfect fallen angel then, a man I couldn't resist and could never get enough of. What the fuck was I going to do without him now?

I dropped my head and shook it, unable to look at Hutch. I didn't want him to see my tears, which I wasn't sure I could stop. Hutch might have been more like a friend, but I was still on this trip for work and I needed to pull myself together. He was counting on me and I didn't want to let him down.

"Catherine, you're not okay. I can see that," Hutch said softly. "I don't know what happened, but I assume Lambourne has everything to do with it. I'm here if you want to talk about it."

"Thanks, I'll be fine. I just need some sleep."

"Why don't you get some then? I'll leave you to it. Can I bring you an aspirin or something?"

"No, I'll be fine."

"Okay, then." Hutch stood up and walked back to the main table.

An aspirin. If it were only that simple. I wished there was a pill to silence my broken heart. The painful ache was deep and without any single point of origin. It was like my whole body felt William's absence, while my every breath, my every thought was about him. I missed him, but I had to remind myself that we were over. He had told me to leave. The last few weeks meant nothing.

But even as I thought this, I knew it wasn't true. William had awakened a part of me I'd thought I'd lost and for that I would always love him—even if he couldn't love me back. I took a quick look around the cabin to make sure no one was paying attention to me. Beckett seemed to be dozing in his seat and Hutch and Emmy were each glued to their tablets. So no one saw me slip on my sunglasses and no one noticed my tears.

*****

Even on a private plane, the flight was long, and I was glad to finally land and walk on solid ground again. I'd managed to get a little bit of sleep, but not nearly enough. Plus, I had that overly tired, dehydrated, sick feeling that was only going to be cured by a full meal, about a gallon of water, and maybe fifteen straight hours of sleep. None of those things were likely to happen over the next few days, so I decided I needed to suck it up and make sure I had a steady stream of *café au lait* to keep me going.

I'd traveled extensively with Jace, and I'd been in the Paris airport for layovers a few times, but I'd never actually been in the city of Paris. It didn't have a beach or surfing, so there was never a reason for Jace and me to spend any time there. I was looking forward to exploring the City of Lights with Beckett now.

The hour was still early in Paris, before nine, but the streets were full of people. Like any tourist, I gaped as the limo holding Beckett, Hutch, Emmy, and I sped through the narrow streets. It was almost surreal to see the Eiffel Tower in the distance and to pass by the Arc de Triomphe. These were iconic monuments I'd only ever seen in pictures.

Fiona Joy had booked us at the Hôtel Plaza Athénée. It was ridiculously grand and across the Seine from the Eiffel Tower. I've never seen so much gilt and marble. It was classy and classic and totally Parisian. I immediately wished I could share it with William and then had to push that thought aside.

While Hutch checked us in, I stared at the sparkling chandelier above us and the exquisitely dressed women and men passing beside us. I'd worn a black long-sleeve cashmere sweater, dark jeans, black ankle boots and a grey coat, but I felt so frumpy next to the true Parisians. Beckett was staring too, and at one point our eyes met and he mouthed, "Oh my God!" and I smiled. I was so glad he was here with me.

"Voila." Hutch handed me a room key. "Are you and Beckett okay sharing a room? They're booked, but I can try arguing."

"Not a problem, we've done it before." Beckett and I had slept in the same bed a million times, and we were happy to do it again in Paris.

Hutch led the way to a bank of elevators.

"How long do I have?" I asked Hutch.

"Rest, freshen up, then let's meet me in the lobby at noon. The line cooks Fiona booked are prepping at the venue already, so I need to get there and get started on a few dishes."

"Sounds good." It actually sounded exhausting, but I wasn't about to complain. I was here to work.

Hutch's room was across from ours, and he disappeared into his door just as Beckett opened ours. The suite was amazing. Marble floors gave way to walls adorned with gold accents, floor-to-ceiling windows lined one wall, and outside there was a cute little balcony. The main room held a plush white couch, two deep red *chaise longues*, and a carved wooden table. Beckett went immediately to the windows and squealed with excitement. The view of the city was unbelievable. We could see the Eiffel Tower, the Seine, and roofs with classic Parisian chimneys. It was breathtaking.

Another door opened into the bedroom, which housed a large four-poster bed awash with pillows. The headboard was stately and covered with a beautiful gold material. A final door led into a bathroom that contained the most glorious tub I had ever seen. It was an oval soaking tub with intricate tile designs climbing up its sides. The whole thing was regal and over the top. I loved everything about it.

"That's it. I'm moving to Paris," Beckett called from the bedroom.

I was content to take in the view from the living area, and Beckett peered around the door. "I'm going to change and head out to some of the bakeries. Morning really is the best time."

"Have fun," I said, finally prying my attention from our amazing view.

"I will. Would you like me to…ahem, pick anything up for you while I'm out?" He raised his brows.

I knew what he was alluding to: a test. I closed my eyes. "No. Let me get through tonight, and I'll worry about that after."

"Fine. But you're going to have to face it at some point."

"Trust me, there's nothing to face. But yes. I'll take the test and prove to you that we're both worried for nothing."

"Who's worried? I can't wait to be Uncle Beckett."

I would have thrown something at him if I'd had anything in my hand. Instead, he retreated into the bedroom, then out the door. I enjoyed the view, then decided to try the bathtub.

A few hours later, Hutch stood in the lobby managing to fit right in without trying at all. He'd dressed in distressed jeans, his trademark Chuck Taylors, a fitted T-shirt, and the motorcycle jacket he'd worn at The Webster. He gave me an appreciative wink. "Very chic."

"*Merci.*" I'd chosen a pair of skinny jeans, a silky, long-sleeve, dark grey T-shirt, and my own black leather motorcycle jacket. I was going to be working, after all, and needed to be able to bend down and move around comfortably. But I was in Paris and this was Fashion Week, so instead of boots, I wore the black Louboutins William had given me for our first date. I'd put my hair up in an artfully messy bun, and applied red matte lipstick. I had my overstuffed camera bag slung over my shoulder.

I was as ready as I'd ever be for my first Parisian photo shoot.

*****

The venue was absolutely stunning. Fiona Joy had booked the atrium rooftop garden of an old bank building. Fiona didn't meet us—I'm sure she had way too much to do getting ready for her show—so one of her assistants showed Hutch and me around. I couldn't help but snap picture after picture of everything from the lush green plants and the colorful flowers to the old iron struts of the atrium's curved glass roof. Behind us, the Eiffel Tower made the perfect backdrop. Tomorrow the room would be filled with white tablecloth–covered tables and lit by twinkling lights when dusk fell. Paris at night—it was going be magical.

I spent the next several hours shooting Hutch at work. The kitchen had been installed on a lower floor, and it was an interesting contrast, old world rustic with top-of-the-line appliances. I knew the way he worked now and could anticipate his movements. It made my job easier, but it also allowed me to be on auto-pilot and stop thinking.

About William.

The time passed quickly and soon enough a line cook swept in and told me the test run had been a success and Hutch was ready to call it a night. I would have paid to listen to him say this in his gorgeous accent over and over again.

As the chaos of the make-shift kitchen started to wind down, I packed up all my gear. I decided to leave my light kit since I'd need it tomorrow and there was no reason to lug it back to the hotel. Hutch walked in just as I was zipping the top of my camera bag. "I have everything I need here." I tapped my camera. "I'm going to head back." I was ready to resume my wallowing.

"You can't run off just yet, darlin'. Someone's gotta help me polish off the test dinner and you look like you could use a good meal about now."

"I look that bad, huh?" I responded.

"You never look bad. I just like it better when you smile."

I quickly changed the subject. "So, are you ready for tomorrow? It's a great space. It's going to photograph beautifully."

"Ah, deflection," Hutch retorted. "I see what you're trying to do. Come on." He waved me to follow him as he started toward the old-fashioned elevator with the manual gate that went up to the rooftop atrium.

I hadn't eaten much all day and, though I wasn't usually one for late-night dining, I was operating on fumes and my body was still on Chicago time. Plus, maybe talking to Hutch wouldn't be so bad. I made a promise to myself not to cry, then said, "Alright, I'll eat."

Hutch and I made our way up to the top floor and sat at a round table in the center of the atrium. It was surreal that we were in a tropical garden on a Paris rooftop on a Wednesday night, sipping wine while the Eiffel Tower's lights sparkled in the distance.

"I'm glad you decided to come, Catherine," Hutch said before he took a bite from a plate holding his signature Flattened Pork Chop with collard greens and caramelized miso butter. I was working on a healthy serving of Hutch's Jambalaya with smoked Tasso, which was hearty and filling and exactly what I needed at the moment.

"I am too. Thanks for asking me. This is really an incredible opportunity and I can't tell you how much I appreciate it. I promise I won't let you down."

"You won't. You might not realize it, but you're the best, Kitty Cat. No one else can make food look sexy the way you can. It's a gift. One of your many that I appreciate."

I laughed, and my cheeks heated at Hutch's flirtiness. It was the first time I'd laughed in days and it felt good.

"There's that smile I've been missin'. I hope you enjoy your time here and that whatever happened between you and Lambourne doesn't overshadow how fucking awesome Paris is. It is awesome, isn't it?" Hutch tipped his head back and looked up at the glass ceiling of the atrium, taking in the stars that twinkled in the clear skies above the City of Lights. I had to agree: Paris was fucking awesome.

"About that. I really don't want to talk about William. Please don't ask me to."

"Fair enough," Hutch responded. "But that does mean the Smiths are off limits too?"

I almost gagged on my fork. I saw where this was going. I hadn't forgotten how Hutch and Zoe had ogled each other at The Webster. I don't know what he saw in her, but anything was better than talking about William right now. "What do you want to know?" I replied.

Hutch looked at me, his eyes sparkling with amusement, and laughed. "I want to know everything."

*****

I felt like walking. Our cab ride from the hotel to the bank building this afternoon had been quick, so I knew I was close. I asked one of the line cooks, who spoke perfect English, for directions and then started on my way. I texted Beckett. Luckily our plans had international coverage.

Stuffed and exhausted and on my way back. You?

Same. See you soon for night cap?

;)

The night was cool, and I had no idea where I was, but I wasn't afraid. It felt good to wander and to be alone with my thoughts. Though it was dark, I was obviously in a chic part of Paris, so I wasn't worried. As I walked along the narrow, winding streets and looked into the shop windows I passed, it hit me that I was alone. *Alone* alone. I'd had a bodyguard for weeks, and I missed Asa's quiet, reassuring presence.

I paused in front of *pharmacie* with a green cross illuminated near its front entrance. I looked down at my watch and it was after ten pm, so I kept walking. But then I made myself go back. Part of me hoped it was closed, but I wasn't that lucky. It was open. *Fine, Universe.*

I strolled through the aisles, perusing the shelves filled with products that looked vaguely familiar. I hadn't put my college French to use for a long time but apparently ibuprofen was the same in every language. But I wasn't looking for the Advil

I must have looked lost because the pharmacist came out from behind a counter and said something, presumably asking me what I was looking for. After some broken English on the pharmacist's part and a lot of gesturing to my belly on my part, I left with a French home pregnancy test in a white paper bag and excited congratulations from the man who sold it to me.

I wasn't sure I wanted congratulations. But I couldn't put it off any longer. Beckett was right.

I had to know.

TWENTY-NINE

I took my time heading back to the hotel. I walked along the Seine for a few blocks, watching barges glide silently along the dark, still water. I loved all the bridges, and when I walked beneath the Pont des Arts, the one with the padlocks cramming every inch of the railings, I sat on a nearby bench for a while and watched as a young couple kissed atop it. When they drew apart, the boy threw something into the Seine—the key to their lock, I guessed, and the gesture a symbol of their love—and the girl looked up at him with a huge smile. Even this late on a midweek night, Paris was overflowing with lovers. I couldn't take it anymore and started to weep.

I was in agony without William. When Jace had died, I had been in agony too, but it was a different kind of pain, one tinged with shock and guilt, with regret, and with finality. Jace was dead, and there was nothing I could do that would change that or bring him back. We'd had no chance to say goodbye, no realization that our 'I love yous' uttered that day would be our last ones, no opportunity to say all the things I wished we could have. It took me a long time to accept all of that, but I had eventually. Jace would never come back to me no matter how much I wished that he would.

But William had had a choice, and the fact that he'd chosen to push me away rather than draw me closer, that he'd had the chance to tell me how he really felt about everything and refused to take it, that he'd withheld his love when he'd promised me his heart, all of those things hurt more than I could have possibly imagined. William hadn't died, but he was lost to me all the same, and it didn't stop me from wishing he would come back to me.

I started walking again, and soon arrived outside my hotel's formidable light stone building with red awnings. I slowly walked through the spectacular lobby, taking in the over-the-top opulence and riots of colors, my heels clicking loudly on the gleaming marble. I took the elevator up to my floor. Taking a deep breath and clutching the *pharmacie* bag tightly in my hand, I pushed the door to the room open.

And dropped the bag.

William stood near the white plush couch, his thumbs looped in the front pockets of his jeans, his leather coat open, facing the door. His eyes immediately met mine, searching my face. He looked like he hadn't shaved for a day or two and his beard was thick and scruffy.

All the breath whooshed out of my body, and I couldn't do anything but stare at him, floored as always by his sheer physical presence.

"Hi," he said.

"Hi," I managed. I pushed the door closed and leaned against it. My heart felt like it was going to jump out of my chest.

"I've surprised you." He gave me a sheepish look I hadn't seen before.

"Yeah, you could say that." I willed myself to take a few deep breaths and calm down. My emotions were so raw, so right at the surface, that I wasn't sure I could hold back a complete and utter breakdown.

I couldn't look directly at him, so I tried to focus on the landscape painting on the wall behind him as I spoke. "What are you doing here? Where's Beckett? I'm supposed to meet him."

He pulled his hands away from his pockets. "I reserved another room for Beckett. I hope you don't mind. I wanted…" He twisted his hands together, a gesture wholly unnatural for him. He looked almost nervous. My head spun, my mind creating a million possibilities for his appearance.

One thought kept repeating itself: *He wants me back.* Did I dare hope for that? The man who cooked for me and made me laugh and knew exactly how to look at me to make my body come alive with desire was *here*, in my hotel room in Paris, and there could only be one reason why. *Right?*

I took another shaky breath.

William down at me, his stormy eyes as troubled as I'd ever seen them. "I came to apologize."

I stared at him now, speechless.

"I was wrong to tell you to go. I was wrong," he swallowed, "I was wrong about so many things. But the one thing I have never been wrong about is you. I love you, beautiful girl. So much."

I didn't even realize I was moving until I was in front of him. "William—"

"No." The look in his eyes was pleading. "Let me say this. Let me finish. I owe it to you."

I nodded. I didn't need to hear it. I loved him too. Nothing he did or could ever do would change that. But William needed to say what he'd come to say.

"I love you, Catherine." We stood facing each other, looking into each other's eyes, not touching.

"I've never felt like this about anyone else. I never *loved* anyone else. Only you. It's been like this from the very beginning and I can't believe I ever lost sight of it, even for a second. All of things I said to you? All of things I promised? I promised you that I'd never leave you, and that I needed to take care of you and you needed to let me. And then I…didn't. I'm so sorry. I know I hurt you. I'm such a fucking idiot."

The anguish he was feeling was so apparent on his face. His eyes were a restless blue, like the sky before a storm.

My first instinct was to reach out to him, to hold him and try to calm the tempest that I could see was raging inside of him. But I didn't. I knew my anguish was apparent on my face too. I stood with my arms folded across my chest and let my tears fall down my cheeks. "You broke my heart, William. When you told me to go…" My voice trailed off.

"I didn't mean it. I don't know what I was thinking. All the shit with the extortion, with Elin and my parents. And Charles. It's such a mess. I thought you'd be better off without me. After everything I put you through, it felt selfish to ask you to stay. But I didn't realize how empty everything would be without you. How empty *I'd* be. I don't care if it's selfish. I need you in my life, Catherine. Please come back to me."

"It's not selfish to let me love you," I whispered.

"Oh, but it is. God damn it, I couldn't protect you. I hate that you were almost hurt because of me. That that crazy bitch wanted to kill you, *because of me*. Of course it's selfish for me to ask you to be with me."

William ran his hands through his thick dark curls, mussing them wildly, a sure sign of his frustration. This big strong man who could take on the world and win was leveled by his loss of me.

"It's all over now. Elin's in jail and all her crazy plotting and threatening and her fucking with us is over. What are you still scared of?" I asked.

His voice was low, holding that same tone of resignation as it had when he'd told me to go. "Of losing you. There will be another one. There always is. That's the price of being with me. I know that, but you need to know it, too."

I gulped. I knew from the start that a relationship with William Maddox Lambourne III would be anything but ordinary. I didn't expect that I'd become the target of a crazy woman during our first few months together, but who could predict these things? All the recent insanity aside, William loved me. That's what I still trusted. And I still trusted him, implicitly. I was willing to take on whatever risks came with the man. They were nothing compared with the risk of living my life without him.

"I'm in," I said, looking up at him.

"What?" William gaped at me, a shocked expression on his face.

"I'm in," I repeated. This time I couldn't help but smile.

He looked at me, and I watched as the storm that had been raging in his beautiful eyes settled, and he returned my smile with one of his own. "Thank God," he said, and he pulled me to him and kissed me deeply.

I was ready for William to sweep me up in his arms and carry me off into the sunset, but he pulled away. "There's one more thing," he managed to say.

"What is it?" I asked.

He started running his hands through his hair again, then he exhaled audibly and paced in front of the couch, like he was getting ready to run a race or head off into battle.

"When I found out about my father, I was floored. I idolized him, you know? I've spent my entire life trying to do everything he would have wanted me to do. Do everything the way he did it. And then, in an instant, he wasn't the man I thought. So I didn't know who I was either."

"I know who you are," I said softly.

He squeezed my hands. "And you never stopped trying to reach me, even when I treated you..." He closed his eyes. "God,

Catherine. I fucked up so bad. I promise, I'm going to spend a lifetime making it up to you."

"You don't need to do that, William. I forgive you. Go on."

"I had a lot of time to think after you left and while I was on the plane." He gripped my hands tighter. "I don't have to be him, I don't have to follow in his footsteps. I've spent my entire life obsessed with something that happened when I was eleven years old. I don't want to focus on the past anymore. They're gone and I have to let them go. I can't give up my future, my life, just so I can figure out their past. My parents, Wyatt, they wouldn't want that for me."

"What are you saying?" My heart was beating wildly. I hadn't expected this.

"I'm making changes. I've already started to dismantle WML Capital Management. I don't want it anymore."

My mouth hung open. I couldn't believe what he was saying. William wasn't walking away from his billions exactly, but he was walking away from the only career he'd ever known, one at which he'd excelled at, all on his own.

"My father lived for the art of the deal. He thrived on the risk of investing. I don't. I do care about the companies I own, so I'll find suitable new owners for all of my major holdings. The deal in Kyoto was just the start. It's going to take a while, but I'll sell off most of it within the next several months."

I finally found my voice. "What are you going to do then?"

"I want to build something for myself."

I nodded. "You should. When we first met, you told me you liked to make things. You *should* build something new, something all your own."

"I will. And on my terms. The vineyard is a small operation, but I like being hands-on, and I love making wine. And I'll keep investing in restaurants. And, I'm going to step up my involvement with the Lambourne Foundation. Come September, I can channel more money into it and then make sure it goes to many more worthy causes."

"That sounds so perfect for you, William. You'll be great."

"I want to, but..." He stopped pacing and walked to stand right in front of me, taking my hands in his.

"But what?"

"But I can't do it alone, Catherine. I want it all. With you. I want spend my life making you happy and watching you smile. When you're ready, I want to marry you. I want us to have a family. I want us to have a fucking incredible life. Together."

Tears stung my eyes, but I blinked them back. These weren't tears of pain but of joy. Complete and utter joy. I smiled. "You won't have to." I wrapped my hands around his neck and pressed against him. "I'm in." The heat of his body flooded into me, and our mouths met in a kiss both tender and filled with longing.

He pulled back. "God, I've missed you. I don't know what to do first—tell you more about my plans or take you to bed."

I laughed. "Oh, take me to bed."

William bent and swept me into his arms, solid and secure around me. I pressed my cheek against his chest, and his scent washed over me. In my ear, his heart thumped steadily.

It beat for me.

He really did love me, just as I loved him.

We passed the wall of windows, and the lights of Paris glittered in the darkness. It was like a dream. But if this was a dream, I never wanted to wake up.

The bedroom door clicked closed behind us, and William lowered me slowly onto the four-poster bed. My head settled on the small mountain of pillows and then William was beside me, his warm, familiar form covering me.

"God, you're so beautiful," he said, his hand stroking over my hair and fanning it over the pillows.

I drew his mouth to mine and slowly feasted on his lips. I took his lower lip between my teeth, gently nipping it, then tracing the seam of his lips until he opened for me. As soon as our tongues met, the blood rushed in my ears, and the last vestiges of my control faded. My hands dug into William's back as he kissed me deeply, passionately, and without reserve.

Gently, he pulled me up and tugged my T-shirt over my head. I toed my shoes off, while William tugged my jeans over my hips. He pulled them down to my ankles then kissed his way back up, pausing to plant butterfly kisses on the back of my knee

He worshipped every inch of my body—the inside of my elbow, the curve of my ankle, the fluttering pulse at my wrist.

"I love you, Catherine," he said, his breath warm against my palm. "I love you."

He quickly undressed then pulled the covers back and settled under them with me. I molded against his big warm body, lit only by starlight and the twinkling lamps of Paris.

His mouth found my shoulder, and he drew the straps of my bra down, one by one. My nipples were hard and swollen, and the material caught on the extended points. William looked down at me, at the scrap of fabric, and took a shaky breath. With trembling hands, he freed my breasts and tossed the bra aside. His hands closed on me, kneading me until my flesh heated and grew heavy. His thumbs rubbed over my extended nipples, and it was like a cord straight to my sex. My hips arched with each slow circle, pressing against his hard cock.

I still wore my panties, but they were soaked, and I knew William felt how much I wanted him.

His mouth traced a path from my collarbone to the swell of my breast, came teasing close to my nipple, and traced the other side. I groaned and arched my back.

William laughed huskily. "I survived the flight by imagining what I'd do to you when I had you in bed again."

"And what did you imagine?"

"It was a long flight." His molten grey eyes met mine. "It would take me years to show you all of it."

"Good. I want years with you."

He palmed my breast again. "But do you know that every single fantasy of mine involved these hard, rosy nipples. Every single fantasy involved me tonguing them." He flicked the tip of his tongue against my tender flesh, and I moaned.

"Licking them." He licked then blew cold air, making me shiver and my clit throb.

"Sucking them." His mouth closed on one hard point, sucking hard, pulling taut that tight cord to my clit.

"William." The word was a plea.

His hands skated down my body, caressing my curves, and hooking into the straps of my panties. He tugged them down then settled himself between my thighs. His cock pressed against my sex with a pleasant heaviness.

I wrapped my legs around him, but he made no move to enter me. Instead, his mouth slid to my neglected nipple, and he took it into his mouth. His fingers found my slick folds, and he cupped me.

He rose up. "You're so wet for me."

"I want you, William. So much."

"I'm yours."

His hands grasped mine, and our fingers twined together. His dark gaze met mine as he slid into me, filling me, completing me. With torturous, beautiful slowness, he thrust into me. His eyes never left mine, and in his eyes I could see every single emotion.

Lust. Need. Love.

He made himself completely vulnerable to me, giving me all of himself with each thrust. My hands closed tightly around his as his thrusts deepened and quickened. He knew how to move, his thick cock sliding inside me, his pelvis pressing against my clit. But it wasn't the act of sex that brought me the most pleasure. It was the look in William's eyes, the fact that he held nothing back.

I felt him swell, saw the muscle in his jaw flex, and I arched up to meet him. My muscles flexed against him as the climax spiraled through me, warm and sweet. With a low groan, he pulsed inside me.

"Catherine." His hands tightened, and his grey eyes darkened impossibly.

"I'm yours, William. Always."

*****

William pulled me close, cradling me in his arms, stroking my hair, my back, my arms. It was as though he couldn't quite believe I was really there beside him. The moment was sweet and tender. Until my stomach rumbled.

I had eaten a full meal with Hutch just a few hours ago, yet I was famished again.

William pulled back, one eyebrow cocked. "I should have fed you dinner before taking you to bed."

"I had dinner. I can't believe I'm hungry again."

Reluctantly, he released me and stood. "How about dessert then? Give me a minute. I'll grab that pastry bag." Naked, he padded to the bedroom door.

I had no idea what pastry bag he meant until he opened the door and walked into the living area.

Pastry bag? *The white bag from the pharmacy!*

"William—"

"What's in here?" he called. "A croissant? A macaron?" He walked back into the bedroom, tugging the bag open, and my heart stopped. For a long moment it seemed the whole world stopped. I didn't breathe. I didn't move. William stared into the bag and went completely still. When he looked up at me, his eyes were dark and his face was pale.

"Are you serious?" he asked.

"I don't know."

In one stride he pulled me into his arms and kissed me hard, taking my breath away. When he released me, he pushed the bag into my hands. "What are you waiting for, beautiful, *beautiful* girl?" he asked with a grin. "Let's find out."

ABOUT THE AUTHOR

Sorcha Grace is an adventurous eater, beach lover and author of scorching contemporary erotic romance. She is also the nom de plume of a nationally bestselling author who publishes in another romance genre. Find her on Facebook and Twitter.

www.facebook.com/SorchaGrace
Twitter: @SorchaGrace